High F
Lisa
first novel – *Dangerous Lies*

MW01126426

"This is the closest novel I've read to Mario Puzo's "Godfather" in decades . . . one of the best finds of this year! . . a story that won't allow you to look away, and it's one that will cause you to laugh and cry right to the last sentence."
The Bookish Dame

"Seduction. Crime. Revenge. One woman's life on-the-edge . . ."
The Morning Call

"This riveting novel is fast-paced and full of intriguing characters. I found myself picking this book up every chance I got just to see how it would end."
Four Stars, Excellent *Romantic Times - Mainstream Fiction.*

"The book is laced with suspense, humor, emotion and lots of twists and turns . . . racy new thriller has two unforgettable protagonists."
Palm Beach Post

" . . . a thriller with just enough steam to captivate . . ."
Parkland Press

". . . a tale of suspense, heartbreak, humor, and love. Smith has style, class and a gift for story telling."
Amazon.com readers award *Dangerous Lies* **Five Stars**

"If Mary Higgins Clark looks over her shoulder she may see Lisa Smith following closely behind. Their books have the same ingredients . . . page turning suspense and a plot that grabs the reader from the first page." ". . . Smith's sly sense of humor puts the frosting on the cake."
Spotlight Magazine

Followed by Equal Enthusiasm for
Exceeding Expectations

"fantastic characters" "well told, well plotted out and executed perfectly." "I was absolutely trapped by this book. " . . . held me right to the very last page." "a surprise at the end that will have you sitting with your mouth hanging open."
Natalie Hillier
http://booksfromthepurplejellybeanchair.blogspot.com

"Smith . . . has woven an intriguingly rich tapestry of delightful well-developed characters into a perfectly balanced plot bursting with riveting mystery, crimes of the petty and the horrible sort, suspenseful twists, and romantic tension complete with love scenes that sizzle and pop."
Cari Pestelak http://audacityshewrote.com

"5 Soaring Stars" ". . . it's the authentic details of the time-periods that make it fun to read . . ." "historical and fictitious characters work in sync as they are perfectly set in these time frames, and midst the transitory madness of WWs I and II Paris." "It's witty, fun and sassy."
Deborah Previte: http://abookishlibrarian.blogspot.com

"This book has it all! . . . romance, mystery, sex and crime. . . . a story that you will not be able to put down."
Charla Wilson http://booktalkswithcharl.blogspot.com

"If you like a thrilling read pick up this book."
http://Alaskanbookcafe.com

"Smith's books have the pace and heat of Jacqueline Susann and the style and sophistication of Dominick Dunne." **Amazon reviewer**

". . . twists, turns and adventures, it keeps readers on the edge of their seat." ". . . suspense, family drama, romantic tension and more, then you want to check out this e-book!"

Paradise Misplaced

Lisa April Smith

Windgate Press

Other books by this author
Dangerous Lies
Exceeding Expectations (the prequel to *Paradise Misplaced*)

For more about
Lisa April Smith
and upcoming projects
visit her website http://www.LisaAprilSmith.com

Acknowledgments

It's common knowledge. Writers spend a lot of time alone. Nevertheless, I believe that no project that takes longer than two hours is done entirely without help. I am indebted to so many people who helped and encouraged me over the years.

Starting with my husband, He-Who-Wishes-To-Remain-Anonymous, who knows that when I'm staring into space and don't respond to his questions, I'm not intentionally ignoring him, I'm simply somewhere else, involved in other people's lives. I'm also incredibly grateful that after a marriage that began when I was eighteen and he was twenty, unprompted, the man tells me that I'm beautiful. You can't put a price tag on that.

Lois Lineal, a former magazine editor who came out of retirement to do so much more than edit my books multiple times. She is my confidante, advisor and wonderful friend. You can't put a price tag on that either.

Many thanks go to my dear friend of twenty years, the talented photographer and graphic designer Sandra Friedkin, who designed the covers for *Exceeding Expectations* and *Paradise Misplaced*.

How would I manage without Dr. Len Pace who graciously advises me on all medical issues in my books?

And then there are my kids, who lovingly believe that their mother is incredibly gifted. That's what they tell me and I'm not about to argue.

~ Chapter 1~

New York City, January, 1964

Careful not to jostle fellow pedestrians with the bulky case that contained her modeling paraphernalia, Charlie threaded her way through the busy Manhattan sidewalk traffic. Reaching a newsstand, she stopped. They had completed the last shoot of the day early, well before the Monday to Friday workforce would file out of skyscrapers and scramble for buses, cars, taxis, and trains. Using her free hand, she paid the vendor and tucked copies of *Women's Wear Daily* and the *Herald Tribune* under her arm. She could read them that evening as she ate dinner. A month ago, she would have enjoyed having the extra hour to prepare dinner and freshen up before Raul came home from work. A year and a half of sharing jokes, chores, petty problems, and personal triumphs. And then for no logical reason, he had packed his things and moved out. 'Needing time to sort things out' was deliberately vague, particularly for a man who had no difficulty expressing his feelings, in not one, but two languages.

Another woman, Charlie decided for the thousandth time. There had to be another woman. That's what Raul needed time to sort out. His law firm had scores of glamorous Broadway and Hollywood celebrities as clients. She envisioned Jayne Mansfield seated at his desk, smiling seductively as she leaned forward, her voluptuous breasts spilling out of her scarlet satin dress, just as in dozens of publicity photos. What man wouldn't succumb? But Raul had too much integrity to cheat. He would leave. And that's what he did. He moved out. What other explanation made sense?

When a young mother pushing a stroller abruptly halted to tend to a crying toddler, Charlie came out of her recurrent daydream to nimbly sidestep the near collision. As she scampered down the dingy subway steps her eyes adjusted to the dim light. A quick glance at the posted signs confirmed the direction needed for the train line that led home. Below the clamor of street traffic and swarming throngs above, sounds from the distant rumbling cars, shuffling footsteps, and multi-lingual conversations were distorted by the echoing tunnels. In the harsh artificial light, objects further than a car length away seemed to be variations of black, white and dingy gray.

From habit, she took stock of her fellow travelers. A lone woman might receive unwelcome attention. A drunk could get surly. A pickpocket could be looking for a target. Although incidents like these were more likely to occur in the first few hours of the morning, when the subways were deserted, it was wise to be alert. Standing nearby were two well-dressed, middle-aged women wearing sensible shoes, carrying B. Altmans' shopping bags. City dwellers who had met for lunch and shopping, Charlie guessed. Fifteen steps to the right was an elderly Asian man, one arm resting on the shoulder of the small boy who stood next to him. The child held a scaled down violin case. Doting grandfather taking his grandson for a music lesson. A gaggle of teenaged girls wearing matching pleated skirts and saddle shoes, carrying overloaded book-bags, discussed plans for the weekend. Probably students from a nearby parochial high school.

Partially obscured by a column, Charlie noticed a bearded man with a dark knit cap pulled low over his brow and ears standing in the shadows. She thought she had seen him earlier when she had stopped to buy newspapers. He was wearing what appeared to be a ratty military-issued overcoat. She found it difficult to look away. The odd coat and beard fascinated her. Unusual attire was common in New York. Thanks to on and off Broadway theaters, television studios, and Madison Square Garden, the city attracted actors and musicians, circus and rodeo performers. And like every city, New York had its share of pimps and prostitutes, hobos and drunks. But something about his beard seemed incongruous – either the color or texture. She decided another casual glance wouldn't be considered rude if she pretended to be looking for someone. When she turned the man's face was blocked from view, but she did see one gloved hand holding a black well-made umbrella – odd for the unseasonably warm and dry day. But then, homeless people often wore and carried bizarre items.

She turned away. A child reaching into a box of Cracker Jacks reminded her that she hadn't eaten anything since breakfast. The distant sound of an approaching train merged with the rumbling in her stomach. Charlie bent to lift her carry case.

A shattering blow on her right shoulder sent her crashing to her knees. A shrill screech ricocheted off the concrete. Outraged by what she perceived as a careless act of exuberance from one of the students, Charlie turned to glare. The bearded man in the military overcoat hovered above her, brandishing the furled umbrella, threatening anyone who dared intervene. His eyes were cold and determined. The grandfather was dragging the bewildered boy with the violin case away. One of the shoppers, blocking her head with her arms, screamed. The schoolgirls covered their faces or clung to one another.

"Run! Get help!" Charlie shouted at the nearest girl, fearing the crazed man would turn on one of them. No one moved. She tried crawling away from the platform's edge. The vicious umbrella was hurling toward her head. As she dove to avoid it, the sharp tip caught her scalp. Blood streamed into her eyes, blurring her vision. "Please! Please! No more!" she begged the crazed man. She could hear the train getting closer over the chilling screams.

"Get back! Back! The train!" a woman yelled. "She's bleeding. If it's money you want, take the damn bag and let her go!"

"The train!" a girl's shrill voice shouted. "Oh my god. Oh my god! Look at the blood. Somebody make him stop!"

"Please! Please!" Charlie tried to shield her head with her arm and caught a wave of punishing blows on her back and shoulders. Her hand felt the platform's edge. She flattened her torso against the concrete and inched away from the terrifying abyss. A violent jab caught her rib. She heard it snap. Instinctively, she drew her knees to her chest and tried to protect her head with her hands. A series of a searing kicks pummeled her arms, hands, and spine. She writhed in pain pleading for her attacker to stop.

And then she was falling. Locked in a fetal position – plummeting into nothingness. The sudden jolting pain of impact. She could hear the echoing thunderous roar of the train, the screeching brakes. Squealing sounds coming from every direction. The vibrating rails beneath her body grew increasingly stronger. A flashing light lit the black tunnel and the oncoming train. She had no time to think. She flung herself at the nearest wall. Her last conscious thought was the rush of air, the earth trembling, and that hideous, grating, steel against steel, endless shriek.

*   *   *

"We're almost there," the man holding her hand promised. Through her swollen eyes Charlie saw the troubled look on his dark lined face. "Hang on," he said. "Just a few more blocks. Damn this rush hour traffic!"

She realized she was in an ambulance. She could hear the wailing siren, feel the vehicle making its way through traffic, slowing to a crawl and accelerating again. Lights flashed through the rear window. The stretcher that supported her felt like a bed of broken glass. Though every crack in the pavement increased her agony, Charlie prayed they would go faster. She was afraid she would die before they reached a hospital and help.

"Damn trucks!" a woman standing next to her said, wearing what appeared to be a man's uniform. "Why don't they pull over? The cops should ticket every bastard who refuses to pull over. Some lousy bum grabs her purse and pushes her in front of a train. He couldn't just take the purse and run. He had to shove her off a subway platform in front of a train."

"Sometimes I hate this lousy city," the man said. "What's her pressure?"

Charlie couldn't hear the response. She wanted to tell them about the bearded man with the umbrella, but when she tried to speak, nothing emerged. She could feel her life slipping away, like a footprint on the beach, grain by grain erased by a receding wave. The pain disappeared when she saw Raul smiling at her. She walked toward his open arms. A stranger's voice kept interrupting, obscuring the image. She tried to ignore the insistent voice that brought the returning pain.

"What's your name? Tell me your name!" the muffled voice said, as though he was talking to her from behind a closed door.

Would you please keep it down, her brain pleaded. She preferred being where it was quiet and she could float.

"I don't like her vital signs. She's lost a lot of blood. Get her back. I'm afraid we're going to lose her," the woman urged.

"My name is Merlin, Merlin the Magician they call me. Now what's your name?" the man's voice said. "We don't have any identification for you. Tell me your name!"

"Charlotte. Charlie."

"Charlie. I got it. Now stay with me, Charlie. Open your eyes and look at me. That's real good. Now, I need your last name."

"Morgan. Please hurry."

"We're going as fast as traffic allows. See, you're doing fine now, Charlie."

If Merlin truly believed that she was doing fine, he couldn't know about the fire consuming her body. "Pain," she whispered.

"Yeah, I know. It hurts real bad. But you lost a lot of blood and you got to stay with me. You hear? Now who do you want me to call? Your husband?"

"Not married."

"What about your parents?"

There was a time she would have said, call Jack Morgan. Call her father. He would know what to do to make the pain stop. But he was gone. "Both dead."

"Don't go closing your eyes! You must have a girlfriend, a boyfriend, sisters, or brothers?"

Not Amelia. Not now. She couldn't do this to her fragile pregnant sister.

"Keep her talking, Merlin," the woman warned. "She's slipping."

"Charlie! You just keep on thinking about me," Merlin coaxed. "We're going to Metropolitan Hospital, where they got the best doctors in the world. They're going to fix you up better than new. But you have to tell me who you want me to call. A pretty girl like you has to have someone."

"Call Raul."

"Raul. That's real good! Now I need Raul's last name."

"Francesco."

"Raul Francesco. Tell me about him. Is Raul your boyfriend or just a good friend?"

"I don't know," she sobbed.

"Okay. Maybe Raul's your boyfriend, maybe not. What do you want me to tell him?"

"If I die, tell him that I love him."

"You're not going to die, Charlie. You're going to live for a very long time."   She closed her eyes, too weak to cry.

"Don't go closing your eyes, Charlie. Keep them open! I need you to stay with me."

"Terrible pain. My legs. Hurry! Please call Raul. Tell him . . ." The entire right side of her body was in flames.

"I'm going to call Raul the minute we get to the hospital,"

Merlin assured her. "But you have to stay with me. I need you to stay with me. Come on. You got to concentrate on this sorry excuse for a face."

Charlie forced herself to find the empathetic brown eyes in the sea of darkness.

"You believe in God? Course you do," Merlin coaxed. "Only fools don't believe in God when they got troubles."

Charlie thought she nodded.

"I'm going to say the Lord's Prayer and you're going to say it with me. It's going to help you handle the pain. Say as many words aloud as you can. Okay?"

She grimaced her response.

"Our Father, who art in Heaven," he said slowly.

She concentrated on the words, whispering as he spoke. At some point she blacked out. When she awoke she was lying on a moving cart. Ceiling lights raced by. Strangers issued anxious orders. Once again, she relinquished control of her body and allowed the welcoming void to engulf her.

*　*　*

Aware of voices around her, Charlie opened her eyes. The glaring overhead fluorescent lights temporarily blinded her. She remembered the attack and then riding in an ambulance. Now she was flat on her back, dizzy, more asleep than awake. This had to be a hospital. Unless it was all a bad dream. Nightmares could seem real. Through the haze she was aware of the all encompassing, scalp-to-toe, pulsating dull pain. This wasn't a dream.

Surrounding her gurney, backed by a white drape, three men were talking.

"And you're sure this wasn't an accident?" the man in the pale green scrubs with his back toward her said.

"We have witnesses that saw her get attacked and pushed, just like we said."

"Jesus Christ, what's happening to the world? First President Kennedy is shot and now this. Have people gone nuts? Forget the gunshots and the stabbings I see. The President of the god-damned United States is killed and then a pretty girl, in broad daylight and not bothering anyone, gets shoved off a subway platform."

"Look, it's very important that we question her now, before she forgets details that may be able to help us catch this lunatic," said a man with a graying mustache and seriously rumpled tweed jacket.

"You get five minutes. She needs to rest," the man in the green scrubs instructed. "Five minutes and not a minute longer, Nurse."

The seriously rumpled jacket moved closer. "We're detectives with the New York City Police Department," he said. "A man attacked you in the subway station with an umbrella. Did you ever see the man before?"

"No," Charlie tried to say. But no sound emerged. Not even a whisper. She needed two additional attempts before she produced an audible sound.

The face above the rumpled jacket with the graying mustache looked at a man of about her age with cropped wiry red hair.

"We can see you're having trouble speaking, so we're going to make this as easy for you as we can. Was there anything familiar about him – his face, his gestures, his walk?"

"No," she croaked.

"Did he say anything to you either before or during the attack? Anything at all?"

"Nothing."

"Some people on the platform thought he wanted your purse or your suitcase and you resisted. Do you think he was trying to take something of yours?"

"I don't know."

"We need the best description of the man that you can give us. Don't bother describing his clothes. Everyone on that platform gave us a description of his clothes. Tell us what else you remember – anything about him that made him special."

She tried to moisten her lips with a dry tongue. "Five foot eleven."

"Five foot eleven," the younger detective repeated. "How can you be so sure?"

"My height. Same as me."

The mustached man's mouth twisted into a wry sympathetic smile. "What about his hair? Eyes?"

A hat covered his hair, but she remembered the exposed portions of his face. "Light eyes. Fair skin. Light hair."

"How do you know that? He was wearing a hat."

"His brows."

"Good! That's the details we're looking for. What about the

umbrella?"

"English. Expensive." Like one her father had owned.

"Okay, we got it. English and expensive."

Where was Raul? she wondered. Did he know she had been hurt? "Raul. Raul Francesco."

"Raul Francesco," the younger detective repeated, his eyes solemn and sincere. "Don't you worry. As soon as we're done here, we're going to go find Mr. Francesco and let him know where you are. We just need your help a little longer."

"Your five minutes are up, Detective," the blurred outline of a woman in white said in a firm voice. "You heard the doctor's orders. This patient needs rest."

"She's being very helpful. Just a few more questions, please."

"You're well past five minutes," the nurse chided.

"You got kids? A dozen or so were standing not five steps away from her," the detective with the mustache said. "He could've gone after one of them. That could've been your kid."

The nurse shrugged. "Okay. But be quick, or her doctor will have my head."

"Please, Charlotte," the younger detective pressed. "Try to give us more. See if you can remember his body or the way he carried himself. How old do you think the guy is?"

She reached into her brain recreating the scene. During the attack, struggling to protect herself, she had seen virtually nothing but the umbrella and his shoes. Before that, she had seen him from a distance. But there were a few seconds when she had looked into his eyes. The skin around them was unlined. She could feel herself sinking into a black sinkhole. Sleep was battling for control. She willed her eyes open. "Young."

"Young, twenty-five, thirty? Or a teenager?"

"Not a teenager."

"Do you think he was drunk?"

She recalled the cold determined eyes. "Not drunk."

"You're doing great, Charlotte. See if you can hang on a little longer. It's important that we stop this guy before he attacks someone else. Can you remember any distinguishing scars?"

"No." Her voice was so faint she could barely hear it. "Beard. Funny beard."

"I'm sorry. Did you say funny or phony?"

That was why the beard looked wrong, she realized. Something about the color or texture didn't seem natural. Phony! It wasn't real. The kind actors wore. Why would a crazed man wear a detachable beard? As a disguise. She could hear the drone of voices in the distance, but couldn't understand what was being said. She opened her mouth to speak. Had her lips moved? The only sounds she could hear were those in her head. The beard wasn't real, she wanted to shout. A disguise, she repeated over and over in her brain until it all seemed unimportant.

*   *   *

Charlie was aware of hands poking and prodding her, tense voices, being jostled, lifted, then floating, hearing unfamiliar sounds, slipping in and out of consciousness. Segments seemed like an endless dream where she was being moved like a sandbag, interrupted by bizarre flashbacks of the attack and President Kennedy. Throughout it all, she knew that she wasn't in her own bed or room.

A woman in a white uniform with salt and pepper hair adjusted a metal contraption over her bed that held her hoisted right leg.

"You're at Metropolitan Hospital. You've had a bad accident," the woman said, "Do you remember?"

"Is President Kennedy really dead or was that all a bad dream? I sort of remember trying to protect him – or maybe he was trying to protect me."

"President Kennedy was killed in November. You were attacked in a subway station yesterday."

"By a man with a beard." The image was returning. The umbrella flailing at her. The subway platform. People watching. Screams. Screeches. Horror. The oncoming train. And then the torturous ambulance that drove too slowly no matter how she begged the attendant to rush.

"I remember." Her voice was feeble and hoarse. When she tried to shift position she discovered her right arm was in a cast and her left arm was connected to an IV next to her bed. She cautiously lifted her left hand to touch her scalp. The top of her head was encased in gauze. Through the gauze she felt a long ridge of bumps. "Nothing hurts. I remember being in horrible pain. Now my entire body feels like Silly Putty."

"You'll feel that way for a while. You've been given a lot of medication for the pain." The nurse removed a clipboard from the foot of the bed and began writing.

Using the tips of her fingers Charlie examined her nose, eyes, jaws, and chin, and discovered a dressing on one cheek and a sizable lump on her forehead. "My face! How do I look?"

"You'll never know how lucky you are that gash on your scalp wasn't your face. Except for a few scratches and bruises, your face is perfect. Don't pay any attention to the discoloration. Give yourself a week or so and you'll be just as pretty as you were before."

"I suppose you think that I'm a silly vain woman, worrying about my face, but I'm a model. That's how I earn a living."

"Don't apologize. Every patient who wakes up with bandages on his head asks the same question. Unfortunately, they're all not as lucky as you."

"Does anybody know where I am?" She remembered telling someone Raul's name and asking for him. "I was hoping . . .'"

"I thought you might ask about that fellow. He hung around for hours. But your doctor told him to go home and come back after you're moved to your room and had a chance to settle. I expect you'll see him later."

Charlie tried to smile. The cut on her lip made it difficult. Using her index finger she examined her teeth. All intact. "I can see my arm is broken. It's in a cast. But why is my leg hanging from that contraption?"

"I can't discuss a patient's medical condition. You'll have to wait to speak to your doctor," the nurse explained.

"When? When will he . . ." she asked, too tired to complete the sentence. The effort to speak and move had exhausted her.

"Your doctor has left for the night. He'll be doing rounds early tomorrow morning. Then you can ask him all the questions you want. In the meantime, try to sleep. You need to rest." The nurse gave the top sheet a parting pat.

The medication wore off sometime during the night. The buzzer to signal a nurse dangled from her right bedrail – well within reach for an arm minus a cast, well within reach for a patient not immobilized by a leg strapped to a scaffold. What seemed like a year or two later, when a passing night-nurse heard her moaning, she got the shot she desperately needed.

*   *   *

The nurse making morning rounds provided a bedpan, but would add nothing to what Charlie had learned the night before about her condition. She would have to speak with her doctor.

A man with close-set owl-like eyes, curly dark hair, and wide hunched shoulders arrived shortly before seven-thirty.

"I'm Dr. Horowitz, one of the surgeons who operated on you last night. I don't suppose you remember me." He bent to inspect the gauze encasing her head and then her face. "You're looking much more alert this morning. How do you feel?"

"Like a mummy."

He laughed as he pulled the curtain that surrounded her bed. "You're a very lucky mummy. You had a bad time of it. We had to do a great deal to get you to this point. Fortunately, we had an excellent team on duty last night, including a talented interning plastic surgeon. You were badly cut."

"On my back and scalp."

"And your shoulders. Dr. Lazaar spent several hours working to make you as near perfect as possible."

Visions of the attack returned. She remembered the point of the umbrella slashing through her coat and flesh.

"The stitches on your scalp will be hidden by your hair. Fortunately your face was untouched."

"My arm is broken. What about my leg?"

"Your leg is more complicated. Let's talk about your arm. You broke the ulna. That's this bone." He pointed to his forearm. "After the cast is removed you'll need therapy. With work you should regain full use of it."

Charlie attempted a deep sigh and was stopped by a sharp pain that bypassed the medication she had received an hour earlier.

"You cracked three ribs." Dr. Horowitz examined her tender midsection, his fingers gently probing. "By some miracle you had minimal internal bleeding. Cracked ribs will heal. Unfortunately, they'll be sore for a while. The best we can do for you is to wrap you up and hope you don't have to sneeze or cough."

"I suppose that includes laughing. Try not to say anything funny."

"You're making jokes. I like patients with a sense of humor. They tend to heal quicker. And even if they don't, they make my day nicer."

"When can I expect to be discharged?"

"What's your hurry? It can't be the food. You haven't eaten yet."

She knew the doctor was withholding something. "The real problem is my leg. That trapeze isn't meant to keep me from running away."

The smile disappeared. He turned to examine the brace and cables gripping her ankle and followed it to the armature above. "You're right. It's not your arm, or the cracked ribs, or the lacerations you received that have us concerned. You fractured your pelvis and a vertebra. The vertebra is impinging upon your spinal column. We treat that with bed rest and traction and give everything a chance to mend."

"And if it doesn't?"

"Do you know something I don't know?" he teased.

"What I'd like to know is will I be able to walk again? Am I going to need a cane, a wheelchair, crutches?"

"We'll know more a month from today. I'm sure I don't have to remind you that you're lucky to be alive."

"I had a slight limp before the accident. Wouldn't it be ironic if this new injury corrected it?" she quipped, trying to keep her fear hidden.

"I'm not surprised you limped. We saw that in your X-rays. You probably were good at hiding it, except when you were tired or tried to rush."

"But now I'll have a noticeable limp, *if* I can walk at all."

"We don't know that as yet. Let's be positive!" he urged with a smile. "You're fit and fairly athletic." He slipped her chart into the holder at the foot of her bed. "You survived a brutal attack that would've been fatal for someone with slower reflexes."

"I was athletic."

"Physical therapy can do wonders. And now there's a very anxious fellow waiting to see you. You were asking for him during surgery."

"Raul?"

"I believe that was the name he gave."

"Could you tell him a tiny white lie and tell him the nurse needs me for the next few minutes. I do want to see him, but I'd like a little time to digest all you've said."

"Of course. Five minutes? Ten?"

"Ten, please."

Charlie watched the doctor exit, gulping back the choked sob that had been lurking below the surface until he was out of earshot. The night before, when she believed she was going to die, she would have given anything to see Raul, to have him embrace her in his comforting arms. But not now. If he thought she might be crippled, he would feel compelled to return. He would view it as his duty. As the only son in a family that had fled Cuba when Fidel Castro took power, he had exaggerated ideas about obligation and honor. She didn't want him to return because of pity. And at that moment she felt pitiful. She might not walk again. No jobs specified a model in a wheelchair. Another choked sob escaped. Charlie deliberately bit the cut lip and winced. Childhood training from her father and English nannies was there to coach her. *Proper young ladies don't inflict their sadness on others, Charlotte. And they most certainly don't cry in public. Now, now. Shoulders back! Chin up!*

Her father had always said, "Don't blubber, Charlotte. Marie Antoinette went to the guillotine like she was going to her coronation." Her father hated to see his daughters cry. It had been easier to bite back the tears than to watch her father's face when she had been hurt.

She would cry later, in private, just as she'd done in the past. She could snivel, and weep and sob until her head ached. But not now. Raul wouldn't find her with red bleary eyes and a runny nose. She did her best to steel herself when he appeared at the door carrying flowers. Despite all efforts, her pulse spiked and her face reddened when she caught sight of his classic features and impossibly boyish smile.

"My very first visitor," she said, offering the side of her face for a kiss. "Aren't you thoughtful to hurry over. Don't be alarmed by the scary beret. I got a nasty scrape on the top of my head. How did you hear that I had an accident?"

"Accident?" he scolded in his silky cello voice. "You were attacked by a madman and shoved off a subway platform in front of an oncoming train. One of our secretaries was listening to the radio right before she was about to leave the office and heard the news. I came to the hospital immediately. They wouldn't let me see you until now."

"I know I look dreadful, but it isn't as bad as it might seem. My arm is broken and a couple of ribs. But they'll heal. Thank God, he missed my face. As for the rest, just a couple of bumps and bruises. Nothing to stop me from returning to work as soon as I lose the cast."

"The newspapers said that you're going to be here for ten to twelve weeks."

"What do newspapers know?" she scoffed, unnerved to hear her injuries were common knowledge. She pointed to her dangling limb. "What kind of misinformation are they supplying about my leg?"

"They said that you had fractured your pelvis and some vertebra. Doctors are concerned that you'll walk again."

"I don't know how they come up with these things."

"They buy information from hospital staff – aides, cleaning people, anyone who might overhear a conversation or have access to your chart."

"Well, they're absolutely mistaken. I spoke with my doctor this morning. He's not concerned that I'll walk again and neither am I. This trapeze thing is strictly a precautionary measure. I'm going to be good as new before you know it."

"A fractured pelvis sounds serious to me," Raul countered.

"I'm not playing the martyr. Do I look concerned?" Charlie gave him her professional model's smile – the one that was expected to sell everything from cars to chewing gum. Then she remembered her sister, pregnant with her first child. "Amelia." Charlie frantically scanned the room for a telephone. "Amelia can't learn about the accident from the papers or some well-meaning neighbor. Please call her and tell her that I'll be fine."

"Don't worry. I'll take care of it. I'll tell her just what she needs to know and no more," he said, his voice businesslike, but his eyes were soft and anxious "And as soon as I leave this room, I'll make certain that you have a telephone so you can call me if you need anything."

"I know you mean well, but . . . I don't know how long I'm going to be here." Charlie took a deep breath and fought back the stabbing pain that had nothing to do with her injuries. "Maybe it would be better if you didn't come too often. It would only confuse both of us."

Raul's smile was forced. "You're probably right. But I'll be a phone call away if you need anything."

"Thank you. A phone would be great." She used her free hand to cover a fake yawn. Another minute of looking at those soulful penetrating eyes and Marie Antoinette's valiant example would be useless. "Now shouldn't you be getting to the office? I don't mean to be rude, but the medicine they give me makes me very sleepy."

"You're going to be fine. It's just going to take time." Raul kissed her cheek and departed.

She was exhausted and drained – too tired for more than a few silent tears before falling into a deep sleep.

~ **Chapter 2** ~

Buenos Aires

Jack wiped his face with one of the towels left for the convenience of the hotel's guests, then draped it around his neck before taking a shaded chair on the terrace overlooking the tennis court. Steps away, two tanned youths in matching khaki shirts and white shorts gathered stray balls. The daily morning lessons were essential for a man in Jack Caine's position. They kept him fit and trim, helped ensure his welcome with the hotel's management, and enabled him to meet tourists. Emilio Castellanos, the hotel's Tennis Director, was more than willing to introduce him to male guests looking for a game and unattached female guests seeking — seeking whatever it was that women vacationing alone sought. The arrangement was advantageous for Castellanos as well. Though the fee Jack paid was half Castellanos' usual hourly rate, it was a guaranteed addition to the modest salary he received from the hotel – particularly appreciated in the off-season winter months.

The Parador Grande had five clay tennis courts, four for guests, and this one, set aside for lessons and exhibition matches. The raised bluestone terrace that abutted it, which now held chairs and umbrella-covered tables, could easily be converted into a small spectators' gallery. In addition to tennis, swimming, shuffleboard, scuba diving, sailing, and innumerable other amenities, the hotel also featured a long beachfront dotted with yellow and white striped canvas cabanas. The Olympic-sized tiled pool, with a connecting in-pool bar was also available, so that those who wished could simultaneously satisfy their exterior and interior needs for liquid refreshment.

Although Jack spent much of his time at the Parador Grande, he was not a registered guest. He slept at a nearby rooming house which provided clean Spartan quarters. Fifteen months earlier, Jack, his two daughters from his first marriage, and Petal Morgan, his third wife, occupied either the Manhattan brownstone, rolling estate in Virginia, or mansion in Palm Beach. He had abandoned that comfortable life and the daughters he adored by staging his suicide. A desperate act of a desperate man, done to protect his daughters from the disgrace that would have resulted from the inevitable disclosure of a crime – a crime he had initially committed due to pressing financial need and had then been blackmailed into continuing. Unwilling to confront his searing loss, Jack permitted himself no doubts or self-pity. While awake, he only allowed himself images of Charlie and Amelia laughing, surrounded by attractive young people in extravagant settings. Asleep, his mind delighted and tortured him with memories of his girls. Occasionally, their mother, who tragically died at twenty-four, joined them.

Buenos Aires had seemed an excellent place to start again. Blessed with abundant natural resources and politics that favored the wealthy, Argentina had produced many great fortunes. And where there were great fortunes, Jack had reasoned, there would be any number of wealthy widows and divorcees grateful for sophisticated virile male companionship, women who would be willing to overlook his inconvenient financial distress. Unfortunately, the aristocratic widows he had encountered thus far – divorcees were rare in Catholic Argentina – were garrisoned behind an impenetrable wall of sons, uncles, brothers, and spiritual advisors. In Argentina, men controlled family fortunes and female members' behavior.

Jack reached for the neatly refolded Argentine newspaper a guest had left behind on the adjoining table. A front-page article delved into Lee Harvey Oswald – the crazed man who shot President Kennedy two weeks earlier – and the time he had spent in Russia. Even here, thousands of miles away, people were consumed with the popular American president's assassination.

"Are you planning to spend the rest of the day with your new American lady-friend?" Castellanos asked as he dropped into the chair beside Jack's. Castellanos was a tall sinewy man with dark, tight curly hair and the confident air of a former international champion.

Jack's new American friend was Sally Heissen Cavanaugh, a tailored blond of about fifty-five with appealing rugged features and an infectious laugh, who was traveling alone. Unmarried women usually traveled in pairs. It was often awkward for him to approach one and not the other. Typically, the women were secretaries and schoolteachers who scrimped and saved throughout the year hoping to find a romantic paradise, if only for a week. As appealing as many of these delightful ladies were, Jack couldn't afford them. What he sought was a woman with Sally's qualities. For in addition to traveling alone, Sally was heir to the formidable Heissen beer fortune, and the widow of Gerald Cavanaugh, the late CEO of Heissen Beer. Jack hadn't made love to her as yet.

"Sally's at the dentist. She chipped a tooth," Jack informed Castellanos.

"Good. Then you have time before she returns to humble a boastful Italian chap. It would give me great pleasure to see him brought down a peg."

"Does he speak English, Spanish, or will I have to try to follow his Italian?"

"Rest easy, my friend. He speaks Italian, Spanish, and English."

The overconfident Italian was Antonio De Luca, a man in his early forties, with thirty extra pounds, a small bald spot at the back of his head, and dark bushy eyebrows. At Jack's suggestion, they decided to play a three set match, loser pays for lunch — a gentleman's wager. The Italian had a formidable first serve when it hit its target, which it rarely did, and a second serve that was embarrassingly simple to whip across his weak backhand. First set ended 6 - 1. Realizing it would be an easy victory, Jack allowed De Luca to take the second set and ended it quickly in the third. Emilio would be pleased.

Donatella De Luca was waiting for them poolside. Despite deeply recessed eyes, she was a handsome woman with a strong chin and full mouth, younger than De Luca by perhaps ten or twelve years. Sally found them as they were having drinks. The dentist had taken a cast and she would return tomorrow.

As always, Jack directed all conversation toward the others. He had fabricated an elaborate past, which he could supply as needed, but he preferred listening. In the hour and a half it took to eat lunch Jack learned a great deal about his companions. De Luca owned factories in Italy and a vineyard that had been in been in the family for generations. They had left their two sons, ages eight and six, with Donatella's family in Rome. Sally had a grown son and daughter. She neglected to mention their ages. The son was married. The daughter was not. She also neglected to mention her family's association with beer. Wine apparently topped beer in prestige.

"Jack is taking me sightseeing this afternoon. Come join us," Sally told the pair as De Luca took the check from the waiter. "Jack knows a number of local artists, some of whom are quite colorful. It'll be fun."

Donatella looked at her husband. It was obvious that she wished to accompany them.

"We wouldn't want to intrude," De Luca said, as he scribbled his name and room number on the check.

"Please. You wouldn't be intruding," Jack assured him. "We'd love to have your company. I have some interesting spots in mind. You can always get a tan."

"Only if you promise to give me a return match tomorrow. I had some trouble today with my first serve. But when it's working . . ."

"It's deadly," Jack acknowledged. "I couldn't do anything to stop you in that second set."

It was settled. The men would shower and change while the women waited for them. The foursome would spend the afternoon together, and what was even better, Sally had suggested the idea and not Jack. No one would suspect the commission he received for items purchased.

Neither Sally nor the De Lucas wished to visit the venerable Ignacio Church that Jack thought they might enjoy. All loudly protested they had seen enough churches in their travels. Nor did they wish to visit the historic fort in Lojan, or Casa Rosada, the pink Presidential Palace. They wanted to be taken to meet the artists that Jack had told them about.

"Don't forget," Jack reminded them before they left the rented car and driver, "you are not obligated to buy anything. Artists love to show off their work. Find something nice to say and they'll be delighted to answer questions. Except for our last stop today, we are visiting studios, not shops. I'm taking you to some genuinely talented artists you'll be hearing more about in the future. Of course, if you decide there's something you want to bring home, you would be purchasing it at a significant savings."

Neither Sally nor the Italian couple had any interest in Pre-Columbian art. But the dealer/restorer was an entertaining fellow, who was willing to share stories about the Incas and their bloodthirsty rites. Jack interpreted as needed. Sally bought a small stone figure. The next stop was a weaver's, a Mestizo woman who spoke little English. She incorporated traditional native designs with natural dyed wool of varying textures into her work. The pieces could be used as wall hangings or rugs. Donatella inquired if a larger item, which intrigued her, could be shipped. Jack assured her the artist was trustworthy and the transaction was completed.

"Where do we go from here, Jack?" Sally asked. "We have time for just one more stop before getting back to the hotel."

"You have your choice. There's a woman artist, a surrealist, very gifted, very avant-garde, just being discovered. Anything you buy of hers will double and triple in value in ten years. I have two of her pieces and I treasure them," Jack said, thinking how different his life would've been if his own limited artistic talent had matched his interest and appreciation.

"And our other choice?" De Luca asked.

"There's a German goldsmith who I think is a genius. But I don't want to praise him too highly. You have to see for yourself."

"Jewelry, now you're talking," Sally said. "What's his specialty? Turquoise, pearls, jade, silver?"

"Nothing like that. He rarely uses gemstones, only gold, twenty-two to twenty-four carat gold. As a young man he fell in love with Scythian art. Most of what he does has a strong Scythian influence. You won't find pieces like it anywhere. His name is Jacob Weiner and he has an interesting story to tell."

As Jack had predicted the three found the diminutive man and his jewelry fascinating. Weiner spoke twelve languages, including Italian. Donatella selected a necklace and matching earrings for herself. De Luca looked at every pair of cufflinks before choosing an impressive set. Sally couldn't decide which pieces she could bear to leave behind. Every niece and nephew required a future birthday or Christmas gift. She wanted Jack's opinion. Did he prefer these cufflinks or those, this ring or the other? There was one ring Jack particularly admired, an understated ring with a unique design and flawlessly executed. He couldn't hide his admiration when she pointed to it.

"It's outstanding. A great choice for a man," Jack agreed.

"Let me buy it for you, a souvenir of our wonderful day?" Sally said.

He held up his bare hands. "I don't wear rings. And I couldn't accept, even if I did."

"Maybe we can go to that other artist you told us about tomorrow," she said.

He slipped his arm around Sally's waist and watched her eyes sparkle like a child at the circus. "What about tonight? I don't want the day to end. What do you feel like having for dinner?" Jack asked his companions. "You are all to be my guests." He could afford the gesture. Thanks to the De Luca's decision to join them, and Sally's extravagant generosity, Jack had earned more than a month's expenses in that single day.

"Isn't this the sweetest man?" Sally gushed to the others before addressing Jack. "I'm surprised they don't call you Sugar Caine. You best be careful, or I'm going to take you home with me in my suitcase."

Over the next five days of her stay Sally would let him know with every way known to women that she would be pleased to be the next Mrs. Caine. Jack thought about it, thought about it often, and with more than a little regret. If Sally had any trepidations as to his assets, or his method of supporting himself, she kept them to herself. He had taken them all to dinner that evening, but that was the last time he paid for anything other than the few lunches he and Sally had away from the hotel. On the evening before she was due to leave Sally slipped out of bed, walked to her half-packed suitcase and removed a small box. In it was the ring he had admired.

"You're not allowed to refuse," she said, handing him the box. "I told you that I want you to have it to remember me."

"As if I need anything to remind me of you. I'm not likely to forget the wonderful times we've had together." He knew what she was waiting to hear, words he couldn't say. As tempting as it was to return to the States as the future husband of the well-heeled and magnanimous Sally Heissen, it was far too dangerous. St. Louis might seem a safe distance from New York or Palm Beach, but today people traveled. And those who could afford to, traveled extensively. Sooner or later someone would recognize the purportedly deceased Jack Morgan. He couldn't return to the United States. He pulled her down beside him, lifted the satin gown, and covered the smooth skin of her pelvis with kisses. She laughed that husky sensuous laugh as she realized what would follow. It was the least he could do.

~ **Chapter 3** ~

Acre, Israel

At various times in its long history the vital port city of Acre had been held by Jews, Romans, Syrians, Persians, Macedonians, Moslems, Crusading Christians, and Ottomans. In 1918, it was captured by the British. In 1948, it became a part of Israel. The site had been repeatedly sacked, rebuilt, and abandoned, fortified with stone walls and forts, and grandly expanded, making its architecture and archeological remains as diverse as its past.

On the outskirts of the city, at a site dating back before the Romans arrived, Naomi rinsed the sand from her body and hair using the improvised field shower filled with sun-warmed water. Unlike the others on her team, she needed a shower and clean clothes before joining them at the last meal of the day. Youthful and trim at forty-four, she had no difficulty doing the arduous digging, sifting, and climbing required at an archeological dig. Work had gone well that day. They had unearthed two shattered but complete storage pots that she knew would be dated two centuries BC when Jews held the area. The extra hands had helped.

In late June they had taken on five American volunteers eager to work on a dig over the summer: four college students, two boys, two girls, and a high school history teacher, named Michael. They had come to Israel to learn and become part of it. As though by handling the earth, replacing their pale pasty coloring with a rugged tan, and uncovering the artifacts of their ancestors, they could establish a link with their past. Naomi knew that she and the history teacher would become lovers. He was married. She didn't know if he had children, nor did she care. She preferred married men. A married man could be counted on to leave at the end of the summer with a minimum of fuss. There would be no talk of staying and finding a permanent job. A passionless good-bye kiss and a soon-to-be-broken promise to write. No entanglements, no regrets.

From habit Naomi checked the small hand mirror. She no longer owned makeup, only salve to protect her lips. Her now-darkened hair was cut short and typically hidden under a hat. Lines from frowning in the sun creased her forehead and the corners of her eyes, but there were no signs of broken bones left to mend unset, no lurid scars or macabre tattoos like many survivors bore. She often thought that her body had fared better than her mind.

Approaching the Spartan dining tent Naomi noticed that Michael had saved a place for her. She filled her plate with food and sat down beside him. Nearby, the two college girls were absorbing wisdom being shared with them by Shaul and Uri, the team's senior members, men more than double their age. Inevitably, they too would become lovers. The two boys would have to find young *sabras*, Israeli-born girls, who would consider their American cousins naïve but exotic strangers. Linda, a red-haired sophomore with a face full of freckles, grinned at Naomi. Her friend Jill, a broad-shouldered girl with dark eyes and braces, was too engrossed to notice her presence.

When she was still Nicole, and after her American husband and children had fled occupied Paris for the United States, she'd insisted on staying behind to aid her wounded brother Philippe, who had foolishly left school to enlist at seventeen to fight for France. While she desperately tried to find him, all her valuables, including her identification, had been stolen. With no money, no passport, and nothing to sell, Nicole went from house to house begging for food and shelter. As the invading army grew in strength and numbers, food became increasingly scarce. She was turned over to the Nazis by a collaborator when he caught her stealing moldy corncobs from his pigsty. Her punishment – forced to be an unpaid prostitute, first servicing ordinary German troops, and later a major who claimed her for himself. Fortunately, she was not suspected of being a Jew, only a thief, or she would have been sent to a concentration camp. A year later she managed to escape.

For nine months she lived by hiding in fields, gleaning scraps of rotting crops and scavenging garbage cans until a farmer found her. She had collapsed while rifling through a shed looking for anything edible. Suspecting she was a Jew, he carried her to his house. He and his wife allowed her to sleep in the barn and gave her food and clean clothing until they grew too frightened to let her stay. The Nazis had shot a neighboring collaborator. When the cold of winter and a persistent racking cough drove her to seek the warmth of a barn, she was again apprehended, this time by a widowed farmer with five children. Seeing her emaciated skeleton he knew she was an escapee: either a criminal or a Jew. It didn't matter which. He needed a woman to cook, clean and warm his bed. She needed a place to hide. Preferring a woman with flesh on her bones, he insisted she eat enough to replace the lost weight. He also beat her when she displeased him. Nicole stayed until the war's end, then once again escaped. This time she made it to an Allied relocation camp.

Queries were made on her behalf. She learned that her brother and parents were all dead. Information about her husband and children took longer. They had lived in Philadelphia, but they had moved and left no forwarding address. Her husband's relatives were unable to assist. Nicole was questioned once again. Did she know where her husband might have taken the children? Without additional information it would take time to locate them. A month passed and then another. Other camp internees located relatives and friends who had survived. One by one Europe's homeless obtained visas and fled: to the United States, England, Brazil, Argentina, Mexico, Canada, Australia, the Caribbean Islands, any perceived safe haven that would have them.

Yet another camp official came to speak to Nicole. Alain and her children had vanished. His sister and brothers didn't know where they were. Could she think of a reason her husband might have for leaving no forwarding address? Had they gotten along well? Had they argued? Often? About money? The children? Other women?

She told him that she didn't know where her husband might have taken her daughters, or why. They had argued. Often. Not about money. About the children. The camp worker frowned and promised to continue searching.

Nicole remembered back to the life she had had with Alain. For three and a half months, from the day she had managed to get rid of the last of his rich whores, to the day Marguerite was born — three and a half months – she had shared Alain with no one. He had been hers alone for fourteen weeks. After that, the only time she had his complete attention was when they made love. She had lost him to her own daughter. If Alain was present there was no one else in the room for Maggie. When they moved into her parents' home, maids, cooks, nannies, all raced to attend to Alain's every whim. Even her cynical, aloof mother had succumbed. No female was immune. If only Michelle had been born a boy, there would have been someone to adore Nicole. And now this. He had taken their daughters and run off. She had suffered and fought to survive for this.

"Look around you," volunteers had lectured her. "You're not the only one who's lost everything. Others are starting new lives. Put aside the past. Live for the future. You're young and you have your health. Others are not so fortunate. You can find another husband. You'll have other children."

Nicole collapsed. A nervous breakdown, the camp doctors called it. But there was nothing nervous about it. It was a calm better than any she had known. No sounds, no nameless faces, no grotesque visions of her brother's exposed bones. No memory of the degradations she had endured, the endless line of men waiting to violate her. No images of her children crying, or of Alain leaving her. Nothing. Peace. Darkness. A black blanket enveloping her, hiding her from the piercing light.

Months later, as the blanket gradually lifted, the camp no longer contained familiar faces. The few people she'd known were gone. Those still there, the ones who lacked a country that would take them in or family seeking them, talked of going to Palestine. They would start their lives again in the promised land. A new beginning. A clean slate. Nothing to remind them of the past. Nicole decided to join them.

Shortly after she arrived in Palestine she was approached by members of the Haganah, the daring underground group fighting for liberation. Nicole was told that she was an ideal candidate: intelligent, fluent in English, beautiful, and mannered. Just the sort of woman British officers stationed in Palestine found irresistible. She could learn information from the British officers that would advance the Jews' fight for a safe homeland. Her people needed her. The Haganah needed her. They trained her. She was taught to kill with anything at hand: a rifle, a pistol, a bayonet, a knife, a pen, a water glass, the mirror from a compact. If working for the Haganah meant using her body for seduction, or if she was to die, it was of no importance to her.

In 1948 Israel became a state and Nicole's special services were no longer needed. She applied to join a kibbutz. Some joined as a means of regaining a family lost in concentration camps. Others because they believed in the lofty ideals of a commune. Naomi joined because she wanted someone other than herself to make daily decisions for her. Swayed by her status as a hero of the Haganah, the kibbutz accepted her. Though she worked as hard as any, without complaint, she was a poor fit for communal life. She lacked the ardor, the zeal, the commitment others had. In 1953, after reading about an ongoing archeological excavation, she impulsively wrote a letter offering her help and describing her interest in history, and her pre-war work with rare books. They invited her to join the project.

She was well suited for the slow-paced, hermetic, exacting work on a dig. She followed procedures, learned quickly, and possessed a keen eye for detail. Her notes were meticulous. Nine years later she was considered a valuable member of the team.

"Jill thinks you're a dead ringer for a girl we saw on television," Linda said, as they washed the dinner dishes.

In the last few minutes before nightfall, mountains in the distance softened and appeared closer.

"A dead ringer?" Naomi inquired.

"It's an expression. It means that you look just like someone else," Linda explained.

"It's true. She does that funny thing you do with your mouth, Naomi." Jill demonstrated the odd pout.

Naomi unconsciously touched her upper lip. "Why was she on television?"

"She was talking about this dumb guy who paints," Jill continued.

"He's not dumb," Linda argued. "He's retarded, but they say he's some kind of a genius. I have a picture in my tent of the model who discovered him. It's an old magazine. She looks like Naomi, around the eyes."

"And the mouth, and the cheekbones, and her entire face," Jill said. "She looks exactly like you, Naomi. Go find the picture, Linda. She simply has to see it."

"That's all right," Naomi said. "There's no need to bother. I'll take your word for it."

Linda stood, quickly followed by Shaul. "You could have family that you don't even know about," Linda said. "She might be a distant cousin. Wouldn't that be exciting? To find a member of your family living in America, after all this time?"

"No one. I have no one."

"I'm going to get that magazine," Linda said. "You be the judge."

Shaul draped his arm over Linda's shoulder. "I'll go with you. It's not wise to walk alone after sundown."

"She's Naomi's double," Jill said, sliding closer to Uri. "I couldn't believe it."

"We'll go too," Michael said, taking Naomi's hand in his. A look passed between them. Unless she objected, that night he would be sleeping in her tent. "I want to see the American model who looks like Naomi."

Could it really be Michelle? Naomi wondered as they made their way in the semi-darkness, their path lit by flashlights reflecting off the stone. She would be twenty-three now. No, twenty-four. It would have to be her younger daughter. Marguerite had favored her father, the pedophile seducer. And in the highly unlikely chance it was Michelle, what would she do after all these years? Would she try to find her daughters? Try to make a place for herself in their lives? Try to regain their love? Or punish the man who had stolen them from her?

~ Chapter 4 ~

Amelia and Hal Holmes, Charlie's sister and brother-in-law, arrived just as her lunch tray was being removed, less than twenty-four hours since she had been wheeled out of surgery and moved to a private room at Metropolitan Hospital. But she didn't need to check the wall clock to tell that it had been three and a half hours since her last shot. Agonizing pain had resurfaced, as predictable as Big Ben. The most minimal contact with her bed – simply brushing her sheet – was agony. It would be another thirty minutes before she could ask for the next shot.

In her seventh month of an uncomfortable pregnancy, petite Amelia looked more like herself as a child than an adult. Her soft blue eyes and small nose were almost lost between her puffy pale cheeks. Hal Holmes was slight, but his shoulders, torso, arms and legs, even his slender head were in proportion, so he appeared taller. Charlie had come to like Hal. He wasn't terribly quick, but he was loyal and caring.

Though private, her room was tiny – Manhattanites measured space by the inch, not the foot – and too small for anyone to move about without occasionally bumping her bed and sending a thousand volts of electricity surging through her body. Unfortunately, kind Hal paced when he was troubled. Apparently, seeing her skewered and suspended like a slaughtered calf troubled Hal.

"Please sit, Hal," Charlie requested for the third time since they had arrived. Hal sat, only to pop up again, like toast, moments later.

"Do sit down, Harold. You're making us dizzy. Look at poor Charlotte. Can't you see she's uncomfortable with your wandering?"

Hal sat once again. "I'm so sorry. I don't know which bothers me more, your leg or bandaged head."

Amelia glared at him. Raul had prepared her, Charlie thought with relief.

"Not your face," Hal continued. "Just the top of your head. Isn't there anything we can do for you? Anything at all?"

"Before you know it I will be as good as new," Charlie assured her sister and brother-in-law. "Now, tell me about your parents. Are they as excited as I am about the new addition to the family?" she asked, hoping to forestall the anticipated resumption of pacing.

"My mother claims that she's taking it all in stride, but that hasn't prevented her from redecorating the entire nursery," Hal admitted. "It's their first grandchild."

Charlie made small talk and pretended not to notice how slowly the wall clock's minute hand advanced. "Please don't worry about me," she said, when she realized her sister and brother-in-law were about to leave. "This is just temporary. You have to concentrate on my future niece or nephew."

"We'll be in New York tomorrow." Amelia took Charlie's hand and pecked her cheek. "I've some shopping to do. Would you prefer we call or visit?"

"Call," she said, hoping she didn't sound as anxious as she felt. "I promise to let you know if there's anything I need."

*   *   *

Detectives Frank Marrone and Ray Kowalski arrived a few hours later, while Charlie was still under the influence of numbing pharmaceutical relief that eased the pain but made it difficult to concentrate. She vaguely remembered the fiftyish man with the graying mustache and deep furrowed brow, but had no recollection of the younger detective, Ray Kowalski, a man in his late twenties with wiry red hair and a narrow freckled face.

Kowalski showed her the portrait a police sketch-artist had done based on the recollections of witnesses and explained they hoped that she could add to or refine the drawing. He waited for her response.

She stared at the roughly penciled image – two cold light eyes, a suggestion of a brow hidden behind a knit hat, a full beard and mustache hiding the bottom half of a face and barely discernable lips. The face in the sketch was chillingly familiar and yet wrong. But in her drug-altered condition she was unable to improve it.

The disappointed detectives thanked her for her help, assured her they would do their best to capture the madman, and left.

*   *   *

Petal Wentworth Morgan's lavish bouquet of tropical flowers arrived that afternoon. The note inside requested that Charlie call when she was well enough to have visitors.

Her relationship with Raul had created an untenable situation for Petal. Long before she began dating Raul Charlie had been well acquainted with her stepmother's views regarding people who weren't white, wealthy, wellborn and Protestant.

Petal's Beliefs:

Given they met the other requirements, Roman Catholics were tolerated. All others: Jews, Hindus, Muslims, Buddhists, heathens, et cetera, were not. If RC's kept their priests in line, married one another and maintained their estates, they made acceptable neighbors. That didn't apply to Jews who thought their academic degrees, financial success, accomplishments and vulgar charitable donations entitled them to access anywhere. Which was absurd. They were pushy upstarts and always would be.

Regarding the needy: poor whites suffered because they, or their forebears, had made unwise choices. Petal worked hard for organizations that helped these unfortunate souls improve their sorry circumstances. Non-whites had created their own problems as a result of being lazy, dirty, slow-witted, intemperate drinkers and breeders. Many were not to be trusted. An alarming number were downright dangerous.

As for Latins, people from Spanish-speaking countries, if they were visitors to the country, i.e. ambassadors, guests, or international tourists, they were treated courteously. Petal believed that recently arrived Latins were naturally servile, and given proper training and supervision, they made better household staff than American negroes.

Raul had been born in Cuba and was therefore Latin. As he was not a visitor to the United States, according to Petal's laws governing social behavior, the moment Charlie began dating him she should have been *dropped* – snubbed and removed from all guest lists. Ironically, thanks to Fidel Castro, the poor woman was continuously presented with a conundrum. The United States of America considered Cubans fleeing the Communist regime *freedom fighters,* and had granted them all sorts of favored treatment. To further complicate the matter, Raul was an attorney with a firm that handled many famous and powerful clients, including Petal. The poor woman was forced to walk a narrow path between ostracism and acceptance. It was far easier to have Amelia for a stepdaughter. Amelia was a sensible girl who had married Protestant, white and well.

Charlie's rules of courtesy, though vastly different from Petal's, were equally rigorous. She called her father's widow to thank her for the lovely bouquet immediately after reading the attached note. Petal's courtesy visit would be a maximum of thirty minutes. Both could survive a half hour of forced meaningless chatter so that society as they knew it might continue.

*   *   *

Petal's timing the following morning was perfect – as Charlie's drug-induced haze was lifting and before the real pain arrived. After she kissed the air above Charlie's cheek, and handed her a beautifully wrapped package from Bonwit Teller, she took the seat closest to the door and waited while Charlie read the card.

Although Petal possessed not one feature that could be described as pretty, she was slender, impeccably groomed and stylish. The fitted gray serge suit she wore flattered her silver hair and yellow-green eyes.

"This is so nice and entirely unnecessary," Charlie said, holding the card aloft. The package contained dusting powder and hand lotion, both by Chanel.

"Dr. Lansing would be happy to take you on as a patient, if I asked him. Would you like me to do so?"

Dr. Lansing was *the* Fifth Avenue physician. A fine doctor, no doubt, but a general practitioner. "How very thoughtful of you. But my case is a bit unusual. My injuries require an orthopedic surgeon."

"And you've found one whom you trust?"

"I'm in very good hands. The Chief Surgeon of Orthopedic Medicine at Metropolitan is treating me." There was no point in mentioning that the Chief Surgeon of Orthopedic Medicine at Metropolitan was Dr. Nathaniel Horowitz. No point at all.

Petal scarcely discussed the nature of her injuries, or the manner in which they had been acquired. To do so would invite a protracted morbid conversation. Far better to discuss those details over cards or cocktails with one's peers. Thanks to newspaper reports, Charlotte Morgan would be the exciting topic of conversation for the next few days.

"You'll never guess who asked for you. Skip Reinhardt," Petal confided. "And that wasn't the first time. You remember Skip, Charlotte. Nice looking young man – favors his mother. And very tall. He graduated a year or so ahead of Amelia. From Yale."

Charlie nodded. "I remember Skip."

"His grandfather did well in gold mining and later real-estate. His parents are T.J. and Lane Reinhardt. Darling people. The Duke and Duchess stayed at their home. T.J. invited your father and me to a dinner in the Duke and Duchess' honor. Nineteen sixty, I believe. Skip was interested in you. Knew you had done some modeling and seemed very impressed. Should I encourage him?"

Charlie remembered hard-drinking Skip Reinhardt. As a college student, he had ignored her and pursued Amelia, who had her eye on Hal. But there had to be a reason for the glowing description of Skip's assets. Obviously, Petal had learned that Charlie and Raul had separated and was attempting to foster a more suitable alliance. It was a thoughtful, if self-serving gesture.

"If Skip asks for me again, just say that I send my best," Charlie said, offering polite acknowledgement but no interest. She looked away as Petal discreetly glanced at her watch.

"Where does the time go? I promised myself that I wouldn't stay long. I'm certain that your doctor wants you to rest as much as possible. You will tell me if there's anything you need."

Charlie promised to let her know if she required anything and thanked her stepmother again. Petal left on the hour, precisely twenty minutes after she had arrived.

*   *   *

The last time she had been hospitalized was the day she was born. As none of her family had ever required hospitalization, Charlie's experience to date with these citadels of healing was negligible. After three days as a patient, she had become well acquainted with hospital culture. Physicians were male and could be distinguished by the stethoscopes that dangled like necklaces or were stuffed in pockets. Some wore white lab coats over slacks, shirts and ties like the interns did. In general, interns were distinguishable from accredited practitioners by their youth, scruffy and sometimes threadbare clothes, and red eyes due to lack of sleep. Nurses were female and clad in white, immaculate starched uniforms, stockings and shoes, and a diverse assortment of headgear. Each nursing school had its own distinctive hat. Despite the impact of the mini skirt that had revolutionized the fashion industry the year before, only the most daring young nurses chose to wear their skirts above the knee. Aides looked much like nurses, minus the distinctive hats. And orderlies, no matter what their size, wore loose fitting pants and shoes with thick rubber heels.

Days were an endless cycle of blood samples, bedpans, tasteless meals, flowers, thank-you notes scribbled with her clumsy left hand, embarrassing intestinal gas, dry skin, itches that were unreachable, thermometers, linen changes and the humbling dependence on others for the simplest need. And she could endure all of this without complaint, were it not for the pain.

Pain dominated her thoughts. Managing it was a full-time activity. Nurses were not permitted to offer medication. The patient had to request it, at four hour intervals or longer. Which she did. Occasionally, she would beg. For some unknown reason, pain medication lost ninety-nine percent of its effect after three and a half hours. The last thirty minutes of an interval were horrible, and every minute beyond that grew increasingly unbearable. Theoretically, Charlie's day was divided into six four-hour segments. In theory, she should have to endure no more than three hours of agony daily – six multiplied by the final half-hour in a segment. But it never worked out that way. The nurse didn't respond immediately to the buzzer as she was otherwise occupied performing life-saving ministrations, or gossiping about a party she had attended the evening before. Eventually, the nurse would respond to the call and leave to prepare the shot. Then, just as she was on her way to administer that merciful injection, she would discover that Charlotte Morgan had been hauled away for additional tests or X-rays, or was being examined by a doctor or intern. Minutes later the doctor, therapist, or nutritionist would leave, and Nurse Nightingale was now occupied doing something else. An hour or so later, the good nurse would remember the requested shot, and provided there were no further interruptions, her now desperate patient would receive the numbing medication. So the targeted six shots daily were never more than five – sometimes as few as four. And the three hours of guaranteed misery were a minimum of seven.

Doctor's orders or hospital policy were the reasons given.

"There has to be a better way than this," Charlie complained to a sympathetic nurse.

"They're afraid patients will become addicted. I wish I could help, but I have to follow hospital policy or I'll lose my job."

Charlie became angry every time she thought about the

accident. She was furious at the man who had attacked her. Furious with herself for not fighting back. And when she wasn't angry, or fighting searing pain, she worried. Friends stopped by in the evening on their way home from work, but there was little to distract her during the day.

She worried that she might never walk again. She worried whether her savings would be enough for her rent, utilities and the extensive hospital and medical expenses that mounted daily. Fearful that her medical insurance wouldn't cover the cost of a private room, she requested a semi-private one. Having clawed her way out of financial devastation when her father had committed suicide, she had no desire to repeat the experience.

Lacking training and practical education, modeling had been her salvation. Now she worried if she would be in demand when she was discharged. A model's income was determined by the size of the fees she could command and the number of jobs offered. Prior to the accident, Charlie was a favorite and commanded excellent fees.

Although models didn't usually receive salaries, there were a few exceptions. Perfecta, a new line of cosmetics, had decided to go with a new concept – one model to represent their entire product line. The two-year contract was the largest dollar amount ever. Charlie had been amazed to learn she had been selected one of five finalists. Her *look* was considered unconventional. Two other finalists, Betsy Daniels and Julie Ranken, were both brunettes and all-American classic beauties. The other natural blond, Sunny Lee Jones, was a former Miss Virginia and possessed a trained soprano voice and eye-riveting cleavage. Insiders said that Brigitta Schwimmer and Charlie had been selected in part for their athletic ability. Brigitta had been an Olympic downhill skier before she had dyed her hair a stunning red and switched to modeling. It was rumored in the industry that an opponent had accused Brigitta of tampering with her skis. Unsubstantiated rumors often followed models the others didn't like. Charlie had met Brigitta at the tryouts for the Perfecta contract, and had found nothing to dislike. She was eager to advance in the competition but then, all the girls were.

If Charlie was chosen to represent Perfecta, the contract would guarantee an impressive income. The likelihood of that happening now was zero. However, photos of all candidates, shot prior to the accident, continued to be used as part of Perfecta's publicity. A few welcome checks should arrive in the mail.

*   *   *

Charlie managed to get her shot before Dr. Horowitz's morning rounds so that she could discuss her progress intelligently. Nine dreary monotonous days had passed since being hospitalized and she was hoping for some encouraging news.

While a young student nurse, wearing no makeup to cheer her gaunt face and colorless complexion silently observed, Dr. Horowitz ran his practiced hand across her bandaged ribcage. "Tell me how it feels when you breathe."

"Almost as good as it did before the accident."

"Oh to be young again. The young heal quickly. Have I told you, according to your latest X-rays, if you give your therapist your complete cooperation, you will be able to walk."

Charlie gasped, heady with relief. "Will my limp be worse than before?"

"Let's not get ahead of ourselves. You might need a cane. You might not. I can't predict how this will affect your limp. Depends on how hard you're willing to work."

"Work doesn't frighten me. I'll do it. Anything. Would it be all right if I kiss you?"

Horowitz's owl eyes twinkled with amusement. "Only if Nurse Rowling promises not to report us. How about it, Nurse Rowling? Can we count on you?"

The student nurse responded first with a confused dazed look then smiled shyly and nodded.

When he bent forward, Charlie pecked the proffered cheek.

"When do I begin therapy? I'm sure you understand how eager I am to get back to work."

"Patience! Therapy isn't a miracle pill – take two and feel better the next morning. But I have some more good news for you. Tomorrow, you're getting a new cast. You'll like it. It's shorter and therefore lighter." He removed the link that maintained traction and slowly lowered her leg. "Now, when did we last look at your scalp?"

"The day before yesterday," she answered, as her calf met the sheet.

"Those last stitches should be ready to go."

"I'm going to lose my mummy hat."

"In ten minutes your mummy hat will be history. You may need a small bandage; we'll have to see. And now you're going to sit up." He reached behind her back. "Nurse, please take her arms and pay attention to the cast. I'll handle the rest. Try not to help. Let us do all the work." Gradually, they repositioned her into a sitting position on the bed and then into a wheel chair.

To be upright after the innumerable hours spent horizontal was wonderful and a bit dizzying. Dr. Horowitz gingerly lifted the layers of tape and gauze before each stitch was cut and gently tugged free. She knew what to expect – first the sting and then the freeing release of tension.

"Don't be looking for your mirror just yet," Dr. Horowitz advised, as he swabbed her scalp with something cool and strong smelling. "There's a lot of ugly clotted material. You can check out Dr. Lazaar's handiwork after your hair is washed."

"My hair, washed. That's going to be pure bliss. When is this going to happen?"

"As soon as I leave. Right, Nurse?"

The serious young woman nodded.

"And tomorrow, after we change your cast, you'll be starting therapy in earnest. I've assigned you to Pat Torres. In my opinion, she's the best there is. Now, do you have any shorts or sweat pants and a polo shirt here at the hospital? I know how you ladies feel about these revealing hospital gowns."

Charlie's mind raced ahead. Clothing. Moving about a gymnasium. She had been so busy doing absolutely nothing, she had forgotten the obvious. With her purse gone, Raul had the only key to her apartment and access to her clothing. And now she would have to contact him. Ask for help. See him again.

"As part of an experiment I'm conducting, you're being paired with another patient. Detective Thorenson was admitted the day before you. " Horowitz lifted both her free left hand and the right one extending from her cast and nodded approvingly.

"Detective Thorenson is a policeman?"

"Yes. One of New York City's finest. Does it bother you that you're being paired with a man?" he asked. "I believe that paired patients recover faster. Thus far, three teams, not under my care, who required similar therapy have proven the theory correct, which is why I'm recommending it for you. But perhaps you're worried that a member of your family, or perhaps your boyfriend, will disapprove? I would be happy to explain my recommendation to anyone you choose. Sometimes a few words to a concerned relative from the patient's doctor . . ."

Charlie assured him that wouldn't be necessary and after one last look at her scalp, he left.

Nurse Helen Rowling rolled her chair to the sink and helped her lean back, using a rolled towel to support her neck. A gentle stream of warm water flowed down her hair and head. Despite the sting where the latest stitches had been removed, the sensation was exhilarating. She closed her eyes to savor the simple pleasure: cool shampoo and gentle fingers massaging and rinsing, until her hair and scalp were clean again.

"Wait until you meet Detective Thorenson," Helen said, as she towel-dried Charlie's hair. "All the nurses think he's dreamy."

"How did he get hurt?" Charlie inquired.

As the nurse gave her a sponge bath and helped change her gown, she described the detective's assault.

Criminals he had been pursuing had thrown him out a sixth story window. People at the scene, and the doctors that later treated Thorenson all agreed. If his fall hadn't been broken by a storefront canvas awning, he surely would been killed or been left a quadriplegic. Miraculously, the officer's injuries were confined to head-to-toe bruises and both his legs shattered.

Once she was back in bed, her leg reattached to the overhead bar, Charlie dialed Raul's office. With physical therapy beginning tomorrow, she didn't have the luxury of preparing and rehearsing a conversation, so she apologized for calling during business hours, assured him she was fine, and explained the favor she needed. Fortunately, he was occupied with a client and had to turn her over to his personal secretary.

"Let me repeat that," Jane said. "Shorts, sweat pants, polo shirts, sneakers, socks, bras, and panties, nightgowns, a light robe, combs, brushes, something to hold your hair and deodorant. What about makeup, moisturizer, hand lotion, cologne and your favorite soap? You should really have a few cardigans. Hospitals can be chilly."

"It's so easy to forget things you don't realize you need until you see them."

"Mr. Francesco didn't have a chance to explain that I'm going to leave early tonight and take care of it. I'll drop those things off tomorrow before work – if that's all right with you."

"That would be great. I can't thank you enough."

"I'm happy that I can help. If you think of anything else, please call."

Charlie checked the wall clock. Seventy-five minutes remained before she could request medication. Approximately forty-five minutes of relative comfort left. Raul had asked Jane to go to the apartment they'd shared and pick out things she had requested and deliver them, she thought. Why? Too busy? Prior engagement? To avoid seeing her? Or did this simply reflect his decision to end their relationship?

What if one of his parents was seriously ill? With a rare untreatable disease. A fatal untreatable disease. His mother. Would he consider it his duty, as her only son, to put aside his happiness and spend all his free time with her before she died? Possibly.

Or it could be what she'd suspected from the first. That he woke up one morning and realized that she was a tall skinny girl with small breasts and uneven features. He was shorter than she was. In high heels, she was a lot taller. Maybe being seen as a lopsided couple bothered him, despite all his protests to the contrary. Particularly if there was another woman – a gorgeous woman, like the curvaceous strawberry blond they saw mornings on their way to work, walking her fluffy white dog. The exchanged smiles had been impossible to miss.

Women were drawn to Raul. They couldn't help themselves. Even women like Gloria Blair, glamorous star of stage and screen. Blond hair, big boobs, breathy voice, no discernible talent. Raul had handled a rental lease for Gloria when she was hired to do a mindless role in a Broadway production still going strong. She had kept asking to meet him after work about contracts she wanted to discuss with someone "not in the business." Talent agents handled contracts. And Raul wasn't an agent. But he might be seeing the calculating tart that evening – taking her to dinner while her understudy filled in for her. And afterward they could return to his apartment for drinks and . . . And a few tricks in bed that Gloria could no doubt teach every man in Manhattan. With luck, the shameless tramp would lose interest in a year or two.

What if there wasn't another woman? What if she was

absolutely and entirely wrong? What if – and the chances were remote – Raul had decided to become a priest and he was testing his resolution with the separation? He had confessed, that when he was a eight or nine years old, he had told his parents that he was going to "give his life to Jesus." And now, disgusted with a decadent society, he decided to follow his first ambition. Father Raul, who left behind the pleasures of the flesh to minister to a parish. Or a monk. Brother Raul, who spent his life in a remote monastery.

Charlie sighed. She was a silly lovesick girl with the overactive imagination she had been accused of having for as long as she could remember. No man who enjoyed sex as much as Raul became a monk. Simply recalling phrases he had whispered, erotic games they had played, orgasmic heights he had taken her to, made her body ache with longing.

Luckily, as the effect of the medication faded, she was distracted by something easier to understand. Physical pain.

*   *   *

Before Charlie could figure out what to do with the two suitcases Jane had left, a stout dark haired nurse whose nametag read Betty Knightly, arrived with an orderly and informed her that she was being transferred to another room.

"Both suitcases are mine," Charlie admitted.

"Make sure her leg stays steady! Comprendez? Her leg. No move," Nurse Knightly said, gesturing to the orderly. "Don't worry, honey. We're coming back for your things. Can't do it all in one trip. And you can save your jokes about the name. I've heard them all. If I knew what I would have to put up with every day of my life, I never would've married that man."

The orderly steadied Charlie's hoisted leg.

"Do you know anything about my new roommate?" Charlie asked.

"I do, but nurses are not allowed to gossip about patients," Nurse Knightly declared. "You'll find out soon enough."

She and the orderly maneuvered the bed through a series of doors, on and off the elevator, and down a hallway. The surroundings had changed noticeably. Doors were farther apart and more likely to be closed.

"Okay. We're here. Be sure to thank Dr. Horowitz the next time you see him." Nurse Knightly steered the bed inside. "You'll be sharing this suite with Detective Kenneth Thorenson. Detective, this is Charlotte Morgan."

Detective Thorenson waved from the bed near the window. "Hi. It's Detective Thorenson only when I'm on duty. Off duty, I'm Ken."

No wonder the young nurse had blushed when she talked about the officer, Charlie thought. From the waist up, Ken Thorenson was a very attractive man. Broad shoulders. Muscled forearms. Thick wavy blond hair. Vibrant blue eyes. Strong jaw. Perhaps thirty. Nevertheless, someone had erred. Hospital rooms were assigned to either men or women. "I'm afraid there's been a mistake," Charlie said. "Dr. Horowitz paired us for therapy, not as roommates."

"There's been no mistake, honey. I'm just following Dr. Horowitz's orders," Nurse Knightly informed her. "He's asked you both to try it as an experiment. Either of you can ask to be moved if you're not happy with the arrangement. And if you're worried about privacy . . ." She pulled a suspended double-sided velveteen drape that divided the expansive area. "That way you have your own room."

It was two rooms. Divided, each room was double the size of the cell she had just left and nothing like it. Except for the rolling hospital tables, the suite could be mistaken for accommodations at an expensive hotel. Furnishings included two tapestry-covered armchairs, lamps and lamp tables, a couch, two dressers and a television set. Natural sunlight from wide windows that overlooked the Hudson River flooded the room.

"This place is usually reserved for heads of state, senators and movie stars," Nurse Knightly explained. "But Detective Thorenson is a decorated police officer injured in the line of duty, and a real live hero. Mayor Lindsay came to visit him *twice*."

"That's very nice," Charlie responded. "But I requested a semi-private room. My insurance won't cover anything like this."

"That's why you have to thank Dr. Horowitz. Since you've been assigned to share it with Detective Thorenson, your half has been temporarily designated semi-private." It was impossible for models to be prudish. Dressing rooms were hastily arranged affairs that provided minimal privacy. Doing runway shows, designers, most of whom were men, were forever checking and tweaking their creations amid a flurry of indifferent half-naked models. As for photographers, they had no qualms about being ruthlessly blunt. Every detail of a model's body was subject to scrutiny, criticism and suggested modification. Plastic surgery, foam-rubber bosom enhancers, and unwanted-hair removal, for example, were routinely discussed.

Still, there were body functions and visiting friends to consider. She was certain to be teased unmercifully. What if Raul visited? He would never approve. "I don't think my family would be comfortable with . . ."

"Tell your husband, or your boyfriend, that he doesn't have to worry about me," Thorenson said. "You couldn't have a safer roommate." He lifted his sheet exposing his legs. Both were in bulky white casts that extended from hip to toe.

"I'm sure that you're a perfect gentleman, with or without the casts."

"Say, I know who you are. Charlotte . . . The model who was pushed off a subway platform. I recognize you from television. Crazy case!"

"I guess we both had bad timing."

"I don't talk in my sleep or snore. At least that's what I'm told,' he said, smiling shyly. "And I'm pretty quiet, sometimes too quiet according to my ex-wife."

It was impossible not to admire the man. He seemed so undaunted by his surroundings or physical condition. Her pain was intense. She forced herself to breathe regularly and smile before checking her watch. Nineteen minutes remained before she could request relief, and then God knew how long until a nurse would arrive with medication. She wondered how long *heroes,* who had been visited *twice* by Mayor Lindsey, had to wait before a buzzer was answered. "I don't suppose you ever have to beg for something to ease the pain."

"I don't understand. The nurses here are first rate. They couldn't do more for me."

"This wing has extra personnel," Nurse Knightly explained. "But even if it didn't, we've been given strict orders to provide Detective Thorenson with the finest care possible."

Let visitors have a good laugh at her expense, Charlie decided. Teasing was nothing compared to pain. She had been paired with a patient who required similar physical therapy by her doctor. That the patient was an attractive man – an unattached attractive man – was a matter of chance and beyond her control. As for Raul, he had abandoned all right to object when he packed his bags and moved out. Should he drop in, he would have to deal with whatever hurtful suspicions rose to trouble him. He didn't have to know that her motive in accepting the arrangement was purely practical.

"Please call me 'Charlie.'"

~ **Chapter 5** ~

A hundred years earlier archeological excavations were little more than organized treasure hunts. Local rulers could be bribed to permit foraging foreigners to mine gravesites and confiscate the irreplaceable artifacts, or to hack off and haul away priceless stonework, just as Lord Elgin did in the early 19th century at the Parthenon. Throughout England and Europe, it was a favored hobby of the wealthy. Enlightened royalty often had been persuaded to finance these so-called scientific expeditions. In return, they received magnificent statuary or other works of art to adorn their palaces or national museums. And if the local rulers couldn't be persuaded, bribed or bought, there was always outright theft or war.

By the twentieth century, virtually every country sought to protect its prized historic identity and national pride. Painstaking modern archeological methods were employed. Sites and related artifacts had to be photographed and recorded. Excavations were typically divided into a grid and an unique ID was assigned to each segment. Retrieved items were labeled with a corresponding address and entered in a log, noting the object, the ID, the depth where found and any other pertinent information. Caches were photographed or sketched before their contents were removed. A body wrapped in finely woven linen, buried with tools and personal adornments, had vastly different connotations from a bare haphazardly-arranged skeleton. As for tools, as soon as the first artifact was uncovered, shovels and picks were replaced by smaller digging devices such as trowels and hand picks. Delicate items were meticulously freed from their confines using a range of implements, from paintbrushes to dental tools, depending upon the material, delicacy, and condition of the find. Loose soil was sifted to find tiny items that might have escaped detection.

At Naomi's site, the stone dwellings and cisterns, as well as the artifact-rich *midden*, or garbage dumps, had all been excavated. No human remains had been found. Sponsors decided, without going down to bedrock, something they were unprepared to do, that the site had revealed all that it would. Two weeks before they were set to leave, while walking, Naomi spotted an object exposed by the elements, jutting out of the sand. Closer inspection revealed a partial jaw and teeth – undeniably human. Naomi ran to find Uri. Without waiting for corroborating carbon dating, feverish excavation began immediately. Two complete skeletons were located nearby. Naomi had found the valuable missing burial ground. The sponsors agreed it would be foolish to stop now. Awarded first choice of location, Naomi selected a spot not far from her original find. Within a month, carbon dating confirmed what the team had suspected – the bones were as old as early artifacts.

Four months had passed since the two American students had given her the magazine containing a picture of the model who so strongly resembled herself when she was young – a woman who might or might not be her daughter. Scanning every American magazine available, Naomi had discovered other pictures and learned her name – Charlie. Perhaps Alain had changed their names, Naomi had reasoned. That would explain the failed attempts to locate him and their daughters.

She had stared at the pictures for hours, trying to compare the toddler she remembered to this glossy mannequin. Some features, such as her oversized upper lip and pronounced cheekbones, were familiar. Others were not. This Charlie was so tall. Would Michelle be that tall? She was two years old the last time Naomi had seen her. Alain was tall, but not exceptionally so. The reverse pout that the summer interns had cited as proof, the peculiar mannerism they shared, was noticeable in only one photo. Surely thousands of people had the habit of occasionally pursing their mouths. And Michelle's eyes were a deeper blue, or perhaps the intervening years had altered Naomi's memory. Four months of torment and she was no closer to a decision. Somewhere in the United States were two women in their twenties who believed their mother unfit, uncaring or dead – whatever lies Alain had fed them.

*   *   *

One Friday, in the early afternoon, as she was examining the contents of her sifting box, Naomi noticed a truck leaving the unpaved road and heading toward them. It was an unlikely time for visitors. At dusk all work would halt for the Sabbath. As the truck neared Naomi recognized the driver. It was Ruben Kane, a widower she had met at a café in town a year ago. Normally Naomi's lovers were handsome, lean, educated, and temporary: soldiers, tourists, summer interns. Ruben Kane was none of these things. He was a brute-like man with a thick neck, thinning coarse curly hair, and a broad nose. Were it not for the unexpected and sudden flashes of fire in his eyes, he might have been quarried from sandstone.

It was incomprehensible to Naomi why she had sat with him, drinking her coffee in the busy café, why she had stayed to listen to his depressing story. He was the son of Polish shopkeeper parents who had relocated to Palestine in the late twenties and purchased land from the local tribal leaders. The family's early years were typical for pioneers, filled with countless disasters and near starvation until the novice farmers learned how to seduce the desert into providing for them. And there were always the unexpected unprovoked attacks like the one that had taken Kane's wife a month earlier. A sniper had shot the young mother. She died before medics could reach her. Naomi never did understand why she had agreed to leave the café with Kane, allowed him to drive her to the outskirts of town and lead her twenty paces off the road onto the sand. Perhaps it was because her Israeli soldier lover had been transferred two months earlier, and the need for sex was strong.

There was nothing tentative or tender in their first sexual encounter; no flattery or foreplay. Which was fine with Naomi, who preferred penetration before her body could prepare, as near to rape as possible. She sought the sting of sudden entry. It fueled the rage she believed she needed to survive. When they finished, the spent man didn't move except to place his head on her breast. She lay there thinking he would soon lift his bulky weight off her. Instead, he began to weep. Soft weeping turned into racking sobs. Not knowing what else to do, Naomi cradled his bearlike frame in her arms and found long forgotten words of comfort in French, the language of her childhood. As she lay beneath him, it began to rain, a light drizzle that quickly turned into a torrential desert downpour. Water dripped from his hair onto her face. The clothes they hadn't bothered to remove were wet and heavy. A bubbling puddle circled them. The cooling rain washed away Kane's tears and he made love to her again, this time not like a drunken soldier on a twenty-four-hour leave, but slowly, gently, like a caring bridegroom with a virgin bride. Despite herself, she responded in kind, almost forgetting the parade of loveless sex in the past. As Kane released his seed deep within her, a fork of lightning lit the sky and the earth below –

followed almost instantly by a deafening crash of thunder. Naomi felt the ground tremble under her, a frightening electric shock followed by dry rain. Another bolt of lightning, miles away, lit the night and allowed them to see the remains of the shattered tower, fifty paces away, that had taken the strike. The dry rain was the bits of flying debris. Had they driven another five seconds they might have been killed. Kane tried to tell her something, but the powerful storm drowned out his words. He helped her to her feet, led her back to his truck, and wordlessly drove her to camp. She hadn't seen him since.

Over the past year she had often thought about the preternatural events of that night and wondered what had happened to him – why he hadn't pursued her. Men generally did. Perhaps he had found someone else, or had remarried. A farmer with three young children needed a wife. Strict Jewish law allowed a widowed man with young children to remarry before the otherwise prescribed year of mourning ended.

"I'm going into town," Kane said as he casually ambled toward her, as though he had seen her the day before. "If we leave now, we can buy provisions before everything closes for the Sabbath. You'll come to my house afterwards."

Uri, who had drifted over as Kane approached, asked, "If you're going into Acre, would you mind if we came too? The back of your truck is empty."

Kane nodded and shrugged his broad shoulders. "Come. As many as can fit."

Automobiles and gasoline were expensive. Hitching rides was common in Israel.

"Give us a few minutes to put away our tools and wash up," Uri said.

Although Naomi feigned indifference, this was an opportunity for a long hot bath with thick towels, and maybe a night in a bed with a mattress. Odds were the farmer would provide a Sabbath dinner meal finer than the camp's plain fare. And the sex would hold her for a while. Ugly as he was, Ruben Kane had the stamina and physical equipment of a bull.

As the others noisily prepared to leave, Naomi replaced her tools, washed her face and hands, and took a seat in the truck's cab.

"You thought that I forgot about you," Kane said over the

truck's rattle and the cheerful singing from the rear cargo area.

"There was nothing to remember," she said.

"You're not going to ask why I didn't come to see you after that night?" he asked, looking amused.

"No."

"Maybe I was killed."

She shrugged. "It's a small country. If you were killed, I would have heard."

He stroked his curly dark beard and smiled to himself. "You found a burial ground. Were there artifacts or just bones?"

"Trinkets. Nothing elaborate."

"Simple cloth wrappings, no signs of mummification or tattoos?"

"Yes."

"Jews," he announced, with more than a touch of pride. "Proof that we were here before."

He was right and he was wrong. Jews had occupied this site, but not every site that contained undefiled human remains indicated Jewish settlements.

"Don't assume because I work with my hands that I'm a mindless beast who lacks feeling for our history. There are many books in my house."

The truck bounced and lurched as it threaded its way down the unpaved road. "You let your beard grow," Naomi said. "You look different."

"Different." He nodded and laughed as though she had made a fine joke. "My children are with my brother and his family for the Sabbath. The house is empty. You'll come home with me tonight. In the morning I'll make you cheese blintzes and sour cream for breakfast."

The mention of the childhood treat made her unconsciously lick her lips. "A farmer who cooks."

"I'm a widower with three children who all like to eat," he said, laughing again.

Naomi couldn't decide if he was mocking her. "I like berries with blintzes," she said, simply to be contrary, annoyed by his good humor and that he took for granted that she would accompany him.

"You like berries with your blintzes. What kind of berries?"

"Strawberries, raspberries, blueberries, any kind of berries." The thought of the juicy ripe berries made her mouth water.

"If we can find berries, I'll buy them for you."

"What about dinner? I'm hungry."

"I'll buy cheese, bread, and chickpeas, cucumbers and some falafel."

"I'm sick of cheese and bread. I want chicken or meat."

"Pick out whatever you like."

"When will your children return?"

"Tomorrow after sundown."

"I want to be back in camp before they return."

He turned to her and grinned. "Anything else you want, my lady? I didn't bring a pencil and paper."

"I'll let you know."

*   *   *

Naomi permitted Kane to show her his home. Compared to her family's Paris residence the house was small. Compared to her room at the kibbutz or the field tent, it was palatial. She hadn't lived in a dwelling reserved for a single family's use in more than two decades. By local standards, it was spacious and comfortable. And for a widower with three school-age children, it was surprisingly neat. But the home-sewn sheer curtains, chair cushions, and decorations, all said they were chosen by his dead wife. The sole exception was Kane's desk and the shelves above it, the latter holding as many as a hundred books, grouped by subjects. Naomi scanned the titles. They were a mixture of agricultural, practical mechanics, and novels, some classics, some contemporary. When they reached the room his sons shared, she managed to view the few toys and personal items with forced detachment. Nor did the sparse master bedroom with its solitary bed trouble her.

"Your wife," she said, pointing to a framed photograph on the nightstand.

Kane leapt to place it face down.

Naomi righted the picture. "You needn't bother. I have no interest in replacing her."

The small flowery room occupied by Kane's daughter caused her knees to buckle. The single doll gazing into space from a child's chair, the teddy bear minus one eye, the ruffled spread, forced her to reach for a wall to steady herself. If Kane observed her reaction, he said nothing. When they left, he closed the door to his daughter's room firmly behind them. She wondered what he knew about her past.

When they returned to the living room, Kane removed a small box from his pocket and handed it to her. "For you. A little gift. A nice hot bath will feel good."

Naomi examined the box. It contained two cakes of lilac-scented soap. She recognized the expensive French label. "Save it for someone else. I don't need fancy soap. Plain soap is fine."

"You asked for berries," he said, refusing the proffered box. "The greengrocer didn't have any. I bought you the soap instead."

She stayed in the tub a decadent forty-five minutes and emerged refreshed and smelling of lilacs.

"I put the television on," he said, his gaze dropping to the part of her breasts not covered by the towel and then returned to her face. "You can watch the news or an American western while I shower."

While most Israeli homeowners owned a television, one was not to be found on a dig. Naomi quickly lost herself in *Gunsmoke*, with its rangy virile sheriff. An hour of watching television was a luxury equal to an unhurried hot bath or a filet mignon.

Kane returned in a worn navy bathrobe, clean-shaven.

"You shaved your beard."

He took the seat next to her on the couch. "I thought you would be pleased."

"Your face is your business."

"Was your American husband clean-shaven?"

He knew she had been married. "Yes."

"Was he handsome?"

"Very handsome." Kane's face was broad and plain with plump cheeks and an incongruous small bow mouth. It was hard to make the comparison without smiling at the absurdity.

"Not like me, eh? I'm forty-two. And you're forty-four, not that you look it. You have the figure of a girl. It's hard to believe that you gave birth to two children."

"How do you know so much about me?" she asked, both curious and annoyed.

"Did you think you were the only one in the Haganah? Three years I served. I know a great deal about your past."

"I've been with hundreds of men, maybe thousands. If that's

what you wanted to know, all you had to do was ask."

"I'm not interested in how many men you've been with. The last time we met we talked about me, my wife, and children. I want to know more about you."

"I don't discuss my life. Not with you. Not with anyone." Naomi stood, deliberately blocked the television screen, and allowed the towel to drop to the floor. She watched his eyes narrow as they slid over her naked breasts, navel, and pubic area. "Isn't this why you brought me here?"

"Partially." He rose and slid his roughened hands down her spine, and gently squeezed her buttocks. "I could have picked you up in town tomorrow night if it was all I wanted. I didn't have to ask my sister-in-law to take my children for a day and a half."

She reached inside his robe, triumphant when his thick semi-erect member engorged and exceeded the width of her hand. "This is why I came. For this, a hot bath, and a decent meal. Don't expect any more from me. I have nothing left to give."

He flung his head back and closed his eyes. "Maybe not. But I can't clear your scent from my nostrils," he said, as though determined to express his thoughts before lust overcame him. "This I know because I've tried. For an entire year, I tried. I blame the lightning. The lightning fused our souls that night."

She pulled his face to hers and sank back onto the couch, taking him with her, guiding his cock, not inside her, but between her legs. "No more talk of lightning. Tell me how the sight of my ass, my tits, my mouth excites you. Talk to me only about fucking."

*　*　*

Following the promised blintzes and sour cream the next morning, Kane proudly showed Naomi the land surrounding his home. A family-sized vegetable garden was adjacent to the house, and lines of citrus trees extended as far as the eye could see. A large metal shed held a tractor, a wall covered with tools, and rows of stacked baskets.

"My brother Avram and I share the tractor."

I"No chickens?"

"No chickens. No sheep. I hate the stench of livestock. Close your eyes and sniff the air. When they bud, when they blossom, when the fruit ripens, citrus trees smell wonderful every day of the year."

Naomi breathed in the scent of the fragrant ripening oranges. They reached a patch of thick grass amongst the trees. "Ruben, make love to me."

"Later. I want to make love to you before I drive you back to camp, so you can think about me in your bed tonight as you wait for sleep."

"Now. Here."

"Come. We'll go back to the house. I have a large collection of records. You can pick out whatever you want to listen to."

She slipped her arms under his and wrapped them about his back. "What sort of music, Israeli or American?"

"I don't know who's worse – French Jews or German Jews. You're impossible snobs. You think you invented culture. I have Chopin, Tchaikovsky, Beethoven, Strauss, Mozart," he said, as she filled his ear with her moist breath. "And if you want American composers, I have Copland and Gershwin – *Rhapsody in Blue*."

She bit his lobe hard enough to sting. "The records will wait. Make love to me now!"

He pinned her against a tree with his wide frame and thrust his groin against hers. "This is what you want. You want me to touch only your body and not your brain. So you can hide from me."

"And tomorrow, I may not want even that."

*   *   *

Naomi did think about Ruben Kane as she waited for sleep, and many other times as well. While she worked, the piercing sun burning through her blouse, she could feel his rough callused hands exploring her body, his thick torso against hers. He was a patient and considerate lover, and yet there was something of an animal about him; the way he sniffed the air and listened for sounds she couldn't hear, the way his never-still eyes took in his surroundings. She was certain, even when he slept, that he could instantly will himself alert. It was a trait many in the Haganah possessed. Perhaps that was his attraction. He was like a fierce mangy lion guarding his pride, ever watchful. She felt oddly safe in his presence.

But Ruben didn't come to camp the following Friday or the Friday after that. Not that he had promised, or implied that he would come. She wondered if another year would pass before their next meeting. Perhaps, she mocked to amuse and console herself, the man only required yearly sex.

~ **Chapter 6** ~

Within twenty-four hours Charlie knew that she no longer had to wait in excruciating pain for medication or was forced to use the unpleasant bedpan. As promised, Ken didn't talk in his sleep or snore. He didn't chatter incessantly. But sharing accommodations with a stranger had many of the problems one could expect to encounter trapped on a raft in the middle of the ocean. They quickly established guidelines for peaceful coexistence.

Regarding the single television, they would draw asterisks beside upcoming programs in *TV Guide* they really wanted to see, and underline general preferences. Stars took precedence over underlines, and the inevitable conflicts were negotiated. Both radios, or the television and a radio, could be played simultaneously only if the volume was kept low and the drape was closed.

When not required for privacy, the dividing drape was left open. The suite became stuffy when it was drawn. Ken's worst injuries, which he casually dismissed, Charlie learned, were his shattered, not merely broken, femurs. Located in the thigh, the femur is the largest bone in the human body. He required help getting out of bed, but once both the bulky cumbersome casts touched the floor, he could transfer himself to a wheelchair if one was provided. With crutches, usually left on the wall near his bed, he could navigate the trip to and from the bathroom. Her right leg still required traction for part of the day, and she wasn't permitted to put any weight on it. She could move in and out of a wheelchair only with assistance. The decision was, whoever was closer to the drape, or more mobile at the time, was in charge of adjusting it.

And with regard to the obvious, without having to discuss it, they automatically turned their eyes skyward if accidentally a part of their companion's anatomy, normally covered, became exposed.

Visitors, unless forewarned, were stunned. After the experimental pairing was explained and the use of the opaque dividing drape demonstrated, they pretended sophisticated indifference.

Most of Ken's visitors were cops, whose conversations with Charlie were oddly formal. She assumed that the hushed comments and unfamiliar snickering from the other side of the drape had something to do with her. That worked both ways. Not surprising, when Ken was out of the room, or sufficiently beyond hearing range, every visiting female guest of hers giggled and whispered their appreciation of Ken's good looks.

*   *   *

"What made you come to New York? Don't they need cops in Wisconsin?" she asked as they ate lunch, about a week after her arrival.

"All that fresh air and dairy products makes for dull criminals." His face took on the lopsided grin she now knew accompanied half-truths and bold-faced lies. "It's a well-known fact that cheese makes you neighborly. Ask anyone from Wisconsin. Now concrete and steel, with no place to park a cigarette, let alone a car, makes for some very interesting bad guys."

"Like the men who tossed you out the window."

Ken couldn't suppress a smirk. "Excellent examples."

"I thought cops traveled in pairs. Where was your partner when you were doing your flying act?"

"Waiting downstairs like I asked him to."

"Shouldn't he have been with you?"

"Not this time. I'd received a call from a snitch I'd used before. He said that he had information about a case I was working on – gave me enough so I knew that he wasn't lying. But I had to come alone. He said he didn't feel safe around my partner. I should've known what was coming the minute I opened the door. The little rat was shaking like he was tied to an electric butter churner. I'm thinking they forced him to do it. Anyway, he was found the next day at a Jersey construction site with his throat slit."

"And his accomplice?"

"Accomplices," Ken corrected. "Two gorillas – men paid to dish out punishment, or in my case, kill someone – are now incarcerated. We have a good idea about who hired them, but so far they haven't talked."

Charlie swallowed. Hearing a new friend describe a horrific act perpetrated against him wasn't the same as listening to reports on the news. Perhaps it was just as well his family lived in Wisconsin, too far to read the daily newspaper reports of crime in Manhattan. "Why were you singled out?"

"They knew that I'm going to testify against them – things I'm not allowed to discuss before the trial." He shrugged and smiled. "How long has it been since you met with someone assigned to your case?"

"I don't know. A while."

"Hmmm," he murmured as he stretched to scratch his toes with a hairbrush he used for that purpose. "Do you remember which cops interviewed you?"

Charlie reached back into memory. "Kowalski and . . . Mallone or Marrone. Detectives."

"It's not the kind of case that gets dropped. Too much publicity. But I bet you'd appreciate hearing from them – just to let you know what's going on."

"Can you do that?" she asked, surprised she hadn't considered the power of her fate-delivered, valuable connection before.

"If I ask nicely. Probably."

*   *   *

The following day when Charlie and Ken were wheeled back from their afternoon therapy session they found Detectives Marrone and Kowalski waiting for them.

"Detective Thorenson can stay in the chair if he wishes," Nurse Knightly advised the accompanying aide. "But it's back to bed and traction for Miss Morgan."

"Fifteen minutes more," Charlie coaxed, dreading return to imprisonment. "I feel fine. Really. And we have company."

"Fifteen minutes." Nurse Knightly shook her head in resignation. "Buzz when they leave and not a minute later. That leg needs to be raised.

"I want this treatment if I go down in the line of duty." Detective Marrone's deep-set eyes swept the suite. "Couple months with nothing to do but worry about what you're going to eat for lunch. Nurses to wait on you. Look at this place. It's the size of my house."

"Ray Kowalski," his partner said, rising to shake Ken's hand. "Nice to meet you."

Essentially ignoring Charlie, who was silently observing the scene, the three men exchanged names, precincts, divisions, superior officers, and quips. Their conversation seemed to be an informal chat among foreigners who shared a common language. Ken's tone had changed. Although he lacked the visiting duo's harsh nasal accent, he spoke in a flat staccato that matched theirs.

"Charlie's waiting to hear how things are going on her case," Ken eventually prompted. "Any suspects?"

Marrone cleared his throat. "I wish we had better news. We checked out every soup kitchen and flophouse trying to find someone who came close to the composite. We asked if anyone had noticed a gutter rose wearing a crazy Army coat. Gutter rose – that's a bum, a hobo," Marrone translated for Charlie's benefit. "We came up with zero. Nada. Nothing."

"We hauled in every gutter rose with a beard and general build, sobered them up if necessary, grilled them, and then put a few in a lineup," Kowalski added. "Nothing. So we checked out recent discharges from the loony bins, but nobody matched the description or M.O."

Charlie had been scrambling to follow the unfamiliar slang. "What if he got rid of the coat and shaved his beard?"

Three pairs of eyes turned to look at her as though she had just suggested her assailant was the Easter Bunny.

"It's winter. Bums don't ditch warm coats in winter," Ken explained. "And one nuts enough to push you off a subway platform loaded with witnesses probably isn't sane enough to shave his beard."

"Did anyone see which way this guy went after the attack?" Ken asked, directing his question at the detectives.

"He jumped onto the tracks on the other side of the platform and took off into the tunnel. No sign of him after that," Kowalski said.

"Let's just say this wasn't a bum or a druggie, but a guy wearing a disguise," Ken suggested. "Is there anyone you can think of who would want to harm you?"

Stunned by the implication, Charlie turned her full attention to Ken. "I'm a model. It's not the sort of occupation that's likely to inspire an attack."

"What about the case you cracked, Charlie?" Ken continued. "What about the guy who put the scheme together? Interpol ever catch up with him?"

"You can't leave out revenge as a motive," Kowalski agreed.

"Fine, but he bore absolutely no resemblance to the man who attacked me," Charlie said, praying the three pairs of eyes hadn't noticed the nervous scarlet flush surging up her neck to her cheek. Only she, Raul, and the diabolical fiend himself knew of her father's involvement in crime, and she intended to keep it that way.

"What about your last boyfriend – the guy you were living with?" Marrone suggested.

Charlie shook her head at the nonsensical idea and laughed. "Raul? Never."

"What did you argue about? Is he the jealous type? Did he ever hit you? Threaten you in any way?" Marrone pressed. "We see these things every day. You don't have to be embarrassed."

"Maybe this is something you should discuss with Charlie in private." Ken inched his wheelchair closer to the door.

"Don't go. I've nothing to hide." Charlie waved Ken back. "We decided that we'd made a mistake and ended it. Besides, my attacker was two inches taller than Raul, and I don't know how many pounds lighter."

Marrone rose and reached for his overcoat. "I wish we had better news for you, Miss Morgan, but as it stands, there's not much we can do."

"I know you guys have fifty cases on your desk," Ken acknowledged, "but I'd really appreciate it if you would hit this one hard."

Before they left, both detectives assured Ken the investigation would remain open and active.

"I was able to follow most of what they said," she told Ken after she was once again in bed and tied to her post. "Vic is victim. Perp is perpetrator. But what's an M.O.?"

"M.O. – modus operandi – the way a criminal commits a crime. Did he wear a mask, shout, tie up his victim in a special way? Did he say anything special? Little quirks help us know if we're dealing with one guy or many."

"And a gutter rose is cop language for a hobo."

Ken laughed. "No. That's Marrone's idea of a joke."

*   *   *

Hugh Downs' face faded into the darkening television screen. Charlie and Ken watched NBC for the news, and then the *Today* show before heading for morning PT. Their days had become a cycle of doctors, nurses, meals, assisted bathing, reading the newspapers, telephone calls to and from the concerned, the eight am, six pm, and eleven o'clock televised news, physical therapy, late afternoon visitors, and the occasional field trip to the X-ray Department.

It was the twice-daily PT that Charlie had come to dread. PT – physical therapy. Over the years, patients had invented a variety of catchphrases for the grueling exercise required to regain the flexibility and strength they had lost: *Plead and Threaten, Punish and Terrorize,* and *Pain and Torture.*

Before being teamed with Ken, Charlie's therapy had been limited to relatively simple exercises. Now, like Ken, she used weights, whirlpools, waist-high parallel bars, tilt tables, and a series of grim machines that resembled instruments of the Inquisition. Pat Torres, considered the most knowledgeable and toughest therapist at the hospital, encouraged, challenged, and when necessary, bullied them to lift, arch, bend, extend, pull, and stretch. Nor was the PT facility the hushed antiseptic sanctuary Charlie had expected. Grunts, growls, moans, complaints, and the occasional shriek echoed off its creamy beige concrete walls and tiled floors. And she hadn't anticipated a therapist knowledgeably exerting pressure on a stiffened joint – a sensation akin to having an exposed nerve cauterized.

Ken appeared to be the only patient who looked forward to therapy. His competitiveness, it seemed to Charlie, bordered on fanaticism. If she did fifteen wrist-curls, he did thirty. She had begun the process of learning to walk again while Ken was still encased in his massive plaster prisons. But she had no doubt, once free, he would do everything humanly possible to breeze past her initial advantage.

"Do we have to listen to your whining?" he said, as Charlie waited for her heart to resume its normal pace and her face to go from presumably blotchy florid to sunless pale before continuing. "Do the ten, or twenty, or thirty reps you're supposed to do and quit whining."

"I don't whine. I negotiate. Sometimes I can't do all the reps."

"*Negotiating* – a fancy five dollar word for whining."

"What about you? You groan. You have no idea how annoying that is."

"Toss me a dry towel, please," he said to a patient near the pile of towels. "It's obvious that you've never been to a gym before. I don't groan. I grunt. You squeal. Athletes grunt when they work out. They don't sound like pigs being dragged to the butcher."

"You're not the only athlete here, you know. I can play golf, ride, swim, and ski, all without disgracing myself."

"No kidding. You ever win anything in high school or college? You have trophies or something?"

"I've won cartons of ribbons for riding." She also had won trophies at camp for good sportsmanship and swimming, but she decided that would not impress.

"Then quit whining and do the drill," Ken challenged.

So now she not only had to do every repetition without grumbling, she had to be careful the sounds she emitted came from the bass portion of her registry, and were unmistakably grunts. If he wasn't such good company, Ken Thorenson would be a real pain in the *butt-lift.*

*   *   *

Having Ken there helped pass the endless hours between therapy and visitors, even though topics for conversation were understandably limited. Unlike Charlie's girlfriends, Ken had no interest in makeup, manicurists, moisturizers, facials, hair stylists, datable single men, disgusting married men who posed as datable single men, tall girl shops, cosmetic surgery, or nightclubs. And she had quickly exhausted her repertoire of stories about demanding, eccentric, or maniacal photographers and designers. As for sports, she lacked Ken's fervor for televised competition. Fortunately, with a little prompting, Ken would discuss police cases where he'd been involved.

"Are you going to stay on the force and go back to what you were doing?" Charlie asked as they ate lunch on portable trays: she sitting up in bed, Ken in his wheelchair. "They could probably find you something safer to do, couldn't they?"

"Sure. But is that what you think I'd be happy doing?"

"I think you love being a cop and taking risks."

"You got that right. What about you? Do you love being a model?"

Charlie scraped the gummy gravy off her wrinkled peas. "I like the money. Sometimes we get to keep the clothing. I don't enjoy the endless time in Hair and Makeup or the waiting around between takes."

"So you're in it for the money and the clothes." Ken took his glass of milk from his empty meal-tray and shoved the cart to the side.

"I love being financially independent. Sometimes, when we travel, we get to spend a little time sightseeing. And there's a certain amount of excitement, glamour, the way people look at me when they learn that I'm a model. I get recognized from magazine layouts – which is flattering. It won't be easy going back to being a tall, gawky girl. But I may not have a choice. By the time I'm walking again, there might not be work waiting for me. It's a quick in and out business for girls in their teens and early twenties."

"No seniority. You'd have seniority if you were a cop."

"Seniority! Hah! That's one word you'll never hear in the fashion industry." Charlie pushed away her tray. New! Young! Exciting! That what magazine editors and photographers want. Provided her limp was no worse than it had been before the attack, she would be lucky to get hired for trade conventions or upscale department store fashion shows – work that was erratic and didn't pay a fraction of what she received doing magazine ads or designer runway jobs. And there was always the possibility that publicity from the attack could invigorate her career and give her another few years.

"What about that art thing? You uncovered some kind of fraud – fakes that were passed off as the real thing," Ken asked, after he finished his lunch. "I would guess a smart girl like you would prefer doing something like that."

Ken's view of career-women was surprisingly out of step with current thought. Most people assumed that at twenty-five she would be frantically seeking a suitable husband to support her. People tended to frown on the independent single woman. It was understood that wives could work until their first child was born – after that, only in cases of dire necessity. Soft-spoken maiden aunts, who relied on male relatives or held low-paying menial jobs, were objects of pity. Even trust-fund debutantes eventually succumbed to pressure to marry and produce heirs. But a single woman past twenty-five, with a serious career, was suspected of being frigid, a clandestine lesbian, or a brazen, amoral advocate of free-love. "I don't have the right training or credentials." "You were interviewed on television. It was in all the papers. They said you were an expert."

"That makes good newspaper headlines, but it doesn't hold any weight with museums or galleries."

Using his powerful arms to lift himself and both casts, Ken transferred himself from the wheelchair to the bed. "So what happened to the gallery that passed the fakes off as real? They ever get charged with aiding and abetting?"

"The owner of Gallery Three Fifty-Two was unaware the paintings were forged," "You mean the DA's office decided not to prosecute because they couldn't make a case."

"No. Madame Ivanavich was as much a victim as her customers. A gallery's reputation is everything. Madame Ivanavich relied on her own and a respected expert's opinion and got flim-flammed."

"Is she still in business or did the bad publicity shut her down?"

"I'm happy to say that she's still in business. After the story broke, to restore her reputation, Raul suggested that she provide my services to anyone who had purchased paintings from the gallery. She offered to refund the purchase price on anything suspected of being *improperly represented*, which is a fancy way of saying *fakes*," Charlie explained, grateful to have found a topic that Ken considered interesting. "I examined over three hundred paintings and found twenty-nine works I considered doubtful."

"How many of those customers wanted their money back?"

"Fourteen asked for refunds. Eight said they were satisfied that their paintings were genuine and insisted their experts were more experienced than I was – which they were, even if they were wrong. And seven wanted to keep the paintings for reasons of their own."

"Okay, how do you spot a fake? What do you look for?"

"It's impossible for me to explain, because it isn't . . . When I look at a painting supposedly done by a famous artist whose work I'm familiar with, I get a peculiar sensation that something isn't right. Sort of dizzy. The way you'd feel if you saw water flowing uphill, or you touched something you expected to be solid, like a shoe or table, and it turned out to be a cloud of smoke."

"Weird!" Ken said, turning to stare at her. "Really weird. Because I sometimes get that at a crime scene. Not the dizziness. More like a feeling that things don't make sense."

"Exactly!" Charlie said, amazed. "And other people don't see what you see?"

"Not unless I can tell them what's wrong, which a lot of times, I can't. When did you first realize you had the *gift*?"

"When I was in my teens, but I never believed . . . It's a hard thing to trust."

"You ever wrong?"

"Not yet."

"Me neither." Ken folded his hands behind his head. "There's got to be big money to be made passing fakes. Maybe millions."

"I suppose."

"Which makes me think there's a need for a person with your talent. You know, the New York City police department has squads assigned to bunko, narcotics, prostitution, homicides, and not one person doing anything about art unless something's reported stolen. And I bet it's pretty much the same with the FBI. They probably have an entire division devoted to counterfeiting, but not one agent assigned to crime involving fake art."

"The FBI has to protect the American dollar. Art fraud isn't a problem of national security."

Ken sat up. "Don't kid yourself. Where there's big money involved, wise guys are sitting up nights figuring out how to take it. There must be a market for someone who can do what you do. You spotted the fakes when the so-called experts didn't. Maybe you don't need modeling. Maybe you have something waiting for you that's better. More interesting. You just told me that modeling is 'a quick in and out business.'"

"I have a bachelor's degree in art history and a peculiar knack that I don't understand for spotting forgeries – some forgeries – done by artists whose work I'm familiar with. That doesn't qualify me as an expert."

"How did you learn in school? You listened to teachers and you read. Get yourself a bunch of books on the subject. I didn't go to school to make detective. I read."

If only it was that easy, Charlie thought. Three of the gallery's clients had asked to hire her to review their collections, but rather than confess her meager expertise, she had refused, claiming she couldn't spare the time. "People study for years in universities, then train with respected mentors. I can't afford that."

"Fine. Give up without trying." Ken punched his pillow – a certain precursor to a nap.

"You don't understand. You like to read. I don't."

"Who said I like to read?"

"Well, I was never a serious student. I got decent grades by paying attention in class and doing the homework assignments. I learn by listening and observing. I don't know how I would have managed if it weren't for Cliff Notes."

There was no response from the Ken's side of the suite and his back faced her. He wasn't interested in continuing the debate. PT, followed by a starchy lunch, had tired him – tired both of them. Even in this protected hospital wing, there were loud noises at night to interrupt sleep. Charlie pulled the sheet over her chest and shoulders. She closed her eyes and invited her outrageous imagination to contemplate what she had vehemently denied – living a fantasy – traveling the globe at the request of serious collectors and noted museum directors, discovering unknown masterpieces and uncovering sensational frauds.

*   *   *

Charlie's usually cheerful PT partner had been quiet and unsmiling since they had been awakened this morning at six. And he had left both his breakfast and lunch half-eaten. Ken normally consumed meals with gusto.

"No offense, but I want to go home," she said, hoping to probe the source of his unhappiness. "I hate the irritating creaking of crepe-soled shoes, being tied to this bed, unable to scratch where it itches, and inedible hospital food."

Ken look away from the television that he had been half-watching. "Are you planning to continue or can I ask you a serious question?"

He was going to confide in her, Charlie thought triumphantly. "I'm all ears."

Ken rolled his wheelchair closer to her bed. "The girls I grew up with all stayed in Minnesota, and so did my sisters," he explained to the radio on Charlie's night table. "There's something that's been bothering me." His voice dropped to a whisper "And it isn't something a guy can discuss with another guy. It's *personal*."

He wanted to discuss something *personal*. Ken didn't have to say another word. She knew. After being together twenty-four hours a day, a woman instinctively knew these things. The topic would either be about female body functions or sex. She prayed it was the former. If this heart-to-heart were about menstruation, menopause, or tampons, she was reasonably confident she could handle it. It wasn't that she was particularly prudish about sex. However, raised as she was in a motherless home, by a devoted but old-fashioned father and a prissy English nanny, sex wasn't a topic for discussion, particularly not with a person of the opposite gender. Charlie glanced at Ken who was still studying her radio. "What is it that you want to ask me?"

"I was married to Fran for two years. The divorce came through nearly six months ago."

Thankfully, he didn't want to discuss sex. Charlie breathed a deep relieved sigh. Ken was probably lonely and ready to begin dating again. "And every unattached female at this hospital has been waltzing in and out of this room vying for your attention. Try convincing me that you haven't noticed."

He couldn't suppress an embarrassed grin. "I'd be a liar if I said that I had trouble getting women to go out with me. But being served with divorce papers makes a man question things. He wonders why a woman gives up a life she said she wanted so she can join a cult."

Cults, Charlie silently cheered. Not sex. She was comfortable discussing cults. People in the creative arts were notoriously unorthodox. Many students she had known in both high school and college had flirted with, or had become part of, anti-mainstream groups. "Was it a religious cult? A group of bohemian artists who spend more time smoking cigarettes and arguing about method than doing actual work? Or more like a Ralph Waldo Emerson, back-to-nature cult, that thinks everyone should grow their own vegetables, stop paying taxes, and share the work?"

"It must have been one of those bohemian groups because they drank a lot and smoked weed – marijuana."

Marijuana. A lot of jazz musicians smoked marijuana, Charlie thought.

"When I first met Fran, she was a righteous Southern Baptist. They believe gambling, alcohol, and dancing are the tools of the devil," Ken continued, looking up at Charlie. "She wanted a house on Long Island with three bedrooms, a full basement, a carport, and kids, like me. That's why we got married."

"But something made her join a cult."

"And she took every penny we had saved. I could forgive that. But the worst part is the guy she left me for – this Daryl guy – a greasy bum who can't keep a regular job. A creep who'd lose to a ferret in a beauty contest."

"You have no idea what she saw in him."

"I know what she liked about him. She told me, all right – screamed it. Made certain all the neighbors heard it too."

"How awful," Charlie said, curious to learn more about Daryl's mysterious attraction.

Ken leaned close. "He *gave head*. I can't believe I'm telling you this, but he *gave head* and I wouldn't."

Charlie could formulate no response. For the first time in her life, she was grateful the fashion industry at times could be exceedingly vulgar. Her friend Brenda had blushingly explained the meaning of that expression in a Ladies room. Having to request the definition of that particular bit of slang, from Ken, was unimaginable.

"I don't think it's natural," he went on, still leaning forward and avoiding eye contact. "I never heard of a decent god-fearing man doing that. And I wasn't about to be the first. Do you think I made a mistake? It's hard to get used to living alone again. Is that what women want? Should I have tried?"

Charlie's face was fiery. Even her ears tingled. How had she gotten herself into this? And how was she going to get herself out? Ken didn't curse – not even when he was in pain. This was a heartfelt plea, but she still didn't know how to answer.

"You brought up a number of issues," she said, looking for a way to stall. "Love and marriage is a complicated subject. It wouldn't be right for me to answer without giving it some thought. Could I get back to you on this?"

"Oh yeah, sure," he said, sighing and slumping back in his chair as though he'd just completed a marathon.

Although Charlie thought she detected as much relief as disappointment in Ken's reaction, she wouldn't be much of a friend if she simply ignored his heartfelt request for help.

Over the next day and a half, she spent a great deal of time reviewing their discussion. After significant consideration, she was virtually certain the cause of the breakup had to be more than their conflicting view on oral sex. In order to limit the length of their conversation, she deliberately reopened the subject a few minutes before they were scheduled to leave the suite for their afternoon PT session.

"I have a question for you," she said. "It's about Fran."

"Yeah."

"Joining a cult that smoked marijuana was a radical move, particularly for someone raised to believe that drinking and dancing are sinful. Are you absolutely certain that Fran had the same values and goals as you, before you married her?"

"I'll have to think on that. Can I get back to you?" Ken asked, using her stall tactic against her.

"Take as long as you like."

*   *   *

Something metal crashed to the tile floor – a bedpan or a tray. The tinny thud echoed through the hall waking Charlie, who had been lightly dozing. Nights brought their usual assortment of discomforts, aches, and routine hospital clatter to interrupt sleep. She turned her clock-radio to face her. The illuminated dial told her that it was forty minutes past three a.m. In the next bed, behind the half-drawn drape, Charlie knew from Ken's breathing that he was awake. She sighed.

"Are you awake?" he whispered.

"Yeah," she whispered back.

"I've been thinking about what you said about Fran and values and goals."

"And?" she scratched her arm as far as the cast allowed and waited.

"I always knew what I wanted. My father is a good man but he leads a boring life. He sells feed and grain. His hobby is taxidermy. Can you believe that? He stuffs dead animals for fun. I'd rather get tossed out of a sixth story window every year rather than sell feed and grain and stuff dead animals. I like being a cop. But being a cop's wife wasn't what Fran wanted. She was always chasing some new thing. Like one day, she decided that she would get on one of those television quiz shows and win a pile of money. Then she was going to be a singer in her own all-girl band. They would all dye their hair blond or wear wigs. I always went along with it because, other than dying her hair blond, she never stuck with an idea long enough to do anything about it. I tried to make her happy. But the house, the car, the kids, they were my dreams. I just convinced myself they were hers."

"Perhaps Fran's leaving was for the best for both of you," Charlie said. "There's a wonderful woman out there who feels about things the way you do. Give yourself a chance. You'll find her." But there was no response from the other side of the drape. Had she supplied a tired cliché when he needed wisdom? Or had Ken's blunt admission drained him? A cart carrying medication rattled down the hall. They could hear the dull footsteps, the click, click, click of the wheels. From the street below, a siren approached, passed under the window, and was lost in the city's din.

"But what about the other thing? I tried to make her happy. Maybe I wanted to do it too often. Should I have . . . Was I wrong not to . . . "

Blessing the anonymity darkness provided, Charlie took a deep breath and slowly released it. "I don't think a person should do anything in bed that they don't feel comfortable doing. There are many ways to please and satisfy a woman. Smoking marijuana may have been the key – being raised the way she was. The marijuana may have helped break down her inhibitions and once that happened . . . "

"Then whatever he did she liked."

"Because she was able to relax and enjoy it. And it was easier to blame you than herself."

"You're not just saying that to make me feel better, are you?"

"I wouldn't lie to you."

"Thanks."

"You're welcome."

*   *   *

"Sorry. I was looking for 1425. I must have the wrong room," Charlie heard the familiar voice say.

"Not if you're looking for Charlie," Ken said. "I'm going to the solarium down the hall."

"Before you go, say 'Hello' to Rosemarie, a scheduler at the agency and my dear friend," Charlie ordered Ken, from her trussed position in bed.

"So how are you doing, kiddo?" Rosemarie bent to kiss Charlie's cheek, before placing a tin on her night table.

"A whole lot better than I look. I only spend a few hours a day in this contraption."

"I like your roommate. Very polite. Better looking in person than in the newspapers, if that's possible. Neil would go nuts if I shared a room with a guy who looked like him."

"We were paired because our injuries required similar therapy. As you can see the suite is really two separate rooms."

"You don't have to sell me," Rosemarie said. "Is he married? Seeing someone?"

"He's divorced. I don't think there's anyone special in his life at the moment."

"Any chance of the two of you . . ." Rosemarie waggled her fingers, suggesting intrigue. "One door closes. Another door opens. I'm a romantic. Is it possible that fate, karma, kismet could've brought you two together?"

Charlie shook her head. "I don't think so. Ken is a very nice guy. Just not my type."

"You're still hoping that Raul will wake up and see that he's an idiot for walking away from the best thing that ever happened to him?"

"Am I being silly, Rosemarie?" Charlie asked. "Should I give up and move on?"

"I don't know, honey. I always thought that when you were together you two could light up Madison Square Garden. But hey, what do I know? I thought Marilyn Monroe and Joe DiMaggio were a forever-after couple until she dumped him for that egghead Arthur Miller. What about Raul? Does he say anything when he comes to visit?"

"I've asked him to stop coming as long as he feels the way he does," Charlie admitted. "But he calls, or he has his secretary call, every few days to see if I need anything."

"Well then you're doing the right thing. Dragging things out doesn't do anything but make a girl feel worse." Rosemarie reached for the tin of pastries. "Here, have a cannoli. I made them myself."

"Only if you have one too," Charlie said. She took a pastry and waited until Rosemarie selected one before biting into the crispy crust that released the sweet filling.

"If you're sure that you're not interested in the cop, I wouldn't mind fixing him up with my niece Toni. You remember Toni, don't you? She came to the office hoping Mr. Glick would hire her. Unfortunately Glick said that she was too short."

Charlie remembered Rosemarie's pretty niece. Mr. Glick had

been untypically tactful. In addition to lacking the mandatory height, Toni was too curvaceous for the demanding fashion industry.

"She has her own shop. When she graduated from the beauty academy my brother Angelo loaned her the money to open it. You can imagine our surprise. My thickheaded brother thinks women are supposed to become nuns or get married and have six kids. But Toni begged and pleaded. And Toni was the baby of the family and the apple of Angie's eye, so he finally gave in. Now she's got two girls working for her. One does hair and the other is the receptionist and helps with shampoos when it's busy."

"You must be very proud of her."

"If only she wasn't dating worthless bums that don't deserve a great girl like her. The latest slob claims that he's a chauffeur. Some chauffeur! He dresses like a punk and has too much time on his hands. I think he does odd jobs for the mob. It's the danger she likes. The bum before this one drove stock cars. We're all praying that Toni will come to her senses before it's too late. She's such a good kid. She deserves better."

"Speaking of jobs, hear anything about who will be chosen to represent Perfecta?"

"It hasn't been released yet," Rosemarie said, lowering her voice. "But I happen to have the inside scoop on what everybody will know in a couple of days. Take a guess."

"Sunny Lee. She's got the winning combination: big boobs, big teeth, and a Southern drawl that drives men mad."

"Wrong! That nasty Brigitta Schwimmer, the skier, got the contract. I told you. I said, 'Perfecta's looking for the new American woman.' It could have been you."

"Why would you call Brigitta *nasty*?"

"Oh honey, you're just a sweetie. You think everyone is nice."

Tired of being told for the thousandth time that she was a terrible judge of character, Charlie changed the subject. "I should be able to return to work in a month or so. Have there been any calls for me?"

Rosemarie's distraught expression said it all.

"As bad as that?"

"I must get asked ten times a day, how's Charlie doing? How's the girl who was pushed off the subway platform? I tell them that you're doing great, that you'll be back in a month, maybe less. But I can't get them to book. It's like they feel real bad for you but . . . I don't know. It's crazy." Rosemarie placed her hand on top of Charlie's. "You going to be all right, sweetie? I got a little pin money that Neil doesn't know about. I could lend you enough to tide you over for a couple of months."

Charlie patted her friend's hand and smiled. "I'll be fine. I've saved a little pin money too. Besides, when I leave here, I can get a job at an art gallery. And galleries don't frown on a few extra pounds, wrinkles or double chins."

"Lucky for you that you got brains, not like some girls I have to work with. Now what about the maniac who attacked you? I can't believe they haven't arrested that crazy bastard. I still shake when I have to use the subway."

"Two detectives are working on it. I expect they'll be making an arrest any day now," Charlie lied, adding another to the mountainous pile.

*   *   *

After she was unhooked from traction, and before Ken returned, Charlie used her new walker to cautiously inch to the window and stare down at the murky Hudson River. The police hadn't identified the lunatic who had nearly killed her. He was still free to attack his next victim. Even if she could learn to walk again without a limp or pain, her career as a high-paid fashion model was over. People purchased the clothes, makeup, and perfume in ads because they envied the models who wore them. They imagined glamour and sophistication would follow as a direct result of possessing the featured clothes, makeup, and perfume. Pity was the antithesis of envy. The assault, the time spent in this hospital, the treatment she received, even the futility of the police investigation, were all fodder for the insatiable media's campaign. The publicity triggered by her part in uncovering art fraud had energized her career; now publicity worked against her. Media attention was a double-edged sword. Crime sold newspapers. Crime victims couldn't sell fashion. Her career was gone. She had always known modeling was a short-lived career – just not this short. Doubtless, some art gallery or auction house would hire her to do something: cataloguing, tracking inventory and sales. She would have to move out of the city and cut her expenses, but she would survive. She had survived worse.

The career she didn't dare dream about required professional training, not a simple BA in art history. *High-fashion model and art expert* the newspaper headlines had labeled her. Newspapers distorted and exaggerated facts. Reporters credited her with more expertise than she merited. The knowledgeable art world was not so trusting.

Still, as Ken had pointed out, minimal attention was given to art fraud, which, with huge sums of money involved, surely existed. Provided she could broaden her knowledge, perhaps there was a place for someone with her bizarre knack. But who would hire someone with her credentials? Not museums. Private collectors? Several of Madame Ivanavich's clients had requested her services. Her stepmother travelled in the right social circles.

The major obstacle remained, Charlie reminded herself. Limited knowledge. Was it possible to expand her scope of artists and their work through reading? It was much easier to attend classes and have organized material and concepts presented in a logical and meaningful way. She had learned nothing about fraudulent art in college. She strongly doubted that she would learn much more about the subject in a Masters program. And attending graduate school involved years and money that she couldn't afford.

But she could afford library books. Trapped in a hospital, she had lots of time to read. The possibility of pursuing an exciting new career made her pulse race. She couldn't remember the last time she last felt so exhilarated, giddy. Amelia, she thought, reaching for the phone, then replaced it. She hadn't given enough thought to precisely what was required. Amelia would buy coffee-table books containing illustrations and perhaps useful background material. Those were easy to find. Charlie owned shelves filled with them. What she needed was specific information on art fraud.

There was only one person who understood the crime, possessed the intelligence and tenacity, and would be willing to spend the time needed at the New York City Library to seek out sources. She would have to forgo all pride and ask for Raul's help.

~ Chapter 7 ~

While New York City enjoyed the crisp fall, Buenos Aires welcomed spring. Despite the mild winter, the season had seemed endless for Jack, with few tourists and fewer commissions. The modest bankroll he had managed to accumulate over the lucrative summer and fall had dropped dangerously low. Gratuities to the hotel personnel had to be maintained or Jack risked losing his status as a welcome unregistered guest. Fortunately, his weekly tennis lessons had been temporarily halted because Emilio worked at an exclusive country club in Westchester, New York. But with their season ending, he would soon return and Jack's lessons would resume.

Cab drivers demanded cash. And as he hadn't paid his rent for the last ten weeks, his landlady could no longer be put off with heartfelt promises and flattery.

To ease his expenses Jack had been reduced to seeking invitations from wealthy friends. More than an acquaintance and less than a trusted confidant, Jack had made himself useful – a fourth for tennis, an extra man to balance a dinner party, a presentable escort at dances – a gentleman who could be relied upon for his cheerful disposition and impeccable manners. He had abandoned hope of being a member of the inner circle of Buenos Aires society, families who had known one another for generations. Many new dynasties owed their fortunes to textiles, rubber, and meatpacking, while old wealth came from the pampas, land that contained an inequitable share of the world's richest topsoil and produced wheat, alfalfa, flax, which in turn fed thousands of swine and cattle. But whether industrialist or rancher, the affluent owned mansions, either in the center of Buenos Aires or in the fashionable suburbs, where they could mingle, shop, and enjoy the pleasures their wealth afforded them.

Though Jack regretted the necessity, being a guest for a long weekend at a grand estate could raise a man's spirits and temporarily reduce his expenses. But the approach had to be artful, a seemingly chance encounter. And likely candidates didn't congregate where the less fortunate did. They played golf, tennis and partied at inaccessible private clubs. They held box seats at concerts and operas. They dined at restaurants Jack could not afford. However, a drink at one of these same establishments was manageable. A chance meeting over a drink could lead to other things: a fine cigar, valuable introductions and tidbits of useful information. It was at one of those chic restaurants that Jack had the good luck to bump into an acquaintance who shared his passion for horses, in the men's room.

"Did you hear, Ramon Biretta broke his collar bone on the polo field?" the plump man with a pockmarked face asked Jack.

Jack had attended a few polo matches when he had lived in the States. His interest in horses had started with his girls. Charlie had become infatuated with horses first, with Amelia and her father quickly following. All three took riding lessons. Amelia soon lost interest in entering competitions, but Charlie had won ribbons at numerous events. Jack could have competed, but he was content sharing the excitement with his girls.

"Bad luck! No, I hadn't heard," Jack said, washing his hands slowly to prolong their conversation. "How long will Ramon be on the sidelines?"

"Six months. Paolo, his younger brother, will be playing for him. Paolo is good, but he's not Ramon."

Jack probed until he learned the location, date, and time of the next event. It was to be held at the Santana estate and hosted by the oldest son, Diego Santana, a man Jack knew only by reputation.

Aware that Ramon Biretta lived near the hotel and would attend the upcoming exhibition, Jack called him. Polo matches didn't require tickets of admission, or printed invitations, only the veneer of one who belonged. After he expressed his deep regret at learning his good friend would not be competing, and patiently listening to the retelling of the chilling accident, Jack asked if he ould share a ride.

"Jack, my friend, it would be my greatest pleasure to have your company. Unfortunately, my car is filled. Try Banco. Banco should have room for you. There is only he and his wife."

Roberto 'Banco' Popularo wouldn't be attending. He would be out of town. But Banco suggested that Jack call another mutual friend. It required three calls before Jack finally had a ride, and more than simple transportation, the implied endorsement of a popular member of the tightly knit group, Eduardo Sanchez. But etiquette demanded, even if another invitation to Sanchez's home was offered, Jack would have to decline. He had been a guest at the estate less than a month ago.

*   *   *

Polo is played with two teams, with four riders and horses each, on a flat grassy tract approximately the area of ten football fields. Similar to hockey, the object is to hit the ball between the opponents' goal posts. As in hockey, players are rotated. In polo, the ponies, as the highly trained horses are called, may be substituted at set intervals or when injured. As every competitor needs four to six trained mounts, though fewer are common, it is not unheard of to have as many as sixty ponies present at a match. In addition to the playing field, a site has to accommodate horses, spectators, handlers, equipment, and the cars and vans that transported both two and four-legged competitors. In Argentina, arenas were usually large expanses, owned by a player or a member of his family.

While it was expected that spectators at matches would wander about greeting friends between chukkers, as the playing periods were called, and before and after the match, Jack knew it was critical to appear reserved. Like most societies, the Argentine upper-class followed sharply drawn rules a casual observer might overlook. For men, raucous laughter in a public setting, or mixed company, was considered frivolous and lacking in decorum. Women were permitted casual behavior only within their family or with female friends. Familiarity with strangers was considered inexcusably gauche. For women, it was interpreted as imprudent or flirtatious. Jack was an outsider – a man who could point neither to family nor land. His pose – a heartbroken childless widower of taste, breeding, and wealth who only wanted a fresh start in this exciting country – had not been challenged. He guessed that some believed and others had doubts. A simple smile

or a nod prior to being formally introduced was considered courteous, but for a man in Jack's position, anything beyond that was not. \

Before the match began Jack left Eduardo Sanchez and headed for the area set aside for riders and their mounts. He knew several of the players competing that day. As this was a friendly exhibition, not a state or international competition, members of the Red and Blue Teams mixed freely. Grooms checked horses and equipment. Occasionally a meticulously braided tail loosened and required attention. Players rapped the leather thongs of their mallets around their hands to test their reliability. Horses stomped their hooves, sidestepped, and whinnied in anticipation. Jack saw Paulo Biretta astride his first mount, a sorrel broad-chested mare, who repeatedly tossed her mane and circled anxiously. Both were apparently unhappy. Jack threaded his way through the undulating mass, patting a horse's neck or flank, nodding at its rider, as he went.

"Jack, please do me a favor," Biretta said. "See if you find my groom. He must be with the other ponies. He's a small man with a twisted leg. His name is Paco. I need him. There's something wrong with this bridle. Look at the way she keeps throwing her head."

Jack caught the mare's head with his hand and scratched the white blaze between her eyes. The mare stopped circling and gazed at him expectantly. "Now, darling girl, let me take a look and we'll see if I can figure out what's bothering you." Jack ran his fingers under the bridle's sidepiece looking for an irritant, but not expecting to find one. Before a competition, horse and rider were apt to be jittery. When his fingers reached a spot near the mare's ear, Jack felt a burr that had attached itself between skin and leather. "I have it." Jack showed Biretta the offending burr and addressed the mare, "Now, girl, I bet that's more comfortable, isn't it?"

"Many thanks, Jack. That damned groom. I should have his hide."

"It's quite possible the mare picked up the burr after she was saddled."

"You are too forgiving." Biretta adjusted his chinstrap and tapped his hat with his riding crop, apparently now ready to leave.

Jack caught the mare's bridle. Opportunities like this didn't occur daily. "The last time we played tennis we clobbered the Onorato brothers in two straight sets. What do you say to another match?" He released the mare.

Biretta's attention was elsewhere. Few horses remained in the staging area. "Sure, Jack, absolutely. Anytime. Call me. We'll set up a game." He didn't wait to hear Jack's response.

Jack walked back to the sidelines and scanned the onlookers.

The audience was scattered over the length of the long playing field, but the identity of the day's host was apparent. Diego Santana and his entourage held court. The expansive family had established their base and were busy settling themselves. Jack took a position between them and Eduardo Sanchez, who was surrounded by a group of people, many of whom Jack didn't recognize.

The players took their positions on the field and the referee started the match. A member of the Red Team tapped the ball to his team member. Seemingly indifferent to the danger of collision and flailing mallets, horses and their riders took off after the ricocheting ball. The action was at the far end of the arena. Spectators, positioned steps from the sidelines, used binoculars to pick out their favorites in the attending cloud of dust. The mass of men and animals grew closer. They could hear horses breathing, snorting, players shouting instructions to one another. The ground vibrated as the horses grew alarmingly close. Jack helped spectators who were grabbing children and moving folding chairs to safety. In a tightly knit pack of pounding hooves, four horses and riders vied for the ball, less than the width of a car from the sidelines. A metal ice cooler containing bottled beverages had been carelessly placed too close to the sideline. An absorbed player could easily miss seeing the obstruction. If a horse tripped on it, the result could be disastrous for both horse and rider. Forgoing his own safety, Jack dove for the cooler, one second ahead of the day's host, Diego Santana.

"You are quick, Senor," Santana said, after they had pulled the heavy cooler away from the sideline. "And courageous. You could have been trampled or kicked."

"No more so than yourself, Senor."

Santana extended his right hand. "Please allow me to introduce myself. I am Diego Santana."

It was the very opportunity Jack had hoped for. "Jack Caine. I am delighted to meet you, Senor Santana. I've heard so much about you."

"And I you. You are a friend to Eduardo Sanchez and Jose Maria Ramirez. And now you must join us." Santana signaled a servant for a chair.

Conversation halted as a rider and horse from the Blue Team broke from the pack and galloped down the field towards the goal line. Both teams raced to catch up. The rider could lose control of the ball. A hoof could send it spinning in any direction. The distance made it hard to distinguish the ball in the flying dust, but spectators could see the mallet rising and striking, could hear the dull thuds above the drum rolls of hooves. For a second it seemed a member of the Red Team was close enough to intercept, but an opposing player successfully blocked his path. The first goal was scored. A spontaneous cheer rose from a few individuals within the crowd and was immediately replaced by laughter, praise, and enthusiastic, but polite applause. Spectators had relatives and friends on both teams. Praise and applause was considered courteous. Cheering or gloating was not.

"Well done," Jack proclaimed to his host.

"Did you play when you lived in the States?"

"Now that I've had the pleasure of seeing it at it's finest, I wish I had. I rode, of course."

When the chukker ended Jack excused himself, explaining there were friends he hadn't greeted as yet. He made his way through the hundred or so people that lined the field, stopping to chat with those he knew before returning to his seat. Isabella Santana had left her female companions and now occupied the chair next to her husband. Jack bent formally from the waist when they were introduced.

"Your Spanish is to be commended," she said, "I'm told that you speak French. Do you speak it as well as you speak Spanish?"

"You are too generous, Senora. I do my best not to humiliate myself in Spanish. I'm more comfortable in French. My late father indulged a foolish son who dreamed of becoming an artist as a young man and permitted him to study in Paris."

Jack had lived in Paris as a young man, as a poor expatriate and minimally talented artist. But he had acquired the language and manners.

"You know we Argentines consider ourselves more European than South American," Senora Santana said. "Buenos Aires is often referred to as the 'Paris of the Southern Hemisphere.'"

"And for excellent reasons, Senora," Jack agreed.

"We are entertaining the French ambassador at a small dinner party in town," Diego Santana explained. "If you have no other plans for that evening, we would be delighted if you could join us. You're staying at the Parador Grande, are you not?"

Accepting messages was part of his arrangement with the hotel's staff. Jack nodded and assured Senor Santana that he would do whatever was necessary to attend, employing the formal term for 'you', as before.

Santana corrected him by repeating the sentence and substituting the more intimate form of the word. "You are to call me 'Diego' and my wife 'Isabella'," he added.

Jack placed his right hand on his heart and dipped his head. "You honor me, Diego."

"Not at all, my friend."

After Jack was dropped at the hotel, and before heading back to his rooming house and the inevitable interrogation from his landlady, he paused to review the day. Simply being around horses was a rare treat, but the day had been more than a pleasant diversion. It had been productive. He would call Paolo Biretta to arrange a tennis match, possibly at the Parador Grande, possibly at Biretta's club. He had met and been befriended by Diego Santana – and invited to a party that the French ambassador would be attending. Though neither invitation would do anything to ease his expenses beyond giving him a fine meal, they could lead to other beneficial occasions. Gatherings of the aristocratic class, events that used to be commonplace in his life, Jack now eagerly sought.

*   *   *

He waited a few days before calling Biretta and leaving a message with a servant. Biretta returned the call to the hotel and missed him. Jack persisted until he finally reached Biretta at his home. "There's no sport in doubles," Biretta grumbled. "Doubles is for women and old men."

Jack ignored the snipe at his superior age. "We can play at the hotel if you'd like."

"Come to my club. It's closer to my office."

Jack immediately agreed. Another opportunity to meet and establish himself in local society. Later Jack found a message waiting for him at the hotel. The date and time had been set for the Santana's party.

"What does this say?" Jack asked the clerk who had illegibly scribbled the message. "I can't make it out."

"It says the dress is formal, Senor Caine. You are to wear a tuxedo."

"Are you certain?"

"I took the message myself. Gentlemen are to wear tuxedos. Madame Santana was most specific."

Jack thanked the clerk and walked away. A tuxedo. Damn! He no long owned tuxedos. He owned bathing, tennis and riding attire, two sports jackets and a dark suit. No tuxedo. In his present financial condition the purchase of a new tuxedo was impossible. Accessories: patent leather shoes, a formal shirt, a cummerbund and tie – doubly impossible.

He needed something to sell or pawn. The ring. The ring that Sally Cavanaugh had given him. The brief moment of relief quickly dissipated as Jack remembered he had sold the ring a month ago to pay the landlady. He had nothing left to sell.

~ **Chapter 8** ~

When Charlie received the first volumes from her collection – those she had purchased in college, plus those she had kept of her father's – she resolved to suppress every demoralizing thought and devote her full attention to learning. While her books contained material on techniques, stylistic schools and general biographical data on specific artists, as well as useful excellent reprints, they had nothing about forgers or forgeries. As feared, material on the subject was limited and difficult to obtain. But after a week or so the first few articles, pamphlets and books joined the growing stack piled next to her favorite chair.

To make the best use of time, available data and her ability to learn and retain, she divided her days into sessions. From the time she awoke until three o'clock, breaking only for PT and meals, she concentrated on a particular artist and read what she could find on his or her life and work. Scouring every illustration by that artist with a magnifying glass, she took in whatever her brain chose to absorb. In a haphazard, and less efficient manner, that was more or less the way she had learned in the past. Countless visits to museums, churches and historic buildings open to the public, countless discussions and comparisons of artists' works with her father, classmates, doyens and college professors, had gone into creating the peculiar knack she ardently hoped to grow.

Because information on art fraud was so scarce and far more intriguing, Charlie rationed it, allowing herself the luxury of studying it after she had completed her less exciting research. If the morning included Parmigianino, Caravaggio and Tintoretto, in the afternoon she rewarded herself with *Art Fakes and Forgeries* by Fritz Mendax. Contentedly ensconced in the maroon armchair, her right leg supported by an ottoman, she read as many chapters as she could before her eyes grew too tired or her brain refused to accept more information. On the suite's equally comfortable couch, Ken simultaneously looked at an issue of *Life* magazine and watched television.

"It goes back as far as that," Charlie mumbled.

"It goes back as far as what?" Ken asked.

She looked up to find Ken ignoring a troupe of acrobats flying across the screen. "Sorry. I didn't realize that I was talking to myself."

"What goes back that far?"

"Fakes, done deliberately. The ancient Phoenicians, Greeks, and Egyptians all produced phony art work."

He tossed the magazine aside. "I don't know why you're surprised. Every age has crime."

"It says here – " She found the page she had been reading moments before. "In 1881, a large black stone was found in a temple in Sippar, now Iraq, with inscriptions dated twenty-three hundred B.C. It was later discovered to have been made in the sixth century B.C, *seventeen centuries* later. British archeologists theorize that sixth century religious leaders paid to have it made, because they wanted to expand the existing temple. The priests felt they needed something to add legitimacy and prestige to the costly project. And lo and behold, they just happened to come across a magnificent religious relic –a seventeen hundred year-old stone icon that required a suitable setting."

"You show me a scam, I'll show you someone making a profit off of it. So who made money off of it?"

Thanks to her reading, Charlie knew the answer. "A bigger and more impressive temple meant more worshipers. More worshipers meant more shekels in the collection baskets. In Europe, a thousand years later, pious Christians made pilgrimages to holy relics and the churches that held them. Some of those relics have to be fake."

"Like I said, some things never change. You gotta love it."

"I guess I do," she admitted.

*   *   *

Wearing old chinos and a T-shirt, Ken was exercising his wrist and forearm with a free weight while watching television. Charlie considered the exercise overkill. It was Sunday, their sole day of rest from PT, and Ken's wrists and forearms – his entire upper body – was sufficiently imposing.

As usual, at this time of day, she was busy studying. Today's book was on counterfeiting. At first, she thought that Raul had mistakenly included it until she found the note inside.

Take a few minutes with this. Fraud is fraud. Something might apply. Raul.

The book was useful. One chapter discussed paper: how it was manufactured, the devious ways counterfeiters obtained credible paper and various techniques for simulating handling and age. Another chapter dealt with distribution, which ranged from a sole traveler dropping twenties as he made his way across the country, to an organized network that sold large sums of American counterfeit currency to foreign crime cartels. The extraordinary lengths criminals would go to in order to achieve their goals was astounding. She set the book aside to consider ways of applying that to art fraud.

Paper and paperboard were frequently used as bases for ink washes, calligraphy, charcoals and watercolors. If a forger wanted a sketch to be credited to Rembrandt, it couldn't look as though it had been done on a new practice pad. She wondered where a forger would locate paper that would convince an expert it was of the correct age and composition. Perhaps from old works by lesser, undistinguished artists that could be erased or covered. She would have to give it some thought, because similar tricks were surely applicable to canvas and board.

*   *   *

Charlie focused on the ceiling as Pat expertly worked the joints in her stiff right wrist, elbow, and shoulder. Having seen daily improvements, she now believed Pat's creed; the right kind of pain today would improve flexibility and mean less ongoing pain later.

"Okay, you're done for today," Pat said. "Let me get you an icepack."

"Tell me where you keep it and I'll get it for her," Detective Marrone's voice said.

Charlie sat up. Ken was also waiting for her, a wet towel draped over his head, accompanied by Detectives Marrone and Kowalski.

Kowalski helped her off the table and into her wheelchair.

"Thanks." Charlie took the icepack from Marrone who had followed Pat to the cooler. "Tell me that you've arrested the man who attacked me."

"I wish." Marrone watched Pat walk around the large room checking the equipment before she left. "Can we talk here or should we find someplace more private?"

"That was the last session today," Ken said. "No one's coming."

"There's been a new twist to your case," Kowalski explained. "We're not looking for a crackpot anymore. Two uniforms working the Bowery spotted a bum wearing the coat. They picked him up and called us."

"But that's good news, isn't it?" Charlie asked. "I suppose you need me to identify him – pick him out of a group. I'm sure that I can be taken to the station."

Marrone set a chair near hers and sat down. "The doper is not our man – too short and the wrong color. He was just dumped out of Bellevue Hospital, admitted the day after you were pushed, carried in when he O.D.'d. Since then, he's been a guest of the city – last stages of hepatitis."

"Doper is my partner's name for a heroin addict and O.D.'d is cop-talk for an overdose – an addict who's taken too much drugs," Kowalski translated.

Marrone cleared his throat. "The addict said that he found the coat rolled up in the subway tunnel, a hundred yards down from where you were pushed."

"What was he doing in a subway tunnel? It hardly seems a restful place to sleep."

"He probably used the niches in the wall along the tracks to stash his kit – his drugs and needles," Ken added. "It's dangerous, which makes it a first-rate hiding spot."

Kowalski addressed Ken, "Now ask me how this half-dead scrawny bastard got enough cash to finance an OD? With five twenties he found in the coat pocket. Five twenties."

"What's important isn't the coat the sorry slob was wearing," Marrone said. "He led us to the umbrella, which like you said, was expensive, and the beard. A detachable beard, a good one, like actors use."

A detachable beard. Her attacker's face came back to her. That first hazy hour in the hospital. She remembered trying to tell someone about the phony beard. Later, when she awoke trussed to the scaffold, she had forgotten.

"That changes everything. The attack on Charlie wasn't random." Ken turned to address Charlie. "It was planned by someone who meant to harm or kill you."

"You got it," Marrone agreed.

Charlie's eyes darted from Marrone to Ken to Kowalski. She could feel the blood leaving her face and her hands and feet growing cold. The idea of being targeted had been unthinkable.

Now it was undeniably real.

"What about the umbrella?" Ken pressed. "Any fingerprints?"

Kowalski frowned. "Nothing. He wore gloves. And he could have lifted it. Easy enough. People are always losing umbrellas."

"Why? Why me? What could I have done that would . . . There has to be some other explanation."

"Nutcases don't wear disguises they later dump," Marrone said.

"And not just any disguise," Ken pointed out. "This guy is smart. He wanted people to think he's a bum. Nobody looks at bums. He picks a coat that attracts more attention than his face, and a hat and beard that covers everything but his nose and eyes. Are you thinking this was a hit?"

Kowalski shook his head. "We don't see it that way. We think it was personal. The guy was obviously mad."

"Maybe you would prefer talking to us in private, Miss Morgan," Marrone said in a flat voice, glancing at Ken. "I'm sure Detective Thorenson understands. Questions get personal and we need you to speak freely."

"Actually, I'd prefer Ken to stay," Charlie said, confident that she had nothing to hide.

Marrone reached inside his jacket and extracted a pad and pen. "Do you gamble? Bet on the ponies? Numbers? Maybe you got in over your head. It happens."

"No, no and no," Charlie replied, laughing nervously.

"We eliminated your last boyfriend," Marrone said. "He has an alibi. Besides, he doesn't fit the description."

"We have to ask if you've ever been threatened by someone you owe money to?" Kowalski interjected. "Have you ever witnessed a crime? Or maybe you heard something that you weren't supposed to hear, and you didn't report it because you were scared or didn't want to get involved?"

Charlie shook her head repeatedly.

"Do you own something that someone wanted to buy and you turned them down?" Marrone asked, returning stares when three heads turned to look at him. "You never heard of the Mafia?" he scolded. "You have a business the Mafia wants to move in on, and they'll go after you."

"Detective Marrone is right," Kowalski acknowledged. "Have you had any dealings with criminal types?"

"Me? No!"

"Let's try another angle." Marrone slumped back in his chair. "What about a fan? Don't go shaking your head without giving what I'm saying some thought. You're a model. Your picture's on the cover of magazines. A guy thinks he knows you. He imagines things."

"What sort of things?"

"He thinks that he's in love with you and that you've rejected him. Could be an ordinary looking guy. He looks sane – quiet – someone you'd pass on the street without a glance. Maybe he sends you love letters, photos, little gifts. You ever get weird mail or gifts from someone you don't know?"

"No! No love letters. No weird mail. No photos. No little gifts," she said, hoping she looked more composed than she felt.

"Before the attack, you ever notice anyone staring at you or following you?" Ken inquired.

"I'm very tall for a woman. I've learned to ignore stares. Did any of you ever handle a case like that?"

"A nutcase fan? A tracker? I did," Marrone volunteered. "You may not realize this, but I'd estimate that nineteen out of twenty rapes or kidnappings with sexual abuse, the vics are good-looking women. Even kids – good-looking kids – are more likely to be targeted. And you're a good-looking woman."

Charlie mouth went dry. The thought of children being victimized was sickening.

"Ever get any obscene calls, or the phone rings and you can hear someone breathing, but no one answers?" Ken asked.

"Occasionally, I answer the phone and the caller hangs up. But this is Manhattan. Some people forget their manners."

"Without possible names or motive, we have nothing to work with." Marrone flipped his pad and clicked his pen closed before replacing them in his inside jacket pocket. "You need to make a list of *anyone* who might have a motive. Let Detective Thorenson help you. He's been living the good life at the taxpayers' expense too long." Marrone started to leave, then stopped. "This guy may not be satisfied with putting you in the hospital. If we don't catch him, he may try again. Do yourself a big favor. Give that list serious attention."

*   *   *

Not long after the hospital dietician left the suite Ken used his crutches to hobble across the room and drop a pad and pen next to Charlie. "Before you get lost in your reading, you need to work on that list Marrone and Kowalski asked you for."

The day before he had strained a groin muscle and had been pretending not to be in pain ever since.

"If I could think of anyone who wanted to hurt me, I would've told the detectives when they were here," Charlie protested, as unwilling to dwell on her assailant as she was to relinquish her studies.

He fell back into the wing chair and winced. "You can't pull a pillow over your head and make this go away."

Knowing that Ken would pester her until she relented, Charlie reached for the pad. "Fine. What do you want me to write?"

"Put down the names of anyone who asked you for a date in the last year or so, and you turned him down, even if it was only for a cup of coffee."

"Now that's just silly."

"Listen, Goldilocks, there really is a big bad wolf who gobbles up little girls who don't follow orders and talk to strangers. Start writing."

Charlie reluctantly scribbled the names as she remembered them. Two clothing manufacturers, one department store owner, two salesmen, an accountant, two attorneys and a judge. And a vile fashion industry icon who suggested that she participate in a ménage a trois.

Ken grunted as he shifted position. "Now add everyone who's cursed, shouted, or threatened you."

"There's a lot of tightly-wound people in the fashion industry. You wouldn't believe the language they use. My boss, Mr. Gluck is the kindest man I know and he shouts at everyone."

"Leave out loudmouths who scream at everyone and write down everyone who got angry with *you*."

Charlie added the most unlikely names, including a photographer who became crazed when she was late due to circumstances beyond her control, and a neurotic designer who insisted that she had torn one of his gowns, which she hadn't.

"Do you really think this is going to help?" she asked.

"You're not finished. Now I want you to write down the owner's name of every phony painting you turned up."

"Now that makes absolutely no sense. Madame Ivanavich offered to refund the full purchase price to anyone who was unhappy, which is parking-meter change for most of her clients. So there's no motive."

"Not to you. Keep writing!"

For the next hour Charlie scoured her memory. "I can't remember them all. I'll have to call the gallery and ask Madame to check her records, even though I think the idea is crazy."

"This guy's reason makes sense to him."

"Do you think the man who attacked me could have been hired to do so?"

"Marrone and Kowalski don't think so and I have to agree. Slashing at you repeatedly indicates anger, rage. Hit men don't take things personally or they wouldn't be hit men."

"In that case I can eliminate three quarters of this list." Charlie quickly drew lines through several names.

"What are you doing?" he objected. "What's wrong with those names?"

Charlie rolled her eyes and smiled sweetly. "My attacker was my height. Allowing an inch or so for error, I eliminated anyone who's either too tall or short."

"I was going to tell you to do that later, but as long as you started, don't forget general body build. Witnesses agree this guy was scrawny, so you can scratch out anyone that isn't."

Charlie was disappointed. She had been expecting praise. For a layman, she considered her reasoning astute. Raul had always been generous with praise. Nevertheless, she wordlessly returned to the list and deleted those who weren't thin. Five names were debatable since her attacker had worn a bulky coat. And his eyes were light – which eliminated anyone with dark eyes. She put a line through four more names. Only six remained – clients she hadn't met or when she'd met them, she couldn't recall the color of their eyes because she had been concentrating on the artwork she had been hired to verify.

"Do you remember anything about his shoes?" Ken asked.

"His shoes?"

"There's a story that goes around the academy. Members of the Ku Klux Klan liked to have pictures taken of themselves standing next to burning crosses, wearing their long robes and masks. But the morons forgot their feet weren't covered. Later, many of them were identified by their shoes. Unusual shoes might be a lead."

"Give me a minute." Charlie closed her eyes and returned to the horror movie burned into her brain. She was on the subway platform and noticed a strange bearded man. At first, she could see only the top half of his body. She reluctantly advanced the film to the attack. The umbrella was slashing, and she was face down on the concrete, blood dripping in her eyes, trying to shield her head with her arms. "Expensive black wingtips. Small. Narrow. Maybe custom-made. And the soles were barely scuffed." Charlie checked her list and deleted the sole candidate whose oversized feet she remembered clearly.

"He's either rich or a working stiff with really bad feet who had to part with big bucks so he can walk. Did you get anything else? What about his voice? Did he say anything?"

"No."

"What about his breath? I bet he didn't stink like a bum."

Charlie tried to recall smelling anything odd, but there was nothing distinctive about the man's body odor. She tried to deduce the color of his hair from his brows, but the cap had been pulled too low and the fake beard hid any potential five o'clock shadow. The fake beard! "Spirit gum! Did they check to see if there were any hairs stuck to the beard or the cap?"

"Marrone didn't mention hairs, so maybe there weren't any. And what's spirit gum?"

"But he said it was 'a good one, like actors wear' not one of those Santa Claus contraptions that are held in place with elastic. I bet it was attached with spirit gum. That's what actors use."

"And you know that from plays you did in high school or college?" he asked, looking amused.

"Yes and I also know about spirit gum because models use it for all sorts of purposes, including keeping a plunging neckline in place. It's also used for fake eyelashes."

"You ever wear fake eyelashes?"

"Sometimes. They can be very flattering. I wear them when I have to look sultry," Charlie said, batting her eyes at him.

He looked away. "Yeah, well you don't need them."

"Detective Thorenson, what a gallant thing to say. Sometimes you surprise me."

"I like the theater angle though. The big black umbrella with a fancy handle. The beard. And an audience. Think about it. This guy worked an audience. Kowalski and Marrone ought to try that angle. Now, are you ready to show me that list?"

Charlie covered the pad with her arm. "Not yet. I still have to speak with Gallery Three Fifty-Two and I need a believable fib."

"A lie?"

"Perhaps you think that I'd have more success with the truth? How does this sound? 'The police have asked me to create a list of possible suspects because they suspect one of your clients may have tried to kill me. Would you be so kind as to give me their names and descriptions?'"

"Okay, I get your point."

Charlie leaned on her walker and inched toward her bed. "If I have to tell a fib, I'm going to need privacy. Do you mind if I close the drape?"

It took fifteen minutes of daydreaming before Charlie was able to produce a plausible fib – one of the clients had asked her to call him and she couldn't recall his name, only what he looked like.

"Darling, how good to hear from you," Helena Ivanavich exclaimed in her throaty Russian accent.

They exchanged small talk until Charlie found the right opportunity to ask her favor, and several names were discussed and eliminated.

"Justin Voyt was a regular customer until about ten years ago," Helena said. "That was when he stopped buying from galleries and switched to a private art supplier, Gustav Kadinski."

"Is there anything you can tell me about Kadinski?" Charlie asked, for no particular reason beyond curiosity.

"I can tell you plenty about Kadinski, but my five o'clock appointment just walked in. Give me your number and I'll get back to you."

Charlie waited until Ken's television program ended, debating what she should tell him about the sole remaining name. When the closing commercial came on, she had decided to go with the unvarnished truth. She pulled the cord that drew back the drape. Ken had returned to bed.

"Does this mean you're ready to go over your list?" he asked, using the remote device to turn off the television set.

"Yes. But first I have to tell you a long story and you have to promise to be patient with me."

"When am I impatient with you?"

She ignored the question. "Are you familiar with the name Justin Voyt?"

"Sure. He's that big shot millionaire who's always calling the mayor's office. We hear about it when he wants something special from the police department. So Justin Voyt made your list. How many names are still on it?"

"You promised to be patient."

He held up his hands. "Sorry."

"Well, Voyt may be an egotistical vulgar braggart, but in the inner world of art, his private collection is considered extraordinary. He used to loan pieces for various exhibits, but he stopped doing that about five or six years ago. Well, I've always wanted to see it. Who didn't? And suddenly I had the perfect excuse, because Justin Voyt had purchased two paintings from Gallery Three Fifty-Two – two potentially suspicious paintings."

"So you met him?"

"Not in person. This may or may not be important. I'll leave it to you to decide."

He punched the pillow behind him. "Go on."

"Well, I called the New York phone number Voyt had given the gallery ten years earlier and was told that Mr. Voyt was out of town. Three months and a dozen phone calls later, Voyt was still out of town and I was starting to wonder if I was ever going to have the opportunity to see his fabulous collection. Then one day as I was walking down 83rd Street, just off of 5th Avenue, I passed his Manhattan address. I knew he had converted the top two floors at the Voyt Pointe into a pied-a-terre. A mischievous little idea occurred to me. I don't usually do things like this, but the idea was *so* tempting. The Gallery had given me a very impressive letter to use as identifying credentials."

"You little sneak. And I always figured you for a goody-two-shoes."

"That's what you think. Wait until you hear how wicked I can be. The next day I put the letter and the original sales certificate personally signed by Justin Voyt in my purse. Then, wearing my most business-like suit, I took a taxi to his residence. The building's concierge rang Voyt's penthouse apartment. He explained to the housekeeper that Miss Morgan, from Gallery Three Fifty-Two, was here to inspect paintings purchased by Mr. Voyt."

"And they let you in," Ken said.

"Absolutely. I was directed to an elevator for Voyt's exclusive use. In seconds I was outside his door. When it opened, I was gazing into an enormous lobby filled with polished marble, oceans of gilt and classical statuary – all calculated to impress, and entirely in keeping with the ostentatious man. His housekeeper, a humorless woman of about fifty – English, I think, who wore no makeup, stared at me.

"'Mr. Voyt purchased two paintings from Gallery Three Fifty-Two in nineteen fifty-five,' I said in the most official and driest manner I could muster, then waved the supporting credentials I had brought with me at her.

She took them from me.

'As you can see, Gallery Three Fifty-Two has asked me to reevaluate the paintings as part of their ongoing service to their most important clients.'

"'There's only a small portion of Mr. Voyt's collection here,' Mrs. Renshaw said, allowing me to enter and returning the letter. Apparently, she was sufficiently satisfied that I posed no threat.

"'I expect the rest of his collection is divided between his homes in California and Chicago,' I said, hoping to sound knowledgeable.

"Mrs. Renshaw sniffed. 'The mansion in Chicago, the estate in La Jolla, a penthouse in Las Vegas, and a villa on Paradise Island. But there's more in the vaults than there are on the walls.'

"'Insurance is so out of hand these days,' I said, demonstrating my sympathy to the irritations of the fabulously wealthy. 'I suppose Mr. Voyt chooses to keep some things locked away.'

"'Mr. Voyt doesn't have to concern himself with the cost of insurance. He has his own reasons, which he doesn't discuss with me. Which paintings are you here to inspect? I have work waiting for me,' she said, having correctly identified me as an employee like herself and not a guest.

"'A Manet and a Pissarro.'

"'Just the two then? I suppose you'd recognize them if you saw them.'

"'I would. The names, dates, and subjects are detailed on this invoice.'

"'Follow me. I'll have to stay with you,' she said. 'Mr. Voyt is very particular about who he permits to visit."

"She briskly walked me through several rooms whose walls displayed a number of works I would have loved to spend time viewing, until I reached a small anteroom that held one of the paintings I was seeking.

"'This is the Manet,' I explained. I moved closer to better examine the work. The subject was a small sailboat in choppy marine-blue water. It reminded me of Manet's *The Escape of the Rochefort,* done in the late nineteenth century. This had more skyline and the boat was set farther back. I moved closer to study the brush strokes. Copyists are slavish, precise. This had Manet's wonderful flow. I was looking at a fine painting – but a forgery, nevertheless.

"'I'm done in this room,' I told Mrs. Renshaw, 'but I still haven't seen the Pissarro. It's a painting about this size set in a flowering garden.'

A uniformed male staff member, doubtless a butler, entered the room and was glaring at me in a manner untypical of a servant.

"'There's only the bedrooms and they don't contain any paintings of gardens,' Mrs. Renshaw said, nervously glancing at the butler. 'You shouldn't be in here with Mr. Voyt out of town. He's very particular about who come to visit.'

"I turned to view the only other painting in the room – a stiff portrait of an elderly man with side whiskers and a stern countenance that I assumed to be Justin Voyt's grandfather. But my stay was clearly over. The unhappy Mrs. Renshaw and the scowling butler had decided it was time for me to leave. My head whipped from one side to the other as I attempted to take advantage of what was certain to be my last chance to view the famous Voyt collection. Unfortunately, seconds later I was at the front door."

"And that's your story?"

"That's it."

"How did you let Voyt know his prize painting was a fake?" Ken asked. "Is that done in person, by phone, or in writing?"

"Usually, a telephone call first, followed up with a letter from the gallery. And I don't do the phone calls. Madame Ivanavich does."

"And do you know how he handled it?"

"As far as I know, fine. Madame explained that she was most anxious to regain him as a customer and offered to buy back the Manet. She even suggested that I return at his convenience to examine the Pissarro, or any other works he wished examined, at no charge and with no obligation. But he told her that he was satisfied his purchases were genuine and thanked her for calling."

"And now you're wondering if Voyt could have anything to with the attack?"

"It sounds crazy," Charlie admitted, shaking her head. "The idea's insane. But he's the only name left on my list, and he's about my height and thin, and his home is a short walk to the station where I was attacked."

"And he can buy a hundred pairs of custom-made shoes and fifty-dollar umbrellas and toss them in the garbage. So what happened to your other names?"

"Too tall, too short, too heavy, wrong eye color. But I can't see how my innocent little prank would anger a person enough to physically attack me."

"We don't need to know his motive yet. Maybe he wasn't trying to kill you. Maybe he just wanted to teach you a lesson not to poke around his house and he lost his temper. Maybe he had another reason. Unfortunately, there's no way he can be brought in for questioning without a positive ID or evidence. He has too much juice – power – and he likes throwing it around. The only thing I can do with what we got is ask Marrone and Kowalski to quietly check out if Voyt was in the New York area the day of the assault. And then we're all going to pray that he was out of town, because convincing a high roller like Voyt to cooperate with a police investigation is damn near impossible."

Charlie listened to Ken's reasoning but a thought remained in the back of her mind. If she could discover the motive, she would know the identity of the man who attacked her. There had to be a limited amount of reasons for a vicious assault: love, hate, fear, revenge, greed.

*　*　*

As promised, Helena Ivanavich called back, but not until the following noon.

Charlie reached for a pad so she could make notes. She had to listen carefully because without seeing her listener's confusion, Helena spoke too fast, forgetting that her accent and mispronunciations made her difficult to understand.

"Kadinski *vas* born in Poland," Helena said. "He *vas* Assistant Director of the Polish National Museum of Cracow before he made his escape. In the US, he vas broker to a few new museums and some serious collectors."

Charlie detected disapproval in Helena's voice. "You don't like him, do you?"

"Kadinski drank heavily, and when he drank, he could get very mean. Our paths crossed from time to time, not that he ever gave me anything to handle for him. If he couldn't make a direct sale, he went to Sothebys with his finds."

"By finds, am I to understand you mean previously uncirculated pieces?"

"Yes. Everyone knew that Kadinski smuggled pieces out from behind the Iron Curtain, using his contacts in Poland. But no one cared. They all looked away."

"Behind the Iron Curtain," Charlie repeated as she scribbled. "A lot of pieces?"

"Many, many pieces from private collections. In Russia, before the revolution, the nobility was rich beyond your wildest imagination. Remember, I was born in St. Petersburg. After the Communists took over, you could be killed for owning a single piece of important art."

"Why?"

"It meant that you were members of the upper class, or the nobility. Even owing an evening gown was dangerous. If exposed, you could be branded a White Russian, a counterrevolutionary. You could be put to death on the spot. To protect themselves, people either hid or abandoned their artwork. Thousands of treasures were destroyed by the ignorant rampaging peasants and soldiers. Communists are atheists. Need I tell you what happened to icons, and chalices, sacred paintings and statuary? Burned! Slashed! Melted down for the gold, silver and gems they contained. The military either destroyed or stole anything of value. We fled with what we could carry. My parents started this business with the little we could bring with us – artwork that had been in my family for generations. Now gone. Sold. But better sold than destroyed."

"I'm so sorry. I didn't know."

"Some daring curators and owners hid treasures behind walls, in basements, even in abandoned mines to protect them. Years would pass and they, or their children, sold them. There are ways to get these things out of the country. You're aware, of course, diplomatic pouches can't be searched. And border guards can be bribed to turn their heads. We all know that illegal activities take place daily."

"And Justin Voyt purchased a number of pieces through Kadinski?"

"Enough to fill a good-sized museum."

"Is there any chance that I could speak with Mr. Kadinski?"

Helena laughed her husky laugh. "Not unless you have special powers. We just learned that he recently drowned in Mexico, while he was there on business. It's hard to believe that hairy drunken tub of lard drowned."

Charlie shuddered after she hung up, trying to put out of her mind the image of a hairy obese man flailing in the tempestuous waves, gasping for air, and ultimately sinking. The ghastly vision faded when she remembered her own grim position. Her hospital stay would soon end. Following Ken's directives had produced a single improbable suspect – and one so powerful the police were unable to question him. She could only pray that her attacker was satisfied with the injuries he had inflicted and would not try again.

*   *   *

Raul's call came as an unnerving surprise. She moved as rapidly as her stiff limbs and the walker allowed, to close the dividing drape so that Ken couldn't continue to observe her reaction. She hadn't seen Raul since his first visit, and they hadn't spoken since she had asked for help. He did the research, but Jane continued to handle deliveries.

"I located a few books that I think might be helpful ," he said in his silky cello voice. "Jane has the flu and will be out the next few days, so I'll be dropping them off myself on my way home from work."

"Would it be possible for you to stay? There's something I would like to discuss. About the attack," she added.

"In that case, I'll bring Chinese food for dinner, unless you'd prefer something else."

"Chinese food would be fantastic," Charlie said, forcing herself to sound relaxed and casual.

Her unplanned decision to ask Raul to stay had been practical. She intended to exploit his keen logical mind. And if Jane hadn't already alerted him, it would be interesting to see if her virile PT partner/suitemate aroused jealousy.

"You have the suite to yourself tonight," Ken informed her when he learned that Raul would be visiting. "There's a game Hank and I want to watch."

Hank was Henry Knobbe, a well-heeled and loud Chicagoan, recuperating from a gall bladder operation two rooms down.

"Raul has access to powerful people and information. I thought I'd ask his help."

"If he wraps up the case before you get to the fortune cookies, you can tell me all about it later."

With an hour to go before Raul's arrival Charlie asked the nurses' aide to deliver Ken's dinner to Knobbe's room, and instead of her dinner, to bring two settings. One brief phone call and a bottle of wine, added to her bill, was sent to her room – another advantage of the hospital wing set aside for the rich and famous. After that, she nervously prepared for Raul's arrival, mentally thanking Jane for the makeup and perfume. If Ken noticed the change in her mood or appearance, he didn't comment. He simply sat quietly reading in the chair next to hers, presumably, his dinner getting cold in the room two doors away.

When Raul arrived at 6:30, a half-hour later than expected, carrying two shopping bags, Charlie introduced them. The men shook hands and politely took stock of each another, before Ken excused himself and left.

Raul set the bags down. "You look great," he said, bending over to kiss the side of her flaming cheek.

"Thanks, and I really appreciate your help. I know that it must've taken a great deal of time."

He smiled and shrugged. "How's your arm? I see a walker, so your walking is obviously improving."

"My arm is coming along great." She raised the lightweight abbreviated cast to demonstrate. "The walker is new. I do laps to and from the solarium at the end of the hall."

"When do you get out of here?"

"I haven't been given an exact date, but I'm guessing two weeks."

"And what about your roommate? He looked fine on those crutches."

"Ken and I will be discharged about the same time. I suppose you heard we were teamed as an experiment."

"So I've heard. Jane was impressed with your accommodations."

"I was very lucky."

"And I want your luck to hold. But what I'm reading in the newspapers worries me. The police found the umbrella and a fake beard, but they've made no arrests and apparently have no suspects – unless you know something that I don't."

"That's why I asked you to stay. There's only one suspect, the most unlikely man you could think of, and he has no motive. Do you want to discuss it now or should we eat first?"

Raul reached for a cardboard container. "I'll serve out the soup, and you're going to start at the beginning and tell me how this lone suspect emerged."

Charlie began with compiling the list, the basis for adding and removing names, and the last remaining candidate – Justin Voyt. Raul listened attentively as she gazed at her hands and repeated what she had learned from Helena Ivanavich, her calculated invasion of Justin Voyt's Manhattan penthouse, as well as the man who supplied much of his artwork, the now deceased Gustav Kadinski.

"Please tell me that my crazy paranoia is simply a product of being cooped up so long," she said, when she noticed Raul staring at her.

"Was Voyt upset with your findings?"

"Madame Helena didn't think so."

"But you saw some of his personal collection and one piece was definitely done by our talented friend."

Charlie smiled and wiped her soiled fingers on a napkin. "Considering the size of his home there was very little important artwork to see. His housekeeper told me that the majority of Voyt's works are vaulted."

"Placed in safes?"

"Yes, either for security purposes or to reduce the cost of insurance. I wondered about that. With Voyt's enormous wealth and ego, you would think he'd want his collection on display where it could be admired."

"Justin Voyt is an arrogant ruthless businessman, but attacking you? I don't know. Nevertheless, if he's the only suspect left . . . Have the detectives assigned to the case checked to see if he was ever picked up for assault, drunkenness?"

"Ken says the police won't investigate someone with Voyt's clout without a clear-cut motive, an eyewitness, or some tangible evidence. We have zero evidence. My adventure doesn't qualify as a motive. And thanks to the disguise, there are no witnesses." Charlie returned to silently eating her shrimp in lobster sauce, aware that Raul's methodical brain was systematically producing and eliminating possibilities.

After several minutes passed he said, "If Voyt's collection has been placed in vaults, it might mean that it's being used as collateral for loans. He's known for being ruthless – he's left a lot of victims in his wake – and he's also known to be daring. He's managed to pull off deals others thought impossible by risking it all and succeeding. And he's beyond heavily mortgaged. If a significant portion of his collateral was discovered to be forgeries, lenders could call in his loans and his entire empire would topple."

"Do you think . . . Me?" Charlie pointed to her chest, in disbelief. "Justin Voyt couldn't possibly be worried about me."

"He doesn't know that you only wanted to see his collection because you are a curious art lover. He might think that you were sent by a vengeful casualty of one of his takeovers. If that were the case, you would be a legitimate threat. Think about it. You attended the right schools. You have access to influential people. There have been stories done about you in the newspapers and on television. You're considered an expert. And you fast-talked your way into his home. Voyt's known to be vindictive. He just might be worried enough to attack the one person who threatens everything it's taken him thirty years to amass."

"But unless a significant portion of the collection are fakes, he has nothing to fear from me or anyone else," Charlie argued.

"It makes me wonder how much of that collection is questionable. How many major pieces would have to be worthless to undermine the value of his loans?"

"A single painting could be worth millions."

"Or nothing, if it was proven to be a forgery. Give me some time to do some discreet investigating. Don't tell anyone what we've discussed, not even the police, and that includes Detective Ken Thorenson. If word were to get out that the value of Voyt's collateral is suspect, and the story could be traced back to one of us, we would be sued for slander. Worse yet, if Voyt is the man who attacked you, he could decide that he has to eliminate you once and for all."

"I won't breathe a word."

"Please be careful. Until someone is arrested, you're still a target."

After Raul left Charlie hobbled across the suite to watch the headlights of cars crossing the George Washington Bridge, to and from New Jersey. Above, airplanes flitted in and out of view as they approached and took off from the city airports.

Having secured Raul's participation was as disturbing as it was comforting. Seeing him had triggered longing and doubt. What was the real message in his eyes, his voice, his words? She had to be on guard not to confuse caring for desire, or concern for love.

~ **Chapter 9** ~

The tennis club Ramon Biretta belonged to was large and lushly appointed for one within a city: four grass courts, six clay, locker rooms, a bar, a small dining room, and a trained staff to provide for a member's every need. Jack had been there only once before.

In the first of three sets, while he was fresh, Jack managed to put on a good show. Both men held serve until the score was three-all. Then Jack's first serve took an inconvenient leave of absence and Biretta soon discovered that Jack's second serve relied heavily on a spinning slice, and his well-placed lobs required too much running for a man of Jack's age. Biretta took the first set 6-3. In the second set Biretta handily took the first two games.

When they changed sides, Jack used the break to drink some water, wipe his brow, retie his sneakers and generally stall for time. Singles favored the young. Biretta was easily twenty-five years his junior and unless Jack figured out something soon, the match would end in a humiliating two-set disaster.

The men returned to the court. Jack saw the confident look on his opponent's face and his swagger. He decided to forgo rushing the net and defend from back center. From this position, he could cut and slice weak returns or ram his powerful backhand shot down the sideline. Fortunately, Jack's forceful first serve resurfaced. Jack took the second set with a combination of determination and strategy. The third set went to Biretta who decided to run his winded opponent from one side of the court to the other. Still, Jack was not unhappy. The match had gone to a respectable three sets, and not the debacle he had feared.

"Good match," Biretta said, leading Jack inside, to the long bar, for cold drinks.

"It was an easy win for you. You barely raised a sweat."

"Don't underestimate yourself. I had to work hard for every point."

An idea crept into Jack's mind after both men had given their orders to the bartender. He had considered the Santana dinner party a diversion, perhaps an opportunity to expand his circle of friends, but it could be more. He steered hotel guests to artists he knew and had profited from it. Why couldn't Buenos Aires' elite be similarly induced? While he was admiring the Santana's home it would be easy to guide the conversation to art, and from there to talented local artists he knew. And why not include a gallery or two? He had considered adding a few galleries to his tours. Surely an ambitious owner could be persuaded to compensate him if he were to personally escort interested patrons to his shop. The only snag was the mandatory tuxedo. Jack appraised Biretta's frame – a size smaller and two inches shorter. Just as well, he thought. No story could mask the desperation of such a request. But a loan? Borrowing money was risky –a delicate endeavor made even more difficult by cultural differences. He had observed men like Biretta playing cards and at gambling tables. They exchanged loans with as much concern as they would give a falling leaf. All he needed was a convincing story.

Biretta signaled the maitre'd from across the room. "I can't stay. A quick shower for me, and then it's back to my desk. But there's no need for you to rush. Have lunch. Maybe you can find another game." Biretta addressed the waiting maitre'd. "Mr. Caine is my guest today. Please see that he gets whatever he wishes."

"That's very kind, but I'm not going to be able to stay past lunch," Jack said. "I have to get to the bank before they close. They are always messing up my accounts. My broker told me the bank should have received the check three weeks ago. It's been an annoying inconvenience. I say, just in case my bank was unable to straighten this thing out, do you think you could loan me a small sum to tide me over?" Jack mentioned a sum equivalent to three hundred American dollars. He watched Biretta's eyes go from surprised to suspicious, and from suspicious to friendly in less time than it took to flick away a piece of lint.

"I'm not sure I have much cash with me. Let me check." Biretta found his wallet in his tennis bag. "It seems I have." He handed Jack the amount requested.

"Thank you, and thanks again for lunch and a great workout. The next time you feel like doubles keep me in mind. My singles game isn't strong enough for a fine player such as yourself."

As Biretta disappeared into the men's locker room Jack checked the wall clock. Noon. He had time to watch four men about his age play before lunch, and perhaps strike up a conversation so that they could recognize him at some future occasion. Jack found a chair in the shade and admired a well-executed shot with a nod and a smile. Thanks to Biretta, he had enough money to buy the tuxedo and give his landlady something towards the rent. But despite the ease in which it had been given, this was not a soon forgotten loan like those he had observed between peers. He knew, in that single-second delay, that he was the outsider. The debt wouldn't be mentioned, never alluded to. But if it wasn't quickly repaid, word would soon spread that he was to be considered a social-climbing deadbeat.

*   *   *

Unlike most of South America where the architecture was heavily influenced by Spain, the Santana's home resembled an elegant chateau. During cocktails in the expansive salon, Isabella Santana introduced Jack to the French ambassador, another member of the diplomatic corps, and their respective wives, explaining as she went that Jack had lived in France and spoke French fluently.

"Our beautiful and gracious hostess is too kind," Jack protested in French.

The ambassador's wife complimented Jack's excellent accent and pressed Jack for details about where and when Jack had lived in France. Jack once again repeated his story of an indulged son who incorrectly imagined himself an artist. The group smiled their appreciation of this self-deprecating humor. Jack remained just long enough to ingratiate himself and no longer. He would have opportunities as the evening progressed to tell a few entertaining stories about one or two celebrated, and now conveniently deceased, French artists he had personally known.

Other than his host family, he recognized few of the eighteen to twenty dinner guests. He spotted Isabella's mother, Luciana Villa, across the room. Unless he was mistaken, the handsome woman of about sixty was widowed. Jack had seen her first at the polo match and later shopping with her daughter. Movies, he thought, looking for a topic with which to begin. American actresses. He could tell her he had met Greta Garbo before she became a recluse. It might be just the thing that could lead to a suggestion they meet for lunch. Argentines were fascinated by Hollywood movie stars.

"Perhaps you remember me, Senora Villa? My name is Jack Caine. We were introduced at a polo match held at your son-in-law's ranch."

Luciana Villa scarcely had a chance to acknowledge their meeting when a man appeared at her side. The smiling man explained that he was Manuel Santana, Diego's brother.

"Senor Caine, what a pleasure. I see you've met Senora Villa. Please allow me to introduce you to some of the others. Luciana, you will excuse us, won't you?"

Senora Villa nodded and smiled.

There would be no quiet little conversation with Luciana Villa, Jack mused, as Manuel Santana led him to the first group of guests. She might as well be sequestered in a convent. Things might have been different if he was a member of their tight knit circle.

The real mission of this dinner party soon became apparent. This was not a simple gathering of friends. While business would not be discussed this evening, the affair would be followed by smaller meetings where imports and exports, taxes and tariffs, and perhaps a fee for smoothing the way, would be negotiated and arranged. His presence at this preliminary meeting was similar to the women's. Thanks to his fluency in French, he was a decorative accessory.

After dinner was announced and seats were taken, Jack was seated between two married women. Apparently, married women were afforded a greater degree of freedom than widows.

"Are you planning to visit Buenos Aires much longer?" a slender dark eyed woman with a small mole above her upper lip inquired.

"I adore Buenos Aires, Senora, particularly her wonderful people. I plan to make it my permanent home as soon as I can clear up a few things in the States."

"And then your family will join you?" she inquired.

"I'm a widower. I lost my wife two years ago, and I regret to say, we had no children."

Serafina Morales, the plump woman on Jack's left, nodded sympathetically. "What brought you to Argentina, if I might ask?"

"A bit of business. I breed horses," Jack said, knowing the word 'business' would end further exploration. Business wasn't a suitable topic for polite conversation between strangers. An Argentine gentleman did not discuss his holdings, occupation or profession with anyone beyond his immediate circle – nor would he inquire directly about another's. And if men didn't, women most certainly wouldn't. "Are you interested in art, Senora?"

"I regret to say I know little about art," the woman with the mole said. "Serafina is the one to talk to about art."

Hearing her name Serafina Alcaya turned and entered the conversation. "I try my hand at watercolors. Nothing to discuss really."

"I've seen her paintings. I think she's very gifted, Senor Caine, but you must judge for yourself."

"My dear cousin is being too kind, though I wouldn't object to hearing an expert's opinion. Are you an artist or a connoisseur?"

"A bit of both. I tried my hand at painting as a very young man, but I've never lost my love for art. A man doesn't need talent to appreciate the genius of others. I would be happy to see your work, if you would permit me."

"If you had nothing else better to do," Serafina murmured, dropping her eyes.

"You have many talented artists right here in Buenos Aires," Jack said. "I am fortunate to know several. I would be delighted to take you to their studios – "

The man to the right of Serafina Morales, probably a relative, though not her husband, interrupted. "Local artists!" he hissed. "They're all depraved. Their work is pagan, evil, decadent. Mayan idolatries. Depictions of drunken saints. They are devils trying to capture our souls."

"There must be some exceptions," Jack said. "The artists I've met seem like god-fearing men to me."

"Those who aren't godless pagans are Communist puppets of Castro," a man across the table continued. "Communists are more dangerous than idolators. They want to reduce this country to rubble. When we wish to purchase art for our homes or museums, we go to Spain or Italy."

"And France," Isabella Santana quickly added. "The finest homes and museums in Argentina proudly display the works of French artists."

"What about English artists?" Jack asked, making the query sound as innocent as he could, unable to resist now that defeat was guaranteed. Spain, Italy, and France were all Catholic countries.

England was not. "Are English artists considered decadent as well?"

"Some English artists are admired," Diego Santana said, standing and raising his glass. "A paltry few compared to the many from France. What country can equal the magnificent artists France has given the world? A toast to our honored guests and to France. Vive La France!"

The French ambassador accepted the tribute with a warm smile and gracefully returned it with one his own.

As for Jack, he joined the others at the table in lifting their Baccarat wine goblets, but his silent toast was more personal. He toasted the demise of his opportunity to placate his landlady, recoup the cost of tuxedo and accessories and repay Biretta's loan.

~ **Chapter 10** ~

Saturday, exactly three weeks after he drove her back to camp, as Naomi sat editing her notes she saw Kane's square frame and deliberate, ambling farmers' stride.

"Rifkah had the flu. I couldn't leave," he said by way of a greeting. "It's lucky that I decided to look for you here. You're usually wandering on Saturdays."

How did he know what she did on Saturdays? They had spent twenty-four hours together. It was arrogant for him to assume that he would find her there waiting for him. "And you should be in synagogue praying."

"A farmer doesn't need to go to synagogue to talk to God. We pray in our fields, in our groves. Benevolent Master of the Universe, send rain! My crops are burning in the sun. Lord on High Who Sees All, grant me a good harvest so I can feed my children. Keep the locusts from my fields and deliver them to my enemies."

"I'm not going to your house."

"I wasn't inviting you to my house. I brought a picnic basket."

"I'm busy. I have things to do."

"I have cheese, warm bread fresh from the bakery, and ripe strawberries, big as plums and red as cherries."

"Where did you get strawberries?" she asked, her mouth already watering.

"I have a friend at a hotel who buys my fruit. I told him that I need berries. They're waiting in my truck."

"You have to promise not to kiss me," she said, irritated and wanting to punish him, but unwilling to give up the prospect of an unanticipated nice lunch, berries and sex. "Not on my mouth, not my face, not my arms, not anywhere. Do you understand?"

"What about your ass? Am I allowed to kiss your tight little ass?"

"Yes or no? Will you agree or not?"

"You don't want to be kissed. I heard you."

*　　*　　*

After they had eaten everything but the berries, Kane lay down beside her on the blanket he had brought for them and breathed deeply. "Smell that? Delicate white lemon blossoms. Lemons: tart to the tongue, indescribably sweet in bloom. Close your eyes and you can imagine yourself floating atop clouds of lemon blossoms."

"Is this your orchard?"

"This field belongs to my father. My brother and I work it for him. When he dies, it will belong to both of us." Kane burrowed his nose in her hair.

His hand moved to her face, the tips of his fingers exploring each feature in turn: her eyes, brows, nose, chin, and mouth. He traced her lips and then delved between them to play with her tongue. Naomi's face grew warm until she realized that Kane was using his fingertips to kiss her. Irate at the successful ploy she pulled away and quickly removed her shorts and cotton underpants.

"You want sex, farmer? Mount me like a bull." Naomi got on all fours and offered her rear.

"A very fine offer if I were a bull," Kane said without moving. "I'm not allowed to kiss you and now you want to be mounted like a cow?"

"Yes."

"You're upset. I couldn't come last week because Rifkah was sick. And the week before my sister-in-law couldn't take the children."

"You think I'm upset? Hah! How you spend your time is of no interest to me. The only reason I agreed to come today was because of the strawberries."

"Ah, the strawberries. I almost forgot the strawberries." He flipped onto his stomach, reached into the basket behind him, and lifted a single large strawberry in the air and placed it in his mouth. "I don't remember the last time I had strawberries and these are especially delicious."

"You brought them for me."

"I told you I had them. I didn't say they were all for you. Strawberries are like kisses. They're meant to be shared. Would you like half of the next one? I put a little powdered sugar on them. I hope you don't mind." He bit the ripened fruit into two pieces and placed half in Naomi's mouth and the other in his own.

Naomi rolled the berry around her mouth giving every taste bud an opportunity to savor the rare treat.

"Lie back and you'll get another."

As kneeling now seemed pointless, Naomi lay down next to him and feigned indifference. Kane placed the next one between his lips and brought his face above hers, brushing her forehead and cheeks with it until she deftly plucked it from his mouth.

"Now shut your eyes and open your mouth."

Naomi closed her eyes and opened her mouth. She could feel the warmth of his face as he dragged a halved strawberry across her cheek. She calculated the berry's position, turned, and grasped the moist morsel. It was sweeter than the first. Sweeter and riper. With the next strawberry he brought his face close enough to touch hers if she moved. Feeling the prick of shaved cheeks, she sought his lips until she once again captured the berry. "It's my turn."

Kane willingly surrendered the ripened fruit. Naomi crushed it in the hollow of his broad neck and with smacking noises nibbled until it was gone. The next she dropped into his mouth.

"Take off your blouse. You'll never get the stains out," he ordered, not unkindly.

She slowly removed both blouse and bra intending to tease and arouse him with her breasts.

He pretended to be absorbed in the remaining berries. "There's only three left," he said, taking a luscious plump berry and pressing it against the length of her arm.

As Naomi licked the sweet juice from her wrist, Kane licked her upper arm. Her head touched his when he neared her elbow. "The next one is mine."

He handed her a strawberry and watched with amusement as she crushed it against his chest. In return, he painted her breasts with the last berry. Like a bird feeding its young, he dropped bits of the pulp into her open mouth. They were both stained crimson. Kane drew her closer with his powerful right arm.

"Take me like a bull," she ordered, aroused by his physical nearness but still unwilling to surrender her power.

"I'm not an animal. I'm a man." He remained motionless. When she began licking the powdered sugar that clung to the hairs on his chest, he stroked the soft crease between her legs. "Don't you have a strawberry that wants to be plucked? I seem to have forgotten where it is. It was around here someplace. Ah, here it is. Just as moist and delectable as I remembered it."

She buried her face in his neck, overcome with the heady

perfume of his natural scent, strawberries, lemon blossoms and her own desire. If only she could suppress her lust and be chaste. Or be satisfied with solitary release. But she couldn't. Fired by his hot breath, Naomi pulled his thick hard body to hers. This was what she needed.

*   *   *

"You can't go back to camp looking like that," Kane said as they lay under the fluttering branches. "Come back to my house for a bath."

Naomi considered the suggestion. He had won the initial battle of coital position, and later in a moment of surrender, they had kissed – but she had enticed him to mount her from behind the second time he had made love to her, so perhaps the kiss couldn't be counted as a loss. "Do you have any operas?"

"A few. Carmen, La Boheme. They belonged to my wife."

"What about Turandot?"

"I'm not familiar with the name, so I must not own it."

"I wouldn't have come even if you did." She sat up.

He pulled her down beside him. "Talk to me. Tell me why you haven't tried to contact the woman in the magazine who could be your daughter."

"Am I to have no privacy in this damned country? Is there anything about my life that you don't know?"

"Yes. I don't know why you haven't tried to contact her. Is it that you don't know how or you're afraid to be disappointed?"

"What if this fancy model is Michelle? What makes you think she or her sister want to see me?"

"What makes you think they wouldn't?"

"For all I know they could hate me."

"Why would they hate you? You're their mother."

"You don't know what Alain told them. Everything is so simple for you. You eat, you drink, you sleep, you fuck. Simple."

"Life is simple. The only thing you left out was love. I loved my wife. I love my children, my parents, my brothers and sisters, my nieces and nephews. I could love you too if you'd let me."

"How fortunate for you," she said, making no attempt at hiding the bitterness. "So many people to love."

"Forget your anger. Try loving again. You could start with me. And after me, who can say what's possible."

"I died. What you see before you is a corpse." She pointed to her face. "You need someone that's alive. There are lots of young pretty women who would be happy to be the wife of a hard-working successful man like you."

"Not just successful and hard-working – virile and lusty — a virile, lusty man like me."

She turned away when he gently pulled her chin so that she would face him.

"Other women are willing, Naomi, delicate as a teacup, prickly as a thorn. But I haven't been able to separate my soul from yours. I blame the lightning that bound us as one."

"Lightning! You may as well blame God."

"And who sends the lightning?"

"Ruben, listen to me. You have to think of your children. I can't be their mother."

"Why not?"

"I'm too selfish to be a mother. I was a terrible mother to my own children. That's why my husband left me. That's what we fought about."

"Tell me in what way you abused your children. You hit them? You screamed at them? You didn't feed them? Tell me what you did."

"I didn't scream at them and didn't hit them. I loved them with all my heart. But I was very young and inexperienced, and all they wanted was their father. From the moment they were born, both worshiped Alain."

"My Leah was the best mother – devoted, hard working, always worried about her children, seeing that they ate right, looking over their homework. My children loved their mother, but still they fought for my attention, particularly my Rifkah. Your daughters loved you. Stop looking for ways to torture yourself."

"Then why did Alain take them from me?"

Kane removed bits of debris from Naomi's hair. "I don't know. Maybe he believed that you were dead. Many names were lost during and after the war."

Naomi rose to leave and began dressing.

"The water will be cold, but we can wash up from a hose, unless you've changed your mind about coming home with me."

"I'm used to cold water. A hose will be fine."

*   *   *

As the weeks passed Naomi worried about what she would do when the project ended – a subject she didn't discuss with Kane, knowing he would argue and try to meddle in her decision. Shaul and Uri would have teaching positions at universities. Lacking formal education, no such positions were open to her. Uri had assured her there would be other digs that would want someone with her experience and skills. But to date, every project she contacted regretfully informed her they had all the paid staff they could afford. She would be welcomed as a volunteer. As for the kibbutz, even if she wanted to return, they wouldn't take her back. Membership to a kibbutz was a lifelong commitment that she had accepted and then rejected. In three months, she would have no job and no place to go. Naomi fantasized about walking into the desert, taking whatever direction she faced until she faded into nothing.

~ **Chapter 11** ~

Charlie looked up from her studies to see Brigitta schussing down a sunny slope on the television screen. Rosemarie had been right. Brigitta had been chosen to be the Perfecta spokeswoman. Lucky Brigitta wasn't stuck in a hospital and facing virtual house arrest when discharged, Charlie thought. Brigitta was gloriously free, in her sherbet-pink ski outfit, soft tendrils of her flame-red hair peeking out of her hood, her cheeks glowing in the frosty air.

Ken lowered the volume so they could talk. "Still thinking about going back to modeling?"

"I doubt if there's any work waiting for me, but the thought has crossed my mind."

"Not a good idea for a while. You're too easy a target. Anyone can call your company and say that he's seen your photos and wants to hire you. You won't know that you've been set up until it's too late."

"I could accept jobs only from well-known photographers and companies we've done business with in the past."

"Don't those photographers and companies have secretaries and assistants? You can't tell who actually called."

Charlie frowned. While no jobs awaited her, hearing how vulnerable she would be was depressing.

"I'm not trying to make you nuts, but you're going to have to learn how to watch your back and not take unnecessary chances. You were attacked in a public place, so avoid subways and busses," Ken cautioned. "If you have to leave your house, ask a friend to drive you or take a cab. And don't stand on a deserted street to wave one down."

"I suppose you think I should hire a bodyguard."

"I prefer seeing you an artwork expert. There's a future for you there. Look at the books you've already read."

"Barely made a dent in what I have to know."

"Which reminds me, have you thought about how you're going to get home Thursday and how you're going to manage all this? Is Francesco going to pick you up?"

There was no way she would ask Raul. "I'll take a cab. The

books and most of my stuff is leaving the day before with a car service. The concierge in my building will hold them until I get home."

"The first thing I'm doing is going to the Carnegie Deli for a corned beef sandwich on rye, side of potato salad and a sour pickle."

Seconds passed before she realized that she was staring.

"I see that you're one of those people who think all that cops eat is donuts, hotdogs, and pizza."

"You left out hamburgers, pretzels, coffee, and beer."

"That settles it. You're coming with me."

Charlie checked her hand mirror. For the last two months, not having to worry about her appearance had been a welcome break. No makeup, comfortable stretch pants, a sweatshirt, and sneakers. Her hospital wardrobe consisted of her oldest and shabbiest things – and if they weren't shabby to begin with, after repeated hard wear, they were now. Her naturally muddy-blond hair, loosely tied in a ponytail, hadn't been cut or lightened in nearly three months. She had two inches of dark unsightly roots. "I'm not going anywhere looking like this."

"I've seen you look worse."

"Thanks."

"What do you like best: corned beef, pastrami, salami or tongue?" Ken taunted. "Of course they have other things too. I've never tried the matzo ball soup, but I'm told that it's wonderful. And don't forget dessert. I'm either having the seven layer cake or their world famous cheesecake. But maybe you'd rather eat the meatloaf and string beans we had for lunch." He thumped his chest with his fist, indicating indigestion. "Sticks with you, doesn't it?"

Reminded of the lumpy meatloaf and string beans with the flavor boiled out of them, Charlie conceded. "You win. I give up." Somehow, she would figure out a way to look presentable. "By the way, Detective, you hide the sadistic side of you very well."

"Something had to be done. It's no fun eating alone."

Charlie's thoughts turned practical. Thanks to Jane, she had a pantsuit and flats for the trip home. Her hair was the real problem. In the early months at modeling, when she was struggling to pay bills, she had learned to color it herself. It was messy, but the results were acceptable. Unfortunately, her skills did not include cutting.

But she had hairpins and she knew how to use them. She could wear her hair up and look sophisticated, instead of like a woman in desperate need of a trim.

After locating a sympathetic aide Charlie had the necessary supplies. The following morning, she advised Ken to find a place to hide and not return for a few hours.

"I'm not squeamish. Have you ever seen a body that was pulled out of a dump after rats got to it?" he said, using his cane to limp of out the suite. "I have. And it's not a pretty sight."

"Just go," she ordered.

*   *   *

The food at the famed Deli was even better than Charlie remembered. The stares and gawking, while hardly a new phenomena for her, were unsettling until she reminded herself that her lunch companion was a New York hero. It wasn't until the police car they were riding in neared her apartment, that felt the blood leaving her face.

Ken scrutinized her with his trained cop's eyes. "You're scared. Before it was all a game and now it's real."

"Just a momentary thing. I'll get over it."

"I'm coming up with you," Ken said when they arrived at the entrance to her building.

"I'll be fine."

"You'll feel better if I check the apartment and so will I. Besides, you have nothing to eat in the house and whatever's in the refrigerator is spoiled. After we check your larder, I'm going out to do some shopping. Don't waste your breath arguing."

"Would you like me to wait?" the officer asked when the car came to a halt in front of her building.

"Not necessary. Thanks for the lift. I'll call the precinct if I need another ride," Ken replied, exiting the car and helping her out even though he needed a cane and she didn't. Reaching her apartment, he followed her inside. "You want to sit down and catch your breath or check to see what you need?

"I don't need to catch my breath. I'm fine. Where are you going?"

"I'm making sure that no one is hiding in the closets," he said as he disappeared .

"Planning to look under the bed?"

"All part of the service provided by New York City's finest."

Charlie glanced at her stock of canned and frozen goods and found that Ken had correctly predicted its deficient state.

"It's over between you and Raul? There's no chance of you patching things up?"

"Nothing's changed," she called back, wondering why Ken asked a question to which he knew the answer.

"This place is nice. Pretty much what I expected."

The one-bedroom apartment had a comfortably sized living room, a dining area that held a breakfront and a table that sat six, and a bath and a half. For Manhattan, the size and location suited a successful couple. Like many young couples, she and Raul had chosen modern furniture. The result was stylish and tasteful, though hardly luxurious by the standards of her childhood.

"Looks like you – organized and neat," Ken said when he returned to the kitchen. "I'm going shopping. Give me your key so I can let myself in. Fix yourself a drink or do whatever it is you do to relax. And don't let anyone you don't know in."

*　*　*

Ken had a beer while Charlie put away the groceries he had brought. She started a pot of water for tea. "Would you consider sleeping here tonight?"

Ken appeared startled by the request. "You're asking me to sleep here and you're not worried that someone would get the wrong idea?"

"Hah! You slept ten feet from me for two months. Who would get the wrong idea after that?"

"Maybe me."

"Stop teasing. You don't think of me that way. You're my PT buddy."

"I'm also a man. Didn't you ever notice how many times I avoided looking at you at the hospital? Ever ask yourself why?"

Never once had she suspected *this* – whatever *this* was. "I thought you were preoccupied."

"Yeh! Preoccupied. It didn't seem strange that I spent a lot of time in the john with the water running?"

Her face glowed from the heat generated by the embarrassing vivid image. "I thought you had gas."

"And I thought you were smart."

"Look, I'm going to be fine. There's a doorman on duty twenty-four hours a day, and I have two telephones. Thanks to you, I have a pantry filled with groceries. I was just being silly."

"Then I better go before I change my mind." Ken rose to leave, with Charlie a step behind.

"Thanks again – for lunch, for the groceries, for everything."

When he reached the door he stopped and put his hand gently behind her head to pull it closer to his. She didn't realize that Ken intended to kiss her until it was too late to avoid it without hurting his feelings. His free arm slid around her back and drew her body to his before he planted his mouth on hers for a tongue-to-tongue sensory explosion that melted all resistance. If she still loved Raul, she shouldn't feel this way, she thought. She would not have matched Ken's fiery intensity with her own. Her response had been undeniably passionate. Did one recover from being dumped by a lover by going on to the next, like getting back on the bike after a bad fall?

"I figured we should do that or we'd always wonder what it would be like," he explained smiling. "I thought it was pretty good. I'm sure, given half a chance, the next one would be better."

Confused, she inched back and turned away rather than make eye contact.

"I'll call you. For now, deadbolt your door, remember to watch your back, and call me for anything."

After Ken left Charlie was keenly aware of being alone. Alone in a city with millions of strangers – one of whom had planned and carried out a brutal attack on her.

~ **Chapter 12** ~

Jack was rapidly approaching the invisibility awarded the destitute when the season's first tourists arrived. The handful of guests registered at the hotel included a reserved Japanese businessman who disappeared shortly after noon and reappeared just before dawn; a large, noisy Brazilian family; three nuns on holiday; an American opera singer accompanied by her manager-husband; and two English sisters traveling together. Out of that limited group, Jack viewed the sisters as his one and only target. Thanks to the bribed hotel staff, by late afternoon the day they checked in, Jack had a reasonable picture of the pair. They had flown in from London and had booked separate rooms – unusual for two women traveling together, particularly sisters. That meant one or both was well-heeled. Edith Hendrix was a college professor, subject and school unknown. Dowdy was inadequate to describe her. She looked like a woman who had been suddenly awakened at three in the morning by a fire alarm and had hastily thrown on someone else's clothes – someone who was much larger. It was her sister, Jean Osborne, who attracted Jack's attention. In her early sixties, with permed and tinted brown hair, she wore clothes that were typically English drab, but well-cut and expensive. She possessed the manicured hands of the idle rich and the manners of a lady accustomed to having her needs met by others. And she signed all their chits – the undisputed indicator of who controlled the finances. Mrs. Osborne had the added attraction of residing in distant England where Jack knew no one and no one knew him.

He realized that marriage was his only hope. Unless he won the national lottery, even his position as part-time art hustler, part-time lothario, part-time society hanger-on would come to an abrupt and sad end. Since he had not been able to repay the paltry debt he owed Paolo Biretta, he was no longer invited anywhere. Borrowing such a small sum had been foolish and short sighted. In hindsight, he should have borrowed a substantial sum. He had eradicated his hard-won social acceptance for the price of a tuxedo and accessories.

Marriage had provided for him before, but now opportunities

were scarce. When a man was thirty-five, forty, or forty-five, it was relatively simple to find and captivate a wealthy older woman. Jack had always genuinely preferred older women. As a young man, he appreciated the fading beauty that other men scorned. But most of all he enjoyed being fussed over, flattered, looked after. However, for a man of fifty-eight, circumstances no longer favored him. Older, rich, single women were scarce. And many unattached wealthy women, whose age exceeded his, no longer felt the need to be protected. In Argentina, widows were surrounded and buffered by the men in their extended families. Achieving his goal would be far easier in Palm Beach or Manhattan, where women lived alone and attending society events without an escort was considered tragic.

But there was another obstacle – one which had nothing to do with geography or demographics. As Jack approached sixty, and the object of his intentions grew older, it had become increasingly difficult to rise to the occasion. That which could always be counted on to perform on command, had of late become sulky and unreliable. So it was indeed fortuitous that Jean Osborne, a woman who met so many of Jack's needs, if one could look past her English notion of fashion, was relatively attractive for her age. Facial lines notwithstanding, she had even features, clear eyes, her own teeth, and Jack's expert eye predicted reasonably taut flesh beneath her clothes. Functioning would be near impossible if he had to hold, embrace and fondle handfuls of hanging flesh. So although Jack knew it was a long shot, considering his desperate circumstances and limited alternatives, Jean Osborne merited undivided attention.

Unfortunately, the sisters' reservations were for a brief ten-day stay. Less than two weeks. Ten short days to meet, court, captivate and win a widow's heart – nine days in reality. The days of arrival and departure could not be counted for more than half. Nor was it wise to approach targets the day they checked in. New travelers were apt to be exhausted and irritable. Instead, Jack used the afternoon to be seen walking around and to arrange an exhibition match with Emilio – something done many times to mutual advantage. Jack would meet new guests under favorable circumstances, apparently unplanned, and Emilio would gain students that he might have otherwise failed to attract. The match would be played at ten, after breakfast and before guests disappeared to sightsee, find a lounge chair on the beach, or shop.

The next morning, at the hotel's breakfast room, Jack sipped his coffee and pretended to read a newspaper as he waited at a nearby table until his designated targets had eaten before introducing himself and personally delivering the invitation.

"I see that you're wearing tennis attire," Jean Osborne said, after glancing at his trim tanned legs. "Will you be a spectator or may we assume that you'll be competing?"

"I'm one of Emilio's pupils," Jack said, aiming his most dazzling smile at her. "I'm relying on his kind nature not to make to a fool out of this poor excuse for an opponent."

"What do you say, dear? I haven't arranged for a taxi as yet," Jean Osborne said to her sister. "We could stay and watch the tennis match and go into town later."

The only makeup Edith Hendrix wore was vermillion lipstick so poorly applied it scarcely resembled her mouth. Fortunately, most of it had disappeared with breakfast and had not been reapplied. "That would be lovely," she agreed, smiling amiably, unaware of the trace of egg yolk on her chin or the crumbs of toast that clung to her cardigan.

"Then it's settled," Jean said. "We'll be courtside at ten."

Jack quickly excused himself explaining that he needed time to warm up. It was best not to appear overanxious.

By ten o'clock three members of the staff and eight or nine guests, including the two sisters, had taken seats facing center court. Jack formally introduced Emilio Diego, taking time to cite a number of Diego's significant early triumphs. Jack explained the renowned tennis player and instructor would address them in Spanish and he would translate in English. This part of their routine was solely for entertainment. Most of their Spanish-speaking spectators spoke English.

Diego told the group, after warming up, that he and Jack would put on an eight game exhibition for their guests' enjoyment.

Jack translated.

"Tennis can be enjoyed at many levels. My students range from beginners to experts," Diego said, lapsing into heavily accented English.

Jack translated, solemn-faced, in Spanish. The small audience laughed on cue.

Diego returned to Spanish with high praise for his fine friend and pupil, Jack Caine, employing words even the dullest language student could understand, words like *amigo*, *magnifico* and *excelente*.

"Emilio wants me to tell you that he tried to locate a stronger opponent," Jack mock translated, "but I was the best he could do on such short notice."

The group chuckled and warmly applauded as the two men took the court. Having warmed up earlier, the next ten minutes was used to give Jack an opportunity to smash a few overheads, put away some easy net shots, and for Diego to deliver several blistering unreturnable serves. Jack won the coin toss and elected to receive serve. Diego took the first game, but not without allowing Jack some flashy points. As a professional familiar with his student's limitations, Diego was able to control the match. He could hit a deep fast shot confident that it would be returned, provided Jack could easily reach it. Or he could send Jack dramatically dashing from one side of the court to the other, if the pace wasn't excessive. This was, after all, only an exhibition. After losing a particularly lengthy point Jack complained to the audience in Spanish. Even members of the staff who had seen the stunt many times before laughed. Jack played to the best of his ability, and his best was good tennis. Emilio didn't need to feign concentration. When the match was six – two, a weak service return allowed Diego to effortlessly put away a shot over his shoulder, his back to the net. Jack somberly placed his racket on the ground and bowed. Even the most reserved guests laughed or cheered.

Jack could see Jean and Edith were enthralled.

After the match Jack allowed himself to be congratulated and praised by the other spectators before walking over to the waiting sisters.

"Well done! Ripping fun!" Jean looked five years younger, having changed from the dull suit he'd seen her in earlier to a bright yellow cotton dress. "I can't remember the last time I attended anything half as entertaining."

"Great fun," her sister added. The bulky cardigan he had seen earlier had lost the toast crumbs, but was now buttoned so that the right side was two inches higher than the left.

"Might I sit down?" he asked. "After that workout I could use a cold drink." He signaled a waiter. "May I get you something, ladies?"

Both demurred, but Jack prevailed and ordered pineapple drinks for the three of them, and later a fourth drink when Diego, who had been talking with the other guests, came over to join them. Nothing was as obvious as the sisters' delight in having not one, but two, attractive men seated at their table engaging them in conversation.

"Get Jack to show you the city," Diego suggested. "He knows every site you'd want to see in Buenos Aires and a dozen more you haven't heard about."

Jean's eyes widened. "Oh my! That would be lovely, but we intended to –"

"Nothing we can't do another day. We have the entire afternoon utterly free," the previously silent Edith interjected.

"But that would be imposing, dear. Mr. Caine must have plans."

"Do you have plans that would prevent you from escorting these two lovely ladies, Jack?" Diego lowered his voice conspiratorially, as though Jack sitting across the small table couldn't hear. "My good friend is more than a tennis player. There isn't a serious artist in Buenos Aires that he doesn't know by his first name. Ask him nicely and he'll take you to meet them."

"And my good friend Emilio seems to think that I need looking after," Jack said. "He's afraid I get lonely for English speaking people. These two innocent ladies are here to relax. They certainly don't need . . . "

"Please, Jack," Jean said, touching his arm. "We would be ever so grateful to have you show us the city."

"Ever so grateful," Edith echoed, as she attempted to rejoin a defiant clump of hair with the gray amoeba shaped lump on the back of her head.

"I would be happy to. Just give me a few minutes to shower and change." As he rose, Jack wondered what deformity lurked beneath Edith's oversized, ill-fitting dress and cardigan.

*   *   *

Jack took the pair to the popular tourist sites in Buenos Aires: the Casa Rosada, the pink Presidential Palace, The Teatro Colon, the magnificent opera house across the way, and La Boca, a brightly decorated section of the city noted for its tin houses, shops, dancers and street performers. As they walked Jack found ample opportunities to take Jean's elbow or lightly guide her with his hand on her back and then back away, careful not to frighten his prey by proceeding too quickly. They made an odd threesome – Jack at Jean's side, while the woman devoid of any vanity trailed behind under the large black umbrella she carried to protect her sensitive skin from the damaging rays of the tropical sun. He guessed that he and Jean looked like a refined upper-class couple who had brought along a dotty eccentric relative out of compassion.

Normally, when compelled to squire more than one woman at a time, Jack played for time until he decided which one to target. After that, the lady selected could be relied on to be a co-conspirator at finding ways they could be alone. With sisters, diplomacy in this area, was all-important. To offend one could be disastrous.

At six o'clock, Jack guided the pair to a nearby restaurant, which he knew had good food, a quiet setting, flattering atmospheric candlelight, and most important, prices that would permit him to pay the bill.

Before Jack returned them to the hotel, they had made plans to meet the next day to visit Argentina's famous cemetery, La Recoleta, and the historic skull-adorned church next to it, the Iglesia del Pilar.

Their second day passed pleasantly with Jack's hope for a successful hunt cautiously growing with every laugh and returned smile. He protested only long enough to be polite when Jean invited him to be their guest for dinner at the hotel.

That evening, as they sipped their aperitifs, Jack reminded the sisters about the talented artists Diego had mentioned. Under ideal circumstances, he would have preferred waiting until midway into their vacation before taking them there. Tourists usually spent more after they had several days to forget the cares of home. But given his present financial predicament, necessity dictated the timing.

"Tomorrow, I would like to take you to visit some studios and meet the artists, if that's all right with you. I think you'd enjoy it."

"That does sound ever so lovely, doesn't it, dear?" Jean gushed, addressing her sister.

"Ever so lovely," Edith repeated, her upper lip stained by her apricot aperitif.

*   *   *

Jack met the sisters in the lobby at one-thirty. He had deliberately scheduled their trip after lunch. Their first night's dinner, as modest as it was, and two days of cab fares and refreshments, had sorely undermined his scant reserves. He was relying on today's commission. If the two women purchased nothing, or very little, he would be forced to abandon his quest for the first Mrs. Jack Caine and attempt to include other guests at the hotel in his guided tours. Nevertheless, he was hopeful as he recited his customary warning as the taxi drove them to their first stop – the weaver's home and workplace.

"Remember, you are not obligated to buy anything. I'm taking you to studios, not shops. Artists appreciate your interest. Of course, if you decide there is something you'd like to take home with you, you would be paying a small fraction of what a gallery would charge."

When possible Jack preferred to have the artists discuss their work while he remained a silent onlooker, but as the shy Mestizo woman didn't speak English he was forced to translate. Jean nodded courteously as he commented on the various pieces, but it was soon apparent she had little interest in the intricate weavings. Edith quietly questioned the artist directly about her designs. Somehow, artist and admirer were able to converse. Jack was willing to wait, but Jean was impatient.

"Let's not keep the nice woman," she said. "Please tell her that we thank her for sharing her splendid rugs with us."

"What language were you speaking?" Jack asked Edith after they'd left. "I recognized a few words."

"Latin."

"Latin is only one of many my clever sister knows. She's an expert on ancient languages," Jean explained. "Aren't you, dear?"

"Then she will probably find our next stop fascinating," Jack said. "You are about to step back in time, before the conquistadors conquered this paradise. My good friend, the artist at the next studio, makes replicas of pre-Columbian art that are sold in museums throughout South America. But he also sells genuine artifacts that have been buried here for centuries. Excavators risk their lives delving deep into the jungles and climbing high into the mountains searching for these treasures."

Jack opened a weather-beaten door that exposed a courtyard filled with statuary, and a small shop behind.

"Jose, allow me to introduce Senora Osborne and Professora

Hendrix, two charming ladies who are very curious to learn about the Incas and the Toltecs," Jack said, introducing his companions. "And this is my good friend, the talented artist Jose Ortega."

Knowing the restorer, replicator, amateur archeologist and occasional grave robber could captivate an audience, Jack took a seat to better contemplate his quarry. What at first seemed a near impossible feat – meeting and winning Jean's heart in ten short days – was starting to seem within reach. It was blatantly apparent that she was more than flattered by his attention. She found every excuse to cling to or lean on his arm. With only five and a half days left, he needed to get Jean alone, away from her sister with the twisted stockings and the inevitable trail of breadcrumbs. If only Edith, a woman who resembled a pile of laundry, would come down with the flu. A mild case of Montezuma's revenge shouldn't be that difficult to arrange. Twenty-four hours of being unable to leave the bathroom, followed by a least one day to fully recover. Too bad he wasn't a man capable of that sort of thing. He would have to have Jean's assistance to rid them of their tagalong. He would have to be bolder this evening – resting his hand on her shoulder and then gently squeezing it – some flattery whispered in her ear when they walked – a sly shared smile. He would suggest dinner at the hotel. Surely Jean would insist on being his host again. But if necessary, he could sign for it. The hotel had obliged him before.

"This is where I keep the authentic pieces," Ortega said, leading them inside his shop. "I know that you'll find the prices far less than what you'd expect."

Edith was apparently absorbed while Jean was polite but displayed little real interest.

"Don't the authorities frown on art leaving the country?" Edith asked the artist.

"Some people would prefer that Argentina's native art didn't leave the country," Ortega explained as he handed a tripod pot to Edith. "But they are very short-sighted people. How is the world to appreciate pre-Columbian art if we selfishly keep it all to ourselves? A nation's art enhances its stature. What would the world know about Egypt, if it weren't for the many splendid Egyptian treasures that can be found in museums in France, England, and the United States?"

"True. And I would like to take home a small memento of our

trip," Edith admitted.

"What if we were found carrying contraband?" Jean protested. "It doesn't sound like a good idea, does it, Jack?"

Thankfully for Jack, Ortega intervened. "As tourists, normally your luggage wouldn't be checked, but just to make certain there's absolutely no chance you would be embarrassed, I'll provide a receipt stating your purchase is a replica. Not one of my customers has ever been bothered. Have you ever heard of an English tourist having difficulties taking home one of my artifacts, Jack?"

"Never!" Jack replied truthfully. Manuel Ortega had the perfect operation. Sixty percent of the *genuine* artifacts he sold were copies. Fifteen percent were ancient heads given new bodies, and another fifteen percent were badly damaged pieces that had been radically repaired. Less than ten percent were authentic museum-quality artifacts, and they usually crossed the borders in trucks, hidden amongst freight. Exiting tourists were never bothered, even when Ortega sold them one of his authentic pieces. Authorities automatically assumed the piece was simply another one of Ortega's replicas.

"Manuel, do you still have the *little treasure* I admired last time?" Jack asked, cuing Ortega to bring out a genuine piece.

"I know exactly the one you're referring to. Give me a moment to find it." Ortega ducked into his back room and soon returned with a figurine of a woman no more than eight inches tall. "First let me explain that the Incas were fascinated with deformities. The Inca king kept a number of freaks in his court, like a human zoo. Now, take a look at this, Mrs. Osborne, Miss Hendrix. Cast your eyes on this fascinating little lady. She has the enlarged earlobes and the patches of coca tucked in her cheeks, but see, she also has a hunchback. And there have been no repairs done on this particularly rare piece. She's just the way we found her."

"It's marvelous," Edith said.

Jack inwardly winced. Announcing one's admiration so soon was the worst possible start of a negotiation. "How much for my dear friend, Professor Edith Hendrix, Manuel?"

Ortega shrugged and named a reasonable sum for the exceptional piece.

Both women turned to Jack. "It's well worth the money and very fine, but the decision has to be yours."

"I'll take it," Edith announced.

"You really shouldn't, dear," Jean said. Edith's face dropped. "But if you're set on having it, let me buy it for you as a gift. I insist upon it."

So the lady could be generous, Jack happily observed. A most endearing trait for a financially-tried man's future wife.

Ortega wrapped the small statue and Edith left the studio a content woman. Their next stop was the most famous artist in Buenos Aires.

"In my opinion, Carlos Alsaya may be the single most remembered South American artist of this century," Jack exuded, entirely candid. "And I'm not alone in this opinion. You may have difficulty at first relating to Alsaya's way of seeing things, but I suggest you leave yourself open to that which is exciting and new."

Alsaya greeted them and gestured at his oversized oils of balloon-like floating figures. "Please, feel free to stay as long as you wish. Let me know if I may be of any assistance."

While the rotund man returned to cleaning his brushes, Jack waited for the women. Edith was pointing at a particular oil and Jean was nodding, but Jack couldn't hear their conversation. In his experience, men were more likely to purchase Alsaya's work, but this dramatic genius was an excellent precursor to their next and last stop – Jacob Weiner and his jewelry. What woman could resist his unique wearable art?

As expected, neither sister expressed more than polite interest in Alsaya's art. And as she learned their next destination Jean declared, "I have a chest filled with brooches, bracelets, and rings that belonged to my mother-in-law, which I never wear. What about you, dear?" she asked Edith. "Is Scythian art one of your many interests?"

Edith looked first at Jack and then her sister. "According to Jack, they're not actually Scythian, but artistic interpretations. Perhaps we should head back to the hotel. What with the change in time zones and diet, travel can be most exhausting. You must be tired. We've done a great deal of walking."

"Then that's what we'll do, dear," Jean said. "We'll return to the hotel and you can go to your room and take a nap while Jack and I have tea."

"But what about you?" Edith asked, apparently surprised to be excluded. "Shouldn't you be resting?"

"Nonsense. I'm fit as a fiddle. A nice cup of tea and I'll be ready to dance until dawn."

Jack was elated. That Jean Osborne had taken it upon herself to arrange for them to be alone more than compensated for the paltry sales. She was clearly interested in him. His immediate challenge would be financing the next five days.

*   *   *

"What would you like to do tomorrow?" Jack asked sotto voce, sliding his chair closer to Jean's, as though the question was one that required privacy. Edith had obediently gone to her room. Except for a lone waiter who appeared sporadically, the deck bordering the pool was deserted. "Name it. Horse racing, sightseeing, shopping, a long walk on one of Buenos Aires spectacular beaches. I am yours for as long as you'd like."

"Then you're certain that we're not imposing?"

Jack found her hand and gently pressed it with his. "Have I done anything to give you that impression? I'd hate myself if I did."

"Don't you usually play tennis in the morning? We'll watch you play."

"Emilio and I rarely do exhibitions like the one you saw. You would probably find one of my practice sessions boring. And as for Edith – "

"Not at all. Edith and I would enjoy watching you play. If the truth be told, it was her idea."

"Is there any chance we can spend some time alone? Perhaps an entire day alone?"

Like an homage to an early thirties movie vamp, Jean dropped her lashes and looked back up at him. "Would you like that?" she asked.

Jack's returned smile was half delight at success and half amusement. "Very much."

"Then I'll arrange it."

*   *   *

At 7:50 the following morning, when Jack approached, Heinrich Dieter was loosening his muscles, stretching and bending by the pair of adjoining courts set aside for guests' use. Between the two courts, the English sisters, seated under an umbrella-shaded table, greeted him. Apparently, they had risen at dawn simply to watch him play, Jack thought, pleased to see them. Jean looked fresh and poised in her dark flowered cotton dress. As for Edith, she had on another of her horrible tent-proportioned muumuus, one even the most die-hard missionary would approve of, and only her signature lopsided vermillion lipstick to enhance her appearance.

"There's no need to rush," the tall man with the receding hairline told him. "We can have the court for as long as we wish."

This time it was Jack's turn to be the gracious winner. Dieter was no competition. Relishing the attention of the two women who enthusiastically applauded every point, Jack put away a clumsy lob with an angled shot Dieter was unable to reach. After an hour and quarter of play, Jack could prolong the lopsided match no further. Winded but still determined, Dieter asked for a rematch. The younger man had two teenaged sons arriving at noon who also played tennis. They were far more skilled than their father. Would Jack be interested in doubles any time after lunch? He and Jack could each take one of the boys as partners.

"I was planning to spend the rest of the day showing these two charming ladies more of Buenos Aires," Jack explained.

"We could sit by the pool," Edith suggested. "Jack would be our guest for lunch, and we could watch the next fine match. Less tiring for us and equally splendid. Don't you agree, dear?" she said, addressing her sister.

Jean agreed.

All was going well, Jack assured himself. The entire day would cost nothing. He would have another opportunity to show off surrounded by fit young men. A change of clothes and dinner would follow. All fine. But what he really needed was the promised full day with Jean, and only Jean. His plan called for a romantic secluded setting, perfect for exchanged confidences. An arm carelessly flung over her shoulder. A friendly hug that would turn into an embrace. Gestures that were too bold for their short acquaintance and her expected British reserve, might be welcomed if they were alone where no one knew her. Underneath the cool façade, Jack sensed suppressed passion.

"Edith loves exploring dusty dull libraries, museums, and universities. I detest them," Jean confided at dinner when Edith left the table for the ladies' room. "I suggested that she spend tomorrow at any of the aforementioned and she agreed. Was that was you wanted?"

"It's exactly what I'd hoped for. Now, are you going to allow me to plan a day for us, or was there something special that you wanted to see or do?"

"I'll leave that up to you."

"Bring a sunhat, swimsuit and wear comfortable shoes. That's all I'm going to say."

*   *   *

The pawnshop, which was supposed to open at nine o'clock, was closed when Jack arrived at nine twenty-five the next morning. He had brought with him the tuxedo, shoes, and accessories he had purchased for the unfortunate Santana soiree. They were the last dispensable possessions he owned that he could sell or pawn. When the dealer finally arrived fifteen minutes later, he offered Jack a fifth of their original cost. Jack accepted. What choice remained? With luck and skill, the meager amount would finance the next two days of his scheme.

*   *   *

Jack had taken great care selecting the pristine site. The sandy beach with the shimmering aqua water was a short walk to the nearest bathroom, and there were no lithe young bodies darting about in skimpy swimsuits to remind a woman of her age. Nor was the site entirely isolated. In the distance, one could see a picturesque fishing village where men were mending their nets.

Jean worked on the small needlepoint she had brought with her while Jack swam. He was proud of his well-exercised physique and welcomed the chance to display it. The swimsuit that she assured him she had brought with her, hadn't surfaced as yet.

"You haven't asked about my wife," he said when he returned to their shaded beach blanket, drying himself with a towel.

She set the half-finished canvas in her lap. "I didn't want to pry."

Jack related a borrowed tragic story told him by his barber in the States. The man had lost his wife to cervical cancer. "I watched Carol slowly slip away from me for two long years."

"I'm so sorry."

Jack's eyes grew moist as he recalled his barber's anguish. "I couldn't deny her anything: nurses twenty-four hours a day, private hospital rooms, experimental treatments, black market drugs to ease the pain, anything to see her smile."

"It must have been dreadful for you."

He allowed himself a long sigh. "So you see, I came to Buenos Aires for two reasons. First, to escape, to see new faces and forget. And second, because living costs are less here. Carol's illness . . . . Virtually everything I had. It doesn't matter. I'm here now . . ." He allowed the sound of the waves and wind to complete the thought.

"I suppose it was easier for me," she confided. "I was spared a long farewell. Of course, it was a great shock at the time. One Monday morning Edgar's clerk found him in his office dead by his own hand. A single gunshot."

"You must have been devastated." Jack patted her hand. "Do you know what made him do such a thing?"

"I discovered his reasons the very next day. You may have read about it. It seems Russian spies had been blackmailing him to deliver government secrets to them. He preferred death to continuing life as a traitor."

"My god! You poor woman. But you haven't said anything about children. Did they take it hard?"

"We had none. Three years after we were married I discovered that Edgar was a poof – a homosexual. Even so, I suppose we could have had children. But it never seemed quite right. And there were scant opportunities, as you well might imagine," she said, the blush making her look younger.

"Yet you remained together," Jack pressed, delighted that she had confided in him and eager to extend that intimacy. "Many women . . ."

"It was a good marriage despite the obvious difficulties. My father delivered mail. Edgar was the only child of a tannery owner and a very kind man. I was able to do what I wanted – go where I wished. Besides, my family is strict Church of England. We don't divorce."

"But did your family . . . Were they aware of your – your husband's condition?"

"Perhaps. It's difficult to say. We didn't discuss such things. And now there's just Edith and myself. Don't be fooled by her disregard to her appearance. What you might not guess is that she's terribly clever. In fact, after we leave Buenos Aires, Edith is being given an award by the Egyptian government for translating some obscure hieroglyphics. We're going to Cairo and then it's off to the Holy

Land. What about you? You must have family in the States."

"Only one sister, her husband and their three sons. But they never liked Carol and they virtually ignored us when she became ill. Not once did they visit her in the hospital. I can't forgive them." Jack lifted Jean's hand and lightly kissed it. "Has anyone ever told you that you're very easy to talk to? I find myself being able to tell you the most troubling things and then feeling better about it afterward."

"I suspect Edith has taken a fancy to you. She would never say anything, but I can read the signs. She can barely form sentences when you're near."

"And I have taken a fancy to her sister. Have you read the signs, or are you going to be coy and pretend that you haven't noticed?"

"You're a very easy man to take to, Jack Caine. I suspect you've captured many a woman's heart. Don't be misled by my apparent strength. My heart is fragile. I have to be mindful of it."

"Are you enjoying the time we've had together?" he asked, searching her eyes with his.

"Very much."

"Then you look after Edith's heart and I promise to be careful with yours." He bent over and softly kissed her mouth – a brief kiss and no more. They silently watched the waves until the sun disappeared behind a cloud. "It's getting cool. Are you ready for tea?"

"If you'd like."

"See the boats to our right? It takes about twenty minutes to walk there. Are you up to it or shall I look for a cab?"

"A leisurely stroll followed by tea would be lovely before we return to the hotel."

"I was hoping to convince you to stay. The village is having a festival celebrating their patron saint. Street vendors will be selling all sorts of local delicacies. There'll be music and rides for the children. It's very festive. We could find a small sidewalk café for dinner and watch the fun."

"What about Edith? She's expecting me for dinner."

"Did I mention the fireworks? When it gets dark, there are fantastic displays of fireworks."

"It sounds delightful. But I do feel responsible for Edith."

"Maybe it's time for you to stop being the mother hen. Edith's a capable woman and university professor. There's no need to treat her like a child. Call her! Tell her there's been a little change in our plans."

"You're right! As her older sister, I'm apt to hover when there's no need. I'll call her."

*   *   *

Jean had returned his kiss in the privacy of the beach, but then maintained a discreet distance once they reached the village. Only when they couldn't be observed did she allow Jack to hold her hand or put his arm about her waist. But it was the fireworks that melted her remaining coolness. As the sky above thundered and exploded in dazzling colors, she nestled in his arms.

"This is much better. I like this," he said, nuzzling her cheek.

"We're not young anymore," she whispered as the last ember turned to ash. "I'm so afraid of appearing foolish."

"Two people who care for one another are never foolish. Are you ready to abandon romance to the young? What have they done to earn it?"

She smiled. "Nothing, I suppose."

"Would you ever consider remarrying?"

She bit her lip and frowned. "We should head back. In twenty minutes the square will be deserted and it may be impossible to find a taxi."

Once in the cab Jean grew increasingly quiet.

Jack ran his hand over the worn upholstery. He had invested his last cent in courting this woman. In four days she would get on a plane and leave, never to return. In three days her mind would be focused on the next leg of her trip. So little time. He cursed British reserve. Any American woman above the age of twenty could be expected to be more responsive. He had hoped to be further along at this point. Tomorrow they would spend the day with her sister –a woman he now knew *fancied* him. With Edith dogging their heels, he would have little opportunity to advance his relationship with Jean. The cab hit a teeth-chattering pothole. "So little time," he repeated absently.

"You asked if I would ever consider remarrying," Jean said in that detached manner she had. "Frankly, I never considered the possibility of remarrying – or that anyone would want me in that way."

"And why not?"

"Oh Jack, I'm not the sort men lust after. I was a girl in my prime when I met and married Edgar. And even he –"

"Stop right there! Just stop right there! I don't claim to be an expert on homosexual men, but Marilyn Monroe wouldn't have been able to arouse your husband. You had nothing to do with his preferences. You're a handsome and desirable woman." A light from a passing car caught her wistful smile. Jack imagined that he could hear the faint tap, tap, tap of opportunity. "Please don't think I'm crazy. I wish I had the time to court you properly – to let the seasons pass and slowly win your heart. But it was our fate to meet like this – under these circumstances – here in Buenos Aires. In four short days, if we act like proper responsible adults, you're going to get on a plane and we'll never see each other again. Are we going to allow this one last opportunity for happiness slip away from us? How likely is it that we'll be given another chance?"

"Have you asked me to marry you?"

Was she angry, shocked, annoyed, amused? He couldn't tell. Damn these Brits and their maddening, stiff upper-lipped reserve. How was he supposed to respond? Best to leave an opening. "Please don't say no. Promise me that you'll think about it."

"I don't have to think about it. Edgar courted me for three years before he proposed. I think that I've spent enough of my life doing the dull dreary things that were expected of me. You were right. We have so little time."

"Did I hear right? Did you say 'yes'?"

Jean coyly nodded.

The taxi shuddered to a stop. "We'll be just a moment," Jack told the driver in Spanish. "This beautiful lady just agreed to marry me. Allow me a moment to kiss my intended."

"Take your time, Senor," the driver agreed. "I can wait. Love shouldn't be rushed."

God bless every Brit who ever drew breath, Jack thought as he poured all his relief and delight into that one long kiss. Thoroughly amazing people. Hitler had to be mad to think he could defeat them. Now all he had to do to seal his future was make love to Jean. He had confessed earlier to having *limited funds*. Before they left for England, Jean had to learn the dismal truth. By then, she had to be utterly committed to him. From experience, Jack knew a happy sated woman was less likely to quibble over the difference between limited funds and abject poverty.

*   *   *

The following morning Jack nearly skipped on his way to meet his fiancée and future sister-in-law for a late breakfast at the hotel. He had accomplished a near-impossible feat: finding, courting, winning the heart, and securing a promise to wed in a matter of days. And not just any woman – a financially independent, moderately attractive, agreeable, sympathetic citizen of the terribly conservative British Empire. Yet, that promise could be worthless – planned, put off, and later forgotten – if he hadn't capped it with lovemaking. God bless ladies who held fast to quaint notions of feminine propriety. They did not take their sexual investments lightly.

Tickled with himself and the world, Jack reviewed the events of the prior evening. Like a seasoned trapeze performer, with danger lurking at every turn, he had met the challenge and conquered it. For a while, it looked as though he might not be able to reach the elusive heights, but then he had concentrated on the graceful nape of Jean's neck, her creamy white skin, and her schoolgirlish pleasure with foreplay and it had happened. And God bless Edgar Osborne, that tragic ill-fated fairy who set the lowest of standards for comparison. While his lovemaking was hardly one of his best performances, it most certainly was one of his most appreciated. Jean had covered him with grateful kisses before he left. After last night, he could tell her that he was wanted for murder in every state in the Union and she wouldn't rescind her decision.

When he reached the hotel's lobby Jack saw Edith sitting on a couch by herself. He hoped Jean would not be long. He was starving. As Edith looked up, Jack noticed her eyes were bloodshot, her skin was blotchy, and no effort whatsoever had been made to contain her unruly mass of hair. The sisters had argued. Jean had told Edith about her intention to marry him and they had a violent quarrel. This absurd woman was trying to destroy his very last chance for happiness. "Where's Jean? Is something wrong?"

"She's gone."

"What do you mean she's gone? Where could she go?"

Edith sniffed and wiped her nose. "I know I shouldn't be crying. She was so brave – so determined not to be pitied. We always knew every day could be her last. I tried to warn her not to exert herself, but she wouldn't hear of it."

"No! You can't be saying . . . It can't be. She was perfectly fine last night when I left. What happened?"

"We both knew this was inevitable. I tried insisting that she rest – that she sit by the pool, take naps in the afternoon. Surely, you must have noticed. But my headstrong sister wouldn't hear of it. Not since we . . . " With this, Edith broke down and sobbed. "But you mustn't blame yourself. You didn't know." She found a handkerchief and loudly blew her nose.

"Jean's been taken to the hospital," Jack insisted.

Edith shook her head and regained her composure. "Jean had a bad heart. It gave out, just as we knew it would. But I wanted to be with her when it happened. The one thing I hoped and prayed for was that she wouldn't die frightened and alone."

"Holy Mother of God," Jack breathed. Jean was dead. Her heart. All that talk about fragile hearts hadn't been silly schoolgirl chatter. She had a bad heart. And he had unwittingly killed her.

~ **Chapter 13** ~

Accepting warnings from both Ken and Raul regarding going out alone, Charlie used a car service three times a week. The driver walked her to and from the hospital door. For the first time she actually looked forward to her formerly dreaded PT sessions. That, and a trip to the hairdresser for the long awaited haircut, were her only excursions. The doorman had conveniently supplied the names of neighborhood merchants that delivered.

Concerned friends had visited when she was in the hospital. Now that she was home, they rarely called. And for those who did, Charlie assured them that she was fine and not a virtual prisoner in her own home. To fill the many long hours the kitchen shelves and both medicine cabinets had been taken apart, washed down and rearranged. The interior and exterior of her refrigerator and oven were spotless. Sorted by season, color, and function, her entire wardrobe was as methodically organized as a pharmacist's pills. Her hated ironing basket was emptied. Bills were paid and the checkbook was up-to-date and healthy, in large part because Raul had thoughtfully paid the rent up to the end of the year.

After reading the last of the material she had on the subject of art fraud, her education consisted of concentrating on her list of un-researched artists' works and biographies.

When she had been home for what felt like months, but was only eight days, Raul's resonant voice on the other end of the phone startled her. But he only called to say that he had made some progress in learning that Berkeley Banking handled the largest part of Justin Voyt's financing. As Berkeley was one of a few remaining family owned banks, it was difficult to approach key people. Family owned banks were tight-knit and virtually impregnable. But he knew people who knew people and was making progress.

The next day, as she was morbidly imagining herself frozen in time while the world raced on without her, Hal Holmes called to say that her nephew had been born the night before. Theodore Andrew Holmes was a healthy, seven pound six ounce baby boy with the standard issue fingers and toes. He would be called Teddy. And despite twelve harrowing hours of labor that ended with a

Caesarean section, Amelia was exhausted but well.

Overjoyed to be an aunt and relieved to hear that her sister's difficult pregnancy had reached a safe and happy conclusion, Charlie debated the best way to visit her sister and Teddy. She could beg a friend to drive her, hire an insanely expensive service, ask her stepmother if she could borrow the limo and chauffeur – which she really didn't want to do – when Ken called. Whether it was excitement at the birth of her nephew, or by hearing Ken's reassuring voice again, she discovered herself babbling inanely. Naturally, Ken asked when and how she would see her sister and nephew and naturally, in her giddy state, she revealed the location, the distance and her frustration at not being with her sister. Luckily for her, he was still on temporary medical leave and thought it would be fun to leave the the city and drive to Connecticut.

As she stood in front of her perfectly arranged closet, still undecided after an hour's deliberation about what to wear, Charlie wondered if a single memorable kiss had affected her ability to make a simple decision.

*　*　*

They found Amelia in what had to be the hospital's most luxurious room. A private duty nurse added the basket of flowers that had dominated the entire back seat of Ken's car to the existing botanical garden. Although he had wanted to wait in the car while she visited her sister, Charlie had insisted Ken accompany her.

After being introduced to Hal, his parents, and Amelia, Ken chose the chair nearest the door, where he remained a silent observer during the usual polite family exchanges regarding health and happiness.

Side conversation ceased when Baby Teddy was brought to the room to be fed – a radical exception to normal hospital regulations, it was explained to Charlie. Normally, newborns weren't permitted in their mother's room if anyone other than the infants' parents were present. Amelia's physician, and her father-in-law's position on the hospital's board of directors, had facilitated this breech of policy.

To the nurse's dismay, and Charlie's delight, she was granted the privilege of giving Teddy his bottle. With his pink eyelids and tiny mouth, he was so helpless, so innocent, so absolutely perfect. Charlie didn't care that everyone laughed when she clumsily tried burping him.

Thirty minutes after their arrival Amelia's smile looked forced. Her face was pale and drawn.

"We're going to leave. You look tired, darling," Charlie said, hoping the others would take the hint. "I'll call you tomorrow."

"I thought Amelia looked well, considering," Charlie said to Ken as they made their way through the parking lot.

"Yeah"

He appeared distracted in the car with little to say, in contrast to the drive up, Charlie thought. He had become distant the minute they had entered the hospital. Everyone present had been cordial to him. Hal had attempted to engage him in conversation, while Ken had responded in monosyllables.

"What's wrong? You're very quiet."

"They're your folks. I was just staying out of the way."

"Try again. I know better."

"We've got to talk about what happened when I brought you home. That kiss," he said, his eyes fixed on the road ahead.

"It's not as though I didn't kiss you back."

"Look, we get along great. But we're different – different in ways you don't understand.

"Now, that's ridiculous."

I'm a New York City cop. I like my job and I'm good at it. You come from another world. And that's the difference. You're champagne and I'm beer. So you can relax. I was wrong to kiss you and it's not going to happen again."

"I enjoy your company. I find you attractive. You find me attractive. That kiss proved there's a noticeable degree of chemistry between us. I fail to see the problem."

"Here's the thing," he continued. "I don't know how it is with you, but guys can have chemistry with women they can't stand."

"Really?" Charlie challenged, doubtful.

"Yeah, really! We're going to be friends because what doesn't happen all the time for me, is finding someone to talk to about things that you can't discuss with anyone else."

Charlie's spirits plummeted. For a moment she considering arguing – If caring and physical attraction didn't provide the basis for romantic love, what did? – before a combination of feminine pride and common sense prevailed.

*   *   *

On the bank's third floor, Charlie glanced over at Raul as they sat in the conservative but luxurious reception area, rifling through dull business periodicals, waiting for Robert Makepeace to see them. She detected an anticipatory impatience in him she recognized from equally tense prior situations. It had taken work, persistence, and the help of a network of trusted associates to arrange this meeting. Her part had been locating respected art experts and learning all she could about Gustav Kadinski's death – he had been forty-five, reasonably healthy and reputed to be a strong swimmer when he drowned.

After twenty-five minutes, they were finally led to the impressive corner office. Robert Makepeace, the founder's great-grandson and CEO of Berkeley Banking, greeted them and motioned to the forest green tufted leather chairs that faced his desk. The fortyish lean man reminded Charlie of a fountain pen, from his shined wing-tipped shoes to the top of his gleaming head.

"Newspaper photographs don't do you justice, Miss Morgan," Makepeace said after all were seated.

Preferring to let Raul handle the conversation when possible, Charlie accepted the compliment with a smile.

"You may recall, the articles that appeared about a year ago involved a case of art fraud, one in which Miss Morgan played a major role," Raul said.

"Yes, of course."

"The scheme had been going on for years, undetected, until she spotted the discrepancies and intervened," Raul continued.

"A number of experts must have been left with egg on their face. And you had a part in that as well," Berkeley said.

Raul shrugged modestly.

"And now my uncle Elliot has informed me that you suspect one of our clients may have been victimized in a way that would adversely affect his loans with this bank."

"We do."

Makepeace silently stared at the framed photographs on his desk for several seconds. "I hope you understand what that sort of accusation could do to Mr. Voyt's reputation, not to mention the financial consequences."

Raul nodded. "We thoroughly understand. That's why we're here, why your uncle decided this private discussion should take place. But before I go into our suspicions, and they are no more than suspicions at this point, may I inquire to what degree the Voyt collection was authenticated before you agreed to use it for collateral?"

"A cursory examination of the actual artwork was done," Makepeace said, leaning back in his chair. "Standard procedure. We have copies of all bills of sale, as well as the insurance policies and associated documentation. Many of the pieces had been exhibited by distinguished museums prior to the loan. As far as this bank is concerned, there has never been a suggestion the works were anything but genuine. What could possibly lead you to believe otherwise?"

"While the collection is extensive, the lion's share of value is based on no more than fifteen paintings, thirteen of which were purchased through Gustav Kadinski. Kadinski claimed to have smuggled them out from behind the Iron Curtain, a plausible option, but, thanks to international politics, impossible to verify. And while it might be helpful to ask Mr. Kadinski how these treasures remained uncirculated for a century or more, before he discovered and subsequently liberated them, unfortunately he's no longer available to question. He drowned under suspicious circumstances a week after Miss Morgan was attacked in a subway station."

"Are you suggesting there might be a correlation between the two incidents?"

Raul gave him a tight-lipped smile. "Frankly, I don't know. What I do know is the man who attacked Miss Morgan with a fine English umbrella, in a subway a short walk from Mr. Voyt's Manhattan residence, was thin, light eyed, approximately five foot eleven, and wore custom-made shoes. Mr. Voyt is thin, light eyed, approximately five foot eleven . . ."

"And can well afford custom-made shoes and a fine English umbrella," Makepeace said, completing the sentence. "While I'm sympathetic to your concerns, do I have to remind you how outrageous the notion of Justin Voyt attacking a woman, in a public place, with the intention of harming or maiming her is? Absurd!"

"There's more. After we exposed the fraud, Gallery Three Fifty-Two, determined to regain its prestige, instituted a policy of examining past questionable sales. As part of that policy, Miss Morgan presented herself, with credentials, at Mr. Voyt's New York brownstone. She examined one of Voyt's paintings, ostensibly a Manet, and determined that it was a forgery. The gallery followed up with a letter and offered to refund the purchase price."

"Did Mr. Voyt accept the offer?"

"No. That took place six weeks prior to the attack, and we believe was the motive that triggered it. We have not as yet discussed our suspicions regarding Mr. Voyt's collection with the police, as we have no intention of acting irresponsibly."

As she watched Raul coolly thrust and parry in this verbal duel, Charlie almost forgot the real motive for this meeting.

"Justin Voyt is a respected businessman," Makepeace said, his tone cold and threatening for the first time. "He's also been this bank's client for years. What you're suggesting is outrageous."

"Which is why we thought it wise to first discuss this with you. Then, if you were unwilling or unable to help us, we would be forced to take this information to the police and let them handle it. I'm sure you're aware that the media has been putting a great deal of pressure on the authorities to solve this case."

Makepeace leaned forward. "Surely there's a way to avoid involving the police. I don't have to remind you, if your accusations turn out to be unfounded, not only would you be harming the reputation of an innocent man, you would doubtless, be sued for slander. I'm certain your firm wouldn't appreciate that sort of publicity."

"We're aware of that," Raul replied with a small confident smile. "But we have a plan that would serve the bank's interest and ours, and furthermore, protect all parties involved."

"And what is the nature of that plan?" Makepeace inquired, stone faced.

"When one of Voyt's notes comes up for renewal, request the collection be reappraised to determine current market value. Reappraisals are not unheard of."

"Go on."

"If it's handled correctly, a reappraisal wouldn't be construed as a lack of faith, but simply sound business practice. The art market fluctuates. The collection could be worth more than its original appraisal."

"I suppose." Makepeace turned his head, apparently considering his next response.

Raul used the opportunity to send a quick smile at Charlie before continuing. "Can you tell us where the collection is stored?"

"Why, right here in this bank's vault."

Another few seconds passed in silence. Charlie watched the two men. Makepeace weighing his alternatives and Raul poised to deflect the next objection.

"And I take it, you, Miss Morgan, are prepared to oversee the appraisal," Makepeace noted. "Not that I'm questioning your knowledge or experience, but if the bank's board members did agree to this, we would expect a team of acknowledged experts with years in the field, in addition to yourself, to examine the collection."

As the remark was directed to Charlie, she responded, "Absolutely. I have identified five excellent people recommended to me by James Rominer, the current director of the Metropolitan Museum. They're all highly regarded and can be trusted to be discreet."

"I see you've done your homework, Miss Morgan. Well, frankly, we are not concerned with righting the errors of the art world. My job is to protect the bank's interests. Would you agree in writing to maintain total secrecy, and immediately halt further investigation the moment you ascertain the collection is equal to, or in excess of, the aggregate stated value?" Makepeace asked. "I see no reason to prolong your activities and risk embarrassing Mr. Voyt unnecessarily."

"Most definitely," Raul granted. "But if the collection turns out to be worth substantially less than appraised, our first concern must be Miss Morgan's safety. I'm sure you understand."

"We would need your assurance in writing, that you would notify us before going to the police. The bank would need time to prepare our response to our shareholders as well as the public. Berkeley Banking scrupulously guards its reputation."

"It was always our intention to advise the bank of our findings before proceeding, whatever those findings may be," Raul assured him.

"Then I'm prepared to discuss this with appropriate board members." Robert Makepeace rose to shake Raul's hand and then Charlie's. "If they agree, as I suspect they will, we'll have the legal paperwork prepared."

When they exited the bank Raul saw her to a taxi with a quick peck on the cheek and then good-bye. How different things were now, Charlie thought. A year ago, after a successful testy confrontation like the one that had just ended, they would be racing to find the nearest bed.

~ **Chapter 14** ~

Naomi agreed to return to Kane's house after he boasted he had a recording of *Turandot,* the French opera she had requested simply to taunt him. It pleased her to learn that a half truckload of oranges had been required in trade for the hard to obtain treasure. But in the weeks that followed, Kane continued to show up unpredictably. He offered no apologies for the missed weekends – only the briefest account of a problem that had unexpectedly arisen and demanded his time. If he showed up on a Saturday, they would spend the day together. If he arrived on a Friday, he expected her to come home with him and stay until the following evening. He made no promises and asked for none.

And he no longer used delicacies and small surprises as bribes for sex, minus her controlling conditions. Apparently aware that her sexual appetite exceeded his, Kane now sought intimacy of a different nature with his gifts. Forcing her to recall the happy times in her childhood, he seemed intent on learning about her past.

"Tell me about yourself when you were eight," he might say as he fed her cubes of iced melon while she soaked in the tub. Always reluctant, she would eventually surrender, her eyes closed, relating memories as the pampered daughter of well-to-do French Jews. The week he massaged fragrant body lotion into her parched shoulders and back, Kane elicited a memory of being taken to the theater, for her tenth birthday, dressed in a frilly blue dress, hooded coat and shiny black patent leather shoes.

Today's setting was the hammock he had hung in his backyard, and they currently shared. The treat, rugeluch, a pastry made with honey, raisins, and nuts, which his sister-in-law had made. The topic, the model, who might or might not be Michelle.

"You found her agency and wrote to them. Did they write back?"

"Her name is Charlie Morgan. Charlie is the name she uses for work."

"One name. I like it. It's abrupt, quick, like Americans." Kane dropped a fat crumb of rugeluch in her mouth with his free hand. The motion caused the hammock to sway. "As for Morgan, your husband could have changed their names if he wanted to hide them. Write her. Call and talk with her. Use my phone. Find out if she's your daughter."

Naomi nestled her face against Kane's soft weathered shirt and allowed the pastry to dissolve in her mouth. "This I can't do."

"Then have a friend call her. You met plenty of people who worked at the dig from the States. Find someone who lives in New York."

"Maybe." Naomi knew someone who lived in New York – Amityville – wherever that was. Howard Levine, the high-school principal who had spent six weeks at the dig, and four weeks as Naomi's lover, lived in New York. What's more, the divorced man had given her his address hoping she would write him.

"Ask him to do you a favor. Tell him you might have a distant relation living in New York that you'd like to contact. Ask him to call her."

Naomi opened her mouth and accepted the next morsel of pastry. "That's crazy. What do I ask him to say?"

"Have him ask if she knows someone named Alain Fitzpatrick. Better yet, ask if she was born in Paris. See what her response is. She may not be your daughter. But if she is, you can decide what you want to do then."

"I can't afford to go to the States. I'm paid barely enough to live on. What would I say to her? How would I explain the missing years? Alain robbed me of my children. What makes you think he didn't poison them against me?"

"One step at a time. Don't try to move an entire building at once. Start with a brick."

"Why is it so important to you that I contact her?"

"Because it's important to you."

"You're a good man, Ruben. I'm sorry that I can't be the woman you deserve."

"Your project ends in seven weeks. When were you planning to tell me?"

She turned away so that he would not see her face. "I've been making inquiries at other digs. I'm waiting to hear from them."

"You don't have to leave. You could stay."

"What would I do to support myself? Don't say 'marry you' because I won't. I don't want to marry anyone.""

"So don't marry me. Move in with me. I'll pay you to look after my house and watch my children."

"Now you're being crazy."

"We're picking them up in an hour. They want to meet you."

"No! Don't force me to do this."

"What can it hurt to meet them? What are you so afraid of?"

"I don't know how to talk to children. They'll hate me."

"If my children hate you, I won't *allow* you to see them again."

When he was distracted she reached around him for the loose sugary crumbs on the plate. "What have you told them about me?"

"I told them that you don't want to be a farmer's wife, or their mother, and that you have no young children of your own for them to play with."

"What about your brother and sister-in-law? What did you tell them?"

"First, open your mouth!" Kane placed a piece of rugeluch the size of a walnut on her tongue. "I told them you're stubborn, sulky, that I have to bribe you to talk and that the only time I see you smile is when we make love."

"That must have impressed them. I bet they can't wait to introduce me to their friends."

Kane chuckled, the sound emanating from deep within his chest. "Should I tell them that lightning welded our souls the night we met and made love on the side of a road? Would you like me to tell them that? Instead, I said that it pleases me to look at your face, into your eyes, to hold your skinny body in my arms, and someday, God willing, you'll remember how to smile."

*   *   *

As they climbed down from their father's truck Kane's children stared at her. Naomi had negotiated a small victory. Instead of facing a formidable group of curious strangers at his brother's home, she had insisted on meeting only the children at his house.

The three formally lined up for introductions. Eight-year-old Rifkah – a girl with small close-set brown eyes, a plain round face and clusters of unruly chestnut ringlets that bounced when she moved – smiled a gummy smile as she shook Naomi's hand.

"I'm very pleased to meet you, Aunt Naomi. Abba told us that we are to call you 'Aunt Naomi.'"

"And I'm very pleased to meet you, Rifkah."

The youngest, six-year-old Moishe, had his father's small bow mouth and wide brow. His upper two front teeth were missing. His animated hazel eyes were uniquely his own. "I've something to show you, Aunt Naomi. I found it on the way to school," he said in one breath as she took his hand. "My teacher said that it's very old, but Abba says that you would know best. I want to be an archeologist, like you, when I grow up. Yitzhak says that I'm too young to know, but I think it's best to decide what you want to be as soon as possible. What do you think?"

"I think you should give your brother a chance to meet our guest before running off with her," Kane reminded the eager boy.

Thirteen-year-old Yitzhak reluctantly stepped forward. His hair was straight and glossy and his wide-set eyes were dark chocolate brown, like his father's. Where Kane's lashes were merely dense, his slender son's lashes were long and curled. Of the three, the handsome young Lancelot looked the least like his father. He mumbled his greeting and retreated.

"May I take her now, Abba?" Moishe asked, his hand already grasping Naomi's.

"You have ten minutes to show her your coin. Then you have to bring her into the kitchen. It's time to start dinner. I'll need your help."

Naomi was quickly led to the boy's room where Moishe produced his precious collection. After checking the coin in question, Naomi was glad she could tell the boy that it was authentic and dated back two thousand years, to the time the Romans ruled over vast areas of the Middle East. Finding an ancient Roman coin exposed by the elements was a rare, but not unheard of event in Israel.

"I knew it. I knew it," Moishe yipped, leaping in the air. "I told Yitzhak that it was real."

"Draw a map of where you found it and store it with your coin," Naomi told the excited boy. "That's what archeologists do."

"Abba was right. I'm a supernatural magical boy. I can make you smile."

"A supernatural magical boy?"

"Abba says that we are all supernatural magical children because we make food disappear and we outgrow our clothes while we sleep. And he also said, if we want you to stay in Acre, we have to make you smile. And we have the power, because we're supernatural."

"Why would you want me to stay?"

"Because we need a mother," he explained, as though amazed at her ignorance. "And Abba needs a wife, and he likes you. He told us so."

"Your father is waiting for us in the kitchen."

They found Rifkah and Yitzhak seated at the table shelling peas.

"Don't sulk, Rifkah," Kane told the girl. "Your aunt was too busy to cut your hair today. You'll wait until tomorrow and I'll do it."

"You don't do it right," the girl grumbled.

"That's enough," Kane cautioned. "What will our guest think of our family?"

Naomi reached for the peas to help and Yitzhak pulled the basket away. Kane rebuked him with his eyes. "You said that she's our guest," the boy said sullenly. "Guests aren't allowed to help."

"Aunt Naomi could cut your hair," Moishe told Rifkah. "I bet she could do it right."

The girl turned to Naomi. "Could you?"

"I don't think so," Naomi said automatically. "I'm afraid I would do it badly and you'd be disappointed."

"Oh." The girl returned to shelling peas.

Naomi could only watch as Kane and his children prepared the meal and set the table. Moishe insisted on sitting next to her. To Naomi's astonishment, Rifkah rushed to claim the other side. Yitzhak avoided all eye contact with her.

"I wish my hair was like yours," the girl confided softly as they ate. "Yours is soft and pretty."

"You have lovely hair." Naomi wrapped a curl around her finger. "It's hard for me to imagine that you want to cut it off."

"It gets wild and knotted when it's this length," Kane said. "She cries when I brush it, no matter how careful I try to be."

"I used to cry when my hair was brushed until I learned how to do it myself," Naomi told the child. "I don't know why, but it doesn't hurt when you brush it yourself."

"I can do the front and sides."

"You just want to be treated like a baby," Yitzhak taunted. "You're eight years old and you still can't brush your hair." He turned to his father. "Rifkah doesn't do half the chores that I'm expected to do."

Rifkah slumped in her chair while Kane appeared not to notice her distress. He addressed only his older son. "You each have chores according to your age and ability. You should be proud that you're assigned more work. That means I consider you strong and capable. You made your bar mitzvah. Would you prefer that I treat you like a child or a young man?"

Yitzhak looked down. "A young man."

"Good. Because there's been talk of unrest in the area. Can I count on you to follow orders? Can I rely on you to protect what is most precious to this family?"

Yitzhak grew in his chair. "Yes, Abba."

"Tonight when I drive your aunt Naomi back to camp, you will take the rifle and stand guard. You're not to leave the house until I return. I don't care if robbers steal everything in the barn, including the tractor. You, your brother and your sister are the most precious things we have. Now show me that you are truly a young man and not a little boy." Kane looked at his daughter and then back to Yitzhak.

Yitzhak look confused until at last he realized what was expected of him. "I'm sorry I called you a baby, Rifkah. It was wrong to hurt your feelings."

Rifkah soberly acknowledged the apology.

"When I was your age my hair was almost as curly as yours, Rifkah," Naomi said to ease the tension. "Maybe I could teach you how to brush the knots out of the back."

"Let her do it," Moishe whispered to his sister behind Naomi's chair.

"I was going to," Rifkah whispered back. "Thank you, Aunt Naomi. I have to dry the dishes and put them away first. Then we can go to my room and you can teach me."

* * *

The child's bedroom unnerved Naomi, but she was relieved to see that Rifkah appeared unaware of her discomfort.

The girl pulled her chair in front of a small mirror and pointed to it. "Sit here and I'll stand behind you. That way I can see what you're doing."

Having received her orders so succinctly, Naomi did as she was instructed. She showed the girl how to divide her thick hair into small sections, secure all but one with a bobby pin, then address the remaining loose hairs. Rifkah was soon able to manage even the hardest to reach locations.

"Now that the knots are gone, would you like to wear it in pigtails or braids?" Naomi asked.

"Which do you think is best?"

"Both are nice. Pigtails are easier, but braids stay neat."

"Then I choose braids."

"Do you have any ribbons?"

Rifkah's top dresser drawer yielded a pair of red ribbons. Naomi tied a bright bow at the bottom of the first braid. "I think that looks very pretty. Red is a good color for you."

Rifkah lovingly stroked the thick braid as Naomi worked the remaining hair.

"Do I remind you of your daughters?" the girl asked, admiring herself in the mirror. "Does it make you sad to be with me?"

The unanticipated direct question stunned Naomi. Kane had told his children about her lost daughters. What else had he told them? She struggled for the equilibrium to reply. "I do miss my daughters, and sometimes it does make me sad. But you don't make me sad. See. Look, I'm smiling."

"I miss my mother. Sometimes I cry at night when I think about her. You're not at all like her. But you're nice in a different sort of way."

"Thank you."

"Abba wants you to stay in Acre. Do you think you will?"

"I don't think so. It depends on a lot of things."

"I hope you stay. Abba said that we must shake your hand and wait for you to hug or kiss us first. But would it be all right if I gave you a kiss for teaching me to how to do my hair?"

What had she done to deserve this unconditional acceptance? Naomi asked herself. Nothing! This child should resent her, as her older and wiser brother did. She was an interloper, someone destined to upend their ordered life. She gazed at the small expectant face looking up at her. "A kiss would be very nice." The girl's silky soft cheek touching hers made her lightheaded.

*   *   *

"I have to admit that I didn't think it would go this well," Kane told Naomi as he drove her back to camp.

"How can you say it went well? Yitzhak hates me."

"My Yitzhak doesn't hate you. Give yourself time to get to know my children – each different, each special. Moishe is my brightest and easiest child. Rifkah is the most spiritual. She's apt to forget chores, not because she's careless but because she daydreams. And Yitzhak? Yitzhak is the best looking, least reliable and most spoiled of the three. He was his mother's favorite and the angriest over her death. Give him time. He'll come around."

"Yet you left him with a rifle. If he's unreliable . . . You said that you heard of unrest."

"Sometimes you tell a little lie. Things have been quiet lately – the local pashas have been bought off. Besides, every child above the age of twelve has to know how to handle a rifle."

"But not Rifkah," Naomi said, recalling the silky warm cheek against hers.

"Because she has an older brother, I can allow my dreamy Rifkah to stay my little girl longer than she should. I have to remind myself that in ten years she joins the army."

"No."

"Have you forgotten where you are? We are surrounded by a hundred million Arabs determined to drive us into the sea. Every Israeli son and daughter enters the army. My children are no different."

Naomi edged closer to the truck's door and leaned her head against the window. The army! Soldiers! Endless soldiers. Men, scarcely more than boys, in filthy tattered uniforms, bleeding, missing limbs, contorted with pain. Fetid bodies rotting in ditches. As she tried to erase the gory images from her mind, each of Kane's children joined the hideous ranks. "I can't see you anymore."

"This is only the first time you've been with the children," Kane said.

"I can't see you again. Don't bother coming to the dig site. I won't go with you."

"But I thought you liked my children. You seemed to get along well with them."

"I do like them – all of them. But I warned you this would happen. I'm not cut out to be a wife or a mother."

"Then be our friend."

"I can't."

~ **Chapter 15** ~

Jean was dead. The one woman who could save him from poverty and certain humiliation was dead and he had killed her. *My heart isn't as sturdy as it appears,* Jean had told him. If she was so concerned about her heart, she had had scores of opportunities to stop. It wasn't as if he had raped her. They had made love, and after he had left, she had closed her eyes for the last time. She could have explained her condition when he proposed. Knowing the brevity of their chaste future, he would gladly have married her. Even so, Jack couldn't shake nagging guilt.

In less than twenty-four hours, his life had been a jet-propelled ride – from tentative hope, to euphoria and then a flaming free-fall before crashing. Monday morning he would be begging for a job as a bus tour guide, hoping for starvation wages and the opportunity to grovel for tips.

"Please sit down," Edith said, looking up at him distressed. "Are you all right? I had no idea you would take my sister's death so hard."

Jack took the seat next to her. In his distress, he had temporarily forgotten the pathetic soul who had lost her only sister, now concerned about him. "It's just a shock. Jean was a lovely woman and so full of life."

"The hotel manager said the local police would be called in to investigate her death. They intend to take her away to do an autopsy. I was informed that's Argentine law."

Argentine law? Probably not, Jack decided. But the police were likely to investigate the death of a foreigner. It was bad for tourism if visiting vacationers arrived vertical and left horizontal. The hint of tainted food could shut down a hotel.

"The manager said they would interrogate me as well, though I can't fathom why," Edith declared, indignant at the notion.

"They'll ask you routine questions to satisfy their superiors. Where you ate and went. People you met." Not to mention, who was the very last person to see her alive? Jack worried. He tried to remember if someone had seen him entering or leaving Jean's room the night before. A couple passed on their way to the elevator. But they were drunk. Would they remember seeing him at such a late hour in their intoxicated state?

"I know that you'll be shocked to hear this, but the manager was most abrupt with me – as though Jean's death was my doing. He wanted to know how long I was staying and how I planned to settle the account."

"Which hotel manager?"

"Senor Hernandez, the short skinny one with the thin mustache."

Alfredo Hernandez was easily flustered, Jack thought. "He had no right to talk to you that way. I'll speak with him."

Two policemen in khaki cotton summer uniforms strode into the lobby.

"I suppose the authorities will have to be dealt with," Edith said. "This would have been so much easier at home, where Jean was known."

"I'll speak with them. Let me handle it." In view of her sister's existing heart condition, a lengthy interrogation might be dispensed with if he could convince the police it was unnecessary – easier to do for someone fluent in Spanish. And then the identity of the last person to see her alive would also be superfluous. "Did Jean take any medication for her condition? Did she carry a copy of her prescriptions with her? Maybe I can clear this up quickly."

"How silly of me to forget the obvious. Several prescriptions. Nitroglycerine, for one. Two or three others as well. It should all be in her nightstand or in her handbag."

"Stay here. I'll join you in a few minutes." Jack intercepted the two young officers and took them back to the manager's office where Alfredo Hernandez paced nervously.

"The cause of death was heart failure," Jack assured the manager and police officers. "Her sister assured me that Mrs. Osborne had a heart condition and was not expected to live long. When you examine her room and belongings, as I'm sure you will, you'll find several medications. Any physician can confirm they're for heart disease."

"Nevertheless, an autopsy will have to be done," the younger and more imposing of the two officers insisted.

"Do what must be done, but do it discreetly. I'm certain the hotel would be most grateful if this can be handled quietly," Jack urged. "There should be no reason for the hotel's name to reach the newspapers because an English tourist chooses this hotel to have a heart attack. Am I not right in this, Alfredo?"

Hernandez nodded to indicate he knew a small sum was expected.

"The medical examiner will confirm the cause of Mrs. Osborne's death," Jack continued. "But please don't trouble Miss Hendrix with questions today. She's had a terrible shock. The sisters were very close. Take her passport, if you must. You can always question her later should that prove necessary."

"The English ladies were scheduled to check out Wednesday, that's only three days –" the manager said.

Jack interrupted. "Arrangements will have to be made to ship the body back to England. It all takes time. Miss Hendrix can well afford to stay and will be here until everything has been settled. I know the hotel will extend every courtesy until then."

"Of course. Be assured, Senor Jack, flowers and a note expressing the hotel's condolences at the passing of her beloved sister, will be sent to Miss Hendrix' room," Hernandez offered, at once the formal courteous employee.

"I know that would be appreciated. And after the police are through, please have a maid pack Mrs. Osborne's belongings and put them in storage. Miss Hendrix will decide what is to be done with them later."

He returned to Edith, who had been writing on a piece of hotel stationery and sipping tea, and relayed only critical parts of his recent conversation. "If there's anything else I can do to help, anything at all, please let me know."

"Are you religious, Jack?" she asked. "I wish I were, but I'm not. It would be a comfort to be religious at a time like this, don't you agree?"

"I'm a lapsed Catholic. I believe in God, though it doesn't give me much comfort." Atheists were misguided idiots, Jack thought. God had to exist. Not a God who created a sinful world and then sent His Son to die on a cross to right the mess He'd made, but a God who delighted in devising practical jokes. Dangle hope in front of a mortal, watch him slobber in anticipation, and then yank it away. As for Edith Hendrix, she *had* to be either one of God's mistakes or a prank. An educated woman completely oblivious to her dress and grooming.

"There are people who will have to be contacted," she explained, just as he was about to escape. "As you know, I don't speak Spanish and international calls are frightfully difficult. I would be so appreciative if you could .. ."

Jack sighed. Feeling somewhat responsible for Jean's death, he couldn't refuse the request. But the mere sight of her reminded him of how much he had lost and the ignominious fate that awaited him.

"I've started a list of those who must be notified," Edith said. "There's the mortuary, and the pastor at our church. Cecily Needham, the president of Jean's gardening circle. And Elliot Chapman, the captain of her backgammon society. And our solicitor, Alfred Wellington. I must ask him to wire some money. The rooms and meals are paid for, but there's no saying for certain how long I'll be here. And then there's Jean's estate. Her affairs were all in order, but it takes time to process these things. Jean warned me to contact him immediately if . . . When . . . "

Jean's estate.

"We have virtually no family. Only some cousins living in Australia. I doubt if they'll attend the funeral. Still, they'd want to be notified."

In his personal despair, Jack had utterly forgotten the marvel of inheritance. Unless Jean was the eccentric sort that would leave a fortune to furry creatures, this disheveled heap might be a wealthy heiress. "I'm sure your dear departed sister was anxious to see that you would be well cared for."

"There's a small sum set aside for Jean's charwoman and a very old gardener who looks after her house when she's away," Edith explained, seemingly grateful for his concern. "The rest goes to me."

"As well it should," he said, "And to who else would a fine sister like yours bequeath her home and all her worldly possessions?"

Like a pilot flying solo who suddenly loses both engines, the unforeseen catastrophe called for a cool head and fast thinking. The pilot had no time to waste worrying what part had failed or which mechanic to blame. Jean was dead. And Edith, her only heir, had a schoolgirl crush on him. Every word, every move could lead to an abrupt and fiery crash. In his favor was that Edith was unlikely to have had many past suitors, and with the loss of her sister, she was doubly vulnerable. Working against him was the lack of time, and her guaranteed perception of the unsuitability of the circumstances. In addition, the project would be doubly impossible if he couldn't face her unkempt and unattractive exterior. But when confronted with imminent catastrophe, a resourceful pilot improvised with what was at hand. For the first time since the sisters arrived in Buenos Aires, Jack gave Edith Hendrix, new heiress, a head to toe appraisal.

Her hair was a disaster, an absolute disaster. Handfuls of mousy graying hair had been twisted into an unruly ball that always seemed ready to explode. She wore no makeup beyond the vermillion lipstick unskillfully applied, causing her skin to appear uncommonly pale. Above her reddened eyes were wild untamed eyebrows, but the nose was good and so were her jaw and chin. As for her body, it was anyone's guess. The only exposed areas between her neck and ankles were her hands – even her calves were hidden by the long voluminous dress. She had slender ankles and wrists, but that proved nothing. Some women were like prize cattle – trim hoofs and well-marbled steak above. He had to find out what lurked beneath that missionaries' notion of proper apparel.

"Do you think you'll keep the house now that your dear sister is no longer with us?"

"It will have to be sold. It's far too large for me."

"Too large now that you're all alone. And there would be so many reminders of Jean there, the furniture she selected, photos, cherished mementos," Jack commiserated, with deliberate purpose. Edith's lip trembled. "Your sister loved you so. You can't imagine how proud Jean was of your accomplishments. She talked about you all the time."

Seeing her cool containment dissolving Jack leaned in to hug her. With his arm at her waist, he felt no undulating flesh underneath clumps of fabric, nor did he find any as his hand rose to the middle of her back. The surprise was the firm full breasts pressed against his chest.

"I have no right to detain you. You're dressed to play tennis. Senor Castellanos must be waiting for you." Edith said, backing away, noticeably flustered and blushing like a teenager.

"Haven't I convinced you that I'm here to help you any way I can?"

"Perhaps we should start on this list," she said, indicating the page of people she wished to call in her hand.

Jack glanced at his watch. It was nearly noon and he was hungry. He was also broke. The hotel would permit him to charge a meal if necessary. "Have you eaten?"

"Not a morsel. I'm not hungry."

Then he remembered something she had said earlier. They were on the American Plan! Three meals a day, paid in advance. He had sold his tuxedo to pay for dinners and they were on the American plan. "I'm starving. Let's have lunch and then we can start making those telephone calls."

"But what about your tennis lesson?"

"I cancelled it. I couldn't possibly leave you alone at a time like this."

As they ate in the El Cabano's dining room, an idea was formulating in Jack's brain. He simply couldn't consider courting a woman as physically unappealing as Edith. Impossible! Every woman he had bedded was well groomed and attractive in her own way. He couldn't look directly at this sorry example of femininity without wincing. As for making make love to her . . . Unimaginable! However, there was no doubt in his mind that Edith's appearance could be improved. A decent hairstyle and the correct application of makeup for a start. Her wardrobe couldn't be worse. As for her ignorance of her continuous state of dishevelment . . . Was it even possible to correct that? She would fight every suggestion – fight with everything she had. But under the circumstances, what choice remained? At least she smelled freshly bathed. Daily personal hygiene was an absolute minimum requirement, even in his desperate state.

"It's Saturday. There's no point in calling your solicitor today," he said. "His office is closed and so is every bank. We'll call Monday morning. I've thought of a better way to spend what's left of today."

"Surely the mortuary is open and I would very much like to call the others. I've been told that international calls can take hours to get through. Perhaps we should get started."

For each call, a minimum of two overseas operators were needed, one at each end. Connections were frequently interrupted by annoying static and were apt to break off at any time. A single international conversation required patience and perseverance. Hours of waiting with nothing to do. Jack's brain leapt into action.

She would fight. But in the end he would have his way. "In that case, I see no point in not using the time in between. Wait here and I'll take care of everything." Before she could question or object, Jack left her there, confused. When he returned fifteen minutes later, their lunch dishes had been cleared.

Taking her elbow, he led her out of the dining room, making innocuous small talk as they passed the elevators that could have taken them to her room, past the front desk, and to the door of the hotel's beauty parlor.

"Where are you taking me?" she asked, stopping abruptly.

He leaned close and brought his mouth to her ear, as though he didn't want to be overheard, even though there was no one in earshot, guessing she would once again be disconcerted by the contact. "I've arranged to make your calls from a small private booth inside."

"But why not call from my room?" she asked, blushing and not moving.

"I thought you might feel a bit uncomfortable having a man in your room," he whispered, purposefully filling her ear with his warm breath. "Besides, this way you can have your hair cut and styled while I deal with the international operators."

Wide-eyed Edith reached for her ear. "I realize that my hairstyle isn't smart, and I'm not clever with it the way other women are, but it hardly seems fitting to fuss over my appearance when I'm in mourning."

Seeing that she had no intention of entering the shop he guided her to a loveseat. "Not fitting? One of the last things your sister confided to me was that she would love to see you take greater pride in your appearance." Jack watched Edith's face and posture for clues. "Perhaps she didn't mention it to you for fear of hurting your feelings."

"Well, I suppose from time to time, Jean did drop hints I might do something with my hair. She was so particular with hers. It might be nice but not now. People will all come by with their kidney pies and long faces, and expect me to look as I've always looked. What will they think?"

"I know what Jean would think. She would want you to look your best."

"Is that what you truly believe?"

Bull's eye! "Just yesterday, your sister asked me what I'd heard about the quality of the staff at hotel's hair salon. When I asked if her interest was for herself, she laughed. She said that she was determined to see you restyled, before you left for . . ." Jack had forgotten their ultimate destination.

"First home and then the Holy Land. But my plans are all sixes and sevens now. The trip will have to be cancelled or rescheduled. Who can say?"

"I can see no reason in doing this last little thing that she's wanted for you. Where's the harm?" Seeing her opposition at a new low, Jack led Edith into the beauty salon before she could change her mind.

In the absent fifteen minutes, Jack had informed the shop's manager what he wished done. No area was to be neglected. Her hair was to be dyed and styled. Edith was to have a facial, manicure, and pedicure. Her legs were to be waxed. Her brows were to be shaped. When all that was complete, makeup would be applied. The charges were all to be billed to Miss Hendrix's room, along with the cost of a bottle of sherry, which was to be brought round immediately.

"No orange tones. No stop lights. A rich warm henna," Jack told the colorist while Edith was changing into a robe. "Do you have something you can show me?"

"I'll be right back." The colorist returned moments later with a several hair swatches just as Edith climbed into the adjustable chair. "What is that?" she demanded. "Does this man intend to dye my hair? I agreed to have it cut, not dyed. I know you mean well, Jack, but I simply couldn't. I'm extremely uncomfortable with this sort of attention."

Jack waved the colorist aside and stroked her now loosened hair, in part to calm her, in part to feel it. Luxuriously thick and healthy. "You're doing the right thing. Trust me. It's going to be beautiful."

Her face turned the color of a crimson chili pepper.

"I never considered altering the color of my hair."

"Did you or did you not have red hair as a girl?"

She looked up at him. "Jean told you!"

"No one needed to tell me. It's all in the skin tones." Jack turned to the colorist. "Can these be blended?"

"Of course."

"Then use these two. I'm looking for a rich mahogany."

In defeat, Edith handed him her list of names and phone numbers and took the proffered glass of sherry handed her. "Start with Maud Wrightsmith, please. If I can reach Maud, she'll help with some of the others."

"Close your eyes and relax. I'll do my best, but this will take time."

Between conversations with operators, Jack flipped through fashion magazines. As he cradled the receiver and listened to crackling and random noises, he discussed his ideas with the shop's best hair stylist who assured him the style he had selected was a good fit for Edith's hair.

"Keep it simple and chic," Jack directed. "No longer than the nape of her neck, and easy to maintain."

Edith found him in the adjoining booth. Mahogany clumped spikes jutted from her head. The nails on one of her hands had been painted. "I've agreed to the coloring and manicure, but a woman apparently thinks she's supposed to pluck my brows. It's frightfully painful. I've asked her to stop but she doesn't seem to understand. Please explain it to her in Spanish."

Jack set down the receiver, poured a second glass of sherry and handed it to Edith. "Sip the sherry if it hurts. The final result will be worth it. I promise. Just allow her do her job."

Edith reluctantly returned to her tormentor. Curious, at intervals, Jack peeked around the booth. When the stylist removed the curlers and brushed out her hair, Edith looked younger, much younger. "I like it. It came out just the way I'd imagined. I may have a flair for this."

"I'm glad you're pleased," Edith said, staring into the mirror with unbelieving eyes. "I don't know what to make of it. It's garish and . . . flamboyant. It most certainly does not look like me."

"Be honest! Your hair looks like it did when you were eighteen or twenty," Jack insisted. "And what's the harm in that?"

"In fairness, I do like what she's done with my brows. I don't appear so stern." Clearly shaken, she turned away from the mirror. "Any luck getting through? I feel badly imposing on you. I had no idea international phone calls could take this long."

"Well, I did and I'm grateful to be of assistance."

A timid young woman approached and attempted to lead Edith away. "Please to walk with me, Senora."

"I've been a good soldier, Jack, but this really has been enough."

"What's next, Senorita?" Jack asked the girl in Spanish.

"The Senora is to have the hair on her legs removed with wax – hot wax."

"Doesn't that hurt?"

The girl shrugged. "Some more than others. It depends how hairy she is."

"You've been a good soldier," Jack said, looking directly into Edith's suspicious eyes. "Now would you do this little favor for me if I asked you?"

"What did she say?" Edith asked.

"She said that men aren't allowed in the room. It just for ladies. But I'll be right outside the door. Here, let me refill your glass. Just a little longer. It's almost over."

"But why?" she asked, lowering her voice and standing so close they almost touched.

"Please don't tell me you're one of those Bolsheviks who think that hair dye and cosmetics are symptoms of all that's evil in society."

She smiled and shook her head. "A Bolshevik? Now you're teasing. I simply can't understand the fuss over an old-maid university professor. I teach students half my age who consider me an eccentric relic. No one cares about the way I look."

"Your sister cared. And apparently, I care or I wouldn't be here." Jack watched whatever protest Edith might have been poised to deliver replaced by embarrassment. "Trust me. Soldier on! We're almost done."

From time to time he could hear muffled yelps through the curtained booth until someone turned on a radio to mask the noise. As he continued to monitor the telephone and listen to scraps of scratchy dialogue between operators, an overly made-up makeup artist found him.

"Set up a chair right here where I can watch," he directed the woman. "Most important, keep it simple and natural looking. She knows nothing about cosmetics. Describe everything that you are doing in detail. I'll translate if your English needs help."

When Edith emerged from the sequestered room she looked spent. Just then, a brief two hours after Jack had first initiated the call, the operator informed him that Mrs. Maud Wrightsmith was waiting to speak with Miss Edith Hendrix. He handed Edith the phone and left her alone to conduct her conversation.

She returned ten minutes later announcing that she had done all she could considering the static and poor connection.

"This isn't going to hurt, is it?" she asked, seeing the makeup artist and her kit of brushes and paint.

"Not a bit! I promise. You have my word," Jack assured her.

Edith sat down and woodenly obeyed instructions. A thin layer of foundation was applied followed by a subtle application of rouge, eyeliner, shadow, and mascara – with Jack translating. When the application and lesson was complete, the shape of Edith's auburn collar-length hair complemented the structure of her face. Combined with the restrained embellishment of her skin, eyes, and mouth, the effect was shocking.

"Perfect!" Jack declared, proud and pleased with his achievement. "Even better than I imagined."

Edith scowled at herself in the hand mirror. "People are certain to stare. I look so different. And I'd never be able to duplicate any of this – even if I wanted to. I'm far too clumsy."

"Nonsense! All it takes is a little practice. And if they stare, it's only in admiration."

"You think this looks . .   That is to say – you think it's becoming?" she asked, growing redder as she spoke. "And suitable for a woman of my age and vocation?"

"Absolutely! I think you look neat, attractive and professional. Give yourself time to get used to it." Jack had deliberately withheld deserved praise. Compared to this morning, Edith's hair, face, and hands looked a thousand percent better, but a stream of superlatives would only heighten her suspicions.

"I expect you have things to do," she commented when they found themselves in the lobby.

"Nothing so important that it can't wait. Besides, under the circumstances, I wouldn't dream of leaving you alone."

"Where should we go? I'd prefer a site where I won't be seen."

"With the time difference it's too late for more calls and it's too early for dinner. How about a walk along the water? The beach is usually deserted at this hour."

They followed the path past the pool to the stairs leading to the striped canvas cabana and when they reached the sand Jack removed his tennis shoes and socks. Edith tried a few steps before seeing the wisdom in removing her own shoes. Despite the warm Argentine summer, she wore ugly thick stockings that Jack pretended not to notice. The afternoon sun glimmered on the water as they permitted the waves to lick their ankles.

"A single phone call took hours to arrange," she said, gazing at the water, when the cabanas and remaining sun worshippers were far behind them. "This trip was prepaid, two rooms with meals, and I don't expect the hotel will offer a refund. But they would have no choice if I chose to assign the accommodations to another person. I know it's a great deal to ask. Forget that I said that. It's horrible of me to take advantage of your kindness – a terrible imposition."

Jack did mental handsprings. He would have twenty-four-hour-a-day access to Edith, plus meals, and it wouldn't cost him a cent. Maybe this was a sign that his luck was changing. "Not at all! It's no imposition. I offered help and I meant it."

"You've already made plans. I wouldn't hear of your altering them."

"You're not to concern yourself," he said as coolly as he could. "You're going to need help for the next few days. The local authorities can strangle you with red tape unless you know how to deal with them. As for arranging changes with the hotel, I'd be happy to handle it. And now, we should be getting back before the mosquitoes come looking for their next meal."

It took Jack about an hour to arrange matters with the hotel's manager, go home, pack a few changes of clothes and toiletries, and return – plus the time to take a shower, shave, and change before meeting Edith for dinner.

As she had predicted, staff and guests who hadn't seen her since the afternoon salon blitz did stare as Jack escorted her into the dining room. When they reached a reserved table in the darkest corner, she chose the chair with her back to the other diners.

From the neck up she looked chic and attractive. She had found the cosmetics that Jack had sent to her room, and somehow managed not to ruin the earlier effect. As for her hair, the wind had ruffled its stiffness, making her look even younger. But everything below her neck was still appalling. The horrid navy dress she had selected was less tentlike, but its flimsy fabric made her bunched, ill-fitting undergarments more noticeable. And her white, thick-soled, laced shoes were hideous.

"If this was Nottingham, I'd be expected to drape myself in black. You can't imagine how conspicuously inappropriate I feel."

"Relax! No one knows you or Jean here. As far as hotel guests are concerned, your sister is out with a friend," Jack lied. Word of Jean's sudden demise had spread like ants at a picnic. But he was determined to have nothing interfere with his plans. Edith would enjoy the evening; her trust in him would grow; and he would do everything he could to inflame any romantic feeling she might harbor towards him. "I know so very little about you. Tell me about yourself."

"There's very little to tell."

"Where do you live? Have you done much traveling? Do you enjoy your work?"

She had a small flat in Nottingham, the home of the fictional sheriff who had pursued Robin Hood. Although she loved to travel, this was her first opportunity in decades to do so. Teaching and her students were her passion. She indulged in research and translation as a hobby. And she had questions for him. How had he acquired his knowledge of art? What had made him decide his talent as an artist was lacking? Had he ever been married? Were there children? How long had he lived in Buenos Aires? Jack replied truthfully when it didn't conflict with his adopted past as the childless man who had lost all while caring for his dying wife.

When they had dined previously, Jack had studiously avoided looking at her. He had seen only the results of those meals: the trace of cereal or egg yolk on her chin, bits of toast on her sweater. However, if by some miracle, he had to spend the next several years of his life in her company, he would have to know what to expect. For a man as fastidious as himself, dining manners were critical. And there was no polite way to say, "Close your mouth when you chew." To his intense relief, Edith knew which fork to use, didn't make rude noises when she drank her vichyssoise, and the contents of her mouth remained unseen. But there it was! A particle from a breadstick stuck to her upper lip. He had to restrain himself from leaning over and removing it, the way one would do in dealing with a toddler. He cautiously pointed to his upper lip.

After a second to process the signal, Edith dabbed the offending spot with her napkin. "Sorry."

"Please don't be upset with me. My late wife used to accuse me of being a perfectionist – a compulsive perfectionist. She was right, of course. It's a dreadful trait."

"You shouldn't be so hard on yourself," she said as their waiter arrived with more bottled water. "You're ever so kind and isn't that what's most important?"

She had accepted his criticism comfortably, Jack thought, smiling warmly at her. Despite her expected arguments, she had gone along with the beauty parlor attack he had launched. All of which made him all the more eager to discover what lurked beneath the ridiculous dress. But no shops would be open until Monday. After coffee was served, when she reached for her mirror and lipstick – not the vermillion war-paint, but the deep coral shade that had been selected to complement her hair, Jack couldn't contain his curiosity a minute longer. He made a great show of stretching his leg, rubbing it and trying to hide a grimace with a forced smile. A brilliant piece of theatrics, he thought.

"You've injured your leg," Edith said, concerned. "Oh no! Could you have done that walking on the sand? Perhaps you should have a physician look at it."

"Just an old riding injury that kicks up from time to time. Nothing helps but a soaking in hot water or a massage." He leaned under the table and slid his hand under her hem. "This spot. Right here." He gingerly felt her calf.

"Really? Oh my!" Edith's eyes went wide while she remained stone still.

"And sometimes here." In an instant, Jack's hand slid from her calf to above her knee and back to his lap. "That's where it's the worst."

She opened her mouth as though to gasp or object and then closed it. Perhaps she didn't wish to cause a scene.

"Did I startle you?" he inquired, all innocence.

"A bit."

"Then I apologize. Please forgive my manners. At times I forget that English ladies are far more demure than their American cousins."

A slim ankle, shapely calf, and firm thigh, Jack told himself. Better than he had dared hope. Monday couldn't come soon enough.

"Will you have to cancel your tennis again tomorrow, two days in a row?"

For the second time that day Edith had mentioned his daily lesson – not an exhibition or even a match, just a dull lesson. The coy minx was clearly infatuated with him. Why else would she want to watch him run, stretch and sweat? "A hot bath and my leg will be good as new. Will you be there? I'd feel better knowing you weren't alone."

"If I rise early, I might."

*   *   *

When Jack reached the tennis court at eight Edith was already there, wearing one of her appalling baggy dresses. But she had tried her hand at the makeup with acceptable results, and her lustrous thick hair, which needed little attention now that it had been properly shaped, caught the sun's rays in a most attractive way.

"You look nice," he said, to encourage future efforts.

Other than the hotel staff engaged in routine tasks, the tennis facility was empty. As Emilio ran him through practice drills, aware that her eyes never left him, Jack found himself playing to an enthralled audience. At the end of the lesson he left the court and took the chair beside her. One of her cheeks was rosier than its mate.

"The rouge. May I?" he asked, wielding the white hand towel the hotel provided for their tennis-playing guests.

"Yes, please," she said, looking first to see that no one was watching before presenting her face.

Jack gently dabbed at her cheek. "There, that's perfect. Now, what about today? I thought we'd go to Parques de Palermo, it's a wonderful park in the center of the city, with lakes, and boats, and picnicking."

"I was thinking of informing some friends at home of Jean's passing. Could we do that first?"

"You reached one friend, but you don't know as yet when you'll be returning," he pointed out. "I can see the need to phone the mortuary and your solicitor tomorrow, but wouldn't it be wiser to hold off calling the others until your plans had dates attached to them?"

"Once again, you're right. I suppose I'm not thinking clearly. And a day in a park does sound lovely."

After receiving Edith's assurance that she could manage without him for the time it took to shower and change, Jack raced for his room. Twenty minutes later, he telephoned the local police. Argentina was known for its leisurely pace and red tape, but every extra day, hour, minute was vital to prevent Edith and her deceased sister from taxiing off the runway of his life. Just in case the Buenos Aires bureaucracy, on this one occasion, proved the model of efficiency, he had a plan.

Officer Gonzales remembered speaking with him at the hotel.

"These matters can't be hurried, Senor," Gonzales cautioned Jack. "An autopsy of a foreign tourist, the official papers to ship the body out of the country, all notarized, air arrangements – at best – a week."

"There seems to be some confusion about who is responsible for the body," Jack told Gonzales. "An English woman called the hotel saying that she's Mrs. Osborne's sister and she's coming to Buenos Aires to bring her sister back to London."

"Then who is Miss Hendrix? I thought *she* was Mrs. Osborne's sister," Gonzales said.

"That's what we all thought. But the maid claims to have seen the two women embracing – " Jack paused for effect " – in a manner unsuitable for sisters."

"Lesbians!" Gonzales spat. "The English – a cold bloodless race."

"The hotel has asked me to help straighten out the situation. I suggest that you hang onto the paperwork a few extra days before releasing the body, to give us a chance to sort this all out. We wouldn't want problems later."

"Thank you for taking the time to advise us on this matter, Senor Caine. The department is very grateful."

*   *   *

Planning a day at the Parques de Palermo was a brilliant idea, Jack congratulated himself as he rowed. No tourist had ever requested a trip to the park. But there couldn't be a woman alive immune to the pleasure derived from gliding atop a picturesque lake on a sunny day. Uncomplicated, guilt-free, sensual pleasure.

Edith dipped her fingers into the water while she gazed at the rippled surface or shoreline, and when she thought he wasn't watching, she studied the muscles in his arms and chest tighten and release. The silly umbrella, she had insisted on bringing, turned out to be practical due the dazzling reflected light and her fair skin.

Later, they strolled a portion of the vast grounds and ate local treats Jack purchased from street vendors with pushcarts. With her hair attractively done and her makeup acceptably applied, her appalling attire garnered minimal unwanted attention. If Edith noticed, it wasn't apparent. Away from the hotel and staff, with nothing to remind her of her deceased sister and the harsh decision she would soon face, Edith was clearly enjoying herself. Just as Jack had intended. Throughout the day, he used every opportunity for physical contact without being obvious. Taking her elbow when they climbed steps. Helping with her cardigan. Sitting too close. Casually brushing against her.

Seeing a vendor selling helium-filled balloons, thinking they would laugh when it escaped or they released it, Jack insisted on purchasing one for her. Instead, before leaving the park, Edith gave it to a grungy little boy and then thoughtfully tied it to his wrist.

They had dinner where they had eaten the evening before, at the hotel, using the sisters' prepaid American plan. It was a long, but not an exhausting day. Unlike most women he entertained, the reserved professor didn't require constant conversation. Lengthy silences were comfortable.

When it was time to take her to her room, Jack asked her a pointless question so that they could linger outside her door, and he could stand too close and pseudo-absentmindedly touch her hair. As hoped, neither his proximity nor the gesture startled her. In truth, she appeared pleased. Nevertheless, Jack wouldn't dream of kissing her. There was a lot more to be done before that first kiss.

*   *   *

In a small alcove off the lobby, starting at 9:00 a.m. Buenos Aires time, as promised, Jack initiated the first international call of the day for Edith. By 12:30, having identified and contacted a mortuary that would handle the deceased's remains, as well as Jean's attorney, both he and Edith decided any additional calls could wait until the next day. Besides, Jack had a very exciting afternoon planned – a surprise.

"You're being very mysterious," Edith said as Jacked helped her into a cab.

"Did you or did you not enjoy yesterday? Simply tell me that you had a dreadful time, and I'll turn this cab around and we'll go back to the hotel."

"I'll do no such thing."

"Good. Because we're going to pick out some clothes for you."

"Purchase new clothes? For me? Together?"

"You do trust me, don't you?"

"I thought you were going to help me select a new frock," Edith said in a low voice as they approached the windowless shop. "This looks like a corsetiere. I can't possibly go in there with you." She stopped and refused to move.

Jack took her hand. "You're not in England. This is Argentina. Argentine men often escort their wives and fiancées shopping. It's the custom. I called ahead and explained that you are to be my wife. I promise, you will be treated with the utmost of respect."

"But that's an outright lie," she hissed, the flush creeping up her neck and panic in her eyes.

"A little white lie, simply to protect your honor. Your hair is lovely and you're improving daily with your makeup. You do that because I asked you to, because it pleases me. Indulge me one more time."

"Altering my hair and cosmetics doesn't require removal of my clothes. As for going in a corsetiere with you. Impossible! It simply isn't done."

"I hope you don't think I planned to accompany you into the fitting room? Never! I wouldn't dream of it. I shall wait outside. A matron will assist you."

The color of her face approached the brilliant redness of her hair. "I don't understand you. There are times . . . Times . . . What is it that you want of me?"

"I want you to look your best."

"For the life of me I can't understand why. I suppose you know that you ask a great deal."

Noting a drop in resolve, Jack didn't wait for the next argument; he led Edith into the store.

A saleswoman approached. "You must be Senor Caine. Our shop is honored with your presence. And this is your fiancée. It will be my profound pleasure to personally assist you, Miss Hendrix.

Please to follow me."

"Go with Senora Esposito and everything will be fine," Jack assured Edith.

Senora Esposito had received detailed instructions. No matter what Miss Hendrix said to the contrary, she was to be fitted with a brassiere that fit and flattered, followed by suitable underpants, and either a garter belt or a girdle, should the latter prove necessary. At that point, Edith was to be covered with a light smock so she could model the results for him. Final decisions were to be his.

Jack could hear Edith's nonstop outraged objections through the curtain. In her distress, she forgot his presence. She balked at the translucent and revealing fabrics, impractical sheer lace, and removing her undergarments in front of this stranger.

Senora Esposito was calm but firm. She was there to help, and she would turn around at any point if Miss Hendrix wished. Senora Esposito cajoled, wheedled, coaxed and flattered.

"Here, now the smock, so that you can see how everything will look under your clothing."

"I look like a trollop and I feel like one as well," Edith's voice said.

"And if a trollop is what I think it is, Senorita, you don't look like one. You look muy elegante, very elegant."

"What about my . . . People are certain to stare. Surely I need a proper corset."

"Believe me, Miss Hendrix, you don't need a corset. If people stare, it's in admiration. You have magnificent bosoms. Magnificent! Step out and see if your fiancé doesn't agree?"

"Oh, my word. Jack. Senor Caine. He's heard every word we said. I shall surely die of humiliation."

"Are you just about ready?" Jack asked, pretending he hadn't overheard. "I was busy looking around the shop."

"As your fiancé, surely Senor Caine has seen you in less," Senora Esposito cajoled. "Have you never gone swimming together?"

Edith crept out of the curtained booth, too embarrassed to look at him. The belted smock hid little. Her arms were lean and graceful, as was her waist. Her hips were deliciously curvaceous. And just as Senora Esposito had exclaimed, Edith Hendrix possessed firm magnificent breasts.

"Oh, my. Oh my, oh my! Edith, you take my breath away." An

agreeable tingle assured Jack that he could expect no difficulty with future sexual performance. "Attractive, yet ladylike. Very nice."

"When I look in the mirror, I see a shameless stranger. It's frightening."

"I'm not going to have *any trouble* getting accustomed to seeing you like this. No trouble whatsoever. Now turn around!"

"Why?" she asked, visibly flustered, but unable to suppress a girlish smirk.

"So I can see you from every perspective."

"Would you like Miss Hendrix to try on anything else, Senor Caine?" Senora Esposito prompted.

"Nothing. I don't need to see any more," Jack declared. "Send around a dozen of whatever of yours she's wearing to the hotel, and a dozen pairs of sheer hosiery as well."

"I took the liberty of adding a half slip."

"Good. She'll need one in white, black, and beige."

Senora Esposito happily scurried off to write up her sale.

As Edith reluctantly pivoted for him, Jack imagined the ill-fitting oversized under-garments Edith must have been wearing. How else could she hide that figure? And that precious rounded rump. Edith Hendrix would never be the beauty she must have been at twenty or thirty – too late for that. But in her early fifties, she was quite a package. "Perfect! Beautiful! I don't care if I embarrass you. You look absolutely gorgeous."

"Now you're being absurd."

"Absurd? I couldn't be more sincere. And now we're going straight to the department store. You're getting a whole new wardrobe."

She laughed. "An entire new wardrobe? I planned to purchase one new frock for the presentation. No one outside the academic linguistic community will even be aware of it."

"It's an international event. There'll be reporters and photographers. Reuters will carry it. The story will be read round the world."

Her amused skeptical eyes scrutinized his face.

"Well, it might. But even if it doesn't, you don't suppose that I am going to allow you to go back to masquerading as a duck now that I've seen the glorious swan?"

~ **Chapter 16** ~

Naomi had lied to Ruben their last day together – before the image of his son in uniform caused her to panic, before she told him not to come for her again; she had denied interest in finding her daughters. A letter to Howard Levine, discussing the possibility of a distant relationship to the haunting model, was hidden at the bottom of her camp chest.

Without Ruben to interrupt her solitude with his prying questions and insistent pressure to change, the days crept by, each identical to the one before. To her relief, her body made less sexual demands of her. She made the trip to Acre solely for necessities, and never on Friday evening, when she knew Ruben would be there to purchase his weekly groceries.

There was only work to distract her – and books. Her tent overflowed with her prized small library. But neither her books nor her work could prevent ghosts from taunting her. Sometimes, as she gazed at the swirling sand, she saw her young daughters playing.

"Come with us," Uri said one Saturday evening as the team prepared to go into town. "They're showing an American movie, with Jerry Lewis. You could use a change."

Since a movie didn't require conversation, Naomi agreed to accompany them. She could ignore the lively singing in the dilapidated van.

When they reached the small town, as the group strolled along the street, she spotted Yitzhak on the sidewalk talking with friends. She turned away too late. Instead of the snub she anticipated, the boy left his companions to run after her.

"Wait! Wait! I have to speak with you."

Naomi halted, dreading an emotional scene. "Go on ahead," she told Shaul and the others, "I'll find you inside."

"It's because of me, isn't it?" Yitzhak accused. "You won't see my father anymore and it's because of me."

In the three months that had passed the boy had grown taller, more manly. She could see the faint trace of a mustache on his upper lip. "My decision not to see your father has nothing to do with you."

"Try telling that to Rifkah and Moishe. They blame me. They say I was rude and that's why you won't come back."

"You weren't rude."

"Then what did we do? What did we say to upset you? Who was it? Me, Rifkah or Moishe?"

"Your father needs a wife. I can't marry anyone. I wish I could explain it better, but you're too young to understand these things."

"Bullshit! That's bullshit and you know it! I'm old enough to understand what goes on with a man and woman."

"I'm sorry. I'm sorry about your father. I'm sorry that your brother and sister blame you. Make them understand, this has nothing to do with you."

"You're sorry? Sorry is worth shit!"

People on the street were staring at them as they passed. "Your father will find someone else."

"My father wants you. He doesn't want anyone else."

"I lost my entire family. My parents, my children, and my husband. The thought of losing another terrifies me," she said, startling herself with the unintended confession.

"You think that you're the only one who lost people they cared for? Look around. Everyone in Israel has lost family. I held my mother's hand and watched her die. For no reason," he shouted. "They shot her for no fucking reason."

Naomi was unable to answer the boy. She could do nothing more than silently absorb his accusation and pray the ranting would end so that she could flee.

"I miss my mother. My father, my brother, my sister, all miss her. But we're alive. And we can't waste our lives running away from it. You know what we say, my friends and I? We say, 'Fuck the bastards! To live and be happy is to win.'" He turned abruptly and raced back to his companions.

In the dark of the theater, Naomi brooded. The boy had so unnerved her that she was unable to lose herself in the movie. Others were able to enjoy it. Viewers on all sides accepted the nonsensical plot and the actor's outrageous antics. They laughed – boisterously, loudly, without restraint. Every person in the audience had lost members of his or her family. A few were the sole survivors of entire villages. And they were able to laugh. Israelis laughed, sang, and danced at the slightest excuse. On the fluttering screen, the madcap comic was frantically struggling to free himself from a can he had stepped in. He pulled. He strained. A snarling bulldog appeared. With his foot still stuck in the can and the bulldog at his heels, Lewis ran, his arms flailing uselessly. The audience howled with laughter. Now cornered, the comic got down on all fours and confronted the startled dog by barking. Nose-to-snout, they faced off until the bewildered canine turned and ran off. The man to Naomi's left smacked his knee and cackled loudly. In the anonymity of the darkened setting, she discovered she too could laugh.

*   *   *

Ruben's arrival at camp a few days later was as unexpected as hail in the desert.

"I have news you should know," he said after they had left the others.

"What news? Something happened to one of the children?" she asked. "We heard nothing."

"My children are fine. A friend who works at the hotel and buys fruit from me told me he saw it in an American newspaper. The woman. The model. Charlie. She's in the hospital."

"What are you saying?"

"She had an accident. A bad accident. She's in the hospital."

"What happened? Tell me! How old was the newspaper?"

"He didn't save it. Maybe he read it a week ago. She may not be your Michelle. It's only a resemblance. Here, sit down on a rock. You're shaking. Have you written her yet?"

"Is she going to be all right?"

"The paper didn't say – only that she was pushed or fell off a metro platform. Now will you write? How can you know whether to worry or not until you know for certain?"

"I wrote. I haven't mailed the letter. I'll mail it tomorrow."

"Good. So I can leave. That's all I came to say."

She watched Kane's lumbering farmer's walk down the incline to his truck. "No! Don't go. Don't go yet," she called, racing after him.

He turned to wait for her. "What is it that you want, Naomi?" he asked when she reached him.

"Come back on Friday? If not Friday, then Saturday. Maybe you could bring the children. I'd like to see them." She shrugged. "Unless you're too busy. If you have something else to do, I understand."

There was a long pause before he answered, and in that time, she could see his eyes narrow suspiciously and appraise her sincerity. "Saturday. I'll pick you up so we can talk, just the two of us. Maybe we'll make love. For this you're ready?"

"For this I'm ready."

"Later, maybe we'll go back to the house and see my children. They ask about you."

As she walked back to her work area, Naomi wondered what it felt like to be part of a normal couple, who held hands when they walked and kissed good-bye.

~ **Chapter 17** ~

Copies of all documentation pertaining to the vaulted Voyt collection they had discussed with Robert Makepeace arrived by a uniformed courier within the week. Simply reviewing the extensive list of inventory rattled Charlie. The collection was far more diverse than she had anticipated. It included approximately two hundred oils, twenty-five sketches, forty or so sculpted pieces, two clocks that had reportedly been owned by Louis XV and a mistress of Louis XVI, two dozen religious artifacts worked in precious metals, a Guttenberg Bible, one of the Faberge eggs that had been exchanged as an Easter present by the Imperial Romanoff family, plus a number of items that defied sweeping classification. No matter how much she could unearth and absorb, it would be impossible to be versed in the entire collection.

She called bookstore after bookstore to locate background information and reprints relating to specific artists, a poor substitute for viewing actual work but better than nothing. When not studying, she devoted her attention to organizing the bills of sale, insurance records and provenances.

Four weeks after their meeting with Makepeace, Raul received the phone call they had been waiting for. Voyt had requested a note be extended and the bank had informed him there would be no automatic renewal, as in the past. Voyt's collection would have to be reappraised. And Voyt had agreed. Not that he had much choice. Any future lender would insist on a new appraisal.

Charlie contacted Susan Armonk and James Elton, curators she had selected. Their combined expertise best covered the range of artists and artwork they would encounter. As arranged with Makepeace, all work would take place at the bank in a secured conference room, on a regular Monday through Friday schedule, until the project was complete. Their decisions would be their own. She would compile and present their combined report after it had been reviewed and signed by all three.

To insure her safety, Makepeace agreed to have one of the bank's security guards pick her up at her building's front door and drive her home at the end of the day.

On Monday, Charlie had her first real look at the famous Voyt collection – an exhilarating but intimidating experience. To aid her, she had shipped her art related library to the bank. Cartons were stacked near a set of library tables, lamps, and chairs in the corner of the vast basement conference room. Susan Armonk and James Elton arrived minutes later, as she was organizing her materials. To her surprise, after a polite but cool greeting, they moved a table, lamp, and two chairs to the far side of the large room.

Charlie guessed Armonk to be about fifty. She was an earth-mother sort: tall, buxom, with wiry dark hair streaked with gray that she wore parted in the center. Her square face was devoid of makeup. Elton was a bit younger, in his mid to late forties, with short legs, longish thinning hair and a neat goatee.

With no knowledge of metal works, clocks, Faberge eggs or rare books, Charlie gave the Bible a cursory glance and proceeded directly to the oils, the area she felt most competent to evaluate. After eight hours of mumbling to herself and battling nausea, she saw a pattern emerging – one which she dared not confide to her colleagues. How could she confess her findings were not intellectual, but based on symptoms similar to seasickness?

Though she had selected the experts, they studiously ignored her. They obviously felt no debt of gratitude that she had chosen them, or worried they might be considered rude as they exchanged whispered comments. But she would have to admit they were thorough. Elton examined every millimeter of each oil with a magnifying glass. He labeled slides, placed minute scrapings of paint on them and bagged them. He scrutinized the backs of paintings, many of which had been reinforced with new backings. But the strangest thing he did before moving on to the next painting, in Charlie's opinion, was to turn it upside down and study it.

Susan Armonk was no less meticulous. She compared paintings to catalogs and books they had brought with them. She too took paint samples, and rather than simply upending a painting and studying it, she added two additional steps by viewing it while it rested on each side.

On Tuesday, since she had to leave early for therapy, Charlie informed Armonk and Elton that she would rejoin them the following morning. They looked at her with as much interest as they would have given a member of the cleaning staff. She swallowed resentment and reminded herself that she was the outsider – the dumb blond model who had been the object of public adulation because she had stumbled upon a case of art fraud. And they were the acknowledged unsung professionals who had spent decades acquiring their expertise, who could never expect that sort of recognition. For that reason, she decided not to share her thoughts unless they requested her opinion or the project was near completion.

Friday afternoon, before she left for therapy, she thought she would try Susan Armonk's ninety-degree test. She began with a lesser work she believed to be authentic. To her amazement, it looked true from every angle. Then she repeated the process with a suspect portrait by Rembrandt. On its side and upside down, the model's features and hands, even the draped background, looked wrong, deliberate, unbalanced. Apparently, there was merit to this insiders' trick.

After nine days of work and eating her bagged lunch alone in her deserted corner, Charlie had examined the works of every artist she felt remotely competent to evaluate. She decided to investigate some of the remaining pieces. A near life-size wooden crucifix, reported to be sixteenth century, crude but beautiful in its rendering, caught her attention. As she cautiously lifted the roughly carved object to turn it, her white cotton glove caught a splinter. Shouldn't a four hundred-year-old artifact be smooth from age and handling? she wondered. Unless . . . Of course. A crucifix of this size would have been hung from a wall and rarely touched, so the rough texture could be explained. She was about to go on to the next item, but couldn't. Something was wrong – inconsistent. She sat down to stare at the object. If it were hung against a flat surface, wouldn't the face be a different shade after being exposed to air and light for four hundred years? But the dark wood on the front of the icon matched the back. And there was something odd about the corona, or halo. Charlie left the crucifix and returned to her books to pore over those that contained old depictions of Christ on the cross. Forty-five minutes of research reinforced her suspicion. This particular corona hadn't been used until the seventeenth century – a hundred years later – and not in conjunction with an interpretation as rustic as this. Her reaction must have been audible because from either side of the chamber both Armonk and Elton stopped their work to gawk at her.

"Sorry," she mumbled.

* * *

The limousine driver expertly wove his way through the dense Friday afternoon traffic as Charlie sat brooding in the back seat. Okay, now what? she asked herself. In her opinion, virtually every oil purchased through Kadinski was fake and also the ostensibly most valued. Based on her research and instinct, many of the other items were as well. But knowing you're right was one thing. Proving it was another. Frustrated didn't begin to describe her mood. She felt like Cassandra, the Trojan princess given the gift of prophecy, and doomed never to be believed.

Above the pedestrians and street-high storefronts, Charlie watched for the poster, half hidden behind a construction scaffold, of Brigitta in a white piqué tennis outfit and visor, holding a racket and radiant in her Perfecta Makeup – the same poster she saw every Monday through Friday on her trips to and from the bank. That was a plum contract! Short hours. Great exposure. Big checks that arrived regularly. No brain work required. No risk. And minimal frustration!

She would go home and eat leftover meatloaf, sliced tomatoes, and canned peas while watching the six o'clock news, a prisoner in her own home. Ken might call if he had nothing else to do. But she couldn't explain what she was doing. Raul called weekly to find out how the work was going. And it was going horribly. Elton and Armonk, who continued ignoring her, seemed at ease with their findings. The formerly dreaded physical therapy was now the awaited highlight of her week. Sequestered nuns had more opportunity for romance than she did. Life could be so unfair.

* * *

Charlie heard the dull insistent ring as she removed her key from her front door. She raced to the phone.

"I'm so glad I reached you. I've been trying all afternoon," Rosemarie's voice said.

"I just got home."

"Well someone called the office and he wants to meet you in person – but it's not about a job. I told him, 'Absolutely not. We do not give out that kind of information about our employees.'"

"Did he say what this was in reference to?"

"Sort of. Maybe it will make sense to you. Here, let me read what I wrote. His name is Howard Levine, and he's a high school principal in Amityville. That's on Long Island. He has a friend in Israel who's looking for a woman that's related to Alan Fitzpatrick."

Charlie's throat closed.

"Are you there, honey?"

Alan Fitzpatrick was her father's baptismal name, before he chose to reinvent himself as Jack Morgan.

"This guy sounds harmless enough. He gave me two phone numbers – one from his home and the other at work. I checked it out. Howard Levine is a high school principal in Amityville. What would you like me to do?"

Charlie took a deep breath. "Repeat everything you just said."

"His name is Howard Levine," Rosemarie began again until she reached the end.

"If Levine is willing, tell him I'll meet him in Schrafft's. It's two doors down from my building."

"When?"

"Tomorrow is Saturday. School's out. Tell him to meet me at one o'clock."

"This is kind of exciting. Anything ever happen between you and that gorgeous cop I met? My niece Toni finally got wise and broke up with that idiot mob chauffeur."

Ken had been undeniably clear about his feelings toward her. Just because she ate her solitary dinner in front of the television didn't mean the entire world had to. "Give me her number. I'll tell him to call her if he's interested."

"That would be fabulous," Rosemarie cooed. "Because I really think they could hit it off. Here, let me give you her number. Oh God, do you really think he'd call her? Remember to say that she's very pretty and she's a hairdresser with her own business."

After Charlie assured Rosemarie that she would glowingly report each and every one of Toni's assets and hung up the phone, she had lots of time to worry about her meeting the following day.

~ **Chapter 18** ~

Edith wore the coral two-piece linen dress that complemented her auburn hair and decorously displayed every curve, which Jack had selected earlier that day.

"I feel so conspicuous," she whispered as they ate their crème brulee.

Word of Jack's latest magic trick had spread through the hotel's staff like news that the preacher was having regular trysts with the librarian. With every employee dancing in attendance for the opportunity to stare, the entire evening, from cocktails to coffee, had played like a scene from a Hollywood movie from the forties. He only had to prompt Edith twice about her appearance during dinner – to dab her mouth with her napkin and to be careful of her sleeve when soup was served.

"Surely you're starting to believe me when I tell you that you look beautiful, aren't you?"

"Not beautiful, better." She reached for the handbag for her lipstick and compact.

"I'm glad to hear that you finally agree that the changes are an improvement."

"That would be telling falsehoods," she said with a shy embarrassed smile.

"Would you like to take a walk before retiring? We could have an after-dinner cordial under the stars. There's a small band and dancing poolside." Jack was in no hurry to end the evening, not after the energy expended to overcome her objections, protestations, and shocked refusals to every change. He was entitled to savor his triumph.

"I thought I'd go to my room early, if that's all right. Since Jean's death, when I'm doing something pleasant, tidal waves of guilt pour over me. I feel like the most contemptible sister in the universe."

"You should never feel that way. That's the last thing your loving sister would want. You know I speak the truth."

She sighed. "My sister could never be cruel."

"Jean's passing was not unexpected. You both knew about her

condition for some time," Jack said, escorting Edith to the elevator.

"Seven long years knowing each day could be her last. But I feel particularly guilty spending so much time with you. She never spoke about it, but I knew Jean was" – Edith dropped her head to stare at the carpet – "smitten with you."

"You were there. Surely you noticed that Jean and I had very little in common. You were the one who enjoyed our trips to workshops and bought your little Aztec statue. Poor Jean did her best not to look bored."

When they reached the door to her room Edith asked, "That last day with Jean, where did you go? I don't want you to blame yourself, you couldn't have known she had a weak heart, but did she do anything arduous?"

"Arduous? Not in the slightest. We went to a beach and later we had dinner. She was fine when I left."

"Which of you suggested that you spend the day alone?"

"Jean did."

"Was it her idea as well, to have dinner alone that night or yours?"

"Hers, primarily. She thought you would appreciate some time alone. Isn't that what she told you?" As Edith had made no attempt to move away or find her key, Jack inched closer.

"Jean was kind but very determined. She always succeeded in getting what she wanted."

"Jean always got what she wanted. What about you? What is it that you want?"

"I suppose I want the same things other women do."

Jack moved close enough to feel her breath. Sensing no resistance, he placed his cheek against hers and gently nuzzled her temple with his lips. "Which is no less than you deserve." He hadn't planned to kiss Edith just yet, let alone ask permission to enter her room, but suddenly, with her leaning into him, conditions seemed favorable. "Wouldn't it be better have this discussion inside? Unless my presence makes you uneasy."

"The list of things you've done that makes me uneasy is ten kilometers long. I haven't noticed that stopping you."

"What if I were to give you my word as a gentleman that I would leave the moment you ask?"

She handed him her key.

He opened the door and allowed her to enter.

Edith turned on the nearest lamp. The single bulb cast shadows on her bed. "To a worldly man like yourself, I must seem a hopelessly silly spinster."

He waited to see what she would do next. Invite him to sit down. Turn on another lamp. But she hovered near the desk, apparently undecided on how to proceed. "Truthfully, I find most everything about you charming."

"Now that you've played Pygmalion to my Galatea."

Galatea was the statue of a woman Pygmalion had created and then fell madly in love with. Jack liked the mythical analogy. "All I did was polish what was already there. I must've been attracted to you as you were or I wouldn't have bothered. And now with your permission, I'd like to remove my jacket and tie. I would be much more comfortable without them."

"Your jacket and tie?"

"With your permission." Hearing no opposition Jack deliberately arranged his jacket on the back of the desk chair and folded his tie over it, then reversed the loveseat so that it faced the terrace and ocean view. "It's peaceful watching the waves. Come and sit beside me." He left just enough room for Edith's compact curvy bottom and patted the cushion.

"You never asked me why I never married. Aren't you curious or simply too well mannered to inquire?"

"Definitely too well mannered," he said, favoring her with his most boyish grin. "I thought that was obvious."

She smiled and shrugged, then took the seat next to him. "I was eighteen when the war ended, innocent and consumed with my studies. England lacked men – men of all ages and stations. Tens of thousands of them never returned. The jolly American soldiers had left. What remained of our lads already had wives or sweethearts waiting for them. And there were many many young widows, some scarcely older than I was, with children to care for, who were desperate for men to replace the husbands they'd lost."

Jack used the opportunity to slide his arm around her shoulder, as if to comfort her. "So you buried yourself in your books and never looked back."

"Yes, except for the occasional flight of fancy."

He kissed her brow near her eye, and when she turned her

head, once more on the lips. These were tender kisses, intended not to alarm. But a semi-comatose man could tell she wanted more. Jack continued kissing her on her mouth with greater intensity. When he licked and nibbled her ear, she moaned. He could feel her marvelous breasts pressed against his chest and his cock growing hard.

Then she gasped and pulled away. "We must stop. Or at the very least pause."

"Why?"

"I've exceeded the limit I set before we entered my room several minutes ago."

"Would you be offended it I laughed?" Jack said, hiding a smile.

"Not at all."

There was no end of surprises with this woman, he thought as he rewrapped his arm around her. "I've wanted to do this and more from the day we met. You can't know how happy it makes me that you return my feelings."

"Really, Jack, it isn't kind to make sport with me. Not kind or gentlemanly."

"May God strike me dead this very minute if I'm not telling the truth," he swore, his hand on his chest, confident of his life expectancy from former false oaths. The All-Seeing God could be relied upon to differentiate between a wee lover's fib and a deliberate challenge to His authority. "Now, was I wrong to think you felt the same way about me?"

"No," she admitted. "But you'll have to be patient with me. In case you hadn't guessed, I'm . . . inexperienced."

Inexperienced! Jesus! A virgin! A virgin, for Christ's sake. That's what she was trying to tell him with her war saga. He hadn't made love to a virgin since . . . Hell, he couldn't remember back that far. "In that case, we have no time to waste." When he kissed her again, she allowed him to part her lips with his tongue.

"I place the blame on the chemicals – the chemicals in the hair coloring," she whispered between kisses and little moans.

Jack chuckled. He had been married three times and only Norma, his second wife, had possessed the gift of humor – a lovely trait. "Don't be blaming chemicals for what comes natural."

He slid his hand from her waist to her bosom.

She bolted upright.

"Edith, men and women were meant to touch one another. It's all part of God's divine plan." It took several soft kisses on the back of her neck until she returned to the position that had earlier alarmed her. Jack caressed her breasts until he could stand no more. "Good Lord, woman, I've got to see them for myself. You've kept these two lovelies hidden long enough."

"Now? Tonight?"

"Then when? Tomorrow at breakfast, or when we're walking down the boulevard? What are you waiting for? The next world war?" He could almost hear the internal debate as her desire fought her conscience. "Yes, now!"

"Then would you please turn out the light?"

"If I must." He rose and turned out the bedside lamp. Reflected light from the patio below and the full moon bathed the room in a silvery glow. "Help me undo this blasted thing before I rip something. You wouldn't want me to ruin your fine new undies, would you?"

The poor thing trembled as together they removed the upper half of her dress and brassiere.

"Glory be to God, that is a breathtaking sight!" Jack said, staring at Edith's silhouette in the moonlight. "You're the goddess Athena and Helen of Troy rolled up into one. You're never to doubt me again when I tell you that you're beautiful."

He didn't need artificial lighting to know that Edith was both flushed and moved. And eager to be held again. She was also a quick study – or an instinctive one, because when he placed his head at the crest of those formidable spheres her index finger made intoxicating circles on his ear. He encountered no further resistance until the hand resting on her knee slipped beneath her skirt.

She caught it with hers. "Are you planning to touch . . . We can't. I can't. This is all progressing too fast."

"Edith, my love, I'm a man with a fire burning inside him. I want to touch you everywhere."

"You did give me your promise as a gentleman that you would leave when I asked."

Jack most certainly didn't want to undo the hard-won intimacy he had worked so hard to gain. He stood. Given her feelings for him and her desire, there was always tomorrow. "I'll go, if that's what you want."

"I wasn't asking you to leave just yet. Simply . . . Your shirt. Unless you'd rather . . . Naturally, I would understand."

He laughed. "Silly girl. I'm surprised that you have to ask."

"In that case, would you consider removing your shirt?"

"My shirt?" he asked, amazed once more.

"Yes. Just your shirt and nothing else – if that would be acceptable."

She wanted to feel her skin against his. He bent over her, his hand in her hair, and kissed her soundly on the mouth. "Make no mistake about it. You're a loving, passionate woman, Edith Hendrix. Perhaps a little late to get started, but a passionate woman nonetheless. Show some mercy and don't make me wait too long. I'm not a young man anymore."

*   *   *

It was past midnight when Jack returned to his room. Edith's knees were locked tighter than the Kremlin – but she had allowed him to caress, stroke, and fondle her everywhere else. With his cock as rigid as a baseball bat the entire time. He grew hard just thinking about it. The coos, the feeble protests, the moans, the way her exciting fingers explored his bare forearms, biceps, chest, and torso. Edith Hendrix: freshly minted heiress and seductress. Merciful Lord Jesus, Jack prayed, let it all continue. Don't let anything happen to ruin his chances –not just to bed Edith, but to capture her heart. She was seven thousand miles from home – the ideal place for an overlooked virgin to have a little fling. It would be so easy for her to leave him behind and excuse the lapse of righteous morality as an impetuous madcap adventure. Far too easy.

*   *   *

Jack's center court tennis lesson the following morning was a waste of time, money, and energy. Not only was Jack's concentration on Edith, who watched from the bluestone patio, it was also focused on a handful of male guests whose interest in her was no longer generated by morbid curiosity. While she was unaware of this, Jack was not. Wearing the cream silk shirtwaist he had chosen the day before, juxtaposed against her sunlit auburn hair, Edith glowed.

"We could have breakfast sent to your room," he suggested, when he ostensibly paused for a long swallow of water. "If you call now, it'll be waiting when we get there. Order anything for me.

Surely you know what I like to eat by now."

She reddened. "I couldn't, Jack. You can imagine what people would think."

He set his glass next to her, intending to graze her cheek with his, but she gracefully moved away at the last second. "They'll think I'm a lucky man to be enjoying the company of a splendid woman such as yourself."

Unable to change her mind, he settled for breakfast in the hotel's casual dining room. Jack was disappointed. He had been hoping for another opportunity to reestablish the intimacy he had won the night before. This morning, her behavior was as formal as it had been two days earlier. Was it her conscience or fear that made her regret her actions?

Jack dropped his gaze to indicate the part of her body concealed by the table. "Dearest, you forgot a button on your dress. Do it now and no one will notice."

"Thank you." She corrected the oversight with no sign of irritation. "This morning I thought we could call the authorities and see how they're progressing. They've had three days and we've heard nothing."

"Three days!" Jack scoffed. "This is Argentina where they move like snails. Your sister died on foreign soil. Let's not forget that there are reels of red tape on both sides of the Atlantic. You can't expect to hear anything for a week or more."

"In that case, perhaps we could do some sightseeing. I'd like to see more of the history and architecture while I'm here."

"We can do that this morning after I shower and change. This afternoon I thought we should continue our shopping."

"I already have more than I need."

"Edith, you have underwear, a pair of pumps for daywear and two dresses that fit you properly. We've only begun."

"But I don't have much more time here. As soon as the coroner completes his report, I'll be returning to chilly London and then it's back to work. I'm afraid my trip to Egypt must be canceled. I thought I'd send a telegram with a letter to follow."

"That's exactly what Jean wouldn't want you to do," Jack argued. The tour for two, already paid for, fit so nicely into his plans. "She was so proud of your award. So very proud."

"How could I drop my sister in the ground and leave less than a fortnight later on a jaunt? I don't care about the award. You know that I would forgo ten awards if I could have my sister another day."

"But nothing will bring her back, and you've been looking forward to seeing Egypt and the Holy Land."

"It can't be helped."

"Then postpone it. Don't cancel anything. Simply postpone it. Surely the Egyptian government would understand. And the airlines give you a year to complete the trip, under the circumstances."

"I suppose they would."

"And you'll agree to go shopping with me?" With his hand concealed by the long tablecloth Jack caressed her firm thigh.

She laughed. "Really! Once you set you mind on something, you're impossible."

*   *   *

They spent the next five days visiting tourist attractions and two afternoons shopping for clothes. With Jack's prodding, Edith agreed to purchase several outfits that would be useful immediately and in the late spring at home.

That day Jack was permitted no gesture more intimate than holding her elbow when they crossed the street, or resting his arm on her chair. At first, he worried that her insistence on formality was indicative of a change in her feelings toward him, but that concern disappeared the same evening.

Soon after they finished dinner at the hotel Edith said good-night, as agreed, and left. Jack waited a few minutes, stretched his legs with a brief walk around the hotel grounds and then took the back stairs to Edith's room. The ploy probably fooled no staff member, but it satisfied Edith.

And Jack wanted nothing more than to satisfy Edith.

For five nights she toyed with a man sorely tried. Each night he returned to his room, their relationship unconsummated. It wasn't from lack of effort. Thanks to his dogged persistence and Edith's untapped passion, she had progressed from interest and curiosity, to a desire to please and a demonstrable delight in as many aspects of foreplay as Jack dared initiate. It was only the night before that he had finally been permitted to unzip his fly and release his swollen throbbing member – and that, only because he had complained of intense pain. Five nights of sweet torture.

*   *   *

With Jean dead eight days, the medical examiner's autopsy complete, and Edith's departure growing closer, Jack knew the time had come to move his plan to the next step. The deserted Cathedral of Saint Ignatius of Loyola, reputed to be the oldest church in the city, seemed a perfect setting to underscore his sincerity and gain a verbal commitment.

He led Edith to the eighteenth century carved wooden altar, a ray of sunlight coming through the porthole above it, and genuflected. Beside the statue of the Holy Mother, he took Edith's hands in his.

Although they were the church's sole occupants, she turned away, embarrassed.

"If I were the richest man on earth, I would feel toward you exactly as I feel now." Jack watched the side of her face for clues. "I would pile diamonds and emeralds at your feet. But sadly, I have nothing to offer you but my heart."

"I know."

The surprise admission halted his prepared speech. "What is it that you know?"

"I know that you don't own a car and that you live at a rooming house. I suppose you could say that I'm aware of your limited finances."

"And who told you that?" he asked, with a soft smile, as though he was teasing. The unexpected sorry truth was presented without malice, but Jack knew he was dangerously close to disaster.

"Not long after we arrived, one evening I was watching children playing across the street from the hotel, and I happened to see you passing by. Jean was in her room. It seemed like a nice night for a stroll, so . . . " Edith sighed.

Jack could fill in the rest. She had followed him. "Your sister said that you were clever." He kneaded his brow. Though some had guessed he lived nearby, no guest of the hotel had learned his true address. How long would it take Edith to surmise the full extent of his poverty, the commissions he received from the grateful artists who benefited from his tours? "So you know the worst. I feel very foolish."

"As do I. I'm a mature woman who has always looked after herself. And I've allowed a man I've known less than a fortnight to redo my appearance, select my apparel, even my undergarments."

Her voice dropped to the thinnest whisper. "And take liberties I've permitted no other man."

"I would never forgive myself if you regretted anything. Never."

"I keep wondering, why would a dashing man like Jack Caine spend so much time with a hopeless dowdy spinster? And I don't like the thoughts that have crossed my mind."

A lesser man might falter at the accusation, but Jack had a response that would be convincing as well as honest. "You're part Irish, aren't you? I can hear it. Something in your speech. The way you form your sentences."

"My maternal grandfather was a Mulduney."

"And me mother was a Sheahy, so I'll be telling you the truth. You're wanting to know what draws me to you? Well, what's the use of my saying that your brain is quick, or you're kind hearted, and you have an interest in the things I do? I expect you know that. We don't often discuss it in polite society, but there's got to be more than that between a man and a woman. So I'm going to do my best to explain myself without being vulgar." He permitted her to see him floundering, while he searched his brain for the right combination of words. "When a man reaches my age, while the mind may be willing, and yes, even eager, there are times the flesh is weak. It refuses to cooperate, or when it does, there's little more there than enthusiasm, if you get my meaning." He waited until her face matched the color of her hair. "That's the thing. I'll be damned if I know how you do it, Edith Hendrix. But from the day we met, my flesh is behaving like a randy seventeen-year-old boy again. And I can hardly wait to prove it to you."

                          *   *   *

That night Jack knew he had to simultaneously end the sweet torture and force a decision. Given more time, he was reasonably certain that he could overcome Edith's reluctance, but he could no longer delay her leaving. In a few days she would depart, with her sister's corpse, new wardrobe, cosmetics, and his last chance to escape poverty.

After their charade of parting for the evening, Jack charged a bottle of brandy from the bar and headed for Edith's room. Welcomed with a kiss that promised more, he presented his offering with a suggestion they toast their lovely day together. He noted as he removed his jacket and tie that the drapes were open, the loveseat faced the ocean, and Edith's own contribution – she had draped silk scarves over the lampshades to soften the lighting.

"I thought you might prefer it to absolute darkness," she said, pointing to the lamps.

"I like it. Now all we need is two glasses." He looked around. "The bathroom. I'll get them." When he returned she was waiting for him on the loveseat, the top half of her dress undone, her compelling cleavage open to view. Jack handed her a glass and sat down beside her. "A toast to our lovely day together."

The torture continued, interrupted only by the consumption of brandy, the doffing of their upper garments, and laughter. After draining a glass and refilling it, Edith giggled when Jack helped remove her shoes and stockings.

"No, no, no," she cautioned, waving her finger at him when he attempted to explore her panty area. Yet minutes later she displayed acute interest when he liberated his engorged member, examining and fondling it. When Jack rose, removed his belt, and dropped his trousers, Edith sank back into the love seat without protest.

Methodically arranging his trousers, shoes, and socks Jack began questioning staying. The purpose of the brandy was to lessen Edith's inhibitions, not render her senseless. Having sex now didn't conform to his self-imposed moral standards. Ignoring Edith's garbled calls for him to return Jack checked the bottle. Less than a third remained. His initial reaction was to kiss her goodbye and leave. But she looked so innocent and appealing with her arms outstretched that he decided instead to tuck her in for the night.

"No, Edith, not tonight. You've had too much to drink. We can try again tomorrow." He turned down the blanket, gently lifted her limp body, and placed her on the expansive bed. The near-comatose woman never flinched as he removed her garter belt and skirt – the sales tag still attached to the waistband. He paused in his efforts to savor this first opportunity to see Edith unclothed and not hiding in shadows.

Was it prudery or childhood trauma that had caused her to hide herself from the world? he wondered. Hers wasn't a flawless figure to his critical artist's eye. The tops of her thighs and her hips were somewhat larger than perfection, and he had caressed less bony shoulders. Her breasts, as delectable as they were, were too full for Greek or Roman sculptors. But there was no denying Edith Hendrix was a damned good-looking and sexy woman.

An extraordinary idea came to him. A brilliant inspired idea. One he considered worthy of a master. He carefully slid the last remaining garment, her panties, down her legs and over her ankles before covering her with the sheet. Right before he turned out the light and crept into bed next to her, he removed his shorts. A light kiss on Edith's silky skin and Jack closed his eyes and drifted to sleep.

When he awoke his watch read 6:30. Edith was snoring softly next to him. Ever so cautiously, Jack wrapped his arm around the sleeping woman. As she hadn't stirred, for added intimacy he placed her hand on his semi-erect member. The organ shuddered. In this position, he no longer could see his watch. Perhaps another twenty minutes passed. He lightly blew on Edith's brow. It twitched. Edith was a sound sleeper. Jack tucked her head under his chin and stroked her hair. How nice it would be to wake up just this way, he thought. What a novel and inspired idea. As creative ploys went, surely this was one of his finest efforts. The fingers resting on his cock lovingly curled around it. The delighted organ engorged, red and throbbing, like a lad a third his age.

"Where am I?" Edith asked, abruptly removing her hand.

"You're right here beside me, my love."

"You're not wearing britches. That was your . . . your . . . What are you doing in my room?" She retreated and thrust the sheet between them. "And what happened to my clothes?"

"I can't believe you don't remember. I, for one, will never forget last night," he said, determined to be technically truthful.

"What happened?"

"Why are you so upset?"

"It was the brandy. I remember drinking too much brandy. I can't believe that you would take advantage of my trust and force yourself . . . How could you?"

"How could I what? Do you see any signs of a struggle here? Check your wrists, arms, ankles. Are you in pain or bruised? No! And I most certainly did not wait until you passed out to force myself on you," Jack declared, theatrically pretending to be gravely wounded. "Whatever took place between us was consensual, as it always has been." He rose and went to the bathroom, conscious her eyes never left his fit nude body.

Once inside, he urinated, leisurely washed and dried his hands and face, and used the hotel's supplied mouthwash to gargle. Before leaving he wrapped a towel around his waist, checked the mirror and pushed back a stray curl.

"Please believe me. I know you wouldn't . . ." she said when he reentered the room.

Jack wordlessly picked up his shorts, dropped the towel, and with his back to her, began dressing.

"You're cross with me," she said.

"You think I'm capable of rape, or if not rape, then vile misuse of your trust. I'm not angry. I'm terribly disappointed."

"I know you're not capable of anything like that. That's not the dear boy I know. Now do come back to bed and say that you forgive me."

Jack looked at the door to the hall, as though weighing her words, and then back at the woman who held the key to his future. "Are you absolutely certain?"

"Absolutely certain." She held up the sheet, adroitly revealing her finest features. "Please. I feel absolutely dreadful." Laughing with relief when he turned and slipped between the sheets, she dotted his face with kisses, saying, "I only wish I remembered what happened."

"Let me remind you."

With Jack's assistance Edith had no difficulty recreating her genuine enthusiastic participation of the night before. Nor did he encounter resistance when he led his pupil beyond earlier boundaries. Four curious hands found new places to explore. At the jubilant moment of entry when she lifted her pelvis to meet his, her moan was triumphant. And all was going incredibly well until Edith suddenly stopped writhing beneath him.

"You bloody bounder. You sly bloody bounder!"

Jack lifted his head so he could study her face. "Edith, my love, what's wrong? What have I done to provoke such profanity?"

"You devious, underhanded fiend. I know what you did. We slept together, but not in the carnal sense. I might've forgotten some of it, but I'd never forget anything that felt like this. Deny it!"

"So then what do you want me to do? Should I leave? I will if you insist," he volunteered, confident she would refuse. Edith may have started late, but she had caught up quickly.

"Remain right where you are, Svengali. You're going to finish what you've begun," she said, wrapping her ankles around his calves and sounding like the schoolteacher she was.

*   *   *

At Jack's suggestion, he hid in the bathroom when the breakfast he had convinced Edith to order was delivered to her room.

"What shall we do today?" she asked as they ate the toast and jam in bed.

Jack removed his tray so he could face Edith. With its sides falling open and her creamy skin exposed, the old-fashioned, dusty-rose chenille robe looked unexpectedly alluring. "I have the perfect idea for today. Let's get married."

She looked back at him with rebuking eyes. "Rascal, you know that's impossible. Maybe a year from now. Then, if we still feel the way we do . . . "

The smile on Jack's face turned to a scowl. She wanted to go home and wait a year – to slip back into her prissy habits and haunts, and he, and the time they'd spent together, allowed to fade to a sweet memory. "No! You can't." Seeing that she was touched he reached back in his memory for the words that had worked so well on her sister. "I wish I had the time to court you properly – to let the seasons pass and slowly win your heart. But it was our fate to meet like this – under these crazy circumstances – here in Buenos Aires. In a few short days, you're going to leave. Are we going to allow this one chance for happiness slip away from us? At our age, are we likely to be given another?"

She patted the sheet atop his thigh. "It would only be a year. Besides, I'm still furious at you for deceiving me."

"A year!" he said, outraged. "Why not ask me to wait a lifetime? I'd give anything not to lose you. I love that you make me laugh. I love everything about you. It's not the marriage certificate. I want to go where you go and be with you always."

She left the bed to pace. "How would it look if I returned home with my sister in a coffin and a strange man beside me? Every busybody would be pointing a finger and saying all sorts of cruel things. The gossip alone would cause me to lose my position."

"Exactly my point." He shifted his legs so that he could sit on the side of the bed. "But if we said that we had met in London several years back, and had been carrying on our courtship by mail, and the reason for your coming to Buenos Aires was to get married, then no one could say for certain that we hadn't married before Jean had passed on." Jack breathed deeply and waited several minutes for her to process the totally unexpected idea, believing every second she delayed answering increased his chances. "I know you can see the logic," he said at last. "You're far too intelligent not to."

"A previous meeting and an extended courtship by post. My sister and sole relative to accompany me. A simple private ceremony. That's really most clever. You are a first-rate liar and an exceedingly dangerous man."

"You see, you know all my bad points; there'll be no disappointments. Pity the poor bride who enters the institution of marriage hopelessly dazzled."

"You're a bloody lying scallywag. Do you really expect me to wed a bloody lying scallywag?"

"Define scallywag."

"Look in the mirror."

He blithely ignored the recommendation and continued to press, convinced that despite a pretense at outrage, Edith was weakening. "Would you prefer that I left you in that hideous spinster's shroud and packed you off to England a sorry virgin, saving all that virtue, and passion, I might add, for absolutely no one?"

She replied with a mean frowning face. "You paint a hard picture, cad."

"I'm the cad who asked you to marry me. Say no and I'll never trouble you again."

"You won't resent having to remind me to wipe my chin or selecting my wardrobe?" she demanded, her eyes still suspicious.

"Not in the least."

"And you'll promise that you won't become cross and impatient and lecture me?"

"And be an irritating know-it-all? Never!" Jack solemnly raised his right hand. "I swear by all that is sacred, I will never do any of those vile things. In fact, I consider improving your appearance, like the removing of crumbs and price tags, my duty as your loving husband."

"You tricked me. You tricked me into . . . Into having intercourse with you. Am I to expect that sort of deceit on a regular basis?"

"By intercourse, I assume you mean 'making love.' Judging by your response, I don't think deceit will be necessary," Jack said, simply to watch her redden.

She approached the bed. "And you're certain that you want to be with me always?"

He pulled her down on top of him and kissed her nose. "Did I say that? I suppose I might've mentioned it in passing."

"Rascal!" She snuggled against his chest. "I shall have to invent something to keep you out of trouble. I can envision you getting into all sorts of scrapes if you're not kept occupied from dawn to dusk."

"Then that will be your wifely duty – keeping me busy and out of trouble."

*   *   *

As a new bride Edith thought herself entitled to a small celebration following the ceremony – tea and sandwiches, sweets and sherry– something that could be quietly arranged. For guests she chose the handful of artisan friends Jack had introduced her to, plus Emilio, and their spouses. As the wedding was to be held in one of the hotel's private dining rooms, Jack playfully suggested they include the helpful employees from the beauty salon. Edith thought it a splendid idea and personally delivered the verbal invitation herself. Within twenty-four hours, so many hotel employees had invited themselves, in a spontaneous gesture of largesse the manager declared the celebration the Parador Grande's wedding gift to the couple.

Edith looked lovely in her new ice-blue lace dress and the silver shoes Jack had selected. Her future husband thought himself debonair in his dark navy suit. A mariachi band, hired by Emilio, stayed long enough to serenade the bride and groom. Having acted as Jack's best man, the tennis pro gave a warm toast, praising both the groom and bride, and wishing them the best of luck. In all, it was a festive, if unconventional, wedding.

That night, before they fell asleep in their new room and queen-sized bed, Edith's last words to Jack were, "Please understand if I look troubled now and again. I suffer dreadful guilt for being this happy. I have so much to be grateful to Jean for. It was her idea to take this trip; her generosity that made it possible. My only consolation is that she never knew how much I resented her for monopolizing your time."

Jack nestling Edith's cozy warm rump was reminded once again that it had been his proposal and their subsequent lovemaking that had killed Jean. But he would keep both his gratitude and guilt to himself.

~ **Chapter 19** ~

At 12:30, thirty minutes before Howard Levine was expected to arrive, Charlie walked into Shraffts and selected a booth that permitted her to see the front door. Sipping hot tea to calm the knot in her stomach, she evaluated every man entering the coffee shop. Who was Levine and what did he want? Was he the man who'd attacked her? Her only source of information about Levine was Rosemarie Rifkin, and the story he had given was that he was seeking someone related to Alan Fitzpatrick – not for himself, for a friend.

A handful of people knew that twenty-two years ago, her father had changed his name to Jack Morgan, reinvented his past, and moved with his daughters from Philadelphia to Palm Beach. Somewhere along the way, he became a reluctant player in a scheme to sell forgeries. Her father was a complicated man. Boyish, open and playful. Dark and secretive. But no parent was more loving, selfless or devoted. When he thought exposure imminent, he chose suicide over disgracing his daughters with a trial and jail.

Was Levine intending to blackmail her? Was he a participant in the fraud, or a victim? Was he looking for money or revenge? And would he instigate another investigation into the ugly portion of a past she had successfully kept hidden?

Suddenly, a man was halfway to her table before Charlie noticed him. Levine looked anything but threatening in his corduroy slacks, plaid shirt, and tie that was too wide to be stylish. True villains walk among us unnoticed, she reminded herself. Sometimes they pass as homeless people. But this man with the bushy hair and dark eyes was clearly not the one who had attacked her.

"Howard Levine," he said, when he reached her. "I'm a friend of Naomi Neir's. I worked at her dig a few summers ago. She was part of an archeological team excavating the site. May I sit down?"

"Yes, please. I'm so sorry to be rude."

Levine unbuttoned his jacket and eased into the booth. "Forgive me for staring at you. It's just that the resemblance is so striking. This is eerie. I could use a cup of coffee." He looked around for someone to take their order. "Wow! And you do that same thing with your mouth as she does."

Charlie instinctively reached for her mouth.

"Let me begin again. I was part of a group that volunteered to work on a dig in Israel. One of the archeologists and I became friends. She's the one who asked me to do her a favor."

A bored waitress arrived and stood next to the table, pencil and pad in hand. "What can I get you?'

"A black coffee and a cruller," Levine said. "How about you? Would you like something with your tea?"

Charlie shook her head.

The waitress left to fill the order.

"There's no doubt in my mind that you two are somehow related. I mean you and my friend," he said.

"This friend. Please repeat the name."

"Naomi Neir."

"I don't know anyone by that name." Liars often told highly convincing half-truths and could appear in the least menacing wrappings. "You mentioned the name Alan Fitzpatrick. Are you a friend of his as well?"

"Nooo," he said, smiling. "I don't know Mr. Fitzpatrick or anything about him. It's simply a name Naomi gave me to pass along to you."

"What is it that your friend wants?"

"Naomi is a very private person. She doesn't discuss her past. Nor did she explain her reasons for wanting the favor. But I do know something about her from the people she worked with. Her birth name was Nicole – Jews who emigrate to Israel often take Hebrew names –and she was born in Paris and lost her family in the war. I was told that she has a husband and two daughters living somewhere in the States."

Charlie summoned the last fragment of her composure. "Please believe me, I don't wish to doubt you, but I have to ask if you have any proof." She knew she was ashen, but only those closest to her would know her legs were trembling and that she was having great difficulty breathing.

Levine smiled, not without sympathy. "I have the letter Naomi wrote me and some pictures of us taken together. Would you like to see them?" He reached into his inner pocket and withdrew a letter and several photographs.

Charlie ignored the letter and reached for the photographs. She too had photographs, taken many years ago when she was an infant. Her hands shook as she examined Levine's photographs. She recognized the face. She wasn't dreaming. The normal sounds one would hear in a coffee shop, people talking, coughing, laughing, the clatter of dishes, were swept away by the rush of gushing water. And the only thing she could see were tiny brilliant lights exploding in the dark.

"Whoa! Take it easy! You're breathing too fast. You're hyperventilating." Levine rushed to Charlie's side of the table. "Someone get me a paper bag," he shouted. "Take deep breaths and blow them out slowly. Put your head down. Don't try to talk."

Charlie put her head down and took deep breaths, and did her best to follow Levine's directions when the paper bag arrived. But as images of old photographs of her mother and Naomi Neir reappeared, so did the symptoms. It seemed like hours passed but eventually the ghostly lights faded, the gushing water receded and she was able to sit up without feeling dizzy. "I'm fine. Really," she said in a voice that sounded unfamiliar and forced.

"I'm so sorry. I didn't mean to upset you. I was hoping this was good news." Levine's deep-set brown eyes searched her face.

Charlie smiled to reassure the concerned man. "It is good news. It's amazing and fantastic news – that I never expected to hear. The woman you know as Naomi Neir is my mother. I grew up believing that she was dead."

"Holy . . . My God! You read about things like this in magazines. You see it on television. Holocaust survivors reunited with members of their family after decades. But you never think you're going to be a part of it."

"Thank you. My sister . . . Thank you."

"You don't have to thank me." He took her limp hand and shook it. "I feel honored to have played a small part in reuniting you with your mother. But who is Alan Fitzpatrick?"

"A man we both knew, who has since died."

                           *   *   *

Charlie paced the limited space in her apartment, alternately shivering so hard her teeth chattered, giggling, and weeping. Her mother was alive. Somehow, she had survived. Perhaps in a concentration camp. Charlie reached for a box of tissues to wipe her eyes and cheeks. Obstinate tears stubbornly refused to stop flowing.

Sinking into a corner of the couch, she fought to correlate what she knew to be true and this abrupt change to her reality. Levine had been unable to furnish additional information about Naomi's past. She had twenty-two years to account for and no one to provide answers.

If her mother had been sent to a concentration camp for the duration of the war, she reasoned, all attempts after the war ended, to locate Alan, Margaret and Michelle Fitzpatrick, would have failed. Her father believed his beloved wife was dead – of that, she was certain. His cranky older sister had assured Charlie of that. His decision to change their identity was probably motivated by a desire to embellish his past and create a better life for the three of them. And then he died before he could learn the truth. Tears dripped down Charlie's cheeks to her blouse.

The only way she could learn more was to write her mother at the address on the envelope Levine had given her. And she wouldn't tell Amelia anything before being positively certain that this wasn't a hideous cruel hoax. Her sister was far too fragile.

* * *

Monday, as Charlie was putting away the remainder of her lunch, Elton and Armonk approached her work area. Between them, they had examined no more than a quarter of the collection and had discussed nothing with her.

"It's apparent you've come to some conclusions. We'd like to hear your thoughts," Elton requested.

Charlie couldn't tell if Elton was smiling or sneering. "Have you received word back from the labs?" she asked, stalling.

"The labs?" Armonk repeated, as though she was speaking a foreign language.

"The laboratories where you sent the paint samples."

"Not as yet. These things take time." Elton cleared his throat and began again. "But we're curious to hear your thoughts."

Charlie wondered if she should soften her response. As she was certain no amount of hedging would alter their opinion of her, or her conclusions, she decided to be candid. "I know virtually nothing about printed material, so I wouldn't dream of commenting about the Bible. And I know little more about clocks, enamels, or metalwork, although I did think the stones in the Russian icons looked fake."

"You're suggesting the genuine stones might have been replaced. Interesting," Susan Armonk commented.

"Not necessarily. Like the Faberge egg, which was very inventive, it all seemed too new to me. I couldn't find the smallest dent or scratch. As for the oils, sketches, and sculptured pieces, while I consider the workmanship impressive, I suspect virtually every item Voyt purchased through Gustav Kadinski is a forgery, except one."

Susan Armonk's attempt at a smile was a melding of a dismissal and a sneer.

"But that's large percent of the collection," Elton reminded her.

"Please remember, I did say 'virtually.' A number of pieces go beyond my scope of expertise." Charlie observed his cold frown. "Obviously, you disagree."

"While we respect your enthusiasm and dedication, and appreciate your selecting us for this assignment, we couldn't possibly support that position," he informed her.

"I'm afraid I'd have to go with James," Armonk added. "Pieces from the Voyt collection have been displayed in museums the world over. The very notion that the majority, and the most valuable pieces in the collection, are not what they're purported to be, would be disputed by every expert who's seen them."

"On what do you base this accusation?" Elton demanded.

"It's hard to explain." Charlie felt it was futile to describe the dizziness and nausea she experienced when viewing a painting that was not done by its presumed creator – futile and unscientific. She would have to rely on the documentation – the only area she could confidently defend. "I would like to show you some things I discovered while reviewing the provenances and bills of sale."

Armonk and Elton watched as she placed the folders containing the documentation that she had organized, as well as the accompanying notes she had prepared, on her worktable.

"Perhaps you would be more comfortable seated. This may take some time."

Armonk reluctantly returned with two chairs.

Charlie opened the first folder. "If you carefully examine the handwriting on items purchased through Gustav Kadinski, you'll find they can be reduced to six handwriting styles. Yet there are forty-three different names attached." She arranged five bills of sale alongside one another, held her magnifying glass over the script and then the signatures. "Compare the handwriting. You don't have to be an expert to see they were written by the same person. Kadinski took great care with his fakes, but he was incredibly sloppy with the supporting documentation."

"I see," Armonk grudgingly conceded. "James, is it possible?"

Charlie reached for the folder labeled *Provenances* for further substantiation.

"Don't be a fool, Susan. We don't need to look further," Elton said, dismissing Charlie's proof with a wave of his hand. "So what if the documentation is fake. Everyone knows Kadinski smuggled pieces out from behind the Iron Curtain. Who knows how and when they were obtained. Kadinski couldn't produce valid substantiating documents, so he forged them – or he had them forged. While your little dog and pony show is very entertaining, Miss Morgan, it doesn't prove anything."

Charlie realized Armonk, formerly willing to reconsider her position, now stood firm with Elton. She was jarred by their stubborn refusal to see what was so obvious to her. James Elton had invented an excuse to refute what a nine-year-old child could understand – and Armonk had gone along with it. With all their scrutinizing, upending, paint scrapings, comparisons, and mumbling, these so-called experts either couldn't see past erroneous accepted wisdom or lacked the courage to defy it.

"Well then, my little dog and pony show is over," Charlie said, reaching for her purse and attaché case. "I have urgent matters to address for the next few weeks. I'm sure I can rely on you to continue as you have been, without me. You can brief me on your findings when I return." She knew they were staring at her back as she walked out the door.

There was nothing to keep her from leaving, she thought as she strode down the hall. No one needed her. The project was doomed. Her modeling career was over. She couldn't leave her apartment without worrying that a madman intent on killing her might be hiding in every shadow. Her social life was nonexistent. She had two handsome attentive male friends, but no lover, boyfriend or dates. Two weeks in historic Israel, where she could safely walk the streets and temporarily forget her problems, seemed a wonderful idea. And if Naomi Neir did turn out to be her mother, as she fervently prayed she would, everything else would be irrelevant.

~ **Chapter 20** ~

The trip from Buenos Aires to London, then on to Nottingham and the site of the cemetery where Jean was subsequently buried, was trying. Added to anticipated traveling time were the delays attached to traveling with a corpse, plus the stop in London that should have been brief, but took eight additional exhausting hours.

Informing both friends and associates of Jean's death was painful for Edith and tiresome for Jack. Explaining Jack's presence and Edith's new marital status required numerous repetitions and reassurances. The long church service and subsequent burial were equally wearing. As the bride and her husband were not expected to be cheerful, Jack was certain they were utterly convincing as the grieving sister and short-lived brother-in-law.

Instead of resuming her former smiling self, in the days that followed, Edith grew more reserved and concerned about proprieties. She complained about the shocked responses her new look had provoked. Disapproving comments were pointed and frequent. She grumbled that she was unfamiliar with finances beyond her own simple requirements and fretted about the added paperwork, legalities, and many unanticipated expenses.

Jack attempted to encourage and comfort when he could, but he was having his own difficulties adjusting to the unfamiliar circumstances. After one month in Nottingham, he missed friendly faces, the warm Argentine sun, his tennis and the year-round resort life he had enjoyed. Perhaps it was the circumstances, but he found the people he met to be glum and formal. He was bored without his normal routine and activities. He was also feeling the pressure of being a husband again: having to account for his time and the added responsibilities, none of them under his control.

And then there was the touchy subject of finances. Within the first week, Jack's ego was wounded when Edith didn't ask him to accompany her the day she met with Jean's solicitor to discuss the terms of the will.

Jack quickly forgot the sad future he had been delighted to leave in Buenos Aires, and only remembered the good times he had enjoyed. With no funds or income of his own, he now had to ask

Edith for even the small sums needed to pay a cab driver or tip a bellboy. Married to Petal, her accountant had deposited a sum into his personal account monthly – an arrangement that allowed a man some dignity. Every day that passed made Jack feel more like a useless appendage.

But their most urgent problem was Edith's one-bedroom flat. Like Edith, before he took charge, it was sloppy and unkempt. Books were piled on every available surface. The closets were crammed and chaotic. A life-long fastidious man, Jack found the place intolerable. Worst of all was the creaky lumpy bed they shared. At best, it could accommodate one tolerant sleeper. A new bed could be purchased, but there was no space for anything larger. The existing furnishings overran the tiny rooms.

But Jack hadn't forgotten Edith's mentioning the spacious house Jean had owned, and that she had lived nearby. Exchanging residences was the logical solution, but Edith put off visiting her sister's home. It wasn't until Jack pointed out that Jean's house would contain important papers, as well as accumulated mail, that Edith reluctantly agreed to take him there the following Saturday.

*   *   *

As Jack parked Edith's black Hillman Minx in front of Jean's house, he appraised the cheerless neighborhood. The Tudor homes were prewar, which meant the construction would be solid; however, unless they had been recently renovated, the plumbing and heating systems were outdated and inadequate. He assumed she would accompany him, but as they were about to enter her late sister's home, Edith asked to wait on the front porch.

The tired looking parlor lacked warmth. Massive cast-iron radiators were half hidden behind dreary furniture enlivened only by yellowing crocheted doilies. Behind the parlor and to the left was a small dining room. A mahogany credenza contained brass candlesticks and unrelated knickknacks. Only the oversized Victorian table and high-backed chairs had any character. The required china cabinet was prissy and second-rate. The adjoining kitchen provided the biggest disappointment thus far. Only the refrigerator was new. Nothing had been redone. The sink had a floral fabric skirt intended to conceal the pipes beneath. Cabinets were few and contained little beyond lifeless cheap china. A door that might have led to a pantry contained only a toilet; the tank high above, a metal pull-chain dangling from its side.

Jack returned to the front of the house and went up the stairs. From the landing, he saw the bedroom that had obviously been occupied by his dead sister-in-law, the woman he had inadvertently killed. Upon entering it, he saw that it held the predictable twin beds divided by a night table, a triple dresser and an upright chest of drawers. The wall was covered with a tacky floral print. The black and white tiled bathroom was across the hall. A second bedroom contained a tailor's dummy, an antique black sewing machine, and stacked cartons. The last room contained a daybed draped in faded chintz, a chest-high wooden file cabinet, and an impressive Jacobean desk. Jack glanced at the contents of its drawers as he casually opened them in succession until he discovered Jean's ledger. Flipping through it, he noted the expenditures, dates, and sums. Edith's sister, it appeared, had been thrifty – extremely thrifty. Beneath the ledger was a box held together with a green ribbon. It held the vital papers one acquires in a lifetime: proof of birth, schooling, and marriage.

"These were Jean's," he said, handing the box and ledger to Edith when he returned to the front porch. "You'll need some of them. Others you'll probably want as keepsakes."

Edith visibly winced as she took them from him.

"There's a good deal more space than your flat," he pointed out before he started the tired automobile. "It must be triple the size. I was thinking the largest bedroom would easily accommodate a queen-sized bed. And the furnishings could be replaced, or not, as you wish. Fresh paint and some tidying up would do wonders."

"I find it troubling being here," she said sighing. "There are too many reminders of Jean. I feel ever so guilty when I think of her."

"Well then, I guess it's out of the question."

"But there's so little room for the two of us in my flat. My bed . . . Our bed . . . "

"Moving would be a vast improvement," he quickly agreed.

"I wish I could. It does make sense, but I can't think about it just yet. Perhaps it would be better to rent it to a stranger for a while until we decide what's to be done with it."

Jack smiled patiently and inwardly groaned. He was starting to believe that the marriage had been a mistake. Marrying a socialite accustomed to wealth, gracious living and spending for whatever she wanted was one thing. Marrying a university professor accustomed to living in a garret and dining on burnt toast and tea was another. The car sputtered as it halted before Edith's home.

As they waited for the balky lift, Edith explained that she had missed nearly a month of work due to Jean's unexpected demise and now wanted to further delay the award she was to receive at the Cairo University.

"The Dean personally offered every courtesy the college could extend at your sister's service," Jack reminded her. "He's very much aware of the prestige this brings the university."

"I suppose," she sighed.

"And we never had a honeymoon. It will be good for us. We need some time together."

"It would mean finding a replacement and that might not be easy."

"Yes, dear, but delay this any more and you'll risk offending the Egyptian government as well as Cairo University."

Jack truly hoped the trip could help resolve their problems. But if not, travel was exciting, and he had always wanted to see the exotic Middle East.

~ **Chapter 21** ~

Charlie fidgeted as the limousine waited for the vehicles in front to maneuver past a double-parked delivery truck blocking traffic. Had she forgotten anything? Her travel agent had taken care of the flight arrangements. She had informed those closest to her that she was taking a vacation and would return in two weeks. The passport that had been temporarily misplaced was now packed.

Nearby, pasted to the side of a building was a Perfecta poster that a graffiti artist had modified with spray paint. The tennis racket had been turned into a crude banjo, and a comical mustache and beard had been added. All that remained of Brigitta's face was the visor that obscured her forehead and brows, her nose and haunting green eyes. Charlie recognized the likeness. It was one she would forever remember.

"I have sinned, Lord. Please forgive me. I have accused the wrong man," she whispered. "Thin. Light eyes. My height. Custom-made shoes." A sick laugh stuck in her chest. "Not custom-made shoes, fool – expensive women's shoes. I have injured an innocent man."

"Excuse me, miss. Were you speaking to me?" the driver asked.

"I have to make an urgent phone call. Is it possible to do that from the car?"

"I wish I could help. This line only goes up and back to our dispatcher. Can it wait until you reach the airport?"

Could it wait? Charlie tapped her foot as she deliberated. Could it wait? "I have to think for a moment. Can you drive around the block or find a place to park for ten minutes or so?"

"Don't you worry," the driver said. "I got to your building twenty minutes early, and you were downstairs waiting for me with your bags. We're not going to have a problem."

Her mind raced. Was she running away –avoiding confronting past decisions – or seeking a mother she had believed dead? She had the rest of her life to punish herself for the error. If possible, it was vital to correct the error before matters got worse. Justin Voyt was innocent. What if Elton and Armonk were right and she was wrong? She had blackmailed the bank into a costly reappraisal and had destroyed whatever standing in the art field she might have had. Would canceling her trip to halt the project correct the wrong? It wouldn't. Nor would her presence influence Elton and Armonk's conclusions.

But what about the woman who had attacked her? Could accusing Brigitta wait until she returned? The disguise had fooled everyone. Months had passed without a hint of suspicion. Perfecta's New Woman had no reason to flee.

And by now the telegram had reached Naomi Neir. If Naomi was her mother, the past twenty plus years had been filled with heartbreaking disappointments. Charlie wouldn't add another. She would call Ken when she reached the airport, inform him of her epiphany, and let him handle it.

"It's all right, driver. You can continue to the airport. I can make my call when I get there."

~ **Chapter 22** ~

As workers unloaded luggage from the rear of the plane, a bus stood poised on the hot tarmac ready to drive passengers to the terminal. Naomi unconsciously checked to see that Ruben was still at her side. Squinting at the glaring sunlight, she fingered the folded telegram in her pocket. She knew its brief contents by heart. She would soon meet the child she had borne, now a woman.

'*FLYING INTO LOD INTERNATIONAL WEDNESDAY stop FLIGHT 1248 stop CHARLIE MICHELLE.*' Michelle: the name Naomi had given her. And Charlie: the name her father had used to hide her.

Ruben had insisted on driving her to the airport in his brother's car and leaving his children home. From the moment the telegram had arrived, Naomi had been too agitated to argue with him about anything.

"Look!" she said, pointing. "Passengers! They're getting off the plane."

"I see."

Naomi compared the silhouettes stepping onto the staircase to the model in the magazine. Too short. Too stout. Too old. Dark haired women. Men. More men. A black robed woman – two black robed women. Finally, a tall slender woman carrying a shoulder bag and a small round case.

"Do you see her?" Ruben asked. "She's behind the two nuns."

People around them were shouting and hugging one another as one after another recognized their visitors. Naomi and Ruben watched the bus fill and make the circuit to the terminal. Passengers disappeared into the terminal and then reappeared to squeals of laughter, shrieks, and tears.

"She can't remember me. Maybe she's angry that I stayed behind when I had the chance to leave. My father wanted me to go. He said I belonged with my husband and children. Only my mother agreed that I should stay behind to rescue Philippe."

"You don't know anything for certain. Try to relax."

"Maybe she thinks that I didn't try to find them – that I walked away from my husband and children and forgot them."

"You don't know what she thinks. Now that she's here, you'll ask and find out."

"Do I kiss her or shake her hand? Maybe I should wait to see what she does first."

If Ruben responded, Naomi could not hear him over the noise as their fellow welcomers greeted and embraced the excited travelers. Deep in her chest, she could feel her heart throbbing. Behind the restraining gate, a tall striking woman in a yellow two-piece dress materialized like a magician's bouquet of flowers and dominated the chaotic scene with her presence. Naomi was light-headed and queasy. She had forgotten to breathe.

"Stop frowning," Ruben ordered, as though he was speaking to one of his children. "You'll frighten her. Wave and smile. Let her know how happy you are that she's here."

Naomi lifted her hand to wave, but Michelle didn't see her. She was walking away from them. Naomi yanked Ruben's sleeve. "She's leaving! Quick! Stop her!"

"Don't worry. She's not going anywhere without us."

Naomi wove her way through the tight crowd with Ruben a half-step behind. Michelle turned and saw them. Naomi froze. What did her daughter believe had happened? Alan could have told her lies. Then Naomi saw the same radiant smile she had seen in the magazines.

When they were near enough to touch the younger woman needed no encouragement. She immediately bent to press Naomi's face against her own. Naomi wanted to say something as the seconds passed and she realized the tears on her cheeks weren't her own, but nothing emerged.

"Shalom! Welcome! Welcome to Israel," Ruben said, using his awkward English. "I'm Ruben Kane – Naomi's good friend. We're very happy to see you." He tentatively extended his hand.

Michelle made the decision for him. She dabbed her eyes with a tissue and kissed his cheek. "Shalom. I'm so happy to meet you. It's very kind of you to come for me."

"Today you're a woman with two first names. Are we to call you Charlie or Michelle?" Ruben asked.

Her eyes still glistened as she turned to Naomi and took her hand. "Charlie, if you wouldn't mind. Michelle still feels odd to me."

Ruben took the carryall. "Naomi is very excited to finally locate you after so many years. She has been unable to talk about anything else since your telegram arrived. Give her a few minutes and she'll find her tongue."

"Welcome," Naomi said hoarsely. They waited for her to continue. "Welcome," she repeated.

Ruben laughed his robust earthy laugh. "Welcome?You speak French, Hebrew, English, and Yiddish. Four languages and that's the best that you can do?"

"Five languages. You forgot Arabic," Naomi rasped. She wished that she could find the appropriate words, but all she could do was clutch the strange woman's manicured hand as they walked.

"Excuse me. You speak five languages," Ruben said, still laughing, now joined by Charlie, who was wiping away tears.

As he drove the winding route to his home, Ruben asked, "So now that you've met, neither one of you have any doubts that you are mother and daughter? Naomi was worried."

Charlie giggled and shook her head. "My father's baptismal name was Alan Fitzgerald and my mother's maiden name was Nicole Strauss. I was born in Paris in 1938."

"Your sister's name is Marguerite," Naomi continued. "She was born in 1936. Your father had three, no four brothers and a sister named Fiona who lived in Philadelphia. You were born with a limp. We had to massage your leg to help it grow straight."

"You see, it all works out the way it was intended," Ruben said. "The Lord King of the Universe has seen fit to bring you together."

Ruben's children were waiting for them outside the house, with their hair brushed and wearing their freshly pressed school clothes. As the eldest, Yitzhak was introduced first. His composed formal greeting was followed by those of his high-spirited siblings. Ruben saw that everyone had refreshments in the tiny garden behind his home before Moishe was permitted to show their guest the artifacts he had found.

When Charlie admitted she was recuperating from a recent accident and a bit wobbly on the uneven ground, it was Yitzhak who first claimed the privilege of helping her.

"Is your sister also a model?" he asked, providing more support to her elbow than needed.

"Yitzhak wants to know if your sister is as pretty as you are," Rifkah explained unnecessarily.

"Amelia doesn't model, but she's much prettier than I am. I've brought pictures of her and her husband Hal, and their new baby Teddy."

"A baby!" Rifkah clapped her hands. "That means Aunt Naomi is a *Bubby*," she gushed, using the Yiddish word for grandmother.

"My teacher says that the new president of the United States is a good friend to Israel," Moishe said in his most grownup voice. "Did you ever meet him?"

Charlie covered her mouth. The others laughed openly.

"We were very upset when your President Kennedy was killed. It was a senseless tragedy," Ruben said.

Charlie nodded.

"Her pictures are in American magazines and newspapers. Abba said that she was on United States television," Moishe said, defending his question. "She could have met the President."

"I haven't met President Johnson, but I have met a senator, several congressmen, and John Lindsey, the mayor of New York City. Do you think your teacher would be sufficiently impressed with that?"

Moishe grinned at his siblings with smug satisfaction.

"We would be very happy to have you and Naomi stay with us while you are in Israel," Ruben said, surprising Naomi. They hadn't discussed where Charlie would stay. Naomi had thought the American model would insist on checking into a fine hotel.

"Where will everybody sleep?" Moishe asked.

Rifkah elbowed her younger brother. "Charlie will take my bed, and I'll use the bedroll. You and Yitzhak will sleep in your room, where you always sleep. And Aunt Naomi will share Abba's room."

Naomi blanched. She had never stayed the night when Ruben's children were present. She had assumed they were unaware that she had. Obviously, it had been a foolish assumption. No child appeared surprised with Rifkah's room assignments.

"You are all so kind," Charlie said. "It embarrasses me to confess that I was selfishly looking forward to having Naomi all to myself – at least for a few days. I hope I haven't upset your plans."

This poised young woman was indeed Alan's daughter, Naomi noted, observing the pleased faces surrounding her. The American had the gift to charm everyone who came in contact with her. They might share her facial features, but the ability to disarm and captivate she had inherited from her father.

"There's a nice hotel a few miles from camp," Ruben suggested. "You and your mother could stay there."

"Don't you normally live at a dig site?" Charlie asked.

"Yes, I live at camp, but the conditions there are primitive. We sleep in tents. We shower with cold water. The food would distress you. Our meals are simple."

"I'm not a picky eater. I'd like to try it," Charlie said. "I think it would be fun sleeping in a tent for a change. If it proves too woolly, we can always check into the hotel."

"Or you could come back here," Moishe reminded her.

"Or we can come back here."

* * *

It was after midnight when the two women arrived at camp, hours after the others had retired. Alone for the first time, by the light of a flickering field-lamp, Naomi laid out the bedroll Ruben had loaned them. "You take the cot. I'm used to the rough conditions, you're not." Naomi instantly regretted the accusation. Having avoided society for so long, she had forgotten simple courtesies.

"Ruben is very kind and his children are smart and fun to be with."

"You must be tired. It's been a long day for you."

"I'm too excited to sleep," Charlie said, sitting on the cot. "Don't you want to ask me why Daddy didn't look for you, why you were unable to find us?"

"If you'd like to tell me," Naomi said, pretending that adjusting her pillow required all her concentration, so she could avoid looking at her daughter.

"Several months after we returned to the United States, Daddy received a letter from your mother saying that you had been killed. We moved away shortly after that. Amelia was almost five and I was two. I don't know the reason Daddy changed our names, but I think he wanted a fresh start. He was devastated when he received Grandmother Strauss's letter."

"Your father told you this?"

"No. My father found the subject too painful to discuss. My aunt Fiona told me."

"Your father changed your names and walked away from his entire family – a sister, four brothers and their families?"

"Yes and I never had the opportunity to ask him why. I didn't learn all this until . . . Daddy died in a horrible car crash almost two years ago. I'm so sorry to have to tell you."

"Alan is dead? Your father is dead?"

"The police told us that he died instantly. He didn't suffer."

Alan was dead. And his daughter worried that she, his wife, would worry that he might have suffered. It was not grief for Alan that Naomi felt. It was fury. He had escaped her wrath. To mask her emotions Naomi busied herself with undressing and folding before she found an old T-shirt to sleep in and crept into the bedroll. "And Marguerite – no, you called her Amelia – what did your sister say when she learned that you were coming to see me?"

"I haven't told her yet. She doesn't know that you survived. I thought I'd tell her about you after I returned."

Polite, warm, and cautious, Naomi thought as she wound her alarm clock. Good. It was wise to be cautious. "You better get into that cot. We rise early."

"There's one thing more that I should tell you. Amelia doesn't know that Daddy isn't her real father, and I see no reason to tell her differently. I hope we can keep that our secret."

Naomi realized that she was staring and smiled. "I'm surprised that your father told you. He never wanted her to know. He worshipped his daughters. I was nothing to him, compared to you and your sister."

"He didn't tell me. I learned what I know about his life as Alan Fitzpatrick from Georgette, an old friend of his from Paris."

Georgette, one of Alan's lovers, Naomi thought bitterly. Georgette would defend him. Women would always defend and protect Alan. Naomi turned off the lamp. It had been an exhausting day. Moonlight shone through the tent's translucent walls. "Are you comfortable? Will you be able to fall asleep?"

"Very comfortable, thank you."

Naomi stared into the semi-darkness and drank in her daughter's scent. Americans smelled different. Their scent was a heady blend of deodorant, fragrant toiletries, and a diet rich in meat. How quickly the young and untroubled fall asleep, she reflected as she listened to Charlie's steady breathing. This confident young woman was part of her, and yet she was a stranger. There was the undeniable resemblance, but what else did they share? No common memories. She could claim no contribution to her child's poise, education or fine manners. Even the name her daughter preferred was not the one that she had chosen. She had not been there to teach, to comfort, to soothe the pain, to celebrate the milestones from infancy to adulthood. Alain had robbed her of this. Twenty-three years had been stolen from her – twenty-three years of birthday parties and skinned knees, holidays and confidences, first days of school and first dates. *All stolen from her.* And now Alain was dead and could no longer be held accountable for the pain he had caused.

*　　*　　*

Despite the obvious difficulty she encountered climbing and descending into open pits, Naomi was amazed that Charlie wanted to explore the entire site. She seemed genuinely interested by the scientific methodology, the recovered artifacts, and the suppositions that could be drawn from them.

"It's hard to believe that you never took at least one course in archeology or anthropology," Uri said, unwilling to release her daughter's arm when they were once again on a flat section.

"I wish I had."

"Don't you remember Linda and Jill, the American interns, told us that Charlie had been interviewed on television?" Naomi reminded Uri, the project's leader. "She uncovered a plot that involved forged paintings. Surely there is a relationship between art and artifacts."

"Art and artifacts. Both proof of the genius of man," Shaul agreed. "Do you teach or are you affiliated with a museum?"

"Neither. I only have a Bachelor's degree in art history and I've done some independent study. What I did was a fluke. I simply observed what I thought were discrepancies and did some investigating."

"A fluke?" Uri repeated. "What is a fluke? My English is not so good. Could you translate?"

"She's being modest, Uri. A 'fluke' is an accident," Shaul explained. "What Charlie did wasn't an accident. It takes a trained expert to recognize artistic discrepancies."

"Naomi, your daughter is remarkable," Shaul proclaimed. "How long are we to have the pleasure of her company?"

"That hasn't been decided," Naomi replied.

"Your friends seem nice," Charlie said, after Uri and Shaul had returned to their work.

"They're lechers! Did you see how they behaved around you? Flattering, fawning. Showing off. Positioning. They pretend to admire your mind to get you into bed. Married men behaving like fools. Disgusting! Uri has two grandchildren and Shaul is old enough to have a dozen. I'll tell them you have a young, handsome, successful fiancé. Maybe then they'll remember to act their age." Naomi immediately noticed the abrupt lapse in Charlie's dependable smile and decided to change the subject. "I want to take you sightseeing tomorrow, but Ruben will be working. We'll have to ask one of the men to take us. I never learned how to drive."

"I know how to drive. We don't need anyone to chauffeur us. But we'll still need a car. Where can we rent one?"

"Nobody rents cars. We borrow them. Ruben will stop by after work to ask if we need anything. We'll tell him that we need a car."

"But you told him not to come by for a few days."

"Ruben never listens to me. You'll see. He'll be here today when he finishes work."

"He's very thoughtful."

"But Ruben doesn't own a car. He owns a truck. The car he used belongs to his brother Avram. If Ruben can't borrow Avram's car, he'll borrow one from a friend, or he'll swap somebody oranges or lemons for one. No one is ashamed to borrow anything in this crazy country. Israelis would share dentures if they could."

Charlie couldn't stifle a giggle. "Maybe crazy, but in a nice way."

"Sometimes."

Naomi moved her chair to a patch of shade. They could hear the steady pattern of a pickaxe striking the earth followed by the intermittent scraping of a shovel. It was understood she wouldn't work for the duration of her daughter's stay. Occasionally, when she thought she wouldn't be observed, Naomi compared the tall lovely woman with the chubby toddler she remembered. Michelle had been a happy baby –always trying to keep up with her older sister and please her elders.

"This is a treat for me," Charlie said. "I haven't been able to spend much time outdoors." She turned her face to the sun and closed her eyes. "You're very different from the way I imagined you when I was growing up."

"I wasn't always so cynical. When I was young, I believed in the natural goodness of man. But that was before . . ." Naomi watched the sun disappear behind a cloud. "In what way am I different?"

"Well, for one thing, you have a career. You're independent. Most of my friends are married or engaged. Not one considered a real career. I'm viewed as an odd duck."

"You were in the hospital a long time. Howard wrote that you were pushed off a metro platform. Is that common in New York?"

"It's very *uncommon*. It's never happened before. Contrary to what you may have heard, New York is a very safe place to live."

Naomi didn't challenge the assertion, nor did she believe it. American cities were violent. Their charismatic president had been shot while riding in a cavalcade as the whole world watched.

"What did your father tell you about me?"

"Nothing. We never discussed you. It wasn't until I started school that I realized other kids had two parents. I can't even remember who told me that you were dead. If we asked about you, Daddy would go into a depression that could last for days. We knew not to question him."

What would his adoring daughters think of him if they knew that before he married their mother, Alain depended on rich mistresses to support him? "Your father enjoyed the company of attractive, wealthy older women. I imagine that description would fit at least one woman in your father's life."

Charlie's lips curled into a wry smile. "That would describe both my stepmothers."

"So your father married twice more. Did your stepmothers treat you and your sister kindly when you were growing up?"

"Exceptionally kindly. Daddy would not have stayed with them if they hadn't. We were given the best of everything."

"Did he return to painting or did he find another way to support you? He was an artist when we met – a starving artist, but an artist nonetheless. I thought he was talented, but then I was young and madly in love."

"To my knowledge, Daddy held no jobs after he left Paris. My stepmothers supported all of us. It seems peculiar now, but all concerned seemed to get what they wanted out of the arrangement. And as the indulged recipient, I suppose it isn't fair of me to judge them."

"In return for their generosity, was your father faithful to your stepmothers?"

"I know that he was unfaithful to my second stepmother, who apparently didn't care what he did as long as he was discreet. As for my first stepmother, I was too young to be aware of his activities. Why do you ask? He was faithful to you. He had a mistress when you met, but he ended the affair soon after."

Naomi was startled to hear her daughter discuss her father's affairs so lightly – startled and irritated. The selfish philanderer didn't deserve his daughter's unquestioning devotion. "How could you know that if he never discussed me?"

"I met Georgette, his mistress in Paris, about two years ago. She told me that his feelings for you were unrivaled and profound. They continued seeing each other after he met you, but only as friends."

"She was trying to spare your feelings."

"I don't think so. I never asked about the nature of their relationship, when it began or ended. She didn't have to tell me anything."

If it was true, it was a surprising discovery. Alain had always insisted her old rival Georgette had been content to be a friend.

"Daddy was a complicated man," Charlie said, as though she didn't expect her thoughts to be overheard. "But he would've done anything for Amelia and me – anything. No sacrifice was too great."

It was pointless to continue filling the air with half-disguised criticisms to a daughter who saw her father's flaws and continued to adore him.

"A lovely young woman like you must have a beau, an admirer, maybe an army of admirers."

"I was seeing someone, but he ended it."

The pained smile on her daughter's face told Naomi not to ask more. So this was the way it felt to be a parent, she thought. Despising her daughter's lover, a man she'd never met. Happy for the intimacy. Sad for the heartache she knew her daughter had experienced. Pleasure and pain. Minutes passed before she spoke again. "Your sister's biological father was a trusted relative who raped me when I was sixteen. Your father married me after she was born. If you think that it's best to let her continue believing that Alain was her true father, we will let that be our secret."

*　　*　　*

Naomi looked up from her writing and saw her daughter wiping her forehead with the back of her hand. She had been at that sitting box for hours. Her shoulders, neck, and back were certain to ache later, if they didn't already. "We could both use a break. Sit here and talk with me."

"I am a little tired," Charlie admitted, taking the canvas chair next to Naomi's.

When they were not visiting tourist sites in borrowed vehicles, her daughter wanted to help with the project. She claimed that she needed exercise; that it was good physical therapy. As they worked, Naomi found herself seeking safe subjects to discuss with her daughter. There could be no more denouncements of Alain. She had been lucky not to cause an unbreachable gap between them.

"I'm happy that you were able to take some time off from your modeling."

"After the accident, there's been very little work waiting for me." Charlie needlessly checked to see if she could be overheard. There was no one within a hundred yards. "I've been trying to learn as much as I can on the subject of art fraud. I've been working on a reappraisal of a collection that I believe is loaded with forgeries."

"How's it going?"

"I'm having problems convincing other members of the team."

As they washed up in preparation for the evening meal, Naomi recalled a former lover who could be useful to her daughter. "Tomorrow, I'm going to take you to someone I know, an artist and stonemason," Naomi said. "Everyone in town knows the man is a *gonif*, a thief. Fabulous finds turn up in his shop daily. I think he could be persuaded to share some of his secrets if we asked."

"A forger? A real forger right here in Acre, and you know him?"

"Yes, I know him. This thief considers himself a ladies' man. Just smile at him and pretend you don't notice when he stares at your legs, and he'll tell you anything you want to know."

Charlie leaned across the chair and tenderly kissed Naomi's cheek. It was unexpected and most pleasant. Naomi touched the spot with her index finger.

"I would very much like to invite Ruben and his children to be my guests for dinner."

"That's neither expected nor necessary."

"It's something that would please me. Ruben has been very

kind. He and the children have made me feel so welcome."

"Ruben's a good man."

"Has he discussed marriage? It's obvious that he cares for you."

"There's nothing to discuss. Ruben knows that I won't marry him. The project will be ending soon. When it does, I'll move on." Naomi watched her daughter's eyes widen and the smile fade.

"Ruben might understand, but what about the children?"

Naomi shrugged. "They'll have to understand. I go where the work takes me. I'm used to looking after myself. Blame it on the war."

"Are you going to tell me how you managed to survive?"

What would this pampered young woman think of a mother who had been violated by an endless line of men, and later had used her body to pry secrets from the hypocritical English occupiers? "What's done is done." Naomi inhaled deeply.

"Was it awful? Too terrible to talk about?"

Naomi squared her shoulders. "I survived. I'm alive and millions aren't."

Charlie reached for her hand and squeezed it. "And I'm so very happy that you did."

~ **Chapter 23** ~

The shelves of the stonemason's tiny street-front shop were stocked with religious and secular items likely to appeal to tourists. A hand-printed sign in elaborate lettering in English, Italian, French, and Hebrew hung from the wall. The English words bragged: *If you don't see what you want –ask!*

Charlie had been looking forward to meeting the sculptor reputed to create and sell forgeries since Naomi first mentioned him.

"This beautiful American is my daughter, so be careful what you say," Naomi cautioned Chaim. "Maybe you've seen her pictures in American magazines. She's interested in learning more about art fraud. Forgeries! Fakes! What can you tell us? And don't worry about shocking her. I already told her that you're a thief."

"A thief? That's how you describe me, your friend? You disappoint me," Chaim said, disappearing behind a faded black curtain and emerging with two chairs. He dusted them with a grimy towel. "Art fraud, beautiful lady. There's art fraud and there's art fraud. What is it that you wish to know?"

Naomi took the nearest chair. "Start with the Byzantine. Surely you know something about Byzantine art. Wasn't your partner a Turk?"

"You think you're so smart. You're trying to get me to say that all Turks are charlatans and swindlers. Well, it's true. My partner was a Turk. He ran off with my wife. She was a lovely creature, not unlike yourself," Chaim informed Charlie. "Do you mind if I sketch you while we're talking?" The gaunt swarthy man with the sooty black eyes reached for a pad.

"My daughter gets paid to model." Naomi rose as if to depart. "Tell us something useful or we leave."

"Please sketch, if you'd like," Charlie encouraged the man who she hoped could help her. "I'd love to see your work."

"See, your daughter doesn't object, why should you? Sit down and don't be so impatient. I can talk while I sketch." His eyes darted back and forth from his pad to her face. "She looks exactly like you, Naomi – except for her smile. See, you could look like this one again, if only you could smile." He reached over to adjust the angle of her shoulders. "Your mother and I fought with the Haganah. That's why I put up with her rudeness and she puts up with mine."

"After a sculptured piece is finished, it looks new. If someone wanted it to look old, what would he do to it?" Charlie prodded.

As claimed, Chaim could simultaneously sketch and talk.

She soon learned that both stone and wood figures could be made to appear older by burying them in acidic soil, applying chemicals, or exposing them to heat. Before being slow-baked, either in a kiln or an oven, it was wise to place them in protective wrapping. The temperature and exposure would be determined by the size of the article and the material. Sometimes more than one aging technique was employed. Scorching, if it wasn't used too often, was particularly useful. It was done, a bit at a time, with a controlled flame. The singed area could conceal flaws, and a treasure rescued from a fire seemed to have special customer appeal.

Chaim explained that what set his masterpieces above others was his use of ancient stones that had been quarried and carved by stonecutters a millennium or two earlier. A fragment of a Roman sarcophagus could be reworked into several smaller and more valuable pieces. Unlike lesser artists, he incorporated the eroded edges, natural cracks, and formations into his creations. As sources for his designs, Chaim often copied from museum catalogs.

"Put down your pencil for a minute and bring out one or two of your better pieces – not the garbage you peddle to gullible tourists," Naomi ordered.

"I am at the mercy of two beautiful women. What can I do?" Chaim shrugged and disappeared again.

"He would never leave his supposedly incredible finds in the open," Naomi explained. "It's all part of the show. No one is interested in something kept in plain view. It has to be hidden and have a story attached to it."

Chaim appeared holding a life-sized bust and a stele, a small stone plaque inscribed on its face, about the size of a box of cereal. Naomi recognized the subject of the former. It was clearly copied from athletes found on Etruscan urns. The ragged stele depicting a shield-bearing Roman warrior looked reliably ancient.

Charlie took the stele to examine it more closely. "You're

talented, Chaim. Very talented."

He bowed from the waist. "Thank you, Mademoiselle. It's an honor to display my work to a knowledgeable person such as yourself."

"Do you ever feel the urge to create something entirely original?" she asked.

"Every artist dreams his art will be his immortality. I've done many pieces that spring solely from my brain. But where are the buyers? Who is willing to pay me for my time, my labor, and my genius? A living artist starves. But there is always a market for the long dead artist, even though my talent is equal to or surpasses his. His belly no longer needs food, but mine, unfortunately, does."

"I suspect that it's not only your belly that motivates you," Charlie teased. "It's also a game for you, isn't it?"

Chaim shook his oversized head. "It's not just money that inspires an artist. I could tell you some fascinating stories if you ladies have time for a cup of coffee."

Charlie assured him that they had both time and interest. Chaim locked the door to his shop and the threesome walked the short block to a sidewalk café that served Turkish coffee. His aversion to all things Byzantine apparently didn't include their coffee.

After the tar-like beverage had been set before him, with the smoke from his ever-present cigarette wafting over his head, Chaim began his tale. "You know, of course, most mummies are not the embalmed carcasses of pharaohs; they are the remains of middle and upper class people."

"I didn't know that," Charlie admitted.

"It wasn't so long ago that Egypt's mummies were so commonplace they were used for cooking fuel," Naomi added. "But don't let me interrupt, Chaim. Go on with your story."

"I don't suppose you've heard of Edwin Sedgwick." He put a new cigarette between his lips and lit it with the burning end of his last one. "Sedgwick was a respected expert with a seemingly bottomless purse who thought that he couldn't be fooled by fakes. He boasted that he could identify ancient wood carvings from forgeries by their smell. By their smell! No matter how skilled the artisan, his nose was infallible. And that was all Abdul Medhi, that flea-bitten camel-thief, needed to hear. He might have had ten thumbs, but that devil Medhi was cunning. He made a soup from mummy parts and boiled his third-rate fakes in it. Sedgwick, and his famous nose, sniffed the stewed fakes and proclaimed them authentic. Of course, they smelled old. They stunk of three thousand year old Egyptian corpses." Chaim paused to sip his coffee and savor the amusement of his listeners.

"What became of the forgeries?" Charlie asked, laughing.

"They're probably in highly regarded collections throughout the world. As for Medhi, that crafty camel-thief, he moved to Paris a very rich, fat man."

"That's a fantastic story," she said. "Do you have more?"

"Perhaps, if you're not in a hurry."

"This man can go on for hours," Naomi assured her. "You have the perfect audience, Chaim. Tell us another."

"Two modern ladies like yourselves, what would you know about chastity belts?" he teased. "You've been told they were used in the Middle Ages. Jealous knights going off to fight in the Crusades forced their wives to wear them. Right?"

"That's what I've heard," Charlie said, blushing.

"Hah! No woman ever wore a chastity belt. Everything you've seen or heard about chastity belts is as believable as the tales of Aladdin's lamp. The examples you saw were crafted and aged by clever metalworkers in the eighteenth and nineteenth century. And to this day, the British Museum displays them as genuine."

"And you're certain about this, Chaim? You're not just toying with us, are you?" Naomi probed.

Chaim scowled. "May I be blinded in both eyes if I'm lying. Not one can be dated earlier. They are a fabrication of the prudish Victorian mind. Imagine yourself a proper Victorian lady for a moment. Under the guise of science, morality, art, and history, chastity belts provided endless, titillating drawing-room conversation. A curator from the Museum told me this himself, after he'd learned to trust me."

Naomi snorted. "Was that before or after you sold him one of your phony masterpieces?"

"Laugh if you like. But everything I told you about chastity belts is the complete and honest truth. Every single word. And the curator, who purchased my phony masterpiece, knew full well that it was a forgery. He went on to make a tidy profit on it. The paltry sum

I received is long gone, but the pleasure I get, knowing my work is displayed in that formidable institution, is beyond measure."

"But why would the British Museum continue to display the belts if they know they're fake?" Charlie asked, hoping to confirm what she suspected.

"Museum officials will do anything rather than admit to the public that they've been taken," Chaim explained. "But if a display becomes too much of an embarrassment, there's always the basement. Museum basements are filled with the errors of experts."

"What is the most complicated scheme you know about? Or the biggest, most outrageous?" Charlie pressed, anxious to have him continue.

"I would be delighted to share my best story with you, but that will require a glass of anisette, a taste I acquired in Italy while studying the masterpieces of Michelangelo and Bernini."

Naomi turned to look for their waiter while Chaim, smiling patiently, waited. At last, the glass was set before him.

"Major swindles take planning, research, patience, artistry, daring, and organization," he began. "And that requires a team. Most important is the Director. It's the Director's job to identify the Target. You might suppose that the Target has to be wealthy, but that isn't always the case. A good Target can persuade others to spend their money. For the right Target, acquiring the treasure has little to do with greed. He craves prestige and power. A good Target might be a private individual who is seeking a particular item missing from his collection. Or he could be a curator who wants to insure his posterity by expanding a particular area in a museum. Or he could be an expert with a burning desire to find solid evidence to back up a disputed theory. He could be a scholar with a thesis that needs substantiating, or an authority looking for the link between established artifacts and a dubious piece. In my opinion, the more arrogance a Target has, the better. Pride cometh before a fall. Always remember, it's the Target who determines what has to be provided."

Charlie's mind darted to the mess she'd left behind. Egotistical Justin Voyt would be a perfect target.

"The best schemes involve a Target who wants something specific. For the example I'm giving you, we'll call it Tutankhamen's Pisspot."

She did her best to laugh without appearing shocked.

"Now that the Target and Tutankhamen's Pisspot have been identified, if the Director is not himself a qualified Artiste, he must locate one. The true Artiste is rare. Many people can produce a passable fake. It requires an Artiste to produce a Tutankhamen's Pisspot that will fool the Target and at least one Expert, unless the Target and the Expert are one and the same. Has your mother ever told you about The Finder's Fable?"

"For your benefit, Chaim is choosing to call it The Finder's Fable," Naomi explained. "It's called a number of names, most not suitable for polite conversation. He's referring to a plausible explanation of how the object came to be in the hands of the dealer."

"The explanation must be impossible to disprove and not point to the Director," Chaim continued. "It's best if the person who originally found the item can't be questioned. Death, earthquakes, war are all excellent reasons. It was found in a cave by a shepherd looking for a stray, or by an illiterate peasant digging in the fields, or by an Arab child at an abandoned excavation. Finder's Fables are not difficult to invent. The difficulty is locating a corroborating Expert."

"But a credible expert wouldn't go along on a scam," Charlie said.

"Not intentionally, but some are thick-headed or quick to defend an area of expertise they shouldn't. But a really sly Director is always searching for a Target who's also an expert. The best scam I know about was the work of Hans Dreissinger, one of the premier Directors of all time. Dreissinger learned of an ideal Target, an elderly chief-conservator at a church in Spain. This Target had often bemoaned the loss of six gold and jewel encrusted chalices dating to the thirteenth century, stolen during World War I. It took some research, but Dreissinger managed to locate prewar photographs of the chalices, and after a bit of digging, he found his Artiste, a gifted jeweler. Now you may not realize it, but it's virtually impossible to scientifically determine the age of crafted gold. All that can be determined with certainty is the alloy, artistry and style. As for twenty-four carat gold, where would one start? Now Dreissinger knew this, so the chalices were perfect for his scheme. For his Finder's Fable, he set in motion a story about a man living in East

Germany who had recently died. His heirs were trying to smuggle the chalices, along with other valuables, out of the country. It took Dreissinger several attempts at sending out this rumor, and nearly a year, but the Target finally traced the story back to Dreissinger.

"'Is it true?" the conservator asked Dreissinger. 'Do you know where the chalices are? Are they willing to sell them?' At first Dreissinger denied any knowledge of the chalices. But after much wheedling, he reluctantly produced photos, brilliantly supplying grainy copies of the original photographs.

"'How much are they asking?' the hungry curator asked.

"Dreissinger gave him an exorbitant figure – double the price the genuine articles were worth. 'Even if they are genuine, where would you get the money to buy them?' he argued.

"'Never mind that!' the indignant Target snapped. 'Get them here. I'll tell you if they're genuine.'

"Dreissinger refused. Smuggling was too dangerous. Not worth the risk. He would have to use his own money to pay for the relics and bribes. But eventually he allowed the *Target* to persuade him and showed the man a single piece.

"The curator's eyes widened as he examined the copy. 'They can forget the price they're asking. It's insane.'

"'It's just an asking price. I'm sure they'll take less.'

"'They have no one to verify its authenticity.' the desperate curator said. "Tell them it's a clumsy fake.'

"'Is it?' Dreissinger asked, fearing that he had played his case too hard.

"'Don't be a fool! You tell them that you know it's a fake and offer them a third of what they're asking. Tell them that you think you can find some idiot Englishman to buy them all if the price is right.'

"After much dickering, the final fee was still a healthy sum. With the help of a local priest, the conservator convinced a wealthy congregant to pay for the miraculously found chalices, and congratulated himself for being a shrewd negotiator. The congregant earned many years of reduced purgatory for his pious generosity. The priest enjoyed the prestige the restored church commanded. Worshippers thanked God for this tangible demonstration of his love for them. And Dreissinger made a small fortune. Best of all, since Dreissinger had never claimed the chalices were genuine, he couldn't be charged with selling fakes."

"And as far as you're concerned, there were no losers in this game," Charlie teased.

"None, unless you consider the master craftsman who fabricated the duplicates. No doubt, he was given a pittance of the profit. But that is the fate of artists. It's the price we pay for our gift."

After Chaim finished he presented one of his signed sketches to Charlie and asked for a signed glossy photograph in return. She over-praised the flattering sketch, thanked Chaim for the enlightening afternoon, and promised to send the headshot as soon as she returned to New York.

On their ride back to camp, a hundred ideas bombarded Charlie's brain as she realized how well Chaim's last story applied to Justin Voyt and his acquisitions. The director and expert was the now deceased Kadinski, the former Assistant Director of the Polish National Museum of Cracow. The necessary finder's fable involved treasures smuggled out of Poland, another country behind the inaccessible Iron Curtain. The artiste, or artistes, as Chaim had bemoaned, were unsung and unknown. Tutankhamen's Pisspot was every piece supplied by Kadinski, minus one – probably the first he sold Voyt. And Voyt was the ideal target: affluent, smug, egotistical, with little knowledge of art and a crazy hunger for prestige and power. Arrogance guaranteed that if a piece was questioned, the Target would deny the challenge and challenger, just as Voyt had done with the fake Manet. Too bad the theory wouldn't convince experts like Armonk and Elton to set aside their biases.

"You enjoyed your day?" Naomi asked as Charlie parked the car near the path leading to camp. "Chaim was helpful?"

"Very helpful. There's a great deal more to manufacturing and passing fake art than I'd ever imagined. Yet you rarely hear about anyone getting arrested, let alone serving time in jail."

Naomi shrugged. "A perfect occupation for a clever scoundrel."

~ **Chapter 24** ~

Their plane sat on the runway in London an hour and a half after boarding due to a malfunctioning emergency light. When they landed in Cairo, Edith's luggage was missing. After two hours of trying to explain the loss to the unsympathetic airline representative it was finally located. Since they arrived well past midnight, the hotel had considered them a no-show and had released their room. By the time they finally entered their newly assigned room the travelers were both exhausted and irritable.

But seven hours of uninterrupted sleep away from pressing realities left Jack and his bride refreshed and ready to embrace new adventures. They ate, leisurely unpacked, read the *Times of London*, and when it was time to leave, found a cab to take them to Cairo University.

Edith seemed surprised and pleased to learn that as many as seventy people would attend the ceremony in her honor: the Deans of the Egyptology and Islamic Archeology Departments, their faculties and some graduate and postgraduate students. The University's President made the actual presentation. A photographer, just as Jack had warned Edith about, took pictures that probably wouldn't be seen outside the academic community. Nevertheless, she was well-turned out, looking feminine, attractive, and tailored in her coral linen suit. Apparently, addressing so many students during her career had well prepared her for public speaking. Her short self-deprecating acceptance speech was delivered in a firm, confident voice. When she concluded by saying that she was inspired by her audience's enthusiasm and that she eagerly looked forward to even greater achievements in the field, the applause was more than simple courtesy demanded.

As Edith had predicted, the presentation was followed by a tea where she was surrounded by eager attendees, who, with two shy exceptions, were all male. All wanted to discuss subjects about which Jack had no expertise and little understanding. He was content to be a bystander and see Edith the center of attention, smiling once again, more relaxed than she had been since they left Argentina.

Just before the event officially ended the Dean of Egyptology informed Jack there would be a small dinner at his home that evening, in Edith's honor. As no such dinner had been previously discussed, Jack surmised that it was a recently made decision. He accepted on Edith's behalf with what he hoped was the formal courtesy the invitation required.

Although the evening ended late, Jack asked if they could share one of the double beds, and was pleased to find Edith receptive to the request and his subsequent advances. For the first time since they left Buenos Aires, they made love with genuine passion.

"Perhaps we should never return to England," he said, half-jokingly, the following morning as they dressed. "We do so much better on vacation."

Edith stopped rummaging through the drawer, dropped her head and bit her lip. Jack instantly regretted the careless quip.

*   *   *

The newlyweds spent the next three days visiting tourist sites within traveling distance from their hotel. They gazed in awe at the Sphinx and the pyramids in Giza. In Memphis, they viewed the old capital and a museum that housed a statue of Ramses the Great. In Saqqara, they gaped at the treasures of Tutankhamen, the boy pharaoh whose premature death had led to his unexpected burial in a quickly assembled tomb – the only royal burial that reached the twentieth century intact. In Cairo, they explored mosques and sites from Egyptian and Roman antiquity.

Edith repeatedly told Jack how delighted she was to finally see, touch, and smell the very wonders that she had visited only in her mind. She bubbled with excitement as she speculated about the social organization needed to create the statuary, obelisks, and colossal monuments, minus modern engineering and equipment. As for Jack, he appreciated the timeless beauty, the lean proportioned bodies, the serene order and balance in the artwork. It was not necessary to know the gods' names to feel their power. Though the young Jesus, the one who attended weddings and drank wine with sinners and preached charity, was very real to him, the earthy deities of the Greeks, Romans, and Egyptians were more appealing than the glum, bloodied Christian saints and martyrs. The colossal stone structures, the pyramids, were as moving as any church. Jack might have shared these heretical ideas with Edith, if he had not cautioned himself to avoid even potentially controversial subjects. For the first time since their plane set down in London, they were having fun.

On their last night in Egypt, they took a twilight sail on the Nile. As they stood on the deck watching the riverbank slip past, the ancient world juxtaposed against the new, they could see sparks from cooking fires and farmers leading their oxen. Off in the distance, stood massive modern buildings illuminated by electricity. The following day they would be in Israel. In four days, they would return to the problems they had left in Nottingham.

"Holidays can't go on forever or they wouldn't be holidays," Edith said, as though reading his thoughts.

"We still have four days."

"I want things to be better when we return home, truly I do."

"So do I." Jack reached for her hand and brought it to his lips to kiss. "A brilliant university professor like you, and a reasonably resourceful fellow like me, should be able to iron out the little snags and bumps that every couple faces."

"I've been thinking, if there are difficulties then we must address them. To start, my flat is far too small for two. I shall have to put aside my childish objections. Jean's house is –"

"Forget Jean's house," Jack said. "Let's start again with everything fresh."

"Can we do that?"

"Why not? We'll sell the house, give up your flat, and buy something that suits both of us."

"A new apartment or a new house?"

"Which would you prefer?"

"A house or a larger flat? I've never considered the possibility of either but the idea is tempting." Edith paused to watch a wind-driven raft that held a docile goat and its owner glide past. "A house! A house, with a garden. Not far from the University. Something simple. Nothing ostentatious or grand. If possible, I'd like one with a sunny porch where we could sit outside on nice days. That would be heavenly."

"You should have an office to yourself," Jack said, recalling her runaway library.

"An office for myself, with a big desk and yards of shelves to hold all my books."

"Absolutely! And a file cabinet."

"If I may be permitted to indulge in a flight of fancy, I'd like a large parlor so that I can invite some of my students round. Just tea and biscuits. Perhaps sandwiches. I've dreamt of doing so many times, but always lacked the space."

"Then that's what you shall have," Jack declared. "A large parlor where we can entertain."

She giggled. "I don't know. You might grow impatient with them. Young people can be monstrously boisterous."

Jack thought about having Edith's students in his home, their home. Eager lads and bright-eyed girls all trying to be heard at once. He not only horribly missed his daughters, he missed the sound of young people's laughter. "Who cares if they make noise? Not me."

"It sounds like a dream – a wonderful impossible dream."

"It's not a dream. We're going to do it."

"The very notion is overwhelming. The house would have to be sold. Emptied first and then sold. All those cartons and packing. We really should keep a few pieces. Some of Jean's things belonged to our parents and grandparents. And then we'd need an estate broker. I'll be busy catching up with my work when we return. I can't see how I'd find the time."

"You wouldn't have to. I promise to handle the entire project," Jack volunteered, his arm around her waist. "From selling the house to packing and unpacking."

"There would be ever so much to do. You'd have to decide what to dispose of and what needs keeping. I suppose an agent would want the shrubs trimmed first. You know all too well that organization is not my strong suit."

Jack wasn't thinking about what had to done. His imagination leapt a dozen steps ahead to a comfortable bed that would easily accommodate two people, and a house with central heat, modern plumbing, and an unending supply of hot water. A recently constructed house, he decided, but not totally devoid of character. He would choose sturdy old furniture that could withstand hard use from Edith's students who would drop by regularly for a free meal and sympathetic ear. "I'll do it all. It'll be worth it."

"We'll be proper newlyweds starting afresh."

"Didn't I tell you that we could iron out the little snags and bumps if we put our heads together?"

"And so you did, my dear." She dipped her head toward his.

Jack lightly kissed her temple. A new more spacious house wasn't the solution to half their problems, but it was a promising start.

~ **Chapter 25** ~

After the children had left for school, as Ruben washed and dried dishes from breakfast, Charlie was allowed the privilege of sweeping the kitchen floor. She had succumbed to the children's pleas and agreed to spend two nights in their home. Naomi was soaking in the bathtub, which Charlie now knew was a favorite indulgence.

While she considered finding and meeting her mother a miracle, getting to know her was an experience quite different from anything she could have anticipated. Reuniting after so many years had made a typical parent-child relationship impossible. Naomi rarely seemed at ease. Her laughs were few and guarded. Charlie's childhood imagination had supplied a television mom, one who was perpetually sunny, loving, gentle and wise. It was only in those odd times, when one of Ruben's children needed or demanded her attention, that she saw the parent Naomi might have been.

As she looked at the kitchen's competing floral designs or the front room's jarring patterns, she realized there was nothing to indicate Naomi's influence. There was no cup with her name on it. No knickknack, nothing with her handwriting, no saved greeting card left on a table. Nothing. Like herself, Naomi was a guest.

When Ruben put the last spoon away, he pointed at the screen door leading to the back of the house. "I took the morning off so I could tell you things you should know."

Charlie followed the composed man out the back door, across the yard, into a tool and machinery shed. He picked up a folded sheet of canvas and continued walking to the ordered grove beyond.

"At what time of year do you pick the fruit?" she asked, careful to watch her footing on the uneven ground.

"I'll tell you as much about my orchards as you have patience to hear, later, after Naomi joins us. For now, we should talk about you and your mother. How is it going with you? Has she talked of her past?"

Charlie had learned Ruben was far too attentive and caring to take offense at his directness. It was as natural to him as his thick weathered boots. But what did she wish to confide? Ruben was the one person who knew Naomi best, so she decided to be absolutely candid. "She does talk with me – never about her past with my father or what happened after they were separated. And she can also go for hours without speaking. I can't tell if she's sad or simply being quiet."

"Naomi thinks bad things that happened to her during the War should be kept buried, so she keeps them inside where they burn a hole in her soul. As her daughter, would you like me to talk to you of these things?"

"I would." She braced herself for what she knew would be painful to hear.

"Tell me what you know." Ruben unfolded the clean canvas for Charlie to sit on while he leaned against a tree.

"After the Nazis invaded France, it was arranged that we leave Paris, all of us, my parents, my sister and me," she began. "At the last minute, the family received word that my mother's brother was wounded. My father desperately wanted her to go with us, but she insisted on staying behind to find and care for him. She was supposed to join us later. Six or seven months later my father received a letter from my grandmother saying that she was dead. He took her death very hard."

Then, in his rough guttural English, Ruben patiently filled in Naomi's horrendous missing years for Charlie.

Charlie wiped away the tears. She had not allowed herself to sob openly because she didn't want to cause Ruben to soften the torturous story.

"Didn't your father ever tell you why he changed your names?" he asked.

"No."

"Naomi thinks . . ."

"I know what she thinks but she's wrong. My father truly believed that she was dead. He was inconsolable – unable to say her name. Naomi knows that. I've told her."

Ruben snapped a thorny twig growing near the tree's base. "Do your best to convince her. It's the anger that burns inside her that won't let her heal."

"What is Haganah? Uri told me she was with the Haganah. When I asked her about it, she said that it was unimportant."

"Unimportant," Ruben snorted. "Hah! I should be so unimportant. The Haganah was the spear that prodded the British who didn't want to live up to their promise to establish a homeland for Jews, because they didn't want to jeopardize their cheap oil. Haganah protects us from fanatic Arabs who are determined to drive us into the sea. Without the Haganah there would be no Israel."

"Naomi was a soldier?"

"You know CIA? KGB? Haganah! Your mother was a spy."

She stared at him.

"Yes! Like Mata Hari. She did whatever she had to do to gain information. If she seems cold or distant at times, be patient with her. She's like a wounded baby porcupine – prickly on the outside, hurt and warm on the inside. I want her to be my wife." Ruben shrugged his Kodiak bear shoulders. "But no. She says she will move away when her project ends. That would be bad for her – bad for all of us."

Charlie nodded. She would be leaving soon and wanted her mother to have people around her who cared for her – a family.

"Make her talk to you. Push her! Make her tell you all that you have a right to know. Break through her silence."

They heard the screen door open and slam close.

"She's coming," Ruben said softly. "We pick limes year round," he continued in a normal voice. "Why limes and not oranges I often ask myself."

"I thought I might find you out here, boring Charlie with talk of your trees."

"Your daughter wanted to learn all she could about citrus trees. She's thinking of buying a tract of land and going into competition with me."

Naomi shook her head. "Other men go on and on about cars, or sports, or politics. Ruben thinks only about his trees and his children. In some ways, I think his trees are his children."

"I asked Ruben why his orchards seem to produce so much fruit."

"Not only more – better, bigger, sweeter," Ruben boasted.

"I made fresh lemonade," Naomi said. "Come back to the house. You can talk there more comfortably."

Forty-five minutes later, as Naomi swung in the hammock and

read a magazine, Charlie learned about citrus production, the Kane children and life in Israel. Ruben explained that if a farmer planted kernels of corn from his best stock the resulting corn would resemble its parent. But plant the seeds from a perfect orange and the trees they generated would predictably produce lesser oranges. With fruit bearing trees, grafting was the only way to guarantee passing on desirable traits. Farmers like himself selected branches from trees that had the juiciest, sweetest, most desirable fruit and grafted them to roots that could best withstand drought, disease, insects and floods. Some rootstocks did better in sandy soil. Some preferred clay. Some lived longer or produced a more reliable yield. There were several methods of grafting, and skilled grafters were valued.

Of Ruben's three children, only Moishe showed true interest in his father's vocation. He was also the most studious and brightest, excelling in all academic subjects. Ruben hoped that Moishe would attend a good university and study agriculture.

Naturally Ruben's children were all expert pickers. It was important to be quick, but speed wasn't everything. A clumsy picker could bruise fruit, as well as destroy the buds that would insure the next season's yield. Yitzhak was the best picker of the three. Moishe was quicker than Rifkah, who worried about injuring her pretty hands.

According to her father, Rifkah was too dreamy to be the student she could be. She did, however, possess a lovely singing voice and was often asked to perform at school functions. When Yitzhak was younger, he showed great aptitude in math and science, but now displayed little interest in continuing his education. Ruben's handsome eldest son talked only of joining the Israeli Air Force and becoming a pilot. This dangerous ambition troubled Ruben greatly.

*   *   *

With only a few days left to her stay, Charlie informed her host family that the hotel in Acre would be the site of a party in their honor. Ruben and Naomi protested, but she, assisted by the children, prevailed.

Saturday afternoon, Charlie sat in the living room, the physical center of the excited preparations, and pretended to read a book. Clothing had to be selected, pressed, and if needed, hemmed.

Moishe volunteered to shine everyone's shoes. Naomi braided ribbons into Rifkah's thick curly hair. An hour before they were to depart, Yitzhak discovered the pants he planned to wear had a small unrepairable tear. A brief spat between him and his father ensued when Ruben asked why hadn't the pants been tried on earlier as requested? The excuse and apology were given and accepted. A telephone call was made. Replacement pants were delivered by Ruben's brother Avram, who stayed long enough to welcome Charlie to Israel and ask if she was enjoying her stay.

*   *   *

Ruben strutted as he led the band of six into the hotel's dining room and assigned seats. As hostess, Charlie was made to take the chair at the head of the table. After the last course was delivered, eaten, and praised, Ruben announced that Rifkah would perform songs she had selected in honor of their American visitor – *My Old Kentucky Home* and *America the Beautiful*. Soon every patron, waiter, and busboy halted to listen to her girlish but unwavering sweet soprano voice. The entire room enthusiastically applauded and cheered at the end of both songs. A flushed but poised Rifkah dipped a polite curtsy to her family and another to the tables behind her.

It was a lovely evening made more festive by many toasts and the children's excited gleaming faces. Charlie noticed that Naomi appeared content but had little to say.

Back at the dig site, she was keenly aware that this night would be her last time alone with her mother. Tomorrow would be spent with Ruben's family and the following day she would return home. With the thinnest sliver of moon and no clouds or artificial light to compete with, the largest amount of stars she had ever seen outside a planetarium lit their path.

"The night sky is magical, isn't it?" she said when they reached Naomi's tent.

"I suppose. It's something I take for granted."

Charlie decided to follow Ruben's advice and push for more information. She would begin with what she thought would be a pleasant memory. "Tell me about yourself as a little girl."

"What is it that you want to know?"

"Anything. Everything."

Naomi sighed deeply and closed her eyes. "We lived in a large house in Paris. I had a younger brother, Philippe, who was my mother's favorite. My mother's name was Hortense and she was very proper. She used a lorgnette that hung on a ribbon and was attached to her dress with a marcasite pin. Her family had lived in France for more than two hundred years. My father was also dignified, but not so stern. Rather handsome, I think, with a precisely clipped mustache and pointed beard. As his favorite, I was allowed to light his pipe and take a sip of wine from his glass." Naomi opened her eyes and sat up. "You must be tired."

Fearing that Naomi wouldn't continue Charlie shook her head vigorously. "You can't understand what this means to me – hearing about our family. It gives me a past." She observed her mother's shoulders had relaxed. "Their name was Strauss. Were they French or German?"

"My father was a naturalized citizen. His family emigrated from Germany to France when he was a boy. Some naturalized Jews changed their names so as not to stand out, but my father was too proud for that."

"What did he do for a living?"

"He bought and sold rare books, the same as his father." Naomi reclined against her pillow.

"Was your brother expected to continue the tradition?" she asked, relieved to see the dialogue would continue.

"Philippe left boarding school to enlist in the French army when he was seventeen. There was no time to ask him what he wanted to do with his life. My father's eyesight became bad. I became my father's assistant. It wasn't just his eyesight. He suffered from terrible headaches that forced him to stay in his room – sometimes for days. The doctors told us he would soon be completely blind."

"You bought and sold rare books?"

"Of course."

"How long have you lived in Israel?"

"I came in nineteen forty-six, a year-and-a-half after the war ended. It was still called Palestine then."

"What made you decide to come?"

"After the war I was taken to a repatriation camp." Naomi watched her face for a reaction before continuing. "Displaced people stayed in camps until Jewish relief organizations could locate their families. Other than you, your sister, and your father, my entire family was dead. After the Nazis captured Paris Alain had taken you and your sister to Philadelphia for safekeeping."

"By that time our names had been changed and we were living in Palm Beach."

"No one knew that. All we knew was that you all had disappeared. They asked me . . . they asked me . . . " Naomi paused to swallow. "They asked me if your father and I had argued. We did argue, your father and me. If he wanted to get away from someone, it was from me."

"Why do you say that?" She reached for her mother's hand. "He would never leave you. He adored you. I don't think he ever loved another woman after you, certainly not my stepmothers. He liked them. He admired them. But he didn't love them."

Naomi silently stared at the tent wall.

"Would you stay in Acre if you could maintain your independence?"

"Maintain my independence." Naomi shrugged. "And how would I do that?"

"Why not deal in rare books, like you did when your father was alive?"

Naomi scowled and remained silent, giving Charlie hope her suggestion was being weighed. "I doubt if there are five people who collect rare books in all of Israel," she said at last. "The country is too young. People here need practical items: trucks, tractors, medical equipment, pipes to carry water."

"What about opening a bookstore?" Charlie countered. "I was looking for a book to read on the plane and I didn't find a single bookstore in Acre."

"I know you'd like to help me, but it won't work. A book here is passed around like a cold. There is no bookstore in Acre because there's no need for one."

"Maybe the town is bigger than you realize. Tourists visit Acre. They buy books. I would give you the money to get started."

"Do you have so much money that you can waste it?" Naomi asked, eyeing her shrewdly.

"I have some money, but Amelia is married to a very rich and generous man. Together, it would be easy for us to do."

"But you haven't told your sister that I'm alive."

"Not yet. I will, as soon as I return. Trust me, she'll be as thrilled to learn that you're alive as I was – as I am. " Charlie pulled back the thin blanket and got into the unforgiving canvas cot.

"You worry about your sister. Despite what you say, you think she may not be happy to hear that her mother is a Jew living in Israel."

"I do worry about Amelia, but not for the reasons you think."

"Do you really know your sister that well? Or your father? Can anyone predict what another person will do? You were viciously attacked. Haven't you accepted there's evil in the world? Or do you believe, if one life is saved, all are saved?"

"If one life is saved, all are saved. What does that mean?"

"Pious Jews believe that saving one life is the same as saving all humanity."

Charlie considered this unique statement of faith. "I think I do believe that. It gives a person hope."

Naomi undressed in semi-darkness and turned off the field lamp. When the darkness engulfed them, she spoke. "How bitter I must sound – bitter and ungrateful. Never think that. That I found you – that you're here beside me – that we can talk – that I can hold your hand in mine – is a miracle for which I give thanks." Her voice had become scratchy and barely audible. "There were times when I thought about ending my life, but now that you . . . I have two daughters again – and a grandson. It's enough for me. More than enough. Can you understand?"

"Yes," Charlie whispered, her throat tight with emotion. "I understand."

~ Chapter 26 ~

To Naomi, it seemed as though she had just walked these corridors and passed the same rows of chairs only yesterday. The days had slipped away like a dream. Her daughter had checked her luggage and was leaving, returning to her life in the United States. Today, there were five people to see her off. Ruben had warned the children that delays were common at the airport due to security. They would have to wait patiently, without complaint, until Charlie's plane took off. Unwilling to miss the excitement, they had chosen to come along.

As the small troupe walked and chatted, Naomi thought her mind was playing a cruel prank. A man riffling through a magazine at a small newspaper and magazine stand reminded her of Alain. He was older than she remembered him. Nearly a quarter of a century had passed since she had last seen him. All the frustration, resentment, and anger returned. Her daughter's insistence that Alain had believed her dead, that he had never stopped loving her, were forgotten in that one moment. It couldn't be Alain, Naomi reassured herself. Alain was dead. Killed in an auto accident. She and Charlie had been talking about him and now she foolishly imagined finding him in an airport. It was a cruel joke played by her over-stimulated psyche.

Just then Rifkah, who had been skipping beside them, fell. The bare corridor echoed with the sound of the child's head striking the hard tile floor. Naomi knelt to examine her. The cut on her upper lip was deep and bloody. Rifkah was doing her best to be brave, but her mouth trembled and her eyes blinked back tears.

"Here! Use my handkerchief," Ruben said.

Charlie, who had also knelt beside the child, handed Naomi Ruben's handkerchief. Naomi took it and patted the angry red lip. Soon the white cloth was red with Rifkah's blood. "We'll take you to the ladies room and put some cold water on it."

"Cold water will make it feel better," Charlie agreed.

Rifkah reached for Naomi's hand.

"I know what will make it feel better," Ruben suggested. "Ice cream! You take Rifkah to the lavatory and stop the bleeding, then we'll all have ice cream."

A few minutes in the lavatory with a cold compress was all that was needed for Rifkah to announce that she was ready for the treat.

"Tell your father to go without us," Charlie told the girl. "We'll join you in a few minutes. I want to talk with Naomi in private."

Naomi wondered, as Rifkah closed the door behind her, what last minute thoughts her daughter wanted to share.

"The children treat you like their mother. Rifkah turned to you when she fell, not her father or her brothers. You."

"I know you mean well, but stop playing matchmaker. I don't want to marry anyone, and if I did, it wouldn't be to an ugly man with hands as rough as limestone, and a beard so wiry you could use his face to grate potatoes. I spend time with Ruben because he's good to me. Because he has a bathtub and hot water. Can't you see that I don't want the responsibility of children?" Naomi had watched her daughter's eyes sadden, but she could do nothing to stop herself. Why had Alain's ghost returned to reignite the fury that she prayed had died with him?

"We should join the others. They'll be wondering what happened to us."

They soon found Ruben and his family eating ice-cream cones. While Ruben and Charlie made small talk, and the children argued about the dimensions and capacity of the plane, Naomi brooded. She had allowed her anger to ruin the bond with her daughter that she so desperately craved.

The plane began boarding. Right before her daughter joined the line of passengers Ruben thoughtfully herded his children away, giving them one last moment of privacy.

"I hate to see you go," Naomi admitted.

"I'm sorry that I interfered," Charlie said, hugging her. "It was wrong of me to assume that I know what's best for you."

"No. No. You meant well. It was I who was wrong. I said things that weren't true. This has been very emotional for me. I hate saying good-bye to you. It's seems as though you just arrived."

Charlie released her and picked up her carryall. "Come and visit us. Amelia and I will be thrilled to send you a ticket."

"Maybe someday," Naomi touched her daughter's arm once more, trying to imprint the love she saw in her eyes forever in her brain.

"You've never been to the United States. Please come and stay with me. We'll do it all. I'll take you anywhere you want to go – Broadway, the Empire State Building, the Statue of Liberty. New York has a hundred museums."

"Someday," Naomi promised. "Someday I'll surprise you."

~ **Chapter 27** ~

Edith and Jack toured as many holy sites in Jerusalem, Tel Aviv, and Galilee as time and their endurance permitted. Their choices were not determined by the popular tourist attractions, as in Egypt, but as Christians who wished to deepen their knowledge of God. In Jerusalem, they visited the Church of the Holy Sepulcher, and walked the last five Stations of the Cross. Edith was able to realize her dream and see the Basilica of the Annunciation, perhaps to stand where Mary had stood when the Archangel Gabriel told her she would bear the Christ Child. They walked the streets of Capernaum, one of the cities where Jesus spoke to his followers, and the Mount of Beatitudes that overlooks the Sea of Galilee, where the Sermon on the Mount was given.

The four days passed quickly and once again they were at the Lod International Airport, dressed for the cooler weather awaiting them in London.

When they learned that a severe thunderstorm expected in Heathrow had delayed their departure for another two hours, Jack looked for something to do in the interim. Edith was satisfied with the book she had brought, but reading bored Jack, so he left his coat on the seat next to hers and went seeking something to divert him. The gift shop provided fifteen minutes or so of distraction. Now thirsty, Jack located a tiny restaurant/bar filled with a group of young American students and their weary chaperones, and nursed a drink until he no longer felt comfortable occupying the sought-after seat.

A shop stocked with newspapers and magazines seemed a place to pass the time. After some perusing, he found two magazines, one in English and one in French, that he hoped would hold his attention until the plane was ready to board. As he approached the counter to pay, he spotted a strangely familiar silhouette approaching. Next to a burly man and a teenage boy, a tall young woman, who had to be his daughter Charlotte, was engaged in conversation. A girl with thick braids and a boy carrying a hatbox skipped in front. Jack stepped back to a protected position, hidden from sight by a display stand. With his heart rebounding like a puck in a frenzied game of ice hockey, his initial reaction at seeing his daughter was absolute delight, until he quickly recalled the consequences of being discovered. There could be no explanation for his being alive or the cruelty he had inflicted. But that didn't lessen the pride he experienced seeing her confident and beautiful. She was dressed in a crisp white belted shirtwaist with the collar up. The pigtail had been replaced by shoulder-length hair the same golden blond it had been when she was a toddler. His daughter had succeeded magnificently, just as he had predicted.

Suddenly, the girl with the thick braids tripped and tumbled forward, her head hitting the bare floor with a chilling, hollow thump. Charlie and a woman who Jack took to be the child's mother, dropped beside her. The child's father and two boys turned to face the downed child. He couldn't hear clearly, except to know the conversation was being conducted in both Hebrew and English. The father urged the child to wipe her face with the handkerchief he proffered. Unwilling to have her accident treated lightly the girl turned to her mother for consolation.

It was at that instant he saw the resemblance between his daughter and the slender woman next to her. Jack's legs buckled beneath him. A searing pain pierced his chest. He fell forward, onto his hands and knees. Nicole! He was hallucinating – asleep and dreaming. He had often dreamed of her. But the hideous burning in his chest told him that this wasn't a dream and he wasn't seeing a ghost. Nicole was alive. Somehow, she had survived. He frantically looked around to see if he had been observed. Had anyone seen him gasping for air and reduced to crawling on the floor? It was unlikely he had not been noticed. The sales clerk rearranging stock on the far side of the shop continued his activities, and people walking by were distracted by the whimpering child with the bloody lip. Jack inched backward into an alcove used for storage and leaned against the wall. He needed time to sort out what he had seen before the terrifying pain that gripped his chest forced him to cry out in pain. He had found Nicole. Surely, this was the miracle he had always prayed for: discovering his beloved wife had somehow triumphed over death, reuniting with their daughters, being a family once again. He tried to steady his breathing, to disregard his burning chest, and think clearly. Look and make sense of what you saw, he ordered his brain. Nicole was with another man. They had children. She had survived unknown horrors and perhaps no longer wanted him. No! Never! his ego insisted. They had argued – silly quarrels like every married couple has – but she would never abandon him or their girls. Fool, idiot, dimwitted jackass, he reviled himself, remembering the past. Nicole had frantically sought them, but he had changed their names. God knows what she went through trying to find them. She had been searching for Alan, Michelle and Margaret Fitzpatrick who lived in Philadelphia, and he had reinvented them. How would she know to look for Jack Morgan and his daughters who wintered in Palm Beach, and when they weren't there, divided the rest of the year between MacLean, Virginia and Manhattan? He had made it impossible for her to locate them. He had robbed Nicole of her daughters and husband, and robbed his daughters of their mother. And why? For Mammon and vanity. He could tell himself that he had wanted to protect them from Jew-killing tyrants. But it was the prospect of an easy life that was too tempting for a despicable lazy coward like himself. Of all his sins, and they were manifold, this had to be his worst. "Heavenly Father, let me die now in the Holy Land. Let this be the fatal heart attack that I deserve. Take me before I can harm another soul." He was still weak, too weak to do anything but cower in a storage area, but God refused to hear his plea. The wracking pain in his chest was subsiding.

Jack wiped the sweat from his brow, desperate to understand the events and fallout of the last twenty-two years. Nicole had made a new life for herself here in Israel. She had a husband and three children. Somehow, mother and daughter had found one another. Mother and daughters. The girls were inseparable. Amelia knew her mother was alive as well.

But the children, with their dark hair and coarse features, looked nothing like delicate fair Nicole, Jack reasoned. What if the man wasn't Nicole's husband, merely a friend who had offered to take Charlie to the airport? Surely, the children were his. What then? Was Jack allowing this heaven-sent opportunity to reunite his family slip away without even attempting to rectify the past? Could he convince his wife and daughters to forgive him – to set aside their justifiable anger? For once, he would tell no self-serving lies. He would confess everything. He would reveal the unvarnished truth: how he changed their identities, the games he had invented until his young daughters' new names were the only ones they remembered. He would relate the scheme he devised to convince the world that he had killed himself, as well as the reason. Let them know that he was being blackmailed for his part in a fraud to pass forged paintings as masterpieces. He would make no excuses and humbly beg their mercy. Charlie and Amelia would forgive him once they knew his sole motive was to protect them. The three women whom he adored, whom he loved more than life itself, would understand and forgive him. Jack rose to his feet and readjusted his jacket.

"There you are," Edith said, appearing out of nowhere and startling him. Jack had almost forgotten her. "I've been looking everywhere for you," she continued. "For a moment I feared that you had deserted me. You're not hiding from me so soon after making me a bride, are you?"

Jack tried his most disarming smile. "I was a bit lightheaded and I was waiting for it to pass. And now it has. How much more time do we have before our flight."

"Never mind! You look frightful. You're pale as a ghost. Come and sit down. Can I get you something?"

"Not here." Still weak, he briskly led Edith back to their gate, every second wondering if they would encounter Charlie or Naomi coming from the other direction, and at the same time, struggling not to appear anxious. When they reached two seats facing a window, their backs to people passing by, the burning pain in his chest had resumed. And there was no hiding it.

"Let me fetch assistance," Edith pleaded. "All the color has left your face and you're having difficulty breathing."

"Stay with me. I'll be fine," he said with a forced smile. "See, don't I look better?"

She checked the temperature of his brow with her wrist, looking unconvinced. "We'll give it a minute and if you don't improve I'm going for a physician."

Gradually the pain subsided. "You see, it was nothing, just indigestion."

"Balderdash! Something happened that alarmed you," she said. "Something or someone you saw. You needn't bother lying. Did this have anything to do with the reason you left the States?"

"I told you why I left the States. My wife died of cancer and – "

"Poppycock! I'm not going to be cross with you for your past fibs. I never believed you left the States because your wife died. A man doesn't move halfway round the world, to a country where he doesn't know a soul, because his wife died. You've done something you'd like to forget. Just tell me if the authorities are looking for you. And please, do be truthful. I can't help you if you lie. Tell me the worst and we'll deal with it."

Jack was shocked. Was he so transparent or was Edith so expert at reading him? "The authorities are not looking for me. You have my word."

"Well, that's a relief, isn't it?" she said, patting his hand. "Then you've seen someone from your past, someone you've wronged. I know you well enough to know that you couldn't have done anything deliberately cruel or truly evil."

"Thank you."

"But you've done something that you'd rather not face. Go on," she urged. "Take a deep breath. You've seen someone from your past. Someone you've wronged."

"Yes."

"Would a generous check make it right?"

"No." Jack shook his head. He wanted Nicole and their daughters returned to him. He wanted the time together they had missed. It was selfish, but that's what he wanted.

"An anonymous exceedingly generous check?"

"Not even an anonymous exceedingly generous check," he assured her.

"I suppose a letter of sincere apology with a promise to reform would be useless."

"Useless."

"Oh, my," she said, sighing and tapping her purse with her polished fingernail. "And you were considering scampering away. My, my! Could you tell me if it was to please the person you hurt, or to relieve your guilt?"

"May I have a moment to answer that question. I really want to be truthful and it's not easy."

"You want to be truthful? What a novel idea. Take as long as you need." She searched the contents of her purse until she found a mirror and lipstick and carefully began repairing her makeup between phrases. "Do remember though – as you weigh your conscience – my needs as well. You've stripped me of my invisibility. You've thrust me into a strange new world – one that I'm not yet prepared to navigate – and you've made it impossible to return to the woman I was. What's more, every friend and colleague has been informed that the dried-up old-maid has wed." Her voice broke here. "I shall look the fool if I return alone."

He hung his head in anguish.

"No! That's not what I wish to say at all." She put down her mirror, faced him, and placed her hand on his thigh. "This is what I want to say. Dear Jack, I need you. You've awakened a part of me that I couldn't bear to be dormant again. So I'm asking this favor. If you can't stay with me forever, then give me a year. One year. A mere three hundred and sixty-five days."

"That's what you want?"

"One year to right myself. After that, I won't say a word in protest if you still wish to leave. During that time, buy whatever home for us that suits you. There's no reason for us to be crammed into my tiny little flat for an entire year."

Jack stared at the educated, attractive, fiendishly clever woman he had selfishly manipulated to avoid destitution. How extraordinary that she should care so deeply for him. A year. A year was so little to ask after the pain he had caused. He could locate Charlie and then Nicole again. He lifted Edith's hand and brought it to his lips for a soft kiss.

"Flight 418 will begin boarding in five minutes," a woman's electrically aided voice announced. "Please note, the gate has been changed. All passengers for the flight to London must go immediately to Gate 9."

They looked around and laughed. Except for the two of them, the seating area was devoid of passengers. The voice they had heard belonged to a flight attendant standing next to a sign that read Gate 9.

"Come, dear. Let's be first on line," Jack said, rising and taking Edith's hand.

Edith's eyes glistened as she gathered her belongings. "Thank you, Jack."

~ **Chapter 28** ~

Charlie hadn't returned the empty suitcases to the upper shelf of the hall closet when the phone rang.

"You must've just gotten home," Ken said over a din of background noise. "I tried you two hours ago, but your answering machine was full."

"Haven't fully unpacked. Just got back very late last night. What about Brigitta – the woman who gave a new twist to the word ambitious?" she asked, anxious to learn the result of her airport-bound enlightenment. "Any progress?"

"Look, it's too crazy to talk here. You in the mood for Italian food or are you too tired? My shift just ended. I could pick you up."

"I adore Italian food. When should I expect you?"

"Be downstairs in thirty minutes."

With a half-hour to wait and a full answering machine, Charlie decided to listen to her messages. They ranged in importance from meaningless to astounding. There were several hang-ups from unknown dialers, one message from the building administrator apologizing for the erratic fire alarm systems that had gone off twice during the night. The system had been repaired and tenants could anticipate no further problems. Fourteen messages from business and personal friends – none urgent. Helena Ivanavich had called three times: the first to say that James Reynold Harrison was trying to reach Charlie Morgan, the second saying newspapers were making broad hints about the validity of a famous art collection, followed by another saying her name was connected to investigating Voyt's collection. Which was very disturbing. The final message was from Raul. They needed to talk. Please call. But best of all were several from friends saying that Brigitta Schwimmer, the Perfecta spokeswoman, had been arrested for attacking a fellow model in a subway station.

She was still scribbling reminder notes when the intercom beeped. It was the concierge informing her that Ken was parked in front and waiting. There wasn't time to speculate about the events that had taken place in her absence.

"It's great to see you," she said, thinking to herself when she saw Ken's reassuring handsome face of the unfairness of his beer/Champagne theory. Why were there dozens of gothic novels with fairytale endings for princes and impoverished governesses, and not one with a romance between a princess and her chauffeur? Didn't chemistry count for something? They had had one memorable sizzling kiss, and if Ken had pressed . . . Had he asked to stay that night . . . But Ken hadn't pressed or asked to stay.

"Great to see you. You're tan. Being outdoors beats being cooped up in a hospital room, doesn't it?"

She pushed a stray hair behind her ear. "Where are we going?"

"I'm going to take you to eat in a favorite place of mine. Not much atmosphere but the food's terrific. You've got to make the trip to Brooklyn for the best Italian food."

"Are you sure you want to put Brooklyn up against Little Italy?"

"Okay, but the parking in Brooklyn beats Mulberry Street. Don't you want to hear what happened when you were gone? Thanks to you we got Brigitta."

"So I've heard. I need details. Who handled it? Are you going to get credit? Did she deny everything?"

"You're going to hear it all. Give me a chance." Stuck behind an unloading van Ken cut off a cabdriver who gave him a New York wave with a middle finger. "The first thing I had to do was smooth things with Marrone and Kowalski. And they were okay with my working with them. Thanks to you, we had the motive. What we needed was opportunity, so I took myself to her agency. And what do you know? Brigitta had asked not to be booked that afternoon – she said that she had a toothache and it was the only time her dentist could see her. On a hunch, I called a buddy at the lab and asked him to check the coat and beard for makeup."

"Makeup?"

"Right! And makeup came up positive on both the coat and beard," Ken continued. "I was convinced that we had the right person, but it might not be enough for a jury. So I go to her house and ask her to come down to the station with me to clear up some things. I tell her, as a friend of yours, she would naturally want to help in any way she could. And she buys it."

"You flirted with her, didn't you?"

"Maybe. Or maybe I was extra polite. Anyway, when I get her to the station, I start off by telling her that we had to wait until Kowalski and Marrone arrive. They'll be there in a few minutes. I get her a soda and we start to talk – and okay, I come on to her a little, just to make her relax. I asked her if she remembers December 9th, and her toothache, and her dentist's appointment. I figured I'd give her enough rope to hang herself. And she falls right into the trap because she comes up with the dentist's name. By this time, Kowalski arrived, so I left her with him while I check with the dentist. Now she tries coming on to Kowalski. He lets her think he's falling for the act. When I get back, I tell her the dentist's office said that hadn't been there in a year. Cool as a cucumber, she comes up with another story. She was confused about the day. That's when I lose the smile and tell her that we have samples of hair and makeup from the beard and coat. And we know all about the Perfecta contract, and the talk was that you had the best odds of getting it. I lower my voice and say, 'Listen Brigitta, this is your last chance to come clean. Maybe you didn't plan to shove Charlie off the platform. You only wanted to keep her from landing the Perfecta contract. A couple whacks with an umbrella is one thing. Premeditated murder is another. If the fall off the subway platform wasn't planned, the DA can go easy. But if we don't get a confession, and it turns out the hair and makeup samples match yours, you can forget any chance of leniency.'"

"Can hair and makeup be used as evidence in court?" Charlie asked.

"Only to eliminate a suspect. Science isn't that good yet. But Miss Brigitta doesn't know that. She's not that smart. Which is why she decides to cut a deal. If you can believe her story, and I got to think it's true, her intention was to put you out of commission for a while, maybe slash your face or break a couple of bones. But you were too quick for her. You fell down and covered your head. She claims that she never intended to have you go over the side. That was an accident."

"So you got your confession. Just like that."

"Just like that? You make it sound easy. It took five hours of interrogation praying she doesn't clam up and ask to see a lawyer, and how many months of working on this case?" Ken expertly backed the car into a space that allowed no more than twelve inches between cars.

"If it wasn't for the graffiti, I never would've suspected Brigitta."

"We're here."

Here was a tiny restaurant – small in size, but rich in imagery. The walls featured unschooled but enthusiastic murals. Charlie and Ken were shown to a table abutting the Coliseum and facing a trellised vineyard. An empty bottle of Chianti containing the unlit stub of a candle, and the wax remains of a thousand candles before, graced the table. But the aroma wafting from the kitchen was an intoxicating mix of oregano, garlic, tomatoes, and olive oil.

"It smells delicious." Charlie picked up her menu. "I'm starved."

"What did I tell you?"

She ordered the lasagna and Ken ordered chicken parmesan.

"Are you still dating Toni? Do you like her? Do you think she likes you?"

"Yeah, we're still going out." Ken laughed. And not a polite well-mannered chuckle. A throaty sensual laugh that dashed any ideas she might have been entertaining.

"And that's all you're going to tell your old PT buddy?" she asked, curious to hear more.

"She's nice and very pretty. And fun. She likes when I talk about the job. What I'm thinking about when I'm chasing a guy who could turn on me. Going after drug dealers and pimps."

"You're the man who wants a house, a station wagon, kids, and a dog. Besides liking danger and the obvious physical attraction, what about the important things?'

"Yeah, we talked about that – talked about it on our first date. Toni's not some dumb party-girl. She's a beautician with her own shop."

"Sounds promising."

"One thing though, she's got a mouth like a truck driver. I'm not used to women talking like that. You may have noticed; I don't curse much or take the Lord's name in vain. A lot of cops curse, but then they're guys, and Toni's a woman. " He took a piece of crusty garlic bread from the basket.

"Perhaps you can discuss it with her. Tell her that you like her, but her language makes you uncomfortable."

"Yeah, maybe."

Their waitress appeared with their dishes. Charlie's lasagna was filled with the freshest ricotta, smothered with delicate mozzarella, and dripping with scrumptious marinara sauce.

"And you saw your mother. It must've been emotional meeting her, after thinking she was dead for so many years."

"It was. Very emotional."

As they ate lunch, Charlie related the high points of her trip: meeting Ruben and his children, visiting tourist sites, the orchards, the tenacity of Israelis, and of course, getting to know her mother. She carefully omitted the darker aspects of Naomi's personality.

"Any chance of you and Raul getting back together?" Ken asked when they were back in his car and a block from her home. "I was hoping to hear you patched things up."

"I don't think so."

"Back in the hospital, he seemed awfully worried about you for a guy who isn't interested. And when he saw you weren't paying attention, those were more than good buddy looks I saw."

"And I hope you can work things out with Toni. About her language," She said to change the subject when Ken stopped his car in front of the entrance to her building. Raul was a subject she didn't want to discuss.

"I shouldn't have mentioned it." Ken grinned his embarrassed lopsided grin. "Because, the way she talks – well, it kind of gets me hot, if you know what I mean."

As it turned out, she knew exactly what he meant.

Charlie walked through the lobby and pressed the elevator button. Now that traveling the streets of New York was finally safe, she was too tired to go anywhere but bed. The suitcases, and the mail and phone calls would have to wait until tomorrow.

* * *

Sunday morning Charlie woke up at 8:55 refreshed and eager to take on life, regardless of what problems awaited her. After preparing a large pot of coffee, she dialed her sister and started her story where it had begun for her – meeting Howard Levine.

"Are you going to be all right?" she asked Amelia. Her own cheeks and chin were wet with tears. It was impossible to say whether her sister was taking it well or not. Amelia was incredibly adept at concealing her feelings. "Would you like me to stop now?"

"I'm fine, dear. It's not as though you're telling me that something tragic happened. Mother is alive. It's wonderful. Please go on. Was she terribly upset when you told her that Daddy was no longer with us?"

"I think she was surprised rather than shocked. But I can't be certain. She's sort of private and doesn't talk much."

"Has she aged well?"

"I think she looks remarkable, particularly considering all she's been through." Charlie used a tissue to blot her face dry.

"You didn't tell her the circumstances of Daddy's death, did you?"

"I saw no reason to keep it from her."

"I'm sorry to have to say this, but it surprises me that you chose to share that. A little white lie would've been kinder."

"I thought Mother deserved to know."

"Never mind! What's done is done."

"I was afraid to tell you anything before checking it out myself, darling. It could have been a cruel hoax," Charlie added. It was so difficult trying to guess what Amelia was really thinking.

"And as always, you showed tremendous strength."

"Did I remember to tell you that I suggested to Naomi that she open a bookshop? Her father, our grandfather, dealt in rare books, and she became his assistant after she'd married Daddy. I desperately want to see Mother happy. I'd like to see her have a home and people to care about her. But she's far too independent to be totally reliant on a man. Owning a bookshop would give her choices."

"So you're hoping that she'll stay where she is and marry the farmer?"

"I suppose I am. I invited her to visit, but I have no idea if or when that will take place. Her project's coming to an end. I know she's conflicted about Ruben and his children. You can call her or write, or fly out to meet her if you decide you don't wish to wait."

"I will definitely write – a nice note telling her how thrilled we are that she's alive and that you've met her."

"I can understand you not wanting to travel right now, with Teddy so little and so dependent on you. But why not call her? I know she would love to hear from you."

"I won't be rushed, Charlie. I'll handle this in my own way."

"You know I wouldn't . . ."

"Oh Sweetheart, now I've said the wrong thing. Try to be patient with me. I'm not as strong as you. You can get thrown from a subway platform in front of an oncoming train, spend two months in the hospital, and get on a plane to meet the mother we thought was dead, while I have difficultly dealing with the servants."

Charlie replaced the phone, happy and relieved that her sister had heard and absorbed the shocking news without incident. She celebrated by rescuing an English muffin from freezer burn by toasting it, and smothering it with butter and raspberry jam before devouring it.

Two important phone messages remained: Helena Ivanavich's and Raul's. Charlie reread the hastily scribbled note she had written to herself the day before. *Helena: newspapers –Voyt collection -- doubt validity -- James Reynold Harrison – wants to talk. Raul: call – sounds important.* She was troubled by the newspaper articles, but it was Sunday and the gallery would be closed. James Reynold Harrison, heir to California gold mines and Hollywood producer, would have to wait as well. Which left Raul, who might have called about the unwanted and potentially dangerous publicity. She dialed his number, but there was no answer.

Charlie decided to sort the large wicker basket filled with two weeks of mail the concierge had given her the day before. She was left with five piles: bills, junk mail, magazines, bank statements, and a fat manila envelope addressed to her in Raul's handwriting. There were also four envelopes from the Multiple Sclerosis Society that still sent Raul's mail to this address. She put a rubber band around the charity's mailings. She would forward them to him. How typical of Raul, now that he was successful, to become involved with a particular charity.

Charlie tore the manila envelope open. Inside was a stack of cut-out newspaper photographs with attached articles, and a two line note.

Welcome home. Hope everything was great. Look these over, but don't worry! Call me.

Raul

The articles contained grainy pictures of Brigitta after she was arrested, the Perfecta tennis ads – the original and the one embellished with graffiti – as well as some of Charlie taken before the attack. The press had left no sensational detail unexplored: from Brigitta's past glories as an Olympic skier, to details of her contract with Perfecta. Charlie was variously described as: *former model,*

model turned art-expert, and *viciously attacked Perfecta candidate.* Only one clipping wasn't about the attack – a particularly unflattering photo of Justin Voyt. No article accompanied it, only a cryptic caption beneath – *Why is this man's fortune under investigation?*

Don't worry! Raul's note read. Charlie worried. Somehow, news of the reevaluation had leaked. James Elton and Susan Armonk, experts that she had personally chosen, believed the collection was exactly what it was purported to be. Brigitta had confessed. Justin Voyt had nothing to do with her attack. Yet his integrity was being publicly questioned and she was the cause. Tomorrow, she would humbly apologize to Elton and Armonk, end the appraisal, and pray that Justin Voyt wouldn't sue her.

Despite it all, a pesty nagging feeling kept insisting that she'd been right. Chaim's tale of directors, targets, finder's fables, artistes and experts fit so perfectly.

*   *   *

Charlie was packing her books in the conference room the bank had provided, preparing to leave for the last time, when Susan Armonk and James Elton arrived.

"We must talk," Elton said with a grave face, when he reached her, Armonk by his side.

"Indeed, we must." Charlie rose, slapped the dust from her hands, and took a deep breath.

"We're wondering if you would share with us how you came to your remarkable conclusions," Elton said, in a pleasant conciliatory voice.

"Besides the accompanying documentation, what made you so certain we were dealing with forgeries?" Elton asked.

Were they mocking her? Charlie wondered. "I'm afraid I don't understand."

"The laboratory reports agree with your analysis," Elton explained. "The paint used wasn't produced until modern times. There are minor disparities, but none that fly in the face of your findings. So we're asking you, how did you know? Was it only the documentation?"

"We are respectfully asking you, as colleagues," Armonk added.

"Why don't we sit down?" Charlie suggested.

Elton produced a chair. "I see you're surprised. No more

surprised than we were. You have to admit, those were damn good forgeries. Did you have some inside knowledge? Were you advised in advance what to look for?"

"I didn't have inside knowledge and no one advised me," Charlie said when they were all seated.

"What is it that you see that others have missed?" Armonk asked, with no trace of rancor.

"I really can't explain it. Something looks wrong. It's more instinct than educated analysis."

"A bachelor's degree in art history and self taught." James Elton turned to Susan Armonk. "You hear about the gift but you never believe it."

"It's all well and good for us to agree," Armonk said, his voice and manner kinder. "I don't know if you're aware, but to declare the vast majority of a noted collection forgeries, even with science to support us, is a tremendous risk – not as much for you, because of your age and prior inexperience, but to us."

"If it were only a matter of a piece or two," Elton went on. "Collectors don't like to be made to look foolish. Justin Voyt will have a legion of experts and laboratories in his employ, who will do everything they can to undermine our findings and destroy our reputations."

"We have more to fear than injuring Justin Voyt's pride," Charlie pointed out to the ivory-tower academicians, who had no inkling of the depth of Voyt's dependence on their evaluation. "If we declare the collection's value to be radically less than previously assessed, Berkley Banking can topple the Voyt empire."

"That's impossible. Justin Voyt is an enormously wealthy man. As an only child he inherited his father's entire fortune," Elton protested.

Charlie nodded. "True, but he lives on a grand scale and his holdings are mortgaged to the hilt. If the bank calls in his notes, Justin Voyt will have to sell holding after holding until he can satisfy his creditors."

"Could Voyt be sent to jail?" Armonk questioned, her eyes filled with awe.

Charlie shrugged. "Only if it can be proved that he was complicit in the deception."

"How could that be proven, Susan?" Elton asked his colleague.

"What we have to fear is Justin Voyt's fury. The rich and powerful devour people like us as bedtime snacks."

"What we have is a moral and ethical dilemma," Charlie reminded them. "Do we look for a safe exit or do we act on principle? Maybe you need time to give it some thought."

"I don't need time," Armonk said, touching Elton's forearm. "Dammit, James, we didn't go into this field to make bargains with the devil. I say, we go conservative but truthful – back it up with as much evidence as we can muster, present a united front and stick to our guns."

"I'm in. Ethics, it is," Elton agreed.

Charlie's shoulders sagged with relief. Sixty minutes earlier, she had been prepared to beg forgiveness. Now she had the confidence of respected professionals. "Let's get to work."

"And this time we want to hear every little thought that goes through your brain," Elton ordered.

Four days later their compiled report was complete. Late Friday afternoon, Charlie left it with Robert Makepeace's private secretary.

~ **Chapter 29** ~

The day after they returned to Nottingham, grateful for Edith's generous acceptance of his lack of explanation of his ignoble past, Jack was determined to fulfill his promise to her. After he left, it would be a consoling sanctuary. And in the year remaining before then, they would have a decent place to live. So while Edith graded her students' exams, lectured and wrote papers on obscure subjects, he studied newspaper ads, compared properties, met with Edith's solicitor, and threw himself into the grubby task of sorting Jean's belongings into items for the sale, trash or to retain.

Meeting with Edith's conservative solicitor they agreed upon an amount that Jean could well afford, to cover the cost of a new home, moving and closing fees, improvements and decoration. In September, Jack located a residence that he felt provided basic necessities and a bit more. Bricked on all sides, the modest two-story home had the large screened porch and sunny garden behind that Edith had requested. Like Jean's home, it had been built pre-war. Unlike hers, the original roof, kitchen, baths and heating system had been updated and/or replaced.

As eager as they both were to escape Edith's cramped flat, he convinced her to wait until the repairs were completed to see it.

Under his direction, carpenters, gardeners, electricians, floor refinishers and painters simultaneously attacked the project. Jack had the screened back porch enclosed so that it could be used in inclement weather, or with its many louvered windows open, when it was pleasant. Now a sunroom, it held an assortment of wicker furniture, all painted a unifying white, and folded colorful quilts that could be used to ward off the perpetual English chill. Jack had never concerned himself with furnishing a home before – that being the domain of previous wives and their arrogant decorators. Nevertheless, combining craftsmanship with proportion and color – fundamental to any good painting – didn't seem difficult for a man with an appreciation of luxury. The real challenge was making intelligent use of limited means. For that, he mixed the best of Edith and Jean's belongings with rescued neglected treasures purchased at the local flea market.

Since he couldn't imagine his absentminded wife doing any formal entertaining, and the kitchen held a dining table that seated four and could hold six if necessary, he combined the former dining room and parlor into one large area that now held an upright piano, loveseats, floor lamps, small square tables and upholstered chairs that could be easily rearranged as needed.

In November, to his amazement, when the project was completed Jack was excited to display the results of his efforts.

"It's lovely, absolutely lovely, Jack. All that I ever dreamed of and more," Edith whispered, her eyes glistening with approval as she walked from the kitchen to the sunroom, and then to the front parlor.

"I tried to make it cozy and unpretentious," he said, delighted. "You said that you wanted a home where you could invite your students. Well, as you can see, there's nothing precious just waiting to get knocked over and broken. No wall-to-wall carpet. Not with these fine solid wood floors. If there are spills, rugs can be picked up and cleaned. As for the furniture, I think it's practical and inviting. We don't need a fancy dining room that will never get used."

"It's perfect. I can easily envision twenty or more students and faculty members spread out and having a jolly good time. I can't decide whom I wish to invite first."

He led her to the stairs. "I want to show you your new office."

Edith entered. "Is this all for me?" she asked, laughing at finding the floor-to-ceiling shelves he had had built, filled with her books and mementos, including her plaque from the Egyptian government. In the center of the room was her sister's refinished walnut desk and an oak swivel chair. She slowly walked around the room, running her fingers over surfaces, opening and closing drawers, as if to convince herself they were real.

"Don't you want to see our new bedroom?" he asked, impatient to show her more.

"Yes, of course. I know that our tiny bed has been frightful."

"Only when it's time to actually sleep in it," Jack teased, knowing all reference to their lovemaking outside their bedroom embarrassed her. "I'm sure you'll have to admit other times it can be very nice."

"Rascal!"

"Wanton Jezebel!" he teased, opening the door to their

bedroom. It was painted a cheery yellow and the queen-sized, poster bed was topped, not with a spread, but a lush feather comforter and multiple pillows.

"My word! I can't believe you did this. Where did you find such splendid furniture?"

Jack was particularly pleased with the dressers and a pair of nightstands he had purchased: all carved mahogany and in excellent condition, roughly the same period and style – now freshly oiled. "Found them at the street market. Best of the last century. Bought them for a song. Nowadays people turn up their noses at Victorian, but they're built to last and beautifully made. Not like the over-priced flimsy trash that's suddenly fashionable today."

The third and last room on the second floor was a guest room, largely comprised of Jean's bedroom furniture with a new box-spring and mattress.

"Everything is perfect. I couldn't ask for more."

"I'm so glad you like it."

"You can be terribly thoughtful – thoughtful and incredibly dear." She presented her lips to be kissed.

And equally hurtful, Jack thought.

*   *   *

"I'm ever so pleased to say that you, and your renovations of this house, our little paradise, has replaced your renovation of me as the preferred topic of conversation at campus functions," Edith said one late afternoon in January, as they sat in the sunroom and watched the sun go down.

"Really?" Jack asked, pretending to be surprised.

"My word, yes! I've heard ever so many compliments on it."

"For a country that boasts 'the sun never sets on the British empire' the people I meet, in contrast to their aristocracy, who adore ostentation, seem to take pride in being remarkably drab."

"My students and colleagues seem to feel that you're a magician."

"No magic involved, Dearest. I started with excellent foundations."

"But now I fear you'll be bored."

"I've been keeping busy, maybe not as busy as before," Jack admitted, suspicious. He looked forward to Wednesdays with Edith's lively students. Even her staid colleagues could be occasionally humorous or enlightening. But that was only one day a week. And he had toured virtually every museum worth exploring within easy traveling distance.

"Precisely. Which is why I thought my little idea might appeal to you. I was wondering if you would consider opening a small art gallery."

"A gallery? And I would run it?" he asked, attempting to hide his excitement.

"You could import works from your talented artist friends in Buenos Aires," she said, smiling back at him. "It would be entirely yours."

"Mine?"

"Naturally! What do I know about art? You would select the pieces, price them, and handle sales and the display."

"It sounds like a serious enterprise. Very serious."

"An art gallery isn't like an apothecary or a grocer. The shop wouldn't have to be open daily – perhaps Fridays and weekends. That should be enough, don't you think?"

"I suppose." And at least two evenings to accommodate the schedules of over-zealous business types and rich sportsmen, he thought. Daylight attracted browsers. The vast majority of sales took place at night, by people in chic evening clothes drinking wine, surreptitiously studying fashionable trendsetters or pretending not to enjoy being observed. Not a bad way to spend one's time and energy. He had worked in a gallery before, many years ago, in Paris, primarily charged with crating and shipping artwork or researching provenances. Never trusted to handle important clients or select artwork or arrange exhibitions. The gallery could have been twice as profitable if the stodgy owner had been willing to promote a few promising newcomers he had recommended, who later achieved great success.

. "There's no guarantee that it would succeed," he warned. "In fact, chances are it would lose money the first year."

"As I understand, artists don't receive payment unless and until their works sell."

True. Apparently, Edith had given her *little idea* serious consideration. "But landlords demand payment. Did you have a store or area in mind?"

"Me?" she scoffed. "Dearest Jack, I have no head for business. It was you who found this lovely home for us and negotiated a fair price. You must choose the location. As for the clerical and manual labor," she continued, "it occurred to me that you could employ a student – some bright young chap who could use a few extra pounds."

That would lighten the burden of tiresome paperwork, as well as lifting heavy statuary and hanging large paintings. "That *bright young chap* would have to be reasonably strong and he wouldn't have to be a student. There have to be loads of talented starving artists in and around this place. In exchange for a few days work a week, I could give him the chance to properly display his work – maybe an entire show once or twice a year."

"How lovely that would be. Imagine yourself launching a brilliant career."

"There could be some money to be made."

"I suppose that would be nice."

"Not at first, of course."

"Naturally. But perhaps, given time, a little profit might be seen."

Jack spent the rest of the evening working out details in his head: contacting his old friends in Buenos Aires, selecting pieces from photographs via the mail, transporting items, choosing the gallery's location, laying it out. Suddenly, he realized Edith's devious unstated goal. Now, innocently propped up in bed reading – unaided by spectacles, looking very attractive in the pale blue satin nightgown he had selected to complement her radiant auburn hair – good Lord, she was clever. The one year she had begged for and he had agreed to, had never been mentioned. Clever and daring. Without knowing his reasons for leaving, without knowing the costs involved in renting retail space and setting up a gallery, she was willing to risk it. Using an art gallery as bait, she was gambling on enticing him to stay with her. Clever, daring and in love with him.

Jack opened the drawer that held his socks instead of the pajamas he sought and closed it. Was he chasing a dream that would create havoc and pain? Nicole had a family. There was no mistaking the hulking man's possessive body language or the three children that had looked to her for direction. In addition to Edith, how many people would he hurt with his actions? By now, his daughters and Nicole had found peace. Surely Charlie had convinced Nicole that he hadn't abandoned her, that he'd never stopped loving her. He had unintentionally caused her grief. Unintentionally stolen more than two decades of life with him and their daughters. But if he didn't interfere, she would have the rest of her life with her new family, in addition to Charlotte and Amelia and their children. She would have all that. And he wouldn't. He would never again experience the pride in his daughters' accomplishments, or share their disappointments or gaze into a grandchild's face or hear the delighted squeals and laughter. It was a decision he had made before to protect them – painful but right.

But he would have Edith, the only woman who recognized his every shameful despicable flaw and still adored him. He would have a brilliant, fine-looking, passionate wife and his precious memories of Nicole and their beautiful daughters – and Wednesday afternoons with Edith's students and colleagues, not to mention his very own art gallery. It was more than a miserable sinner like himself deserved. Far more!

"Can't find something, dear?" Edith asked when Jack slammed the third drawer that didn't contain what he sought shut.

"What man needs pajamas if he has a loving wife to keep him warm?" Jack slipped under the down comforter and sidled up to Edith's inviting body.

"You'll miss them in the morning when you have to leave the bed and it's chilly," she cautioned.

"Edith, look at me." He waited until her eyes met his so that she could see his sincerity. "I will never leave you. Not next June. Not ever. You'll have to throw me out bodily if you want to be rid of me."

"Truly, Jack?"

"Yes, Dearest Girl, truly."

~ **Chapter 30** ~

Charlie and Raul sat in Robert Makepeace's outer office – this time at the CEO's request. She had spent weeks in the building's basement examining Voyt's collection and this would only be the second time she would actually talk with Makepeace. She was very much aware that had Brigitta already been arrested, or even if she had been just a suspect, there would've been no reason for a first meeting. She and Raul had coerced the bank into paying for a costly reappraisal for no reason, and then presented the bank with a report saying they had a vault filled with forgeries. She tried to guess Makepeace's response as well as Raul's mood. Charlie looked for familiar signs in Raul: the anticipatory set of his shoulders, the confident half concealed smile, the tilt of his head. They were present, but subdued. He used to revel in this sort of challenge.

"Mr. Makepeace can see you now," his secretary informed them.

"Miss Morgan, Mr. Francesco, good to see you again," Makepeace said as he led them to the tufted leather couch and matching chairs. "Would you like some coffee or tea?"

Raul and Charlie declined the offer.

"Now that the person responsible for Miss Morgan's attack has been arrested," Raul said, "I'm sure you can see why it was so difficult for the police to determine her identity. Every witness described a man. Our suggestion for a reappraisal was driven by well-founded concern for Miss Morgan's safety."

Makepeace smiled. "To say it was an unexpected turn of events is an understatement. Whether you're at a coffee shop or the Four Seasons, it's all people are talking about."

Raul returned the smile. "You must've been equally surprised to learn Mr. Voyt's collection is largely composed of forgeries."

Makepeace nodded.

"The media has been hinting at fraud." Raul leaned back in his chair. "You have my word, the information was not leaked by me, Miss Morgan, or her team."

"I was always confident of that," Makepeace assured them. "You have fine reputations."

"Now, I assume Berkeley will come to a private agreement with Mr. Voyt," Raul suggested. "Something that will satisfy both parties."

"I see you understand the subtleties of finance, Mr. Francesco," Makepeace said, addressing first Raul and then Charlie. "Those discussions began over the weekend, and let me assure you, when the dust settles the bank will not be the injured party."

"Then we shouldn't be taking up any more of your time," Raul acknowledged, leaning forward to rise, to Charlie's surprise. Apparently, the meeting was over.

Makepeace stood to shake first her hand and then Raul's. "And whenever possible, we plan to ask you, Miss Morgan, to advise us on assets of an artistic nature being offered for collateral. This sort of thing will never happen again."

"Could I ask a small favor, Mr. Makepeace?" she asked on impulse. "Could we have the use of an office for a half hour or so? Mr. Francesco has to get back to work and there's something I have to discuss with him."

"By all means. My secretary will be happy to assist."

Makepeace's secretary walked them down the hall to a smaller but well-appointed office. The sign on the door indicated it belonged to Alexander Lowell, V. Pres. "Take as much time as you need. No one will disturb you. Mr. Lowell is on vacation."

"That went well," Charlie said after Raul closed the door and they were alone. Her face reddened as she remembered what they would be doing if this was a year earlier. They would be rushing back to the apartment and tumbling into bed for some serious celebratory love-making. Successfully repressed longings returned in bewildering waves. Was it possible that Raul's feelings were limited to friendship? she wondered. He appeared not to notice her discomfort.

"You're curious to know what sort of private agreement will take place between Voyt and the bank." Raul leaned against the desk, his hands behind him.

She ignored the chair and remained standing. "True."

"Voyt will have to sell a few of his holdings, maybe some real estate, maybe a lot of real estate, depending on how much they've been mortgaged."

"Why was Makepeace so quick to accept your word that we hadn't spoken to the media?"

"Because the bank probably leaked it themselves. It's possible Berkeley doesn't want to be seen gobbling up corporations that owe them money or forcing bankruptcy. It's bad for business. But if masterpieces turn out to be fakes and they've been lied to … "

"They can't be criticized," Charlie said, finishing his sentence. "Did you know all this when we began?"

"Some, not all. In the beginning, I would've sworn they would want secrecy. But I'm glad this all worked out the way it did. This will jumpstart your art career. You're sure to get offers for work now."

"I already have. James Reynold Harrison wants to hire me. He's in the process of designing a museum that will eventually be turned over to the state of California. Harrison wants me to examine his present collection and oversee a number of additional acquisitions. While at the San Bernardino estate, I would be treated as his houseguest. Foreign travel is anticipated. The contract is to go for a year, with a possible extension."

"James Harrison! Impressive. Naturally, you're going to take it."

"It's tempting, but I haven't decided as yet."

"Could your friend Thorenson be the reason for your indecision?" Raul smiled, but not fast enough to hide the momentary flicker of jealousy in his eyes.

Charlie's pulse spiked. Platonic friends weren't jealous of another man's interest. "I introduced Ken to Rosemarie Rifkin's niece Toni. And it seems that I'm a first-rate matchmaker. What about you? You've had plenty of time to find someone."

"I've dated some."

"The tabloids say that you're seeing Gloria Blair."

"Gloria Blair is my client. Instead of meeting her in the office, I take her to lunch. Being seen with a man younger than herself gets her publicity."

And the hungry look in his eyes returned. In that instant, Charlie understood everything. She moved within inches of him, vividly aware of the exchange of electricity. He wasn't shaving his head and joining a monastery. There was no other woman. He still wanted her. The letters from the Multiple Sclerosis Society that she had forwarded to his new address –they weren't asking him to chair a project. They were supplying information, requested either by him or his doctor. She locked her eyes on his. "You can't hide this from me. I have a right to know."

"What is it that you think you know?"

"You have MS."

Neither moved nor spoke. They remained staring at each other until Raul was forced to respond. "If you still care about me, leave me some pride," he said in his warm tenor voice. "I couldn't bear to see pity on your face."

Despite the grief and anger for a cruel unjust fate, she willed herself calm, her face resolved and untroubled. If those dark disturbing eyes saw weakness, she would lose him. "Has the diagnosis been confirmed?" she asked in a even voice.

"Yes. Confirmed." He turned away. "You're too young to be saddled with a husband who'll eventually lose his ability to talk, walk, or even think – who'll be dependent on you for the rest of his life."

"Wasn't it you who said we made a good team? Ask me anything about Toulouse- Lautrec. Anything! But what do I know about banking? What went on there, I couldn't have done that without you."

"I'll always be there for you. You know that."

"What happened to the man who said, when he made love to me, he felt like Superman? He could carry us over mountains and into the clouds." She dipped her head under his to find his eyes again. "I can't get there without you. You don't have the right to skip out on me. You made promises."

He shook his head. "Why do you have to be so damned gorgeous and so god-damned thick-headed at the same time? I'm giving you a way out because I love you."

"You don't get off the hook so easily." She lightly brushed his cheek with her forefinger. "You're the one who's being thick-headed. You're going to be my Superman, whether you're seated, standing, or flat on your back."

"It's a downhill slide that can't be stopped," he said, leaning away from her. "You have to be certain this is what you want."

"Back out on me, buster, and I'll sue you for breach of promise."

"God, you're tough."

Relieved and triumphant when she saw him return to an upright position, smiling provocatively, she thrust her pelvis against his and reached for his belt buckle. "Now how long, do you suppose, we have this office before someone gets curious?"

"Here? Now?" He reached for her derrière to pull her close and bury his face in her hair. "Horny?" he half whispered, half crooned.

"Are you kidding? After all this time? The horniest!"

~ **Chapter 31** ~

Naomi paced nervously. A houseful of Ruben's relatives were arriving the following day. It wasn't that she didn't like Ruben's outgoing family as individuals, or that they went out of their way to make her feel the outsider. On the contrary, they did everything they could to make her feel welcome, including encouraging her little bookshop that consumed her time and barely broke even. Nevertheless, the thought of entertaining the noisy exuberant mob unsettled her.

To calm her nerves she went into the bedroom to reread the letter for the thousandth time she kept in a lacquered box. Of all the correspondence she had received from her daughters, this one was the most precious. She had wept uncontrollably when she first read it. It soothed when she was anxious or apprehensive and lifted her spirits when she temporarily lost her ongoing battle with depression.

Dearest Mother,

It was as though a thorn had been plucked from my heart when I learned you were alive. I rejoice. Hallelujah! I give thanks to the Lord for this miracle.

As impossible as it might seem for a four-year-old child to remember a person or event, I remember you kissing me good-bye. One night Daddy heard me crying in bed when I was six or seven. He asked what was wrong. I told him that I dreamt about you saying good-bye and promising to come. But you never came. He told me that you were in heaven watching over us, and that made me cry harder. Daddy confessed that he sometimes cried because he too missed you, but he tried to be brave and smile, because that would make you happy. If I wanted to talk about you, I should come to him, not Charlie. Charlie wasn't sad because she was too little to remember you, and that was best for her. It was our secret. How it grieves me, as it must grieve you, that you found us too late for a complete reunion.

Now that you've met Charlie, doesn't she remind you of Daddy? Strong. Resilient. Optimistic. Full of fun. They shared so many interests: their love of horses, sports, art, museums. I have no interest in art or museums, no talent for athletics, and I never completely lost my fear of horses.

I don't know if Charlie told you, but after Daddy died, I had a nervous breakdown and had to be hospitalized. My loyal sister never gave up on me. She was there through my darkest hours. Young, totally unprepared, penniless, and all alone, she found a way to support both of us. You must be so proud of her. I am – proud and a little envious. I'm so fortunate to have a gentle caring man like Hal for my husband.

Charlie told me about your kind friend Ruben and his family. She says that you prefer your independence to marriage. It seems that I'm a relic – a member of a dying breed of women who choose to rely on men. With Charlie so much like Daddy, I was half-hoping that you would be more like me.

You can see that I've enclosed photos of our son, and your grandson, Teddy. He is the happiest, most wonderful baby. Hal and I can't stop congratulating ourselves for having produced this perfect child. I don't want Teddy, or any of our children (there will be a minimum of five) to grow up fearful and timid, as I was. They will never see my cowardly face. I shall be the best actress and make them believe that I'm wise, just and brave. Hal's parents insist Teddy is the image of Hal as a baby. I think Teddy favors our side of the family, but I have no baby photographs to show them. You remember Charlie and me when we were infants. What do you think?

I was saddened to hear that Charlie told you that Daddy took his life. His letter to us said it was to protect us. There was something he had done when he was a young man that he was ashamed of. We never learned what that was. Daddy was not without flaws, as I'm sure you know, but he was a wonderful parent. You chose the right man to be your children's father.

You will also see I've enclosed a check for ten thousand dollars. Half is a gift from Charlie; half is from Hal and me. We want you to open a bookstore with it. We hope you will select some books to be given to poor deserving children. In this small way, we would like to honor your parents and brother. Perhaps someday we can expand this to a library in their name.

For now, adieu. Your loving daughter, Amelia.

Naomi refolded the letter, returned it to its envelope, and placed it in the lacquered box. You were wise and I was young and naive, Alain, she told his ghost. Who knows what would have happened to our daughters if you hadn't insisted on taking them to America? Tens of thousands of people in Paris died during the war, and not just Jews at the hands of the Nazis, but from the scarcity of necessities: medicine, food and fuel to heat their homes. Her parent had not survived. She had been too stupid and stubborn to acknowledge the danger. It was only fair to credit Alain for their daughters' safety, and later, for raising them to be educated accomplished women. Where would they be now if it wasn't for his foresight and devotion?

"Naomi," Ruben called from another room. "The children have set the table, washed their hands, and combed their hair. We're waiting for you to say the *shabbos* prayer."

"I'm coming." Naomi reached for the delicate white lace scarf she used to cover her head when she lit candles. It was as similar as she could locate to the one her mother had used for the same purpose. She walked toward the kitchen and her waiting family. They didn't light candles before she moved in. Ruben considered the practice founded on superstition and outdated. But if she was to be the woman heading this home, this family would observe at least some traditions.

Finis

Dangerous Lies
By Lisa April Smith

Chapter 1

April 1979

The trial had everything an ambitious prosecuting attorney could want: a solid case against a known crime-lord and a seductively beautiful witness with a steamy past — ingredients guaranteed to pack a courtroom. From the minute the first photographer had caught a glimpse of Tina Davis the courtroom had been swarming with reporters. It was a plum assignment awarded for Jake Stern's fourteen years with the District Attorney's office and his impressive ratio of convictions. He should be savoring the certain win everyone had been predicting, jubilant with the publicity. Instead, as he watched her testify, he was irritated and agitated — irritated, agitated, and aroused — again.

He had specifically told her to dress conservatively — nothing low-cut or too short — appearances influenced juries. Today she was wearing a white knit turtleneck dress that flaunted every provocative curve — another outfit destined to make the six o'clock news. They couldn't get enough of her: the sexy walk, the clothes, the face. Her face. Each feature in itself was memorable: high cheekbones, delicately carved nose, precisely drawn mouth, and enormous, violet, heavy-lashed eyes. A mass of dark brown, writhing curls framed her face. Reporters battled one another describing her. One reporter insisted that she 'combined the sensual and the serene'. But despite their overblown sketches they all used the same label to identify her: *Tina Davis, Former Mob-Mistress*.

From the time she was fifteen until she was twenty-nine, Tina Davis, born Bettina Berenson thirty-nine years earlier, was the mistress of several underworld titans. At thirty-one, she had married Laurence Paxton Davis, flower-child turned drug-dealer. Jake had deliberately outlined her history in his opening statement. He had no intention of giving the defense an opportunity to shock the jury with the lurid details after she testified. Jake knew, if he told the jury right up front that Tina Davis had chosen to consort with the scum of the universe, they might not like her, but they would believe her. The maneuver seemed to be working. The eight men and four women of the jury nodded sympathetically as she testified. And she was a good witness; she spoke slowly and distinctly and her story was consistent.

The defendant's attorney was unable to hide his growing frustration. "You've testified that your late husband was a drug dealer. Wasn't he also an addict?"

Jake stood. "Objection, Your Honor. It's already been established that Larry Davis used drugs. Mr. Willard is repeating himself in an attempt to badger the witness."

The judge shot the cynical stare Her Honor was noted for at Tom Willard. "Objection sustained. Please get on with it, Mr. Willard."

Jake allowed himself a pleased inner smile, confident his stony face would mask his thoughts. It was almost fun watching him sputter like a defective firecracker as he attempted to derail her. Back in law school, Willard was an arrogant, pretentious ass — an ass who enjoyed waving his money in everyone's face. But he was no fool. The slightest indication of weakness and he would go for the jugular.

"You claim, Mrs. Davis, your husband died owing my client twenty-five thousand dollars, and that my client tried to collect the debt from *you*. Supposedly, he sent the two men who testified earlier, to threaten you. We've heard a lot of fuzzy, distorted tapes that supposedly support your assertion. May I remind you, those two convicted criminals have admitted, under oath, they're receiving consideration in the form of *reduced sentences* for their testimony?"

"Is there a question here, Mr. Willard?" the judge prodded.

"Just getting to that, Your Honor. As I was saying, twenty-five thousand dollars is a lot of money to most people. It certainly is to me," Willard informed the jury. "But as Mr. Stern pointed out, you have some powerful *intimate associates.*" A number of people, including three members of the jury, tittered. "Intimate associates with considerable financial resources. If what you claim is true, why didn't one of your *very close friends* come to your aid?"

Jake didn't wait for Willard to complete the sentence before standing. "Irrelevant, Your Honor."

"Sustained," the judge declared.

Jake would have loved to hear the answer to that one. Why hadn't she gone to one of her former playmates for help? Jake was aware of two who outranked the defendant. Either one could drop twenty-five thousand dollars on a bet and never flinch. Surely one of them could have given or loaned her the money, or at the very least, pressured the defendant to cut her a deal.

Instead she had waltzed into the nearest precinct and offered to get the cops enough evidence for a conviction — volunteered to wear a wire. Volunteers always made Jake nervous. Nervous and suspicious. What made her so anxious to repeatedly risk her life? Over a period of three months, with a recording device neatly tucked in her handbag, Davis had strolled into parts of the city that seasoned officers were reluctant to patrol. Then she had to pretend not to understand or hear, so the threats would have to be repeated. That sort of hot-dog heroics could have gotten her killed.

Jake shook his head. The cops she worked with idolized her. How could cops admire a woman who had chosen to live with gangsters, the very men they saw as their enemies? But cops have their own set of rules. If they had to list the traits they admired most, 'courage' would be at the top. Of course, her looks didn't hurt. When the detectives had first played a few of the tapes for him, they stood around laughing and punching each other — like kids reliving a Halloween prank. Jake knew they viewed most prosecutors as educated, spineless, chicken-shits who got in their way — and that didn't exclude him.

Normally women with her sort of background had horrendous childhoods. But Davis' mother wasn't a prostitute and her father wasn't a pimp. She was born into a typical middle-class family — two parents, a brother, a sister — a family like the one Jake had lost. And she had grown up in Queens, less than three miles from his old neighborhood.

"My husband died trying to stop a fight," Davis said in answer to Willard's latest question. She crossed her legs and replaced a curl behind her ear. "My husband was a pacifist."

The gesture made the bulge in Jake's shorts quiver. She *was* a beautiful woman, an exceptionally beautiful woman. But he had a girlfriend, who was everything he wanted in a woman: educated, young, from a good family, attractive — not just attractive, pretty, very pretty. Tina Davis was not a person he would choose as a friend, much less a date. Maybe he could be more sympathetic if she was stupid or just ignorant, like most of the city's sidewalk hostesses. But she was neither stupid nor ignorant. During preparation for the trial, Jake had had a number of conversations with her. She asked intelligent questions and anticipated his strategies while taunting him with those searing eyes or smiling that knowing smile. And she always carried a book with her — good books, not junk — Tolstoy, Joyce, Proust. A Jewish mob-bimbo who read Proust. Nothing about Tina Davis made sense.

The judge consulted her watch. It was four o'clock on a Friday afternoon, an unseasonably hot Friday afternoon. They were minutes away from halting for the weekend. During their last break, the two detectives who had worked with Davis had unnerving news for Jake. There was a contract out on her.

She was gutsy, but she wasn't going to laugh that throaty little laugh when Jake informed her that someone planned to silence her permanently.

# # #